Mrs. Dodson motioned for us to come closer to her. "Listen. I've been thinking about some of the strange doings in the theater. I'm starting a task force."

"You're starting what?" I asked, but I knew the answer would just keep me awake at night.

She tapped her cane. "You heard me. This confirms Duke was not a suicide. I think someone is trying to kill Royce and make it look like an accident. There is a murderer amongst us and Duke might have been in the wrong place at the wrong time. It's up to us to bring the ruffian to justice."

"Ladies, we need to take these suspicions to the police."

"Police? *Pshh*." Aunt Ginny put her hand in the middle. "I'm in."

"No, no, you can't be in. We just got you out of trouble a few months ago."

Mother Gibson put her hand on top of Aunt Ginny's. "I'm in too."

I felt hysteria growing inside me. "Ladies, I really don't want anyone to get hurt."

The other two joined their hands to the pile and four sharp sets of eyes turned my way. "Are you in?"

It wasn't my proudest moment, being shaken down by four old ladies.

I caved.

Books by Libby Klein

CLASS REUNIONS ARE MURDER

MIDNIGHT SNACKS ARE MURDER

RESTAURANT WEEKS ARE MURDER

THEATER NIGHTS ARE MURDER

Published by Kensington Publishing Corporation

Theater Nights
Are
MURDER

LIBBY KLEIN

KENSINGTON BOOKS
www.kensingtonbooks.com

KENSINGTON BOOKS are published by

Kensington Publishing Corp.
119 West 40th Street
New York, NY 10018

All Kensington titles, imprints, and distributed lines are available at special quantity discounts for bulk purchases for sales promotion, premiums, fund-raising, educational, or institutional use.

Special book excerpts or customized printings can also be created to fit specific needs. For details, write or phone the office of the Kensington Sales Manager: Attn.: Sales Department. Kensington Publishing Corp., 119 West 40th Street, New York, NY 10018. Phone: 1-800-221-2647.

Kensington and the K logo Reg. U.S. Pat. & TM Off.

First Printing: January 2020

ISBN-13: 978-1-4967-2337-6
ISBN-10: 1-4967-2337-6

ISBN-13: 978-1-4967-2338-3 (ebook)
ISBN-10: 1-4967-2338-4 (ebook)

10 9 8 7 6 5 4 3 2 1

Printed in the United States of America

Dedicated to Itty Bitty Smitty
You are dearly loved and missed

Acknowledgments

Thank you to the Queen Victoria Bed and Breakfast for letting me reference their lovely home in my story. You truly are one of the most beautiful Victorian bed-and-breakfasts in Cape May.

Chapter One

"I can't believe you pulled the fire alarm." I was standing outside L'Ecole des Chefs, the community college culinary wing where I'd spent a traumatic week and a half in South Jersey's first annual, *and my last forever*, Restaurant Week competition. I was a little stunned when Tim declared that he'd always loved me and asked me to "give it a go" with him. I was a little stunned, the way Miss Piggy was a little self-involved. Snow flurries danced and played on the air and the temperatures were dipping with the setting sun, causing me to shiver. Or maybe that was just my nerves. The only thing I knew for sure was that I was freezing my butt off in the crowded parking lot while sirens were ringing out all around me.

Aunt Ginny wrapped her fur coat tight around her pink leather hot pants and white go-go boots. "I had to do something to get you out of there. Tim looked like he was about to get down on one knee and there was panic in your eyes. I was afraid you were going to flee."

Is that still an option? I scanned the chefs for Tim while considering life in the rejection protection program. If that didn't exist, it should. "I considered it. My life hasn't turned out the way I expected."

Aunt Ginny watched the crowd filing out of the college and put a papery hand on my arm. "Nobody's does, honey. Nobody's does."

Two fire trucks screamed into the parking lot, followed by an ambulance. I took a deep breath and let it out slow, watching the white fog leave my mouth and swirl out in front of me like puffs from a sleeping dragon. I had seen the hope in Tim's eyes, his heart on his sleeve. I had dreamed of this moment for twenty-five years and now that it was here, I felt like I was signing a waiver for plastic surgery. *What if something goes horribly wrong? What if I wake up and my belly button is missing? Maybe chunky will come back into fashion right after I have all my fat sucked out and I'll have missed my chance to be beautiful. I think I'm willing to take that chance. Wait? What was I thinking about?*

A police car thundered into the parking lot and Aunt Ginny tightened her grip on her fur coat. "Uh-oh."

Uh-oh was right. We'd seen the police more often than the mailman in the four short months I'd been home. Aunt Ginny was somewhere in her eighties, but somehow the feisty redhead got into more trouble than a five-year-old after a sugar binge. I considered our recent luck with law enforcement. "Maybe we should go. I can come back later to get my things."

"Come on. I know a back way out of here." Aunt Ginny backed away from the flashing lights and pivoted toward the parked cars. "What are you going to say to Tim when he comes looking for an answer?"

"I don't know. I can't put him off for long."

"You don't need to rush it either. You'll know when you know. Time is the greatest revealer of men's hearts."

I sighed. "I hope so, Aunt Ginny. I really hope so. Nobody likes a love triangle."

Chapter Two

I woke up the next morning a bundle of nerves with a mouthful of fur. "Figaro, get off of my head." I slid the purring ball of fluff to the side, where orange slits creaked open to glare at me for disturbing his royal beauty rest. Sir Figaro Newton was definitely beautiful, so the sleeping eighteen hours a day was really paying off. If only there was a good behavior nap for the black smoke Persian, we'd be in business.

"I feel like we've fallen down the rabbit hole since coming here, Fig. Do you miss our home in Virginia?"

Figaro yawned and lifted a back leg to clean his undercarriage.

"I'll take that as a no." I stretched and twisted to the side. "No matter where we are, everything eventually goes sideways. Why do you think that is?"

Figaro was judging me under his raised leg with a look that said, *Oh, I'm pretty sure I know where the problem is.*

"Poppy!" Aunt Ginny hammered on the bedroom door before throwing it open. "Why are you still in bed?!"

"Uh, because it's six in the morning."

"Isn't Tim coming over to talk about your feelings?"

"In *four hours*."

"Wash and cream your face and find something that isn't wrinkled to put on. And wrap your hair up in some hot rollers."

"I'm working on it."

"Come on, girl, work faster. No matter what you tell him, you want to look your best!"

"You're still in your housecoat!"

"My first boyfriend didn't just declare his love to me after a lifetime apart. Hop to!"

What happened to you don't need to rush it?

Aunt Ginny trotted down the stairs, followed by Figaro, who saw this as an opening to fill his belly with some gourmet fish goo.

"Really, Fig. You're just going to leave me here?" I flipped the covers off while muttering to myself. "You're supposed to be my best friend. I was the one who stayed up with you all night when you ate that suspicious bug. As soon as we moved in with Aunt Ginny, you switched sides. Traitor."

I picked up the silver picture frame that sat on the nightstand by my bed. It was a photo of me and my late husband taken at some formal society event my mother-in-law, Georgina, had no doubt pressured us into attending. John was wearing a tuxedo and my silver heels were dangling from his fingers. I was wearing an emerald-green, floor-length gown and walking barefoot. I had to use both hands to hold the skirt up so it didn't drag on the ground. We were looking at each other and laughing because he had just made some joke I couldn't remember anymore. We were so happy. I put the frame back in its position. *I would give anything to remember what he'd said to make me laugh like that.*

My heart was split into three pieces, each belonging to someone else. My late husband's smiling face was etched on a big chunk, watching me. John was encouraging me to live life and be happy even though he was gone. *How can I ever be happy without you?* There was a piece that had always been Tim's since we met in high school thirty years ago. First love was hard to extinguish no matter how much I'd screwed it up. I had buried it in the corner and refused to look at it. Then there was Gia. *Where had that come from?* My feelings for the sexy Italian barista were unexpected. His kindness and friendship had made my first few months back in South Jersey tolerable. Maybe even happy. I wasn't sure why he was drawn to a plus-size, middle-aged gal like me when he could have his pick from the parade of short skirts and cleavage I'd seen throw themselves at him every day, but somehow, he seemed to really like me. I would rather die than hurt either of them.

I got in the shower and let the hot water melt my anxiety and calm my mind. What was I going to say to Tim? The problem wasn't love. I'd always loved him. The problem was every time I saw myself saying yes to Tim, Gia popped into my head and my heart broke. But when I saw myself with Gia, I relived the day I told Tim I'd cheated, and he dropped me faster than Oprah lost her first hundred pounds.

I didn't want to decide anything right now. Truth be told, I kind of liked things the way they were. I never dreamed anyone would be interested in me for the rest of my life. Part of me was worried it was a hoax. Like that time Greg Eisler asked me to the school dance in the sixth grade, then laughed in my face when I said yes. The little weasel had feathered hair and thought he was David Cassidy. The joke was on him when he stopped growing at twelve. *Not such a hotshot now at five foot two, are you, Greg?*

I blow-dried my hair, checking the auburn for traces of silver. So far, so good. I applied some makeup, then dressed in teal leggings and a long black tunic. My skinny jeans were way too tight after my brief stint as pastry chef for Tim's restaurant, Maxine's. Who knew a little gluten and dairy would inflate me like a hot-air balloon? So now I'm back to my Paleo sentence and only eating what comes out of the dirt. Festive.

Thoughts of Tim brought the heaviness back. He was the first man I ever fell in love with. I almost married him. Being exclusive seemed like an obvious choice, but I needed more time. John hadn't even been gone a year. I had just started my life over. I'd only stayed in Cape May to take care of Aunt Ginny and keep her out of the assisted living facility she called Old Lady Lockdown because of her . . . let's just say *peculiarities*. We really needed the Butterfly Wings Bed and Breakfast to take flight if we were going to pay for luxuries like water and electricity. This Grand Victorian had been in our family for almost a hundred and fifty years, and the taxes on it were nearly equal to a pop diva's touring glitter budget. Our only options were to sell it or strike it rich on *Survivor*. Since there was no amount of money that would get me to eat a spider, it looked like me and Aunt Ginny were going to be serving waffles to tourists for the foreseeable future.

The grande dame of the McAllister clan was in the kitchen wearing a fuchsia track suit with the word HOTTIE bedazzled on the back and eating a bowl of Cap'n Crunch that she thought I wouldn't notice. *You underestimate me, madam!* I had every sugar cereal memorized and ranked by color, shape, and texture. I knew my stuff and crunch berries were at the top of my list.

"It's about time you rolled out of bed."

"The sun is still yawning."

"Do you want some coffee to settle your nerves?"

"No. I think I'm going to head over to La Dolce Vita to make a couple of batches of muffins for Gia to sell to his weekend crowd. I'll get coffee there."

Aunt Ginny raised an eyebrow. "You think time around a

sexy Italian will help you decide if you're ready to commit to Tim?"

"I think if anyone is able to make me forget about Tim, it's Gia. And that in itself is a red flag."

Aunt Ginny drummed her fingers on the table. "You know I'm here for you, whatever you decide. I just don't want you to make yourself crazy over a man."

"Duly noted." I grabbed my purse and headed for the front door. Figaro sat on the narrow table in the hall where we had a dish of hard candy, a bowl for keys, and a plant that he liked to knock over when he didn't think he was getting enough attention. He gave me a meow as I grabbed my coat off the rack. I rubbed his ears and he pushed against my hand. "You are the only man I need in my life, Fig, but you wouldn't mind if we add someone else to the mix, would you?"

Figaro sat up tall and batted a butterscotch out of the candy dish. It landed at my feet with a thud. It seemed everyone had a definite opinion about my love life except me.

I decided to walk the two and a half blocks to the Washington Street Mall. You don't get much more off in the off season than January in Cape May. The streets were dark and misty, and many of the bed-and-breakfasts were closed for the month so the owners could have their own vacations before the new season began. The few stores that opened had reduced hours, some only open on weekends. Gia opened the coffee shop at eight to accommodate early morning churchgoers on their way to Mass at Our Lady Star of the Sea at the end of the Mall. We'd been pretty busy filling special orders since I'd been making allergy-friendly baked goods to expand clientele. It seemed all the kids born in the last ten years were allergic to something.

I used my key to let myself in the back to the kitchen. Gia was sitting in his little office staring at the blank screen of his laptop, drinking a cappuccino. He looked up when he heard the door close and his eyebrows shot up to his wavy dark hair. He didn't speak at first, his eyes searching mine. We were frozen, letting the silence hang between us.

"I came to make some muffins."

Gia nodded.

"I thought I would do Paleo Mexican Chocolate and Apple Pie Crumble."

After a moment of silence, he stood up. "Do you want a latte?"

"Yes."

He headed to the espresso bar in the front room but paused in front of me. He pulled me into a hug and held on like it was the last time we would see each other. He broke away and left the room without a word.

I set out ingredients for the baking I wanted to try and willed my heart to slow down. Maybe this was a bad idea. There was a reckless part of me that would take off with Gia and never look back. All he had to do was say the word. I measured and mixed batter with shaky hands and a heavy heart until he brought me a coconut almond milk latte that he had created just for me.

"So." He leaned against the counter.

"So." I took a sip of my coffee.

"Are you exclusive with Tim now?"

"I haven't given him an answer yet."

Gia lifted a hand and tucked a shock of my hair that had come loose from my ponytail behind my ear. "So, it's not too late."

"I don't know what I'm going to do."

"What is your heart telling you?"

"That everyone is going to get hurt."

"I don't care about everyone. I just care about you. What do you want?"

"I don't know yet. I don't want to decide right now."

Gia pulled me into his arms. "Then don't. Wait until you are sure."

"What if I never know?"

Gia laughed softly, and I felt his breath against my forehead. "You will."

I pulled back and looked into his smiling eyes. A rush of heat flew up to my cheeks. There was a part of me that loved this attention. Two men were fighting over me. I was both exhilarated and ashamed of myself for being exhilarated. "How long will you wait?"

He grinned. "I don't see a ring on your finger, so there's still time to make you mine."

I returned his smile. "So, you won't give up until I'm engaged?"

Gia brought his face close and brushed his lips against mine. "Bella, I won't give up until you're married."

Chapter Three

I left Gia with four dozen muffins and another little piece of my heart and walked home with my third latte of the morning. I contemplated the many ways my life would change if I entered into a committed relationship with Tim. I mean, it wasn't a marriage proposal. It was a let's-give-it-a-go-by-officially-dating proposal. A proposal to finally see what might have been with my first love, Tim. The one whose heart I recklessly broke twenty-five years ago. If I screwed it up this time, there would be no coming back. What was my heart telling me? It was telling me to run far, far away and hide out in the woods with some cookie-baking elves. Tim's Kia was parked in front of Aunt Ginny's house. He was early.

I wiped my boots on the mat at the front door so long I shaved off a layer of the soles and finally had to go in.

Tim was standing on the other side of the door in his striped chef pants and a black T-shirt with a bouquet of lavender roses. He gave me a big grin, then saw the La

Dolce Vita cup in my hands and his grin shrank half a size. "Hey, gorgeous. I wanted to surprise you." He leaned down and gave me a quick kiss. "I didn't realize you'd be with *him* this morning." His eyes slid to the coffee cup again.

I took the roses in one hand and slipped my coffee cup down on the key table behind him with the other. "I'm just getting back from making the gluten-free muffins." I started to shrug out of my coat when Aunt Ginny breezed into the foyer.

"Welcome home. I told Tim he didn't have to wait in here. He was welcome to come into the kitchen with me, but he wanted to meet you at the door." Aunt Ginny took the roses. "I'll put these in water so you two can talk." She started toward the kitchen, but not before searching my face for clues as to what I was going to say.

Tim smiled down at me. He spied something behind me and his eyes lit up. "Wow." He walked over to a wooden bird hanging on the wall in the sitting room. "You still have that?"

Memories flew at me like dandelion seeds on the wind. "That was my ninth-grade shop project."

"Okay." Tim took it off its peg. "Don't you mean this was *my* project?"

I laughed and tried to get it away from him. "Hey, I got that B fair and square."

He held it out of my reach. "Because I carved it for you after class. You were trying to fake an illness to get out of it."

"Who needs wood-carving skills in real life?"

"Dwarfs, clog makers, whittlers," he teased me.

"Professional whittlers? Really?"

Tim turned it around. "Look, I secretly signed it." He pointed to a tiny heart hidden in the bird's feathers.

"I never noticed that before."

"I knew even then that I wanted you to be my girlfriend."

My throat closed up, and Tim put the carved bird back on its hook. He shot off across the foyer into the library. "Remember when we played that epic, four-hour game of Monopoly?"

"I remember you tried to get me to pay my rent on your Park Place hotel by taking my shirt off."

Tim grinned. "Oh yeah. And that's when your grandmother decided to do her crocheting in here with us."

We both laughed, then gave birth to a moment of awkward silence.

Tim gestured to the fireplace. "You want me to light a fire?"

"Sure." I sat on the couch and took a couple of deep breaths to calm my nerves. Figaro peeked around the corner to see what was going on. His ears pinned to his head at the sight of Tim. A hand appeared and nudged Figaro into the room. *Subtle.* I wondered if Aunt Ginny had bugged his collar.

Tim joined me on the couch and we watched the fire dance over the kindling until the logs roared to life. "I'm sorry if I put you on the spot yesterday."

"I definitely didn't see it coming." Gigi didn't see it either. She had flames shooting out of her eyes when Tim said he wasn't interested in her *that* way.

Tim took my hand in his. "I know things didn't work out when we were teenagers, but I never stopped loving you. I thought about you every day."

"I've always loved you too . . ." I didn't get to finish because we were interrupted when a gray ball thudded onto the couch. Figaro turned so his backside was in Tim's face and gave me a long meow.

"Figaro!"

Tim gathered Figaro's tail out of his mouth and looked around to catch my eye.

Fig was insistent. "Merrrroww."

I scooped the gray pouf into my lap, but instead of settling down, he repositioned himself between Tim and me.

Tim struggled to get a cat hair out of his mouth. "What were you saying . . . before . . ."

"I'm sorry. I was just going to say that I–I've always loved you too . . . but . . ."

Figaro lifted his back leg to do some detail work in Tim's direction.

Tim's eyebrows shot up. "I see you went for the full neutering. Good choice."

I grabbed Fig around the middle and pulled him to me. "I am so sorry. He's not normally   actually, he's always like this. I'm just sorry you have to be on the receiving end of it." I placed Figaro on the floor at my feet. He narrowed his eyes and flicked his tail at me.

I pointed at him to behave.

He flopped over.

Tim shifted in his seat and wiped his palms back and forth over his legs. "You've always loved me, but . . . ?"

"Well . . . I've been gone a long time and . . ."

Figaro mistakenly assumed Tim was baiting him and pounced, rapid-fire batting Tim's hands.

Tim pulled his hands away. "Ahh! Stop it!"

Figaro bolted around the back of the couch to regroup. This was not going well.

I put my hand on Tim's arm. "It's just that I don't think I'm ready . . ."

Tim's eyes lost their sparkle and he ran his hand through his hair and sighed. "I don't want you to be pressured, Mack. It's not like I was asking you to marry me or anything."

"Oh no, of course I didn't think that . . ."

He crossed his arms over his chest and gave a mirthless laugh. "Heck no. We've only been reacquainted for a few weeks really. Much too soon for any kind of long-term commitment."

"Oh. I thought . . . When you told Gigi that you were only interested in me . . ."

Tim's face blossomed pink up to his ears and he looked at the fire. "Oh, that? Well, what I meant was . . . you know. As a chef."

"As a chef?"

Figaro was doing figure eights against Tim's black pants. Every couple of swipes he would stop and inspect his work to see how much gray fur he'd left behind matching the narrow stripes.

Tim cleared his throat. "Yeah. Um, why don't you come to work for me? As my full-time pastry chef."

I felt my heart slide two inches lower in my ribs. Tim wasn't asking me to be his girlfriend. I should have been relieved, and yet I wasn't as elated as I'd expected. I felt the heat rise to my face. *What is wrong with me?* "You weren't looking for a relationship?"

Tim grinned. "I am if you are." He leaned in and put a hand on my leg. "I want to be with you." He turned my chin up and kissed me. He searched my eyes for a moment, then dropped my chin. "But it's not like I'm looking to get engaged. Let's just keep things loose for now."

There was something in the way his eyes shifted to the side that made me wonder if he was backpedaling. *How is he going to pay me to be a full-time pastry chef? He's barely in the black as it is. That was the whole reason we did that cockamamie Restaurant Week competition.* "What exactly would you want me to do as your pastry chef?"

Tim thought for a minute. "Well . . . you and I would

work very closely together to plan the menu. You'd need to come in very early to make the desserts and be finished before the line comes in to get lunch prepped."

"Would you be there with me?"

"Ah . . . no. Not every day. I usually come in after prep and work from lunch to around ten. I don't get off until around two a.m. in the summer."

"So, I wouldn't really see you."

Tim took my hand in his. "That's the biz, babe. That's what we'd be doing if we had our own restaurant."

That doesn't sound like fun at all. "Well, I'd love to make your desserts, but I don't think I can keep that schedule plus my commitment to La Dolce Vita."

Tim dropped my hand. "Oh, you're still planning on doing that?"

"Well, yeah. I've promised to make Gia's baked goods first. Plus, I have the B&B to run. We only have the occasional weekend booking right now, but in a couple of months I think we'll be full when the season officially starts."

Tim nodded and chewed his bottom lip.

Figaro swatted at Tim's shoelace. I tried to nudge him away, but he bit my foot.

Tim smiled wistfully. "We always planned to run our own place together, remember?"

"I didn't have to take care of Aunt Ginny in that dream."

"I'll tell you what." He perked up. "What if you make the desserts here at home? You have a certified kitchen. You could make a few things each week and bring them in when we run low. That way we could still work together, and if you get too busy to make a few muffins for Gia"—he practically choked on his name—"maybe then it would be time to let him find someone else and you and I can make it a permanent thing."

"We can make what a permanent thing?"

Tim smiled. "Everything." He gave me another kiss that lingered until we heard a throat clear from just outside the door.

I sat up straight and Tim stood up. Both of his shoelaces were untied, and Figaro had mysteriously disappeared.

Tim leaned down to tie his shoes. "What do you say? Want to come work for me, Mack?"

I let out an obvious sigh of relief like an open pressure cooker valve. I had no idea when I was going to find the time to make Tim's desserts, Gia's allergy-friendly baked goods, and run my bed-and-breakfast. I *had* made plans with Tim many years ago to run our own restaurant. Of course, that promise had come with a diamond engagement ring, a joint checking account, and fringe bedroom benefits. I'd blindly jumped into situations in the past, and some of them had changed the course of my whole life. I didn't want to make that mistake again. I wasn't ready to make any life-altering decisions, but Tim was offering me time to figure out my heart, and that was good enough.

"Deal." I tucked myself into his arms and hugged him.

We walked to the front door, and Aunt Ginny tried to make herself look busy examining a picture of an old lady cutting a pear that had been hanging in the foyer for fifty years. "Oh, are you two all finished with your talk already?"

I cut my eyes at Aunt Ginny and gave her a look that I was on to her. She blinked and returned giant eyes of innocence.

Tim smiled at me. "For now."

"Good." She took a sip of her coffee and looked over the rim at me. "You guys are so young. You know I hate to see you get all jumbled up in drama over relationship stuff."

Tim gave me a quick kiss. "I'll call you later." He opened the door and had to take a step back.

Huddled in the doorway were three fleecy-haired old biddies. Aunt Ginny's lifelong besties, Mrs. Dodson, Mrs. Davis, and Mother Gibson. They were silent, but their bright eyes were all atwitter.

Mrs. Dodson double tapped her cane on the porch. "Ginny, he's back!"

Aunt Ginny turned pale. Her eyes fluttered, and the coffee cup dropped from her hands and shattered.

Chapter Four

"Aunt Ginny, you're shaking." I rubbed her hands with mine to be sure she wasn't going to pass out or have a stroke.

Figaro rushed to sniff out what had been in that coffee cup while the ladies tut-tutted and shook their heads in a show of support. Tim gave me a subtle head nod and slipped out while I led Aunt Ginny to a tufted chair in the sitting room to compose herself.

Aunt Ginny fiddled with the locket around her neck and stared off into her memories. "I can't believe it. After all this time."

I got the broom and dustpan out of the hall closet. "After all this time what?"

Mrs. Davis took a hankie out of her purse and passed it to Aunt Ginny. "Word on the street is, he's here to stay."

I picked through the larger pieces of pottery and tossed them into the wastebasket. "Who's here to stay?"

Aunt Ginny waved her hand like she was swatting a mosquito. "*Pshh*. We'll see. He's probably having a contract dispute."

I swept the fragments into the dustpan. "Contract dispute about what?"

Mother Gibson patted Aunt Ginny on the shoulder. "You know how he is. He always thought he was a hotshot."

I emptied the dustpan into the wastebasket. "Who's a hotshot?"

Aunt Ginny shook her head. "Yeah, but he really is now. Four Tonys."

I shot to my feet. "Ladies! Who are we talking about?"

Four sets of sharp eyes snapped to me. Mrs. Dodson gave me a love-suffers-long kind of look. "Ginny's first boyfriend, Royce Hansen."

Aunt Ginny woke from her haze with a roll of her eyes. "That's not true. My first boyfriend was Duffy Collins and he was an idiot. With Royce it was love at first sight."

I recalled Aunt Ginny's words just before Tim left. "So, all this *drama* is over a man?" I gave Aunt Ginny a sarcastic look and she had the decency to blush. "I'll go make us some coffee."

Aunt Ginny called weakly after me, "Thank you, honey."

"And bring some cookies!" Mrs. Davis hollered. "You can't gripe about an ex-boyfriend properly without cookies."

I went to the kitchen to boil water for the commiseration session. *So, Aunt Ginny had a high school boyfriend she hasn't seen in years. And, apparently, he's a Broadway actor. Unless four Tonys means something else to her generation. I'd better find that out before I say anything.* I placed a bunch of Easy Peanut Butter cookies on a tray with all the necessary accouterment and willed the water to boil faster. Gossip was happening in the next room and I didn't want to miss it. I had grown up in this house and this was the first I'd ever heard about a long-lost first love. I poured the almost-boiling water over the freshly ground coffee, set the timer for four minutes, and took it with me as I crept back to the front parlor to join the circle.

Mrs. Davis, the giggliest of the biddies, with pink hair, was asking Aunt Ginny if she'd kept up with Royce's career.

Aunt Ginny played with the zipper on her track suit jacket. "I have a couple of newspaper articles. Nothing much."

The ebony-skinned Mother Gibson was usually the voice of reason. "I thought you subscribed to *Variety* so you could keep track of his shows."

Aunt Ginny pinked around the neck. "Is it a crime to enjoy the theater?"

Mrs. Dodson, the most proper and dignified of the crew, gave Aunt Ginny a penetrating gaze down her nose. "I thought you had an entire scrapbook devoted to his publicity shots."

Aunt Ginny shifted in her chair. "Well, I have to keep them somewhere, don't I?!"

I realized something just then. "Is that why you get the *Broadway Buzz* newsletter?"

Aunt Ginny pursed her lips and shot a couple of daggers my way. The timer went off and she jumped a mile.

I gave her a sheepish grin. "Coffee's ready."

Aunt Ginny took a cup from me. "I don't know why I'm so nervous. He probably won't even remember me."

Mother Gibson and Mrs. Davis rolled their eyes at each other.

I passed around the plate of cookies and took a seat on the piano bench. "How did you meet Royce?"

Mrs. Davis put two cookies on a napkin on her lap. "They met in high school."

"They were sweethearts right from the start. Insepara-ble." Mother Gibson took three cookies, then asked for Mrs.

Davis to pass the Splenda. "Don't want my blood sugar to be too high."

"We were not inseparable," Aunt Ginny defended.

"Oh, you were too. We all saw you," Mrs. Davis retorted. "Pass me the cream."

Aunt Ginny crossed her arms in front of her and tried to disappear into the chair.

Mrs. Dodson stirred her coffee and tapped her spoon three times on the side of her cup. "At least until Moira got her claws into him."

"Ooh, who's Moira?"

Aunt Ginny took a deep breath and let it out slowly. "Moira Finklebaum." The words ground out like gravel. "Although she goes by Blanche Carrigan now."

All three ladies said, "*Pshh*," shook their heads, and took a sip of their coffees.

Aunt Ginny shrugged her shoulders. "If you must know, Royce and I were going steady, and I thought we were going to get married when we graduated. He had pinned me at the Christmas dance our senior year."

Oh God, does that mean what it sounds like?

"Get that look off your face. It means I wore his high school fraternity pin. You kids today have promise rings."

"I don't think we do."

Mrs. Davis leaned toward me. "Royce was in every play that Cape May High did in our four years. *H.M.S Pinafore*, *Porgy and Bess*, what were the others?"

Mrs. Dodson tipped her head to the side. "*Pirates of Penzance*."

Mrs. Davis shook her head. "I thought that was the same as *H.M.S Pinafore*."

Aunt Ginny gave me a droll look and grabbed a cookie.

Mother Gibson leaned into the conversation. "No, I think they're two different musicals about sailors on boats."

Mrs. Davis sat back flustered. "Well, that's just excessive."

Mrs. Dodson considered the ladies, then turned her attention to me. "Anyway, he loved the theater. He was good too. And then came *Romeo and Juliet*."

Mother Gibson bobbed her head and her bosom bounced in time. "And that hussy, Moira Finklebaum."

Mrs. Davis sang out, "Bla-anche."

The ladies looked at Aunt Ginny to pick up the story.

She took a long drink from her cup, as if trying to absorb courage in the form of Colombian Medium Roast. "Our senior year, Royce was cast in the lead role of Romeo, and Moira Finklebaum beat me out for the role of Juliet. They were reviewed in the local paper as 'gifted' for giving a 'Broadway-quality performance,' and it went right to their heads."

"Oh no. What happened?"

Aunt Ginny fiddled with her locket some more. "Right after graduation, Royce said he had something important to tell me. I put on my best dress and rouged my cheeks . . ." Aunt Ginny's voice caught. She turned her head and looked out the window.

Figaro crept into the room and his hair bristled as if he picked up on the tension. He jumped on Aunt Ginny's lap and spun around a couple of times before settling down facing the cookies.

I prompted Aunt Ginny to go on. "He didn't ask you to marry him?"

She shook her head no. "He told me he was leaving in the morning with Moira for New York. They were going to try out for a Broadway production of *Our Town*."

Mrs. Dodson picked up the story with a tap of her cane. "We never saw Royce again. Moira returned a few years later and told everyone she'd changed her name to Blanche

Carrigan. She said she was retiring from theater life and settling down. A bunch of hogwash, if you ask me."

Oh, poor Aunt Ginny. I wanted to put my head in her lap and let her stroke my hair like when I was little. She looked so sad and forlorn.

Figaro, the opportunist, took advantage of our distraction and shot out a gray fluffy paw, snagging a peanut butter cookie before anyone could stop him. He hurtled through the room, keeping to the perimeter with the cookie in his mouth, while the ladies grabbed their coffee and cookies and held them aloft with cries of "What in the world!" and "Good gracious!"

Aunt Ginny let out a cackle of delight and the mood was instantly lifted. I was so grateful to see her smile that I decided to let the little terror keep his ill-gotten treat.

Aunt Ginny set her coffee back in the saucer with a tiny clink. "So, every now and then there would be an article in the paper about some play Royce was starring in or an award he received. I hadn't heard anything for a while and thought he'd retired."

Mrs. Davis giggled. "Well, he's back now, so who knows. Maybe this is your second chance at love." She wiggled her eyebrows.

Aunt Ginny narrowed her eyes. "What are you, some kinda nut? I don't need a man at this age. What would I do with him?"

Mother Gibson grinned. "Same thing you used to do with them, only now it takes longer."

Aunt Ginny blushed. "Lila!"

Mrs. Davis shook her head. "Oh no, she's right. And sometimes you need props."

My face was getting hot.

Aunt Ginny glanced at me and tried to change the subject. "Well, I'm not interested in that life anymore. Love is for the young. That's why old ladies like me are never the heroines of romance novels or leading ladies in those romper movies Poppy likes."

I looked up from my coffee. "Rom-coms."

Aunt Ginny tossed her head. "Rom-coms."

Aunt Ginny was right. *You almost never see a romance starring the more mature. That's hardly fair. Geez, even AARP thinks senior life starts at fifty. My God, I'm only seven years away from that. Am I really almost a senior citizen? I'm running out of time. What have I done with my life? Who's going to take care of me when I have to have hip replacement surgery?*

"Poppy!"

I looked up. "What?"

"Are you listening to me?"

"Uh, yes?"

"Do you think I should try out?"

I looked at each of the biddies in turn. They were all watching me, waiting for an answer. "Try out for what?"

Mrs. Dodson *tsk*ed and shook her head. Mother Gibson chuckled. Mrs. Davis picked up another cookie and Aunt Ginny sighed. "Now that Royce is supposedly retired and living with his sister in Cape May, the Senior Center is finally putting on that musical we've been asking for. Do you think I should try out?"

I was seven years away from being a senior citizen, but Aunt Ginny . . . I couldn't even finish the thought. "I think you should do whatever you want and embrace your life to the fullest!"

Aunt Ginny's eyebrows flicked together, and she gave me a look like I was disturbed. "Okay, settle down. It's just the Senior Center. It's not Andrew Lloyd Webber."

Mrs. Davis giggled. "Besides, we want to see if Royce has lost his hair or grown a hump or anything."

Aunt Ginny clasped her locket again. "Well, I'm sure he won't remember me. Besides, I'm not interested, and I'm not going to any special trouble to impress him."

Mrs. Dodson tapped her cane. "Sure."

Mother Gibson nodded. "Perfectly reasonable."

Mrs. Davis giggled. "Uh-huh."

Aunt Ginny bounced her foot. Then checked her watch. Then stood and started to leave the room.

"Where are you going?" I asked.

"To make a hair appointment." Aunt Ginny touched her perfectly red hair. "It's my regular time to have my roots done."

Chapter Five

My life had become a series of wrestling matches. Wrestling with bill collectors to give me time to launch the B&B. Wrestling with my heart over Tim and Gia. Wrestling with discipline to eat kale and grilled chicken instead of jelly doughnuts and Yoo-hoo. And wrestling with the zipper on my jeans that was currently mocking me with every illicit bite from my Restaurant Week baking.

I lay on the bed sweating and cursing, having lost the match. Figaro sat close by, mildly amused. I had two choices. Pull all my larger-size clothes out of storage, where I'd optimistically hidden them from myself, or buy Spanx. I peeled off the jeans and threw them in the corner until they'd had time to think about their treachery, then fired up my laptop. There were many styles of Spanx to choose from. One was a corset that ran from bra to hip bone. I'd have that sucker rolled up like a headband within an hour. The other extreme was ankle to shoulders. My ankles were probably fine sans compression, and I knew my bladder did not have the fight it once had to withstand a twenty-minute spandex peel-off in an emergency situation, so I picked something in between. The link opened to a discount website selling knockoff Spanx—or Spunks. They looked the same and the price was way better, so I bought two pair. Then I fished around my dresser for a pair of yoga pants for today because breathing was high on my list of priorities.

I unrolled my yoga mat and did a few sun salutations. Maybe I would feel less like a failure in downward-facing dog. While I hung upside down, my mind wandered back to Gia and Tim. They were both getting serious. If only I could split myself in half to be with both of them. I was really starting to feel uncomfortable kissing two different men. Don't get me wrong, I was enjoying it. I just wasn't enjoying how it made me feel about myself.

I closed my eyes and breathed in a snootful of whiskers. "What are you doing?"

Fig gave me a nose bonk and did a few figure eights through my hair.

I rose to warrior II pose and he lay down on the middle of my mat in loaf position.

"I know what you're up to, and you're just going to have to wait."

I did another downward dog into child's pose, nudging Fig out of the way.

Fifteen pounds of menace hopped up his persistence, and my back lowered like a pressure plate.

Fig stood on me, purring as I lay with my face smashed into the yoga mat, considering my life.

With a sigh, I grumbled, "Eat."

Ffwomp. "Merow. Merow."

We both knew who was in charge.

Aunt Ginny was in the kitchen fiddling and fussing with the blender pitcher. "Why can't I get this doohickey to work!"

I took the pitcher of fruit and yogurt from where she was trying to cram it onto the wrong base and moved it over to the Ninja.

"I feel like a cat on the freeway." She shook her hands in front of her.

"Why are you so wound up?"

"Tryouts are this afternoon. What if Royce is there? What if he sees me?"

"I thought that was the whole point."

"I don't know what I was thinking! This is a mistake. I'm going to tell the girls I changed my mind."

"If Royce has really moved back to Cape May, you're going to see him eventually."

"Oh no I won't. I don't ever have to leave this house again. What is taking so long for that smoothie?!"

I reached over and flicked the switch, turning the blender on. It surged to life and Aunt Ginny put her head in her hands.

"I can't do it. What if I make a fool of myself?"

I turned off the blender and tapped Aunt Ginny's smoothie into a glass. "I don't remember you being worried about that when you signed up for belly dancing classes."

"Royce wasn't in the class, and that wasn't my first time belly dancing."

"Oh." *Let me file that away.* I handed her the glass. "What are those red and orange pieces?"

"Fruity Pebbles. Will you please come with me this afternoon? For moral support."

"Of course."

Aunt Ginny's shoulders relaxed, and she sank a straw in her questionable breakfast. "Oh good. It's supposed to be *Mamma Mia!* I'm trying out for the part of the sexy best friend, Tanya. I sure hope they typecast."

"What time are tryouts?"

"Right after dinner."

"So . . . five o'clock?"

Aunt Ginny looked up from her straw and nodded.

I tried to choose my next words carefully. "*Mamma Mia!* seems a bit of a challenge for the Senior Center. How are they going to fill the younger parts?"

Aunt Ginny shrugged. "We have a lot of young people. Some of our folks are only in their sixties."

"Uh-huh." *I should probably check that our hospitalization is up to date.* "Are you better now?"

She slurped on her sugar smoothie. "Yeah. I think I was just hungry. I'm feeling much better as long as you're going to be there to cheer me on. And if Moira—sorry, *Blanche*—should happen to show up for tryouts, maybe you could distract her away from the audition."

"How am I gonna do that?"

"I don't know. Get a hot dog on a string and lure her out to the hall."

"Oh yeah, that can't fail." I put the water on for coffee.

"I don't know what I'll do if she beats me out for a part again."

"Maybe she won't even be there."

Aunt Ginny raised her eyebrows. "Right. And maybe this smoothie isn't full of chocolate syrup."

I got two coffee cups down from the cabinet and took out the coffee beans and broached a subject that had been heavy on my heart. "I'm starting to feel guilty about kissing both Gia and Tim when I don't know which one I want to commit to."

Aunt Ginny made a face and shook her head. "You're too young to worry about that. And I don't see a ring on your finger, so just have fun."

I'd been warming up to the big question, but every time I tried to get it out the words stuck in my throat. "Aunt Ginny, did people back in your day ever . . . have sex before marriage?"

Aunt Ginny started choking and I had to pat her on the

back. "What? You can't ask me stuff like that before nine a.m. Good lord, no! Absolutely not. Any lady of quality would never give the milk away for free. We waited until our wedding night."

"Oh." *I see.* "That's what I thought." I took the kettle off the burner and hit the button on the coffee grinder. "What about before their second marriage?"

Aunt Ginny blushed up to the roots of her red hair. "Oh, my lord . . . Is that . . . what time is it? I'm going to be late to the salon. I can't keep Mr. Charles waiting." Aunt Ginny coughed and backed out of the room, leaving me with a whole new set of questions.

Chapter Six

I sat in the sunroom checking email on my phone while I waited for Aunt Ginny to emerge from her boudoir. I didn't know what was going on in there, but it sounded like quite the undertaking. Even Figaro had come running through the kitchen with his tail between his legs after a particularly fretful-sounding procedure. Finally, I heard high heels clacking through the kitchen, but nothing could have prepared me for the vision that came around the corner. Aunt Ginny was dressed in a tailored white pantsuit with a double-breasted jacket and had square-cut emeralds the color of her eyes dangling from her ears. Her hair was a deeper shade of red than it had been in the morning, and her beehive was gone. She was all spiky on the top and pointy down to her jaw.

"Mr. Charles called it the Sharon Osbourne. What do you think?" With a freshly manicured hand, she smoothed her bangs.

"I think you look fabulous! Royce is going to be blown away."

Figaro took a step toward Aunt Ginny in full sniff mode.

She raised her finger in his direction. "Don't touch me!"

He flopped over and stared into space.

She checked the time on her gold watch. "Close your mouth. You look like a fish."

I snapped my jaw shut, still mesmerized by her transformation.

Aunt Ginny handed me a baguette-style handbag. "Here, hold my pocketbook while I touch up my lipstick in the natural light."

I took the small, white purse and almost dropped it. "What do you have in here?"

She smacked her lips together to blot her burgundy lipstick. "Brass knuckles."

I was unable to formulate a follow-up.

"Always be prepared when Moira Finklebaum is in the mix." She took her purse back and donned a new pair of Donna Karan rose-gold sunglasses. "Okay, let's get this over with."

I grabbed my keys and coat from the foyer. Aunt Ginny wrapped a white wool cape around her shoulders, being careful not to smudge her makeup or unsettle her hair. And with one final look down the hall to Figaro, whose tongue was now hanging out of his mouth, we were out the door.

The Senior Center may as well have rolled out a literal red carpet and rented spotlights, because the ladies of Cape May were dressed for the Academy Awards. Mrs. Davis's pink hair had grown several inches through the magic of extensions, and she was tightly encased in leopard-print leggings and a red bustier. A couple of newly platinum blondes had poured themselves into XXL leather miniskirts paired with orthopedic shoes. Even Mrs. Dodson had bedazzled her cane for the occasion. Everyone was sporting the teased-up bouffant of having just come from the beauty parlor. The yellow craft room was alive with perm solution, Aqua Net, and Old Spice.

The tables were laden with beads and glue, felt, and spools of yarn. The back of the room offered a vending machine selling minipacks of Lorna Doones and Pecan Sandies and the like, and another selling water, soft drinks, and nutritional shakes for the elderly.

Mr. Ricardo, the silver-haired salsa instructor, was dressed in black tuxedo pants and a ruffled red shirt that was open to the waist. He had two ladies on each arm and was laying down a thick layer of suave and offering to show off his appendix scar.

Mother Gibson joined me in her usual cargo capris and a World's Best Grandma T-shirt. "Woo, child, Mr. Charles has been busy."

I grinned. "How come you're not all decked out?"

She shook her salt-and-pepper fade. "I don't need to impress anyone. And I'm glad to see you don't either."

I brushed some muffin crumbs off my chest. *How long had that been there?*

One of the men shuffled into the room with a fat manila packet. He had close-cropped white hair in a military buzz cut and a pointy goatee. I had seen him around a few times when I'd brought Aunt Ginny up for activities, but we'd never officially met. He worked his way around the room, passing out booklets.

Mrs. Davis fished a pair of reading glasses out of her bustier and peered down her nose at the booklet. "What is this, Duke?"

Aunt Ginny took one. "Is this the play? I thought we were doing *Mamma Mia!*?"

Mr. Ricardo kept his arms folded. "That says *The Naked Burg*. I don't do naked unless I get top billing."

"Just take one." He shoved a booklet at Mr. Ricardo.

My neighbors from down the street, Mr. and Mrs. Shein- berg, entered the room, and Duke passed them a booklet.

"What's this meshuggener?"

"Just keep an open mind."

Mrs. Dodson reluctantly took hers. "What does that mean?"

As he came by, he handed me one. The cover was faded and worn on the edges. The tagline read *My life on the mean streets of Sea Isle*. I gave it a flip through. It was a script.

"It means I wrote this. This is my play." Duke grinned broadly.

Mr. Sheinberg threw his script on the activity table. "Not interested."

Everyone else added their copies to the stack in rapid succession. I didn't want to be rude, so I dropped my copy in my tote bag to throw it away at home.

Duke held out his arms. "Oh come on! You haven't even given it a chance!"

Mrs. Davis crossed her arms over the ruffle of her bustier. "We're doing *Mamma Mia!*"

Duke waved his manila packet. "But this is so much bet- ter than that drivel."

He was snatching his scripts back and telling everyone off when a statuesque beauty entered the room in a cloud of pale pink silk. She wore her hair in a graceful silver bob, and when she walked, not a hair dared to flutter, as if her lithe, dancer's body had hidden wings while I was forced to stamp around like a barn animal.

Mother Gibson jabbed me in the side with her elbow. "That's Blanche Carrigan."

The gossip lowered to a hush and all eyes turned to Aunt Ginny.

"Moira."

The angel smiled serenely and took Aunt Ginny's hands in hers. "Ginny, it's so good to see you. And please, Moira was so long ago. I go by Blanche now. I'm surprised you're still around. Have you been unwell?" She looked Aunt Ginny up and down with a shade of pity.

Aunt Ginny returned an insincere smile. "I'm fit as ever. I'm glad to see the twelve-step program is working. We hadn't expected you to be sober tonight."

Mother Gibson trilled under her breath, "Woo-hoo."

Blanche's smile cracked at the edges and her pale blue eyes flashed a sharp pang of irritation. She dropped Aunt Ginny's hand and opened her mouth to say something.

Suddenly, all eyes swiveled in my direction. I was at first flattered and wished I'd worn my dressy yoga pants; then I realized they were looking behind me at the very dashing gentleman with a head full of fluffy white hair. He was wearing a tan linen Italian suit with a crisp white shirt and tan-and-white loafers. He was lightly bronzed and smiling like he'd just arrived by yacht from sunny Tuscany.

I whispered, "I gather that's Royce. He sure doesn't look like he's in his eighties."

Mother Gibson whispered back, "Good genes."

Aunt Ginny whispered a little more loudly, "Botox."

Mr. Ricardo scowled as the room broke into applause and his ladies left him to turn their attentions toward the dashing newcomer.

Blanche floated to the tall man and air-kissed him on each cheek. "Royce. How good to see you again. Are you settling in okay?"

She crooked her arm around Royce's and gave a triumphant look to Aunt Ginny.

Her triumph didn't last long, because a little toad of a woman with pinkish-red hair and a thick coating of blue paste on her eyelids removed Blanche's arm from Royce and snapped hers in its place. She wore a garishly bold print of Technicolor cats and had on a shade of orange lipstick that made her skin look like egg custard.

Royce looked down at the round little toad and gave her a gleam of pearly whites. He patted her stubby hand with his own.

She grinned back, and her painted-on eyebrows scrunched down to her flat nose.

Royce turned a warm smile on the roomful of strangers. "It's good to be home. I see some friendly faces." His eyes lingered on Aunt Ginny for just a moment longer than everyone else. "You all remember my sister, Fiona. And her son, Ignatius." Royce looked around confused. "Where'd he go?"

Fiona tipped her head back and screeched, "Iggy!"

A brooding hulk with rounded shoulders, a swayback, and a paunch appeared in the doorway under an invisible gray cloud. He ran his hand through the few wisps of black hair that did little to hide his bald spot no matter how far they were combed over. "What?"

Fiona jabbed him in his faded MÖTLEY CRÜE T-shirt. "Iggy, Uncle Royce wants to introduce you."

Iggy mumbled a frosty "Whatever."

Royce gave the room a sheepish grin and cocked his head. "Iggy, everybody."

I raised my hand and started to say, "Hi, Iggy," but all the ladies started talking at once and rushing to get a piece of Royce's attention. Fiona clutched his sleeve, creating trenches in the linen. Only Aunt Ginny and Mr. Ricardo stayed where they were. One was being aloof and the other was pouting.

"Aren't you going to go over and say hi?"

Aunt Ginny returned my innocent question with a glare. "I'd rather set myself on fire."

Everyone was talking at once, peppering Royce with questions about Broadway and other famous stars they'd read about in gossip magazines.

"What's it like to work with Liza Minnelli?"

"She's delightful."

"Do you know Barbra Streisand?"

"No, I don't believe so."

"I saw you perform with Carol Channing in *Sugar Babies*!"

"Oh my, that was forty years ago!"

Royce was taking it all in stride, nodding, smiling, and signing autographs, but Fiona had taken to swatting at people like flies. "Get back! Get back! Royce didn't come here to be mauled. My brother is only here as a favor to Neil. Get back!"

Royce patted his sister on the shoulder. "That's all right, Fee. I don't mind. I spent a lot of years on tour and didn't get back as often as I would have liked."

Blanche smiled brightly. "Or at all."

Fiona jabbed her tube of lipstick at Blanche. "Hey, my brother toured with the Royal Shakespeare Company in London. Only the very best actors get that honor. Every director wanted him. He couldn't come home whenever the mood struck like some two-bit extra." She applied another layer of coral to her thin lips.

Blanche remained perfectly composed except for the death grip on her handbag. Her knuckles were white and one of the rhinestones popped off the clutch and rolled under the paint cabinet.

Royce began to wax poetic. "Oh, to be on tour with the Bard again. Those were the glory days. 'All the world's a stage, and all the men and women merely players.'"

Fiona gave a smug look to the room. "That was Shakespeare."

Royce gave a modest chuckle. "Well, I don't know if I would say I'm a superstar . . ."

Aunt Ginny muttered next to me. "No one else said it either."

Duke was trying to shove one of his booklets into Royce's hands when Neil Rockford, the new Senior Center director, appeared.

"Good afternoon, ladies and gentlemen! Just wait till you see what I have in store for you!"

Chapter Seven

"**H**ey! You made it." Neil Rockford thrust his hand into Royce's. He was tall and thin. His hair was white, and he looked like he was about fifty. He had the physique of someone who was naturally athletic. In the few months since he had taken over as director of the Senior Center, he had done a marvelous job of making it a place full of fun activities for Cape May County's elderly. Although I suspected many of the ladies faithfully came to the events because Neil was handsome, and they liked to keep their flirting skills sharp. He shook Royce's hand with vigor. "This is quite an honor, sir. Quite an honor."

Royce allowed his hand to be pumped and smiled affably. "Good, good. Well, anything I can do to help local thespians."

Neil continued to hold Royce's hand. "Wonderful. Just wonderful. This is going to be the best production the Cape May Senior Center has ever put on."

Royce liberated his hand and Fiona promptly reclaimed

his arm. "Oh? I was under the impression that this would be your first play."

Neil crossed his arms around himself. "Well, yes. But it will set the bar very high."

Royce grinned and patted Fiona's hand.

"Besides," Neil continued, "now that you're back in town, how could we *not* put on a play?"

Blanche snapped her fingers in front of Neil's face and sang out, "Daylight's wasting, dahling. Where do you want us?"

Neil set his eyes on Blanche. "You look lovely tonight, dear."

Aunt Ginny turned and tried to walk out the emergency exit, but I caught her by the elbow. "Uh-uh."

Neil took Blanche's hand and tucked it in his arm and started leading the procession down the hall. "I convinced the county to let me turn the assembly room into a proper theater. It's a project that's been in the mix for several months, but my contractor assures me it will be completed in time for opening night."

Duke called out from the middle of the procession, "What if we don't want to do *Mamma Mia!*?"

Everyone but Neil shushed him.

We picked our way down the long hall, Neil escorting Blanche, followed by Royce with Fiona embedded into his side like a bright orange tumor. A morose Iggy plodded behind them, followed very closely by the rest of the seniors, trying not to let Royce get out of fawning distance. Aunt Ginny and I brought up the rear, mostly because Aunt Ginny was trying to escape and I was determined not to let her do something she'd regret later.

The old assembly room had been converted into a little theater with a large stage and two-story red velvet curtains at one end, a modest backstage area with a booth to operate lights and sound effects, and six rows of off-set seating for about seventy-two patrons with an aisle down the center. There was a scaffolding set up, and some of the lights rested on the floor waiting to be hung.

Neil hopped up on the stage and held out his arms. "The seats were bought from a theater in Atlanta that was being torn down, and most of the equipment is refurbished. I got the curtains on Etsy, and the piano was donated by the Methodists when they raised enough money for their new baby grand."

The seniors *ooh*ed and *aah*ed over the plush red seats and tried them out, bouncing and testing the springs.

"Hey!" Mr. Sheinberg popped up from the second row. "This one poked me in the keister."

Neil grinned. "Yeah, some of them do that. Now, if I can get everyone's eyes on me for just a minute . . . yes. I know you are all excited to get going with the auditions." He chuckled. "I mean, you've been hounding me since I got here to put on a play. I think you're going to love *Mamma Mia!* The costumes alone . . ."

Duke held up his booklets. "Let's do something more dramatic!"

Someone threw a pack of Tic Tacs at Duke's head. "Sit down!"

Duke dropped into a theater seat with a loud squeak.

Neil ignored him. "*Mamma Mia!* is a story about love and second chances . . ."

Duke hollered through the pages of his script that he'd turned into a tube. "Lame!"

Neil shot Duke a look.

Duke jumped up. "Mine has everything. Drugs. Guns. Betrayal. Crime. Car chases. Gambling. Redemption."

Mr. Sheinberg imitated Duke. "Fencing. Fighting. Torture. Revenge. Meh."

About fifteen seniors shouted, "No!"

Duke flopped back in his seat and sulked.

Neil went on like nothing had happened. "I picked *Mamma Mia!* because there are a lot of parts for both men and women, and you all know most of the songs already."

Mother Gibson stage-whispered, "If we can remember them."

Mrs. Davis whispered back, "I saw ABBA in New York in '79."

Mrs. Dodson narrowed her eyes. "You did not."

Mrs. Davis narrowed her eyes right back. "I did too. I saw them getting out of a cab at a Beanie's Pizza."

Mother Gibson snorted, and Aunt Ginny groaned and looked for the exit.

Neil jumped down from the stage and took a stack of papers from the top of the piano that he began handing out. "I've chosen two scenes for readings, and for the vocal try-outs, Mr. Iggy Sharpe has graciously volunteered to play the musical numbers for us."

Iggy mumbled, "No, I didn't."

Fiona poked him in the butt and growled through gritted teeth, "Ignatius Jeremiah! Get up there."

Iggy dragged himself over to the piano with all the effort of a slug in a footrace for free salt.

Neil handed Royce two pages and flashed him a brilliant smile. "Of course, you will be playing the lead role of Sam, but I'd love it if you'd read across from the ladies as they try out."

Royce took the pages and returned a brilliant smile of his own. "I'd be delighted."

Duke groused when Neil handed him his lines, and he tried to swap Neil a copy of his script.

I whispered to Aunt Ginny, "I wonder what part he's picked for you to read."

I didn't have to wonder long because Neil paused when he got to Aunt Ginny. He looked deep into her eyes with bright intensity. "I know you will do especially well, Mrs. Frankowski."

Aunt Ginny blushed. "Call me Ginny."

Neil flashed his brilliant smile. "Ginny." He winked at her before moving on to Mrs. Dodson and Mrs. Davis.

Mother Gibson waved him off. "I'm not trying out. I'm just here to watch."

Neil put his arm around the woman who might have been old enough to be his grandmother. "Do you know what I need most of all?"

Mother Gibson shook her head.

"Someone to be in charge of the stage crew."

Mother Gibson's face lit up. "Well, I don't know what stage crew does, honey, but I love to be in charge. I'll do it!"

Neil squeezed her shoulder. "Excellent."

He turned to address the room. "I'll call you in the order that you signed up. Royce, would you please take your mark on the stage?" Then Neil turned and sat in the first seat of the front row.

Royce took his place center stage. Aunt Ginny and I took our seats and Fiona plopped down next to us.

"Iggy is just delighted to be a part of his uncle's play."

Aunt Ginny and I leaned forward to look at Iggy, who was slumped over with his forehead resting on the top of the piano. Fiona didn't seem to notice. She was beaming. "Just wait till you hear him play. My Iggy has a master's degree in piano."

Aunt Ginny didn't look convinced. "Does he?"

Blanche was called to the stage and made a big production with her entrance. With her arms outstretched, she swept onto the platform with a flourish. "Together again at last. This is quite a treat for all of you. Royce and I made a great team on stage during our very successful Broadway careers, didn't we, partner?"

Royce's eyebrows shot up, but he declined to answer.

Fiona snorted. "Stupid cow. She didn't have a Broadway career. She tried to ride my brother's coattails until she was finally chased out of New York. It serves her right for taking my brother away from me. If she hadn't enticed him to go to the city, he could have stayed home and worked in the family welding business."

Welding? That would be a hard no.

Aunt Ginny muttered under her breath, "He would have *loved* that."

Mrs. Davis and Mrs. Dodson turned around in their seats to properly gossip and snub Blanche. Mrs. Davis whispered, "I heard she came home early because she couldn't even get a part as an off-Broadway extra."

Fiona leaned forward in her seat. "Royce said that no one would work with her. He had to escape to London before she ruined both of their careers. That's why he signed up to apprentice with the Shakespeare people."

Mrs. Dodson put a hand on her bosom "Well, I don't normally like to gossip."

I almost choked, but I managed to hold it together. Aunt Ginny had less success, and I had to pat her on the back a few times.

Mrs. Dodson glared at us before continuing on. "I heard she came home flat broke and with a little prob-lem." Mrs. Dodson nodded and made the sign for kicking back a shot. "Had to do a stint in Cape Rehab."

Fiona looked from side to side. "She was singing a different tune back then. There was none of this my-old-partner-Royce stuff. She called our house every night and made herself a menace, demanding that if we ever heard from him to tell him she needed to speak to him right away. She said he owed her that much. Can you believe?"

Mrs. Davis shook her head. "The nerve."

Aunt Ginny finally piped in. "I don't know where all her money came from, but it wasn't her fame as an actress."

Fiona's painted-on eyebrows leaned toward each other, making a pinkish-red seagull on her forehead. "Ha! I'll tell you where the money came from. It came from her second husband."

A loud "Ahem!" came from the stage. We looked up to see Blanche scowling in our direction. Apparently, she expected a rapt audience while she auditioned.

Fiona ignored her. "That poor man—Vernon, I think his name was. Or maybe it was Victor. Anyway, she didn't have a pot to pee in before she met him."

Mrs. Davis said, "He must have been loaded, because after he died she was rolling in it."

Aunt Ginny stiffened beside me. "Oh no."

"What's wrong?"

With trembling hands, she handed me her audition pages. "Look what scene we have to perform."

I scanned the pages. It was the scene where Sam and Donna fight about their breakup. I had no words. I took a long look at Aunt Ginny squirming in her seat. Iggy started to play "SOS" for Blanche's audition. I handed the pages back. "What do you want to do? If you're going to regret not trying out, I think you should go for it. But if it's too much considering . . . I can get us out of here with any number of fake emergencies. It's your call."

Aunt Ginny watched the stage. Blanche was very good when she wasn't off-key, and Royce was still trying to get into the rhythm of the song. Next to us, Fiona was enumerating all the productions Royce had been a part of on Broadway and London's West End.

Mr. Ricardo appeared and threw himself down on the other side of Aunt Ginny in a huff. "I don't see what all the fuss is about. He's not Hugh Jackman."

I kept my eyes on Aunt Ginny but asked Mr. Ricardo, "What scene are the men reading?"

He held up his pages. "The scene where someone named Sophie asks me if I'm her father."

Aunt Ginny squared her shoulders and bit her lip. "I'll do it. I'm not backing out."

I patted her knee. "You're going to be great."

Mr. Ricardo threw his arm over Aunt Ginny's chair. "What do you have to worry about? You have a great voice. Blanche has made the piano player start over three times. She told him *he* was off-key."

Iggy was effortlessly teasing "SOS" out of the keys, and Blanche kept stepping in front of Royce to deliver her lines.

Royce threw his hands up and took a further step back. He let Blanche sing her lines and his. When her audition was over, only Neil's applause was more than polite. Blanche seemed very confident in her performance and took an opening-night bow.

The auditions progressed in a similar fashion from there. The ladies all read for the part of Donna across from Royce to keep things simple. Many of them flirted with Royce, and Neil had to remind them that Donna wouldn't be throwing herself at Sam. Mrs. Davis was allowed to sing Tanya's number, "Does Your Mother Know," because she told Neil she would rather be in the chorus than play Donna, and because Neil was tired of fighting with the ladies. Mrs. Dodson made a bit of a fuss that she didn't want to try out for Donna either, and if she got the part, she would refuse to do it. She wanted to try out for Rosie, the chubby cookbook author. She rather tanked the delivery of her lines across from Royce, but she made up for it with a fantastic rendition of "Take a Chance on Me" and surprised everyone when she ditched her cane and threw some seventies dance moves in with the number.

Finally, Aunt Ginny was called to the stage. She wouldn't

look at Royce, and she couldn't hide her nerves. Royce delivered his lines with more feeling than he had with any other audition, and I found I was on the edge of my seat with my heart pounding. I knew I wasn't the only one. The room was still, and all eyes were on the stage. Even Iggy missed his cue to begin the music. At one point in the song, Royce spun Aunt Ginny to face him, and every jaw dropped as we thought he was going to kiss her right there, but she spun away with her next line.

"Brilliant!" Neil was on his feet when the number was over. "That's the emotion I'm talking about!"

Yeah, well, I guess it would be since they've lived the part.

Aunt Ginny was flushed with excitement and relief when she retook her seat. "How was I?"

I hugged her. "You were the best."

Mrs. Dodson and Mrs. Davis turned around on their seats and giggled excitedly. "That was fantastic. There's no way you're not Donna."

Aunt Ginny played with a gold locket she wore around her neck. "Donna? I don't want to be Donna. I want to be Tanya."

Mother Gibson patted her on the shoulder. "We know, honey."

Even Fiona was full of praise. "Nice job. You didn't upstage Royce."

We sat through two long hours of tryouts with the same lines and the same songs. In the end, I think Neil was regretting the whole idea. The one moment of comedy was when Duke took the stage and chose an avant-garde scene from his play, *The Naked Burg*, instead of reading the lines he was given. They were the wrong words, but, I mean, they were delivered really well. Even Royce applauded his efforts.

It was a long night and we were all happy to wrap things up. We stretched and gathered our things. The ladies were discussing going out to celebrate before the results were posted and had the potential to bring any hard feelings. I told them I thought that was a great idea, so they suggested that I drive them. *Once again, snared by my helpfulness.*

Neil hugged his notes to his chest. "You have all done very well. You should be proud of yourselves. It will be a hard decision, but I'll have the parts posted in the morning. We can't put on a production without a team behind the scenes, so if you didn't get a part this time around, I hope you will consider volunteering to work on the stage crew. This play can bring a lot of money into the Center for more programs. The county gives us a very small budget for special events, so we need some donations to pay for most of our activities and supplies." Then Neil looked from me to Iggy. "We especially need some young muscle to do the heavy lifting."

I shifted my gaze to avoid eye contact. *Good luck with that.*

Iggy slumped over so hard I was afraid he'd pop a vertebra.

Neil stopped to grab Aunt Ginny's hand on his way by. "You were wonderful, Ginny." He winked at her and headed up the center aisle.

Blanche noticed the exchange and sneered.

Aunt Ginny stuck her tongue out in return.

While Aunt Ginny had her tongue out, she was interrupted by a certain ex-boyfriend. "Ginny, you were fantastic."

Aunt Ginny froze and snapped her tongue back into her mouth. Her voice lilted as she responded. "Oh, why, thank you, Royce. We'll see how it all turns out in the morning, I suppose."

Royce's eyes roved to Aunt Ginny's neck and he smiled. "You still have the locket I gave you on prom night."

Aunt Ginny froze with her hand on the chain. "Oh, this old thing? I forgot I was wearing it."

Fiona was pulling on Royce's sleeve, but he was fixed on Aunt Ginny. "Would you care to join me for a drink sometime?"

Blanche was a few feet away, but she was leaning hard around Duke, watching.

Aunt Ginny blinked a couple of times. "Oh, well . . . I . . ."

Fiona yanked on Royce's arm and pulled him down the aisle toward the door. "No, sir! You've been away from home long enough! Iggy and I need some time with you."

Royce winked at Aunt Ginny. "I'll see you tomorrow, Ginger."

I nudged Aunt Ginny. "Ooh, Ginger, is that his pet name for you?"

Aunt Ginny waved me off. "It's been too long, who remembers?" Her face broke into a wide grin.

Chapter Eight

I had to drag myself out of bed to go make the muffins. My head was pounding. Aunt Ginny and her friends kept me out until two a.m. celebrating their successful auditions and preloading some good vibes before the results were posted. Aunt Ginny was still sleeping it off, and Figaro cracked an eye open, then rolled over and went back to sleep. I was on my own this morning, so I got dressed, ran a brush through my teeth and another through my hair, threw on some tinted foundation and mascara, and now I was sitting at the coffee bar of La Dolce Vita with my eyes closed.

"Okay, Bella. Open your eyes and tell me what you think of this." Gia was holding a steaming cappuccino mug.

"Mmm." I blew on it and sipped. "Ooh, that's good. What is it? Strawberry?"

Gia cocked his head to the side and gave me a single nod. He was waiting for something else.

"And chocolate?" I took another sip. "Is this the coconut almond milk you usually use?"

Gia wiggled his eyebrows. "Cashew milk. I made it yesterday after you left."

"I love it. This would be perfect for Valentine's Day."

"You are reading my mind."

"I'm going to have to come up with some Valentine's goodies for the pastry case. What do you think about a Paleo chocolate-strawberry muffin to pair with this latte?"

Gia leaned against the back counter and crossed his arms. "Sounds great."

"Ooh, I know. How about a strawberry muffin with white chocolate chips and a chocolate muffin with strawberry pieces? We can call them Stud Muffins and Baby Cakes."

Gia shook his head and chuckled. "I love it. *È perfetto.*"

"I can also make some Paleo linzer hearts with seedless raspberry jam for the sweets."

"Very nice. What do you think about some rose macarons?"

"I think you're trying to kill me."

Gia laughed softly and came toward me. "You obsess too much. Your macarons are perfect."

"I'm not sure they're ready for sale."

He took my hands in his. "You have made thousands. And the seagulls are so fat from eating the ones you threw out in the alley, they can hardly lift off the ground. Stop worrying." He kissed my hands. "I promise to love them with all my heart."

I tried to swallow, but a lump was caught in my throat. Gia leaned in to kiss me. My brain screamed, *Stop it, you might be leading him on!* But my heart screamed back, *Can't hear you, la la la!*

Before Gia's lips touched mine, we heard the disgruntled snort of the Northern Italian Rhino, "Bah!" followed by a string of Italian obscenities. I could swear I heard the word "fornicator" in there.

"Momma." Gia walked around the bar to wrap his mother in a bear hug. She stood about four foot ten up and down, and another four foot ten from side to side. With a tight gray bun over an ever-present scowl. Somehow, she managed to smile beatifically at Gia with one eye while putting a hex on me with the other. She was accompanied today with a rail of an old man in a brown suit carrying a matching, beat-up brown briefcase.

"Zio Alfio, this is Poppy. Poppy, my uncle Alfio. He is here to draw up some papers for me."

I put out my hand to shake Zio Alfio's, but the man looked me up and down like a wolf at a jackrabbit buffet. Zio Alfio made some gestures and head bobbles that clearly meant something about my boobs.

Momma smacked Zio Alfio on the back of the head.

Gia stepped in between us, laughing nervously. "Hey, okay, Zio. *Va bene*, no?"

Gia led his uncle to a polished wood table in the front room and I waved a tentative hello to Mrs. Larusso. Momma returned her usual reply of antipathy.

"Well, I'd better get to the kitchen and start to workin'. Those muffins aren't gonna make themselves." *Good lord, I sound like a hillbilly, gonna catch me a possum.*

Momma turned and headed for the front door. I grabbed my latte and got out of there. *Can you imagine her being someone's mother-in-law?* That thought stopped me in my tracks and I almost dropped my latte. *Score one point for Team Tim. His mother hates me, but she lives in Florida.*

I set out my gluten-free ingredients for the morning. I was making cozy Hot Cocoa muffins with mini marshmallows, Cinnamon Crumb cakes, and a pan of Blueberry Bliss bars for tonight. I was chopping and measuring when Gia's sister blew in the back door.

"I see Momma was in."

"You just missed her."

Karla's waist was impossibly small, her makeup impeccably applied, and her lush, mink-brown hair wrapped in a perfect topknot. "Heard all about your near miss with debauchery."

I dropped my knife. "What?!"

Karla laughed and wrapped an apron around her designer jeans. "Momma said she got here just in time to prevent you from defiling her precious baby boy."

"I did not . . . He . . ." *Okay. Count to ten. Measure your almond meal. Imagine winning the lottery and sending Karla and Momma to Naples for the rest of their lives.*

Karla didn't care. She just wanted to fluster me. She tossed her hand over her head and went out to wipe down the counters.

A minute later, Gia came in and stood very close to me with his back against the counter. He had a cryptic grin on his face.

I laughed and took a step to the left to make some room. He followed me with a step closer.

"What are you doing?"

"Nothing." He popped a couple of blueberries in his mouth and grinned. "So, the *nonnas* had you out past your bedtime last night?"

I measured and stirred sour cream into the cake batter. "Those ladies are exhausting. First of all, Mrs. Davis could drink a Marine under the table on his best days. Mrs. Dodson, who won't broker any nonsense, made forty-seven dollars in tips dancing the hustle on top of the bar. And Aunt Ginny convinced the DJ to let her take over for an hour while he went on an extended break."

"How'd she make that happen?"

"She bribed him. The bar liked her style so much, they're thinking about starting Motown Mondays as a weekly theme."

Gia was laughing so hard, he was holding his sides. "What were you doing while all this was going on?"

"Oh, I was busy. Yeah. Mr. Ricardo asked me to be his wing-man while he tried to pick up a couple college girls two tables over."

"Did he succeed?"

"I saw one of them considering it and called her an Uber."

"I wish I could have seen that."

"You'll have to come with us next time." I poured the cake batter into my pan and sprinkled it with the filling.

Gia gently wiped some flour off my cheek and ran his thumb over my lips.

My knees shook and my heart galloped around the kitchen before coming back to my chest.

I layered the rest of the batter over the filling and Gia helped me sprinkle it with the crumb topping.

He took the sheet pan and popped it in the oven for me. "How did the audition go?"

"Aunt Ginny did great. I can't imagine her not getting the lead. But if she does, she'll be playing across from a Broad-way star who spent his life onstage."

"What's he doing here in the old people show?"

I shrugged. "*Pfft.* Apparently, he grew up here, and now he's retired. He's also"—I paused for effect—"Aunt Ginny's old boyfriend from high school."

Gia's jaw dropped. "No!"

I nodded and started whisking the eggs into the muffin batter. "Aunt Ginny is very nervous about being in the play with him. She doesn't want to get the lead role in the love story because she has some unresolved feelings of her own."

"Sure. Sometimes it's better for the past to stay in the past."

"True, but a piece of her heart will always be his. Old flames are hard to extinguish."

Gia popped another blueberry in his mouth. "Mm-hmm.

Maybe if it was meant to be, it would have worked out the first time."

I whipped the batter against the side of the bowl. "I guess. But don't you think sometimes the timing is just off? What if this is finally their chance to be together?"

"Don't you think if he really loved her he would have fought for her the first time around?"

"What if he just didn't know how? What if she messed things up so badly his heart was too broken?"

"How deep was his love if he couldn't man up after some heartbreak to win her back?"

"What if he *was* wrong? Maybe the fact that he's here now means she should make it right." I whacked the bowl on the counter to deflate some of the air bubbles.

"If he could spend all those years apart from her and not be in agony, he doesn't deserve her."

"Maybe he's just realizing that now. Maybe she's supposed to give him a second chance."

"Or maybe there's someone else she's supposed to be with."

"How is she supposed to know which one to choose!" The room was silent but for the deafening sound of my heart thudding in my ears.

Gia cradled the back of my head in his hands and brought his lips down to still the trembling of mine. "Bella, you should choose who your heart tells you to."

Chapter Nine

I flew home after making Gia's baked goods. My heart was sick. I planned to curl up in bed and hide under the covers until I knew what I wanted. Of course, by the time I realized what I wanted, what I wanted might not want me back anymore.

A gust of wind caught the storm door and it burst from my hand, hitting the wooden siding with a bang. Figaro shot across the foyer like a bullet train from the library to the dining room. I was hanging up my coat when Aunt Ginny hollered from the kitchen. "Poppy, is that you?"

"Yes." *Who else would it be?* I shut the front door and considered kicking it.

Aunt Ginny came down the hallway wiping her hands on an apron. "Thelma texted me that they were on their way over with news. Either that or they're coming with pies. Thelma doesn't know how to text. Anyway, I thought maybe you were them. You look pale. Did something happen at the coffee shop?"

"No." My lip trembled.

Aunt Ginny tilted her head and looked at me through sad eyes. She patted my arm. "Give yourself time. You've only been home a few months."

I was about to head to bed to spend the day wallowing when a fracas rambled its way up the front walk.

First, Mrs. Davis was loudly whispering, "I just don't know how she'll take the news."

Then we heard Mother Gibson say, "She's going to find out one way or another. Better to come from us."

That was followed with the loud tap-tap of Mrs. Dodson's cane. A sign that she was in deep thought about what to add to the conversation.

We exchanged nervous glances, and Aunt Ginny steeled herself for the fallout. The biddies were camped on the porch not-so-quietly discussing which of them was to break the news to her.

"Should I just put them out of their misery?"

Aunt Ginny nodded. "Let's get this over with."

I flung the door open on a very surprised trio.

After a jump, Mother Gibson forced a smile. "Well, don't you look lovely today, Ginny. Is that a new blouse?"

Mrs. Dodson held up a small carrot cake and grinned, showing a full set of dentures.

"Is that a consolation cake?" Aunt Ginny looked from one lady to the next. Mrs. Davis's lips turned down to a frown and trembled slightly. "This is why you're all terrible card players. Get in here."

Aunt Ginny took the cake while I helped Mrs. Dodson out of her coat and hung it up. "I'll go make some coffee."

I said a silent prayer for Aunt Ginny to be able to weather the storm about to come while I boiled the water and made up the tray with various creams and sugars. By the time I joined the somber crew in the dining room, they'd laid the table with a china dessert setting for five. I raised my eyebrows at Aunt Ginny.

She shrugged. "Paper plates never cheer anyone up."

I sat expectantly, awaiting the results of the cast list Mrs. Dodson held up. "We all agreed this would not come between us."

Each of the ladies gave a nod, but they all watched Aunt Ginny as they did.

Mrs. Dodson continued. "It seems that I have been cast in the role of Rosie, the chef and cookbook author."

Aunt Ginny nodded and shifted her gaze to Mrs. Davis.

Mrs. Davis swallowed hard. "And I'll be performing the part of Tanya, the sexy friend."

Uh-oh.

Aunt Ginny nodded again. "And . . ."

Mrs. Dodson smoothed the paper in her hands. "And Blanche Carrigan will be the part of Donna, across from Royce."

I sucked in a lungful of air and held it.

Aunt Ginny narrowed her eyes. "What did I get? Sophie?"

The three ladies shook their heads no.

"Old Greek lady number one?"

The ladies shook their heads again.

"Two?" Aunt Ginny's eyes were darting around the table.

Mrs. Dodson handed her the cast list.

Aunt Ginny took it with trembling hands. Her eyes narrowed. "Blanche Carrigan's understudy!" She balled up the paper and threw it across the table.

Figaro came out of nowhere and skidded across the table, batting the ball into the kitchen. We could hear the paper skittering over the porcelain tile.

"Blanche Carrigan can kiss my . . ."

Beep-beep-beep. The timer went off for the coffee and I plunged the French press.

"Forget it! I'm not doing it." Aunt Ginny picked up the knife and hacked into the carrot cake.

Mother Gibson took out another sheet of paper and passed it down.

I took the knife away from Aunt Ginny before she hacked off something important and finished cutting the cake for the ladies.

Aunt Ginny waved the paper over her head. "What is this?"

Mother Gibson wiped a bit of icing from her cheek, where it had been flung. "That's my stage manager punch list. Honey, Neil put you in charge of painting the backdrops."

I poured five cups of coffee. "Well, see now, he must have heard what a gifted painter you are. I bet that's why he gave the part of Donna to Blanche. So you'd have more time to work on the scenery."

Aunt Ginny gave me a dry look that said she wasn't buying it.

Figaro batted the wad of paper back into the dining room under the table.

"Did you ladies happen to see who got the other parts?" I passed around the china and the girls started making their coffees.

Mrs. Davis passed around the plates. "Well, you know Royce is Sam."

I waved off the cake, determined to be faithful to my diet. "Of course."

Mrs. Davis continued, "Duke is Bill, and Mr. Ricardo is Harry."

Mrs. Dodson tapped her cup with her spoon. "Can you believe Duke got a prime role after all the fuss he put up about doing a different play? And I think I'm supposed to kiss him at the end." Mrs. Dodson scrunched up her nose.

Mother Gibson snickered. "I think he's cute for a little white man."

Mrs. Davis giggled. "Neil is playing Sky, the groom, and Sol Sheinberg is the understudy for all the men."

Aunt Ginny dug into her cake with ferocity. *I see now where I got my tendency to eat my feelings.* I handed her a napkin. "What about Mrs. Sheinberg?"

Mrs. Dodson pointed to the punch list. "She signed up to sew the costumes."

I gave the list a once-over. "Hey, how did I get signed up to do the lights?"

Figaro jumped up on the chair next to Aunt Ginny and patted her arm to get a lick of frosting. She indulged him, against my better judgment. "I signed you up. I thought it would be good to keep you busy so you have less time to obsess over the men in your life."

Mrs. Davis, Mrs. Dodson, and Mother Gibson all *ooh*ed me in unison.

I felt my cheeks get hot and I knew I was blushing again. Revlon really needs to make a heat-sensitive foundation for redheads. "I wouldn't say I've been obsessing." *Where am I supposed to find the time to do this?*

Aunt Ginny lifted her coffee and blew off the steam. "Besides, if I'm going to be up there around Moira Finklebaum every day, I might need you to keep me from shooting her with the staple gun."

I would have laughed except I knew she wasn't kidding. "I'm surprised Iggy is playing piano for rehearsals. I got the impression he'd rather be home watching *Garage Wars*."

Mrs. Dodson waved her hand. "Honey, please. He's been volun*told*. His momma signed him up. Can you believe he still lives at home at his age? Fiona always was a weird one."

Mother Gibson shook her head. "My lord, he's one of those people who's always miserable and doesn't know how to keep his misery to himself. He's going to pout his way through every rehearsal."

Mrs. Dodson crossed her arms over her bosom. "I can tell you this, there is no way I'd let Charlotte still live at home at that age. I'd make her get her own place."

Aunt Ginny snickered. Looked at me. Then cleared her throat.

"What?"

Aunt Ginny shrugged. "Nothing."

Mrs. Davis cast a look around the room. "I heard this play is going to be a big deal because Royce is starring in it. Do you think there'll be talent scouts in the audience?"

Mrs. Dodson looked down her chin at Mrs. Davis. "Get a hold of yourself. The only one who anyone will care about is Royce. Apparently, he's a Broadway legend."

Then why is he doing community theater in Cape May?

"Still," Mrs. Davis continued, "it doesn't hurt to prepare. My character has had a lot of work done. Do you think I have time to get a boob job and a butt lift before we open on Valentine's Day?"

The other ladies appraised Mrs. Davis's assets in consideration.

She lifted her blouse and flashed us, so we could make a more informed decision.

I accidentally spit my coffee out.

"I think it could help me get into character."

Aunt Ginny handed me back my napkin. "I'm not sure a month is going to be enough time." She smashed her cake with her fork. "Moira!"

Mrs. Davis readjusted her blouse. "Are you going to be okay with this, Ginny?"

Aunt Ginny narrowed her eyes and grinned. It wasn't a happy grin. It was a grin that caused chills to run up my arms, and Mother Gibson to start praying. "I'm going to be just fine. You wait and see. I swore that Moira Finklebaum would never get the better of me again. That's a promise I mean to keep. Oh yes, a lesson is well overdue."

Chapter Ten

I was about to throw my Fitbit exercise tracker in the trash, then take the trash to the driveway so I could back over it with the car a few times before setting it on fire. I'd been walking three miles a day and dieting faithfully for almost a month now and hadn't lost a single pound. I'd changed the batteries in my scale. Twice. Then I swapped it with Aunt Ginny's scale. The next day, Aunt Ginny had come into the kitchen and announced that she had mysteriously lost five pounds overnight and she needed a milkshake to prevent bone loss. I threw a refined fit and decided to log every bite for the next two weeks. I wasn't giving up this time. I wasn't giving in to the call of the Oreos. I was committed. But I'd better start seeing some results soon. I was getting Spanx burn from my knockoffs. They were like wearing an inner tube under my clothes. It rained the other day on my way home from the coffee shop and the water just beaded up on my shirt and rolled off. If that wasn't enough to throw me into a royal funk, now I had several hours of baking desserts I wasn't allowed to eat ahead of me.

I put eight bars of soft cream cheese in the bowl of my stand mixer and started it on Low. Tim and I had come up with a dessert menu that included a chocolate Grand Marnier cheesecake in a chocolate crust. I checked the business email for reservation requests while the mixer did its job. I had teamed up with a local spa for a contest that included a stay at our B&B, and I had a couple from Cape Cod who wanted to book a suite with our romance package for Valentine's week. Finally! My property taxes were due soon and the tax fairy must have skipped our house. I scrolled through my saved travel websites to check our reviews. Someone had left the Butterfly Wings B&B one star on TripAdvisor. The report was scathing. "The sheets were scratchy, the towels threadbare and musty, breakfast was day-old muffins and moldy fruit. And the worst part was the snotty innkeeper." *What the heck!* None of those things were remotely true. And we hadn't had a guest in weeks. I checked the reviewer. Travelguy95 had left ten other reviews for restaurants and shops in Cape May. Everything was five star except us. *I'm not going to let it bother me. He's obviously a jerk. I'm not even going to think about it again.*

I put my phone away and stopped the mixer. *The nerve of that guy. People have no idea how damaging their careless words can be to a new business. I wonder if it's that weatherman who stayed here.* I obsessed some more over who Travelguy95 could be while I measured my sugar and scraped my orange peel into the cheese. The front door opened, and I heard the ladies return from morning rehearsal down at the Senior Center as I was cracking my eggs.

"It's a terrible day to open," Aunt Ginny said.

"It has to be why we're cursed."

"We aren't cursed, Thelma. You're letting your imagination run away with you again."

"Well, somebody is up to something, you mark my words. There is sabotage afoot."

That last voice was Mrs. Dodson as the ladies rounded the corner into the kitchen. Figaro the opportunistic trotted behind Aunt Ginny looking for a treat.

"Poppy, you'll never believe what happened." Aunt Ginny opened the cabinet to get four glasses.

"Someone snuck in and added to your painting again?"

Mother Gibson shook her head. "Child, you don't know the half of it."

Mrs. Davis spied the plate of cranberry oatmeal bars sitting by the coffeepot. "Are these for everybody?"

"Help yourself." I removed the mixing bowl and stirred my filling by hand, so the ladies could fill me in on their latest scandal.

Aunt Ginny poured four glasses of tea and motioned to me did I want any. I nodded, so she got down a fifth glass. "Not only did someone paint a giant mermaid with big boobies on my Greek ocean backdrop, but they stole all the props. The rowboat, the watering can, the guitar, everything."

Mrs. Dodson hefted herself up on a barstool at the island. "And that whole yacht piece that Royce enters from the catwalk, gone."

"Oh no." I folded the melted chocolate into the cheese mixture. "Who do you think is doing it?"

The ladies all said in unison, "Duke."

Then Mrs. Davis continued. "He won't stop going on about that play he wrote. Keeps shoving scripts in everyone's hands. He says it's an urban mystery."

Mother Gibson rolled her eyes. "In Sea Isle, that hotbed of corruption? What's the big mystery? Break-in at Yum Yum's ice cream?" The retired Sunday school teacher snickered. "Nobody got time for that."

Aunt Ginny put the tea back in the fridge. "Just wait. I'm setting a trap for him. If he tries to mess with my paints this afternoon, he'll regret it."

"Are you sure it's Duke?" I asked.

Mrs. Dodson answered me. "Who else would try to sabotage the play?"

Aunt Ginny pulled up a barstool and joined the other ladies. "I know one thing. I am so tired of repainting those scenes and learning lines for a part I'm never going to have. And if I have to hear Blanche explain one more time that she's a Method actor and needs to stay in character, I might fly into a rage." Aunt Ginny took a long drink of her iced tea. "And you'll never guess who Neil called in to rebuild that yacht." Aunt Ginny gave me a pointed look over her glass.

"No?"

"Oh yes. Itty Bitty Smitty."

I stifled a laugh. "Does he know you open in a week?"

Mother Gibson threw her head back and laughed. "Honey, he knows. Everybody knows. This may be the first play in history that opens on Friday the thirteenth."

Aunt Ginny looked at the ladies and grinned. "Do you remember the look on Royce's face when he found out?"

"Fiona had to come up and fan him." Mrs. Dodson giggled.

Aunt Ginny turned back to me. "Apparently, theater people are very superstitious. You'll see this afternoon when you come to the technical rehearsal to learn the lights."

The doorbell rang, and Aunt Ginny slapped the counter. "Hee! They're here!" She jumped down and practically skipped from the room.

"What is that all about?" I asked the ladies.

They put on innocent faces and shrugged. Aunt Ginny returned, giggling, with a package. "Just a little special order to help me get into the spirit of things." She tucked the package into her bedroom and came back out with her eyes shining with mischief.

I can't believe I got roped into this. I ladled cheesecake into the waiting springform pans and put them in the oven. Then I started making the crust for Tim's Peanut Butter Mousse pies. "How are things going between Royce and Blanche onstage?"

Mrs. Dodson shook her head. "The woman has no shame. Pawing all over Royce like that. It's unseemly."

Mrs. Davis joined in. "And Neil isn't doing anything to stop it. He just lets it happen."

Mother Gibson waved her hands in the air. "Honey, you could hang your laundry on the tension shooting out of Fiona. She does not like Royce giving attention to anyone but her."

Aunt Ginny set her glass down with a thud. "She's getting on my nerves."

"Fiona?" I asked.

"Both of them. They're demanding and selfish and make the whole thing a lot less fun than it could be."

Mrs. Davis helped herself to another half of a cranberry oatmeal bar. "The only scene Blanche wants to practice is the one where she and Royce kiss."

Aunt Ginny took the other half and it crumbled in her grip.

I took out a mixing bowl for the mousse filling and opened the jar of peanut butter. Figaro appeared like magic at my feet, rubbing against my ankles. "You've been seeing a lot of Royce lately. How does he feel about Blanche?"

The ladies whipped their heads around to Aunt Ginny, who blushed.

She gave me a wild look and said through gritted teeth, "That was a secret, Poppy."

I looked up from my mousse. "Oh, sorry."

Aunt Ginny shrugged for the ladies' benefit. "We've been meeting for coffee. No big deal."

"Ooh," the ladies sang out together.

"It's nothing." Aunt Ginny waved them off but couldn't keep a tiny smile from forming.

Mrs. Dodson nodded sagely. "Mm-hmm. And when do you meet your gentleman caller next?"

"This afternoon." Aunt Ginny giggled. "We've been going to that little café in West Cape May."

"Are you and Royce dating again?" Mrs. Davis's eyes lit up.

I apologized to the ladies and turned on the mixer to whip the bowl of cream for the mousse. It only took a minute and they continued where they left off as if nothing happened.

"Well, I wouldn't say dating, since we have yet to go somewhere without Fiona and Iggy tagging along. I've had moles removed that were less attached."

"Maybe you could take Poppy along and she could find a way to distract Iggy while you and Royce get to know one another."

Say what now? "Oh no. Leave me out of this. I have enough trouble with the two men I've got in my life. I don't need to add a middle-aged child to the mix." I took the jar of peanut butter away from Aunt Ginny and scooped it into a bowl with some mascarpone.

"That's a good idea." Aunt Ginny smacked the island with her hands. "Poppy, you can be my wingman!"

"I don't think you know what a wingman is."

Aunt Ginny sat up to her full height of about five foot nothin'. "Honey, we invented the wingman."

Before I could come up with a sassy response, the front door chimed, and Sawyer called out from the foyer, "I got four roses!"

I continued folding my mousse and we waited for Sawyer to bounce into the kitchen. Her chestnut hair was wind-whipped and her cheeks were rosy from the cold. Her green eyes sparkled and danced with delight as she held up four long-stemmed red roses.

"Same as the others; they were outside my front door tied with a ribbon."

Sawyer had been my best friend since I moved to Cape May in the fifth grade, and Aunt Ginny had been tormenting her at least that long. "Did you check to see if anything was missing?"

Sawyer blinked. "No, why?"

"Maybe it was a cat burglar. They sometimes leave tokens behind."

The other biddies nodded along in support of Aunt Ginny.

Mrs. Dodson nodded to the roses. "Gentleman Johnny was a cat burglar in the seventies who broke into ladies' bedrooms and stole their jewelry right off their nightstands. He always left a rose."

Sawyer nervously turned her green eyes on me. "I've gotten roses four days in a row."

Aunt Ginny made a good show of appearing alarmed. "Oh no. Did you check your jewelry this morning?"

Mother Gibson had to hide her face.

Sawyer's arm dropped to her side. "I don't think anything was missing."

Sawyer was gorgeous. It wasn't hard to believe that she would have a secret admirer. She was also very sweet and very gullible. Not a good combination around Aunt Ginny and her accomplices. I laughed. "They're teasing you, Sawyer. Was there a note this time?"

Sawyer side-eyed Aunt Ginny, who had my jar again and was letting Figaro lick peanut butter off her spoon. "No, they're from a secret admirer."

"You better not put that spoon in there again." I mixed my peanut butter mousse. "Who do you think it is?"

"It has to be Adrian. We've been dating since Restaurant Week."

"Then it's not much of a secret," Mrs. Dodson pointed out.

"But it is very sweet," Mrs. Davis comforted. "Maybe you and he could double-date with Poppy and Iggy."

My mixing bowl slipped and banged the counter.

The ladies cackled, and Sawyer gave me a confused look. "Who's Iggy?"

I shook my head at the biddies. "Why are you all so naughty?"

Aunt Ginny closed the peanut butter. "Oh honey, if you think this is bad, just wait till opening night. You ain't seen nothing yet."

Chapter Eleven

Everyone was gone. Sawyer to her bookstore, Aunt Ginny to her coffee date, and the biddies to reign terror on other unsuspecting victims. I walked Tim's desserts out to my Corolla to carefully arrange them in the trunk. Two trips and one sneak attack by Figaro later, I was heading for Maxine's down by the harbor. The boats were moored for the winter, but they were bobbing with vigor today as the brisk wind was making the water especially choppy. My car crunched over the broken shells as I parked in the back, where two of Tim's line cooks were standing at the kitchen door taking a break between prep and the dinner rush. They crushed their cigarettes in a stone urn and rushed to the car to help me carry in the desserts.

I will not make out with Tim. I was determined not to give in to my lust for either man until I knew what my heart wanted. Until I figured things out, I'd just be leading one of them on. Then I saw him. Tim was at the sauté station flipping around a skillet of shrimp in butter like a culinary god.

"There's my girl. You're just in time for lunch." He threw

a couple of large handfuls of cooked linguine into the skillet and tossed it in the shrimp and butter.

I looked at the time on my cell phone. "Lunch? It's almost four."

Tim plated the shrimp and linguine in a pasta bowl while he laughed at the joke I didn't realize I was making. "This is when we get to eat."

Macie, one of the line chefs, helped herself to a serving of pasta. "Dinner is served around eleven tonight, in case you're around." She gave me a smile, then turned on her heel to find a place to sit.

Juan and Chuck brought in the last of the cheesecakes and Peanut Butter Mousse pies and showed them to Tim.

"Poppy, they look fantastic!" Tim leaned down to kiss me, and with my heart pounding, I dodged him by grabbing a Peanut Butter Mousse.

"I'd better put this in the walk-in so it doesn't melt."

Tim picked up a fork. "Chuck, help her with the other one."

Chuck already had a plate in one hand and pasta tongs in the other. He looked longingly at the platter and back at me.

"Don't worry. I got this." I loaded the dessert shelf while Juan brought the last tray of crème brûlées in from the car.

Tim and his crew were making quick work of the scampi when one of his servers arrived. She was a petite blonde dressed in the customary black pants and white dress shirt. Her hair was up in a long ponytail. "All right. Just in time."

Tim motioned to the platter. "Poppy, are you sure you don't want some? Chuck will eat all of it if you don't get in here."

Chuck nodded with a mouthful of pasta.

I giggled and politely declined.

Tim's eyes flashed and his brow drooped. "Oh, wait. I'm sorry. You can't have this because it has gluten in it. You want me to make you some gluten-free pasta? I can boil fresh water."

"No, it's fine. Really. I had lunch hours ago. I'll be picking up a salad on the way to the Senior Center."

Macie muttered, "Bakers. So lucky."

Tim put his empty plate on the counter. "How's it going over there? Has Aunt Ginny caught the backdrop bandit yet?"

"Not yet, but they struck again last night."

"Have they called in Miss Marple to investigate?"

"I get the impression they're doing that themselves."

Tim started to walk toward me and the hairs on my arm stood up. *Must not let him entice me.* I grabbed my sheet pan and held it in front of me.

"You don't have to go already, do you? Why don't you stick around and watch me cook?"

Sexy music started playing in my mind, and an image of Tim wearing nothing but an apron sautéing over an open flame flashed before my eyes.

"Why are you blushing?"

"What? Nothing. Who is?" *Just . . . chef porn.*

Tim narrowed his eyes and slanted his head while laughing at me. He grabbed my wrist and pulled me to him.

Uh-oh.

"You're so funny."

I leaned back, away from the sexy chef. "That's me. I'm funny."

"Come on, can't you stay? I miss you." He leaned in to kiss me and I turned my head, so he kissed my neck.

Whoa! Abort, abort! Big mistake! I started giggling uncontrollably and tried twisting away from him.

Tim thought it was a game and started trying to tickle me. Luckily, we were interrupted by Chuck.

"Uh . . . Chef?"

Tim didn't try to hide the irritation in his voice. "What?!"

I looked around Tim. "Hey, Chuck, you're not interrupting. Come on over."

"Uh . . . There's a guy . . . says he needs to talk to you . . . about a fish order . . ."

Tim dropped his arms reluctantly. "I'll be right there." Then to me: "It's always something. This is why chefs die young."

"Fish salesmen?" I grinned.

"Eighty-hour workweeks and Chucks."

"Well, I have to go anyway. I have to be at the Senior Center in twenty minutes. Tonight is my first technical rehearsal to learn the lights."

He snuck a kiss in before I could dodge him. I floated to the door with the electricity of a thunderstorm.

"I'm surprised the Senior Center wants you involved given your recent track record with people dying whenever you're around."

"These seniors like to live dangerously."

Chapter Twelve

The Senior Center was a beehive of activity. Some of the stage crew were painting props in the craft room two doors down, seniors carried set pieces from the game room into the theater, and in the middle, a familiar face was leading choreography in the activity room wearing booty shorts and size thirteen glitter heels.

"Honey, you've got to swing your hips," Bebe said in a husky voice.

"These hips fought in Korea. That's as far as they swing."

"Well, put your rump into it. Poppy, hey girl! Look at you!"

"Bebe! What are you doing here?" I hadn't seen my caramel-skinned friend since I bailed Aunt Ginny out of jail a couple of months back. Come to think of it, I'd never seen Bebe on this side of the iron bars.

Bebe left her geriatric partner and enveloped me in a hug as long as her purple hair. "I'm turning over a new leaf. The boss man advertised in the *Shoppee* that he was looking for a choreographer." She held out her arms and flashed a brilliant smile. "Ta-daaa!"

I giggled. "Well, you've done wonders with Mr. Sheinberg there." Mr. Sheinberg had swiveled himself into a corner and was stuck in a potted fern.

"Oh, good lord, hold on." Bebe rushed over and shifted Mr. Sheinberg's trajectory until he worked his way back to the center. "What are you still doing in Cape May? I thought you were on your way back to Virginia after you cleared your aunt."

"Yeah, things have changed. I'm here to stay. Someone has to keep Aunt Ginny out of trouble."

"Speaking of your aunt, where is that shyster? I want a chance to win my diamond pinkie ring back."

"On the stage, painting the backdrops."

"The ones with the topless mermaids?"

"I believe those additions were made without her oversight."

Mr. Sheinberg had swiveled himself into a frenzy. "I think I've got it, but now I can't make it stop."

Bebe gave me an I-gotta-go look. "I'll see you down there when we rehearse the dance number in a bit." She waved a set of long, silver fingernails and held Mr. Sheinberg by the waist until the rest of his body swiveled to a stop.

I spotted Smitty in the game room, measuring some plywood for set construction. He made a note on the wood, then looked closer at the tape measure, grunted, then spun it around upside right. He saw me and gave a salute.

I arrived in the theater, where Royce was on stage with Mr. Ricardo. Duke and Blanche were off to the side, rehearsing a scene. I looked around for Aunt Ginny. Her spiky red hair was sticking out from behind a backdrop. She slowly peeked out, saw me standing in the back, and put a finger to her lips. Then she crooked her finger for me to join her.

I climbed behind the stage curtains and wedged myself next to her. "What's going on?"

"Shh!" She was crouched behind the canvas-covered frame, spying on someone in the audience.

I whispered, "Who are we looking at?"

"We don't know yet," she hissed. "See that little guy near the back row?"

I tried to look around the backdrop, but she pulled me back in. "Don't let him see you."

Because creeping around this painting is so much more discreet. I indulged her and inched my eyes out to scan the audience. "The man wearing the round glasses and the fancy suit with the pink tie?"

"Yes!" she hissed.

"The one who Mrs. Davis is lying behind on the floor?"

"How did you know Thelma was behind him?"

"Her shoes are sticking out in the aisle. What's she doing?"

"She's spying on Piglet."

"You're calling him Piglet?"

"He's all pink and nervous. Too many weird things have been happening this week and no one's been caught yet." Aunt Ginny picked up a roll of electrical tape and wound it around some matches and a firecracker. "This guy's been hanging around since Tuesday. Who knows what he's been up to when we're not here? We're looking in to him."

"What are you doing?"

Aunt Ginny glanced at me, then taped a matchbox striker and metal ring to the firecracker. "Setting a trap. I'm going to catch Duke in the act the next time he tries to paint boobies on my backdrop. Hand me that trip wire."

I handed Aunt Ginny the roll of fishing line. I giggled. "You're making a booby trap." I took another look around the backdrop and saw Mrs. Dodson's head rise up to the bridge of her nose just over the man's shoulder. She must have gotten too close, because the man swatted at his shoulder like a fly was buzzing around. She was saved when, onstage, Royce belted out, "Hear my soul speak, the very instant that I saw you did my heart fly to your service."

"Cut!" Neil jumped on the stage to stop the scene, and Mrs. Dodson dropped back down behind Piglet, I mean, the little man. "The line is, *no she's still Donna.*" Neil held up a script.

Royce smiled and rocked back on his heels. "Are you sure?"

"Yes, I'm quite sure. It's written right here on these pages."

"Oh. Well, what did I say?"

"You were quoting Shakespeare again."

Royce chuckled. "It's in my blood."

Fiona announced to no one in particular, "He was wonderful in *Hamlet*."

Royce nodded and held up his hand. "Five curtain calls."

Neil put an arm around Royce's shoulders. "Maybe we could run lines together later, just you and me."

"Oh, that would be jolly fun." Royce clapped his hands.

I was about to ask Aunt Ginny how Royce had been doing with learning his lines, when I noticed what she was wearing for the first time. "You changed your clothes."

Aunt Ginny gave me a sly grin and held out her T-shirt, so I could read it. It was bright pink and had the words *YOU'RE A HAS-BEEN* written in gold foil.

"I take it that's for Blanche's benefit?" Blanche was onstage glaring in Aunt Ginny's direction.

Aunt Ginny giggled. "I'd say it's open to interpretation."

The emergency-exit door down by the stage cracked open and two burly gorillas in suits tiptoed into the theater. They looked around the room like they were trying to spot someone, then creaked open the end seats on the second aisle and wedged themselves down.

Neil glanced at the men, who looked like a Hummer crashed into a compact parking spot, then turned his attention back to the scene onstage. "Let's move on to the musical number."

Iggy lumbered over to the piano while the actors took their places with Bebe in the front, towering over everyone, arms up to begin the dance routine. Aunt Ginny and I carefully climbed out from around the curtains so we could watch from the audience. Iggy started banging on the piano, but what came out wasn't ABBA. He stopped and started again. Nope, he still sounded like a three-year-old running loose in the sanctuary.

Aunt Ginny whispered in my ear, "He sounds like he's playing a cat in heat."

Murmurs scuttled through the theater like crabs at low tide.

Fiona shot to her feet and pointed at the piano. "Someone has sabotaged my Iggy. This isn't his doing! He has a master's degree!"

Neil turned in Fiona's direction. He sounded more confused than disturbed. "What?"

Iggy held up his hands. "Dude, I think someone jacked up the piano during lunch. It's badly out of tune." He lifted the lid and looked inside.

Aunt Ginny whispered again, "If he pulls a cat out of there, I'm going to lose my mind."

Iggy shook his head and closed the lid. "You need to get a professional tuner before I can play again. It's not good for the piano to continue now."

Mrs. Davis joined us from her hiding spot. "Well, that's awfully convenient, don't you think? He didn't want to be here anyway."

Neil jumped off the stage. "Take the scene from the top,

where Donna makes her entrance. I'll go call the Methodists." He started up the aisle but stopped long enough to take Aunt Ginny's hands in his. "Ginny, you have done a lovely job with the backdrops. I had no idea you were such a gifted painter."

Aunt Ginny ducked her chin. "I'm so glad you approve."

"I'm blown away by them. Does artistic ability run in your family?"

"I believe my grandmother used to paint a little." Aunt Ginny shrugged coyly. "Mostly bowls of fruit and flowers."

"How wonderful." Neil patted Aunt Ginny's hand. "I'd better go make that call." Neil continued down the aisle, the little man in glasses Aunt Ginny had dubbed Piglet jumping out to follow him while wringing his hands together.

"That was actually a pretty good nickname."

Aunt Ginny knocked my arm. "See."

As soon as Neil was out of the room, the oversize loads down in front wrenched their way out of the seats and left by the same emergency exit they had entered from. Mr. Ricardo pushed the button on an old boom box and started playing a Latin number, and the seniors paired up to dance. Bebe led Mr. Sheinberg around and Aunt Ginny was whisked off by Royce in a fit of giggles. I warmed on the inside to see her so happy. Blanche, on the other hand, had a look that would frighten a tiny North Korean dictator.

I felt a tap-tap-tap on my shoulder. *Oh God, please don't be Iggy.* I looked behind me and found Duke McCready. "Come on, let's join the others."

I was so relieved not to see the morose man-child that I agreed. Duke led me up to the stage. "Have you had a chance to read my play?"

"I'm afraid not. I'm sure it's very good." *Okay, that was a bald-faced lie. I hope he can't tell.*

Duke narrowed his eyes but kept stepping in time to the music.

Darn. I smiled brightly.

Duke shrugged. "At least I got Royce Hansen to take a look. It wasn't a real look. It was half a look. He said he skimmed it."

"That's something. Did he like it?"

"He said it was lacking the zing he usually looks for in a script."

"Oh, what kind of zing is he looking for?"

"The kind where he plays the lead."

"Oh." I laughed. "Well, I think it really is too late at this point. *Mamma Mia!* opens in a week. Why don't you pitch your play in a couple of months, when this one is over?"

"It's all political. It was my idea to do a play in the first place." Duke sighed. "That's too late anyway. My grandson is coming to visit, and I told him we were doing the play I wrote. For the first time in my life, he thought I was cool. Now he's going to go back to calling me Geezer Gramps. I hate that name."

"Aww, I'm sorry. But you are playing Bill in *Mamma Mia!* That's a lead role. I'm sure he'll be impressed with that."

"I don't know. Kids today. The only way to impress them is to beep and buzz on their phones."

Behind Duke, Blanche was leading Mr. Ricardo into a crossfire with Aunt Ginny and Royce.

Oh, that will not end well.

In a brazen breach of etiquette, Blanche tapped Aunt Ginny on the shoulder, then stepped aside to switch partners. Royce did not recover quickly. Blanche spun him around and led him away.

Aunt Ginny stormed off the stage, leaving Mr. Ricardo dancing the merengue solo, which he didn't seem to realize for several bars.

I excused myself from Duke and found Aunt Ginny fuming to her crew. "Of all the cheek I have ever witnessed, that has to be some of the nerviest gall."

Mother Gibson put an arm around Aunt Ginny and gave a supportive murmur. "Mm-hmm."

Mrs. Dodson sniffed. "I think it's a disgrace. It looks like Blanche is after husband number three."

Fiona shot a dark look at the stage. "Over my dead body."

Mrs. Davis murmured, "You may not want to say that too loud near Poppy."

"Hey. I had nothing to do with those other ones."

Aunt Ginny looked around. "I still wouldn't chance it."

A weird shiver crept its way up my arm. I tried to brush it off, then it spoke to me. "Hey."

I about jumped out of my skin when I saw that it was Iggy. "Oh, hi."

"Do uh . . . do you want . . . uh . . . to dance or something?"

Mrs. Davis snickered.

Fiona called out from across the aisle, "He's really good. He has a master's degree in interpretive movement."

What the crap? "Oh, thank you, but I need to stay with my aunt. She's not feeling well." I grabbed Aunt Ginny's arm.

"I'm much better now. You can go."

I glared into Benedict Arnold's green eyes. "No, you're not. You're old. You get confused."

Mrs. Davis snickered again. Mother Gibson was hiding her face behind her stage crew clipboard.

I gave Iggy what I hoped was a polite smile. I didn't want to hurt him. "Can I get a rain check?"

He stomped off. "I told you!"

Fiona screeched across the aisle, "Well, you must have done it wrong."

"What are you all doing?!" Neil had emerged from his office. "You're supposed to be practicing the dance number to *Mamma Mia!*"

Everyone stopped dancing and the room sobered like a pop quiz had been announced.

"Take your places, everyone. Where is Royce?"

Everyone looked around, but Royce was nowhere.

Then we heard a scream come from backstage. Royce ran onstage waving a slip of paper. "I quit! I can't do the play!"

Neil paled. "What do you mean, you can't do the play? We've advertised and sold tickets. You can't drop out now."

"I want to help you with your production, but it's not worth dying over."

A murmur shot through the room.

Fiona took the note from Royce's hand.

"It says 'drop out of the play or die.'"

Chapter Thirteen

R oyce reached into his pocket for a monogrammed handkerchief and patted his forehead.

Neil took the note and reread it. "Where did you get this?"

"From my dressing room," Royce answered meekly.

There was a moment of stillness where everyone tried to absorb the information, then they focused on what was truly important. "Royce has a dressing room?! Where is it? Why don't we all have one? What's in it?"

Neil held up his hands. "Okay, settle down, everyone. Yes, Royce has a dressing room. It was the least I could offer him. This man is a Broadway legend and he's agreed to do the Cape May Senior Center musical. Doesn't he at the very least deserve a table and chair in the costume closet?"

Blanche threw her hands to her hips and glared at Royce.

He shrugged. "What? I've had worse. Besides, you have that special stash of grapefruit sodas."

"It's in my contract!" Blanche retorted.

Royce glared back. "What contract? You're in the play because you live in Cape May and you're old."

Bebe put a hand on Neil's arm. "Wait. There's a costume closet? I'll be right back."

Duke slipped into cop mode. "How many of you knew about the dressing room?"

Everyone shook their head except Neil, who half raised his hand. That's when we turned into an imaginary ping-pong match, our heads swiveling back and forth with accusations and answers.

"Did anyone accompany you to your dressing room at any time?"

Royce shook his head no. "Except for my sister, Fee."

The seniors gasped. Blanche pointed at Fiona. "So, that note had to come from you or Neil?"

Neil sputtered. "Just a minute!"

Fiona's eyes took on a hard glint. "Why would I threaten my big brother to drop out of the play?"

Blanche shrugged. "As far as I can tell, you don't want to share him."

Aunt Ginny jabbed me in the side. "That's a fair point."

I nodded and whispered back, "What happened to Piglet and the two big guys? Where did they go?"

Fiona pinked from her bosom up to her earlobes. "I would never . . . !"

Mrs. Davis slowly lifted her cell phone over Duke's shoulder and snapped a picture of the offending note.

Duke raised his voice. "All right, that's enough. Calm down, everybody." Then he asked Royce, "Why would someone want you to drop out of the play?"

Royce shrugged. "I can't imagine."

Mrs. Dodson tapped her cane. "Unless they wanted to do a play that they wrote instead."

All eyes turned to Duke. He let the insult roll off his

back. "Stand down, Edith." Duke folded the note and placed it in his breast pocket. "I still have friends on the force. I'll give this to them and see what they make of it. Probably just a harmless prank."

Mrs. Davis pointed to Duke's chest. "But if you left the note, aren't you just tampering with the evidence?"

"I didn't leave the note."

"How do we know that?" Mother Gibson asked.

"I'm a cop."

"You haven't been a cop for years," Mr. Sheinberg pointed out.

Neil whistled. "We're getting nowhere accusing one another like this. Let's break for dinner. How about everyone be back here in thirty minutes, okay?"

The seniors begrudgingly agreed. Neil took a minute to reassure Royce that he was safe and they couldn't do the play without him. Then Fiona grabbed Royce protectively by the arm and led him out. Royce stopped and called to Aunt Ginny, who joined them. Iggy slumped down in a seat to pout, but Fiona noticed. "Iggy!"

With a heavy sigh, Iggy heaved himself up and lumbered after them.

Some of the folks decided to go to Westside Market for Italian hoagies. Others stayed back to eat sandwiches they'd brought from home. I had a grilled chicken salad I'd brought with me. *How many salads should the average person eat in a lifetime? I think I'm way over the safe limit on iceberg.* I was digging through my tote bag for my fork when a short little man with a wide nose and fuzzy caterpillar eyebrows yanked on my sleeve.

"Excuse me, but can you tell me where I might find Royce Hansen?"

"I think Royce has gone to dinner. He should be back soon, though. Do you want to wait for him or have me give him a message?"

The man had thick lips that rested in a half smile and crinkles at the corners of his eyes, giving him a perpetually amused expression. He ran a hand through the horseshoe pattern of hair that ran around the back and sides of his head while he took in the little theater. "No, thank you. I'll just wait here for him, if that's okay."

"I'm sure Neil won't mind." *He hasn't chased anyone out yet.* "I'm sorry, I didn't get your name."

The little man smiled at me and a wrinkle formed over the bridge of his nose. "That's right, you didn't."

Then he left me and wound his way through the seats, choosing one on the end of the third row center. He took off his sport coat, draped it over the back of the seat next to him, then gave me a tinkling wave.

Sure. That's not weird at all. I picked up my salad and was about to take a seat when I caught the biddies in a suspicious huddle watching the new little man. *Oh no.* I was going to ask them what they were up to but was interrupted by Neil's tap on the arm.

"Poppy, how about I give you that tour of the light booth now?"

"Sure." *I wasn't exactly in a hurry to get to that salad anyway.* I tossed another look over my shoulder at the biddies. Mrs. Dodson gave me an openmouthed wink.

Neil took me behind the red curtain on the side of the stage. "This is what we call stage left."

"But we're on the right-hand side of the room."

Neil gave me an easy smile. "Common mistake. Stage directions are always from the actor's point of view. Stage right is to the actor's right when he's looking out into the house. That means the audience. Stage left is to the actor's left. The 'cage,' as we call the light booth, is stage left."

This didn't bode well. I was confused already, and we hadn't even started yet. "You really know your theater stuff."

"Well," Neil puffed out his chest, "I've studied it a bit. Let's look at the light board."

"Why are there Xs taped all over the stage?"

"Don't worry about that. The ones that glow in the dark are spikes for the stage crew to see where to put the props, and those different-colored ones are for the actors to know where to stand for certain scenes. The audience can't see any of them."

We entered the cage, which was the size of a walk-in closet. Inside sat a wooden board on a high table. It was covered with toggles and dials, all labeled to corresponding lights. Neil ran me through a few practice scenes. Then showed me the master kill switch, which he said not to touch. A series of cables and wires wound from the back of the board to an electrical box where several large cords were plugged in. I had a unique vantage from the cage to be able to see the entire span of the stage and backstage behind the scenery, plus several rows of the audience from the center to stage right. *Or was it stage left?* I'd forgotten already. I was trying to run the complex equation to determine what side of the stage I was on when I saw Mother Gibson carry a plant down to the fourth row, reach her hand through the plant into the newcomer's sport coat, and dig around.

"What's wrong?" Neil started to follow my obviously shocked gaze and I grabbed his arm in a panic.

"The kill switch. Tell me again why I can't touch that."

His eyebrows flicked together for a moment. "Because nothing will work if that's turned off."

"Oh, right. Of course." Mother Gibson extracted a wallet from the jacket, threw a thumbs-up to someone, and the tree started to move out of view again.

I breathed a sigh of relief that Neil mistook for nerves and he patted me on the shoulder. "Don't worry, you'll get the hang of it."

"I hope so."

"Your technical script is right there. It has all your cues and settings."

"I'll do my best."

"I'm sure you will. You and your aunt both seem like you're great at whatever you do."

What? "Oh, uh . . . thanks. We try." *Is he hitting on me . . . or Aunt Ginny?*

Neil paged through the script on the light board. "So, you and your aunt are close?"

"Thick as thieves." *Hmm. I hope I don't regret that analogy when I see what those biddies are up to.*

"Does everyone in your family have red hair?"

"Technically yes, since it's just me and Aunt Ginny." *I'm not going to count my mother because I haven't seen her in thirty years. Plus, she's a brunette.*

"Really? You don't have any brothers or sisters?"

"Nope."

"No cousins?"

"Nope. How about you?"

"Oh, yeah. I grew up with a big family. Six sisters. No redheads."

All I could do was nod along. *He definitely has a thing about red hair. If he asks me if he can touch it, I'm outta here.*

"*Psst.*" Over on the other side of the stage, Mrs. Davis and Mrs. Dodson were trying to hide themselves behind a very small curtain. Mrs. Davis's butt was sticking out one side and Mrs. Dodson's butt was sticking out the other. Mrs. Dodson was jerking her head for me to come to them.

Neil looked past me down in the audience. "Oh good, they're back. We can get started."

I pulled the side curtain back to see that Aunt Ginny, Royce, and Fiona had returned with Iggy. Aunt Ginny had Royce by one arm and Fiona had the other, like they were trying to split him in half. The newcomer popped up with arms wide and hugged Royce like they were old friends and Neil went down to be introduced.

Bebe reappeared from a successful campaign to the costume closet wearing silver shorts and a black-sequined tube top that I thought was supposed to be a skirt and spun around. "What do you think?"

I nodded. "Shiny."

"Girl, I make this look good! I'm going to see if the boss man will let me keep it as part of my paycheck." She flounced down the steps and over to the growing group by the piano.

I took the opportunity to scamper across to Mrs. Davis and Mrs. Dodson, who were about to throw their backs out covertly calling me over.

"What is Mother Gibson doing?" I hissed.

They grabbed me and pulled me into the little area behind the ineffective curtain. "Recon." Mrs. Dodson stuck her head out and looked around. "We're trying to find out who the new fella is."

"I hope you're going to put his wallet back."

Mrs. Dodson cocked her head to the side and gave me a single nod. "Already on it."

I looked out from behind the curtain and saw Mother Gibson dragging a stuffed sheep down the aisle. When the sheep was close enough to the third row, Mother Gibson paused, and it looked like the sheep pooped out a fat brown wallet on the floor next to Aunt Ginny's foot. Aunt Ginny kicked her foot to the side and the wallet slid under the row of seats and the sport coat. Mother Gibson sped up her descent to place the sheep onstage.

Oh my God. They're going to kill me before this play opens.

Mrs. Dodson grabbed my wrist. "There's another thing."

"That shifty pair is back," Mrs. Davis whispered.

I looked at the quartet down by the piano.

"Not them, the two big men who were here earlier."

Mrs. Dodson stood back on her cane. "You know what I think?" She placed a finger by her nose.

"What?"

She gave me a stern look and tapped the side of her nose again.

"Oh. You think they're in the Mafia."

Mrs. Davis grabbed my arm. "*Shhh!* They'll hear you. They're right outside the emergency exit."

I craned my head around to see the door was still closed. *I don't know how they're supposed to hear me through steel, but okay.* "What are they doing?"

Mrs. Dodson tipped her chin up and gave me a grave look. "Loitering."

Oh no, not that. I stifled a giggle.

Mrs. Davis threw her hands to her hips. "This is serious, Poppy. They could be hired hit men here to whack someone."

"Who would they be here to whack?"

Aunt Ginny walked up behind me smelling like capicola ham, oregano, and provolone. "Who could be hit men?"

Mrs. Dodson leaned in until their heads were almost touching. "The beefcakes."

Aunt Ginny nodded. "The two that look like the bouncers from that club we went to last summer?"

What? What club?

Mrs. Davis giggled and nodded. "Yep."

Mrs. Dodson tapped her cane. "What do you think they're up to?"

Aunt Ginny looked around the corner. "I don't know, but here they come now."

A shaft of light punctured the dimly lit front row of seats and the two men reentered and gingerly angled themselves down with a pained *squeech.*

Aunt Ginny watched them from behind her backdrop. "Those seats will have to be replaced after the show if they make this a habit."

Neil called the room together and the biddies scurried off to what they called the "trust circle."

The seniors held hands and chanted something I couldn't make out. Then they clapped.

Aunt Ginny looked at me and rolled her eyes. "Actors."

I gave her a look that said, *I'm on to you.* "I know where you went."

She blushed and cleared her throat. "How was the salad?"

"I don't know. I haven't had it yet."

"Oh. So, at this point, still in the hopeful category."

Neil hopped to the center of the stage and consulted a clipboard. "Since we can't go over the musical number until tomorrow, let's go through the scene where the men arrive and meet Sophie."

I found my way to the light booth and searched the script for the right scene. "Sunset, Pink Fresnel @ 8." *What the heck is a Fresnel?* I found the dial on the board and turned it to line the number eight up with the hash mark. A red light cast a warm glow on the stage. *Okay, that's not too difficult.*

Blanche and Neil sat in the front row, while Mr. Ricardo and Duke took their places on the Xs. Royce was making his way across the catwalk for his big entrance down the mast onto the dock.

Mr. Ricardo tied a thick rope around the dock peg next to Aunt Ginny's flat. "I'm glad to get off that boat."

Duke brandished an oar from the prop rowboat. "Ah, that was nothing. You should try a kayak in the Okanama swamps."

Mr. Ricardo threw his hand out toward Duke. "Oh yes! I read your book, *A Bloke in a Boat in Botswana*."

Duke tossed the oar from hand to hand. "Thanks. I heard I'd sold a copy somewhere."

Royce looked around the set. "Do you want to hear something really interesting? So, you see this . . . this . . ."

The men nodded for Royce to go on. Everyone waited.

Royce belted out, "This royal throne of kings, this sceptered isle . . . This blessed plot . . ."

Neil rolled up his script and called through it, "Royce, the word you're looking for is 'taverna.' "

Royce shield his eyes from the stage lights. "Oh dear. You don't want me to start over, do you? It's not easy getting up to the catwalk."

Neil circled his hand in the air. "That's okay, let's keep going."

Duke picked up his cue. "There was this time in Kalahari." He turned and swung his prop oar and whacked Royce in the back of the head with a loud crack.

Royce dropped to his knees. "Ow!" He grabbed his head in his hands.

I wasn't sure if that was part of the play or not, so I looked at Aunt Ginny. Her hand covered her mouth and she ran to Royce.

Royce's hand came away from his head red with blood. Fiona screamed. Neil vaulted up on the stage and rushed to Royce's side.

Mr. Ricardo looked from the oar in Duke's hand to Royce's head. "Good God, man! What did you do?!"

Duke stood limply holding the prop oar. "That's not supposed to happen."

Blanche shot to her feet and pointed at Duke. "That was an attack! You all saw it!"

Duke held the oar away from himself like it was poisonous. "It was an accident. I thought it was supposed to be padded at the end."

Fiona pointed a trembling hand. "He attacked my brother because he's jealous. He's been out to get him from the start!"

Neil grabbed the oar to inspect it. "Lila!"

Mother Gibson was out of her seat in the audience and already rushing up to the stage. "Ooh. No, no, no. This isn't right."

Mr. Sheinberg called from the audience, "What kind of *farkakte* play is this?!"

Neil was on his knees next to Royce. "Somebody get him an ice pack!"

Mrs. Sheinberg threw down the costume she'd been working on and took off down the aisle at a snail's pace. "I'll get it!"

Neil shouted, "Somebody who didn't just have hip replacement surgery!"

Bebe took off after Mrs. Sheinberg, propelling herself by waving her hands in the air. "Look out, honey! These shoes aren't made for rushing!"

Mother Gibson took the oar from Duke. "This isn't my prop. The paddle on my oar is made out of Styrofoam and painted brown. This is solid wood."

Everyone looked at Duke, who timidly shrugged. "I thought it was kinda heavy, but it was in the boat, so I thought it must be right."

I was out of the cage and next to Neil with my cell phone in my hand and had already dialed the 9 and the 1. "Should I call an ambulance?"

Neil shouted, "No!" He leaned down to Royce's ear. "Do you think you'll be all right?"

"I'm feeling faint."

Blanche shouted, "For the love of God, Neil. Let her call an ambulance."

Neil looked nervously at Piglet. His expression clouded over.

Piglet was punching keys on his tablet.

Mrs. Davis slow walked toward Royce. "Let me see. I

was a nurse." She inspected the back of Royce's head for a couple of minutes and blotted the wound with a handkerchief. "You'll have a heck of a headache for the rest of the day, but I don't think you need stitches."

Neil breathed a huge sigh of relief, and he and Aunt Ginny helped Royce to his feet just as Bebe returned with the ice pack.

Fiona took her brother's hand. "Are you all right, Boodaloo? I told you this play was a bad idea."

Royce was pale and shaken. "I think someone's trying to kill me."

Chapter Fourteen

"This wouldn't have happened in my play." Duke crossed his arms and shook his head. "No way."

Blanche jabbed Duke in the shoulder. "You're the one who hit him! What difference does it make whose play it is?"

Duke held out his palms. "That was supposed to be a foam prop! My play doesn't have any dangerous weapons."

Fiona was rubbing Royce's back. "How about the guns?"

Duke shoved his hands in his pockets. "Well, yeah, but that's it. Besides, cops know how to properly handle firearms so they aren't dangerous."

Mother Gibson tucked the wooden oar under her arm and shot Duke a look of her own. "Mm-hmm. I got some relatives would disagree with you." She spun around and took the oar offstage.

Even Mr. Ricardo was incensed for Royce's sake. "You just couldn't stand it that we weren't doing your cop drama, so you had to attack one of the stars. Was I next?"

Duke took a step back from everyone. "I'm sorry. It was an accident. I found it with the other props, so I figured it was one of those trick props like a glass bottle. How was I supposed to know it would hurt him?"

Neil helped Royce sit on the dock. "Take a few good breaths and let me know if you're dizzy at all."

"I think . . . I think I'm okay. The show must go on."

Fiona and Aunt Ginny started to protest, but Neil cut them off. "No, I think we're going to call it a day. I want everyone to go home and get some rest tonight and come back refreshed tomorrow. Let's start thirty minutes earlier and go through some trust exercises."

Everyone agreed and started to leave the stage. The little man in the third row stood to his feet and applauded. "Bravo, Royce. Great job, as always."

Mother Gibson returned and with the other biddies went to Aunt Ginny's side and huddled up. I ambled over and inserted myself just as Mother Gibson was giving the others her report. "His name is Ernie Frick and his driver's license says he's from New York."

Mrs. Dodson nodded along. "What's he doing down here?"

"Well, he had a laminated card like the ones you get at Mr. Chow's Winghouse, says he was with the Actors' Equity Association. Poppy, what is that?"

"I don't know." I pulled out my phone and Googled it. "Apparently, it's a union for Broadway actors."

Aunt Ginny screwed up her face. "So, he's an actor?"

We unhuddled and watched Royce and Ernie. Mrs. Davis whispered, "Is he one of those little people?"

Aunt Ginny, who was only a couple of inches taller than Ernie, stood a little straighter. "No, I think he's just short."

Royce saw Aunt Ginny looking in his direction and waved her over. "Ginny, come meet my agent."

Fiona scowled at Aunt Ginny. She clutched Royce's arm tighter. "Careful, Boodaloo. You don't want your head to start bleeding again."

Royce tenderly placed the ice pack back on the top of his head.

Aunt Ginny went to join Royce. The biddies and I followed her in a tight group. I felt like we should be snapping.

Royce patted his agent on the back. "Can you believe Ernie went to high school just up the road from us?"

Ernie took Aunt Ginny's hand in his and smiled. At least I think he smiled; his face was kind of always smiling. Maybe it was stuck. "It's true. I grew up in Margate, right here in South Jersey. I got my first job in Atlantic City representing the exotic dancer Lola Giamecco."

They need representing?

"How about that," Aunt Ginny said. "What a small world." Aunt Ginny grabbed Duke and Mr. Ricardo on their way up the aisle. "Have you all met Royce's agent, Ernie Frick?"

Mr. Ricardo shook Ernie's hand, but Duke just stared at the little guy. "Have we met?"

Ernie chuckled. "I don't think so. Do you get to New York City very often?"

Duke shook his head. "I thought you looked familiar. My mistake."

Ernie chuckled again and looked around at each of us. He held his hand out to me. "We didn't get properly introduced earlier."

"No, we didn't."

Ernie laughed. "Okay, I deserve that. I've just arrived in town this afternoon to see how my number one client is settling in."

"Where are you staying?" I asked.

"I'm at the Queen Victoria; beautiful place." Ernie grabbed Royce's arm. "In fact, I'm here because I have great news, Royce. It's the opportunity of a lifetime. I have a contract to bring you back for a one-man show. Of course, it would be a limited engagement, depending on how long you want the run to be."

Fiona narrowed her eyes at Ernie and I was afraid she was preparing to lunge at his throat.

Royce chuckled. "No, no. I'm retired now. Just doing this community theater for a bit of fun and to raise some money for charity."

Charity? What charity?

Ernie patted Royce on the back of the arm. "Come now, Royce. You can't give up the theater for this little . . . well . . . it's not exactly Broadway, now is it?" Ernie chuckled to himself. "Besides, it's exactly the kind of script you like. You're the lead and you have all the lines."

Royce's eyes widened. "Really?"

Neil rushed into the conversation. "Royce is irreplaceable. We couldn't possibly do our show without him."

Fiona yanked Royce's arm. "Now, Royce, you said you were home to stay, remember? You can't go back on your word. Besides . . ."

Royce looked into Fiona's eyes and words were left unspoken, but their meaning passed between them. Royce rolled back on his heels and looked at the carpet. "Fee's right. I couldn't possibly return."

Fiona grinned, as Aunt Ginny would say, like the cat that got the cream.

Aunt Ginny grunted on one side of me and Blanche grunted on the other. Blanche muttered under her breath, "Are you afraid he'll evaporate if you take your hands off him?"

Fiona shot her a threatening look. With her heavy makeup and garishly pink-red hair, she looked like the nightmare clown that waited under your bed to kill you in the middle of the night. Blanche took a protective step back. Fiona turned and started to pull Royce's arm. "Come, big brother. We need to get you home to rest. If today proves anything, it's that you may not be safe here."

Ernie sputtered off a couple more "buts" that went ignored as Royce patted Fiona on the arm.

Blanche took a step toward Royce and put a hand on his back. "Why don't you come to my house tonight to run lines? Just the two of us?"

Aunt Ginny gritted her teeth. "Aren't most of your scenes musical numbers?"

Blanche craned her neck to scowl back at Aunt Ginny. "So, we'll sing them." She turned an angelic smile on Royce. "What do you say?"

Fiona swatted at Blanche's hand. "Get off him. You're the reason he was gone for sixty years!"

Royce, oblivious to the tension in the room, looked around the quarrel to grin at Aunt Ginny. "Hey, Ginger, how about I take you to dinner tomorrow night, for old times' sake?"

Aunt Ginny gave Royce a flirtatious smile. "Old times' sake would be necking at the Point."

Royce wiggled his eyebrows. "Then let's make it an early dinner."

Aunt Ginny giggled, then cleared her throat when she saw the biddies grinning at her with raised eyebrows.

Fiona practically dragged Royce out of the theater, purring that she would take care of him and he was safe with her. He never spoke a word to contradict her. Iggy followed without so much as a look back.

Ernie Frick cocked his head and furrowed his caterpillars. "Hm." He shrugged and grinned. "She certainly does have the upper hand, doesn't she?" He giggled. "I guess I'll be back tomorrow. Good night, everyone."

When we were alone, I turned to Aunt Ginny. "What do you think that's all about? Royce and Fiona?"

Aunt Ginny pursed her lips to the side of her mouth. "I don't know. She has a lot of control over him for some reason. She won't let him make one move without her approval."

"But why is he letting her? That's the question."

Aunt Ginny shook her head. "It's not the Royce I remember. He would never have let Fiona order him around like that."

"Did you see that look on her face when she saw that note?"

"She was practically gleeful. It was all she talked about over our hoag . . . spinach smoothies." Aunt Ginny gave me the side-eye.

"You still smell like salami."

"Fiona is obsessed with Royce staying home with her and Iggy."

"Do you think she wants him to herself bad enough that she would try to scare him into dropping out?"

"I don't know, but if she does to him what she's done with her son, Royce will cave before opening night."

Chapter Fifteen

I'd been up since five to work out, check email, bake for Tim, and drink a spinach smoothie. I was in a foul mood and didn't want to go to the Senior Center for an all-day rehearsal. "Saturday mornings should be for lounging in bed with coffee and a book. Not spending the day watching Mr. Sheinberg pick his teeth with a script. Isn't that why we survive adolescence? So we can grow up and do whatever the heck we want?"

Aunt Ginny handed me a shiny pink travel mug. "Hear, hear. That's why I live my life the way I do. I've earned the right to not have anyone boss me around. I come and go as I please and I do what makes me happy."

"Maybe I've earned that right too. I'm going back to bed for a couple of hours."

Aunt Ginny spun me around and pushed me toward the hall. "No, you're not. You can assert your independence when the play is over. Now go get in the car."

I could feel Figaro laughing at me all the way down the hall. Doing the lights for this play was not my idea and I didn't want to spend the day at the Senior Center. I was like a four-year-old on my second hour of a shoe-shopping spree and I could feel a tantrum building.

I had just about worked up a powerful whine when the front door flew open and Sawyer whacked me in the shoulder. "I got more roses today!" She held five long-stemmed roses under my nose.

"Beautiful." I shoved my injured arm into my coat.

Sawyer frowned. I obviously wasn't showing the proper amount of enthusiasm.

Aunt Ginny patted Sawyer on the arm. "Don't worry about her. She's being a grump today."

I drooped my shoulders and whimpered. "I'm so tired."

Aunt Ginny cooed at me. "I know, honey. And you have spinach in your teeth."

Sawyer took out a compact and shone it in my face so I could get myself under control. "That's twenty-eight roses in seven days." She giggled. "I wonder how long this is going to go on."

Aunt Ginny shook her keys next to my ear. "We have to go."

Sawyer's eyes grew even bigger. "Ooh. What if it's a dozen roses on Valentine's Day? How romantic."

"Mm-hmm." I gave her what I hoped was an enthusiastic nod. "Are you sure you want to come with us? It's going to be a really long rehearsal."

Sawyer stroked the velvety petals. "I feel like I haven't seen you in forever. And I want to talk about your Valentine's Day plans."

"Valentine's Day?"

"It's a week away. Do you know what you're doing, or . . . who . . . you're doing it with?"

"I know I have two different couples booked for romance packages."

Sawyer frowned. "That's not what I meant. Do you have plans with . . . Tim?" She arched an eyebrow.

I knew that look. "Is this another junior high school do you like him–reconnaissance type of situation?"

Sawyer blushed. "It is entirely possible that someone has asked me to discreetly find out about your plans, yes."

I shook my head. "I am not aware of any Valentine's Day plans yet. On either side." I looked at Aunt Ginny, who was jiggling the doorknob and tapping her foot. "Why do you have your keys? Don't you want me to drive?"

"No. It's been a while since I took Bessie out. Come on, who wants to go with me?"

I heard Sawyer gulp in some air. "I–I wouldn't want to take that honor away from Poppy."

I narrowed my eyes at her. "But it's your turn. I want to be fair."

Sawyer paled. "I couldn't possibly."

Aunt Ginny yanked the front door open and marched onto the porch. "Come on, you slug-a-bugs. Get the lead out. First one to the car decides who gets to ride shotgun and who has to drive themselves."

Sawyer and I took one last look at each other before flying out of the house to save ourselves. She pulled me by the hood of my coat to hold me back on the porch, but I caught up and gave her a hip check into the hydrangeas.

Aunt Ginny locked the front door and spun her key ring in circles on her finger as she minced her way over the flagstones. "That's more like it."

Sawyer had climbed out of the bushes and caught up to me. She grabbed me by the waistband of my yoga pants, but I already had my hand on the door of the detached garage. She jumped on my back and hissed in my ear, "I can't die now, I have a boyfriend."

Aunt Ginny's keys jingled that she was getting closer.

I hissed back, "I can't do it. I don't want to die wearing knockoff Spanx." My grip on the doorknob slipped for a moment, but I twisted around and shoved Sawyer into the side of the garage. She lost her hold on my neck and slid off. And I threw the door open. I was home free.

Sawyer hollered out in pain, "Ow! My wrist! I think it snapped!"

"Yeah, I'm not falling for that." *Not again anyway.*

Aunt Ginny rumbled the garage bay door open. "Why is Sawyer lying on the ground crying?"

"What?" *Oh my God, maybe I really hurt her.* I ran back to the door to help my best friend.

"Go, Sawyer, go!" Aunt Ginny double-crossed me, and Sawyer ran in through the large bay door and tagged the red-and-white Corvette.

I spun around to face them. "You both cheated."

Sawyer grinned. "I'll see you up there."

I buckled myself in and said a prayer. Aunt Ginny carefully backed out of the garage and down the driveway, then ran up over the curb and knocked the head off the garden gnome that sat by the mailbox. She hit the gas instead of the brake and knocked the Butterfly Wings B&B sign to a forty-five-degree angle. She craned the wheel to the right and pulled onto the street, colliding with three trash cans that I should have taken in last night. They ricocheted into the Dorseys' yard. The recycle bin got stuck under the bumper, and Aunt Ginny had to throw the car in reverse to dislodge it. It got caught on the license plate, which launched it toward Mr. Winston's yard and splintered his mailbox that was still being held together with duct tape from our last outing. I took one last mournful look toward the house, where Figaro was sitting in the front window watching us. I could almost swear he lifted a paw and touched the glass pane as Aunt Ginny hurtled through the stop sign, dragging the Sheinbergs' pink flamingo sparking down the block wedged in the tailpipe.

Aunt Ginny slapped her thigh. "We should have put the top down."

I was white-knuckling the dashboard as we spun through the blinking red light on Beach Avenue without pause. "It's forty-five degrees out."

"Yeah, but just think of how alive you'd feel when we got there."

Aunt Ginny rode up on the curb to avoid a paper bag and nearly sideswiped a row of parking meters. A yellow bicycle wasn't so lucky. I took out my cell phone to check email and compose a briskly written last will and testament. *Maybe if I don't see death coming, it will soften the blow.*

My stomach bottomed out when I saw an alert from Google. SurferChickNJ had left me a one-star review. She claimed that she stayed with me for a girlfriends' winter get-away and they all got food poisoning. She'd left the same review on Yelp, Twitter, Facebook, and my website. *Who the heck is SurferChickNJ?!* Three couples had stayed with us since the disastrous week of local celebrities. No groups of girls. No friends. All married couples. *What is going on?!* My head hit the side window as Aunt Ginny took a left turn too fast and we sailed past the Angel of the Sea.

I didn't have time to reply with a counterassault. Aunt Ginny launched over a speed bump into the Senior Center parking lot and my cell phone flew out of my hands and hit the dashboard, knocking the protective plastic case off. She slingshot the 1958 convertible in a doughnut until it slid to a stop into three parking spots. "Wee, that was fun!"

I blinked a couple of times until the Grim Reaper disappeared from my line of sight. Someone tapped on my window. I unlocked the door and Smitty opened it and offered me his hand.

"Heya, boss. I see you're riding in the death seat today."

I tried to focus on the little bald man in the Philadelphia Eagles ball cap and Three Stooges sweatshirt. "Am I alive or dead?"

Smitty made a face, "Nyaaaaah. You are pretty green around the gills."

Aunt Ginny knocked her door shut and came around to the passenger side. "It must be the spinach."

Smitty shifted his eyes from me to Aunt Ginny and back again. "Well, don't get sick now. You're going to have company soon."

Oh no. I should have gone back to bed.

Aunt Ginny shot upright. "Are you kidding me?! That vain badger was just here."

Smitty grinned and wiggled his eyebrows. "Georgie will be here tomorrow night. She's coming up for Valentine's Day." He gave a wave and danced into the Senior Center like a vaudeville act leaving the stage.

Where'd that Grim Reaper go when you need him?

Chapter Sixteen

A unt Ginny tramped into the Senior Center in a huff and I lugged behind her. I spotted Fiona and Iggy getting coffee and doughnuts in the activity room. Iggy met my eye. It was like looking into a mirror. I was having a bad day, but he'd had a lifetime of being under Fiona's thumb. I felt a sudden wave of sympathy for him. Still not enough to go out with him, though.

Sawyer entered the room carrying a coconut almond latte from La Dolce Vita with a big heart drawn around the pet name Bella. "Gia says hi and he misses you."

I took the coffee like a lifeline and rubbed the cup against my cheek. "Did you give him your report, Agent 99?"

Sawyer was suddenly engrossed in reading the "caution hot" notice on her coffee cup.

Aunt Ginny grabbed me by one arm and Sawyer by the other. "Come on. I need to check on my backdrops."

She dragged us down the hall to the new theater. Most of the seniors were onstage with Bebe going over one of the big ensemble numbers. Piglet was in his usual seat, currently cleaning his wire-rimmed glasses with his pink silk tie. The two big guys were wedged in their seats down front watching Smitty install the replacement set piece for the yacht on the left side of the stage. They were offering advice that, by the look of it, Smitty was ignoring. Smitty stood back to survey the makeshift yacht and the mast pole fell over. He grunted and took his hat off and rubbed his head with it. After a minute he dug in his toolbox for a drill.

Royce's agent, Ernie Frick, was giving Royce a prerehearsal pep talk. They were running through vocal warmups. "Toy boat toy boat toy boat. A proper copper coffeepot. A proper copper coffeepot."

Blanche breezed by us wearing dark sunglasses and a floor-length, silver fox coat. "I told you not to bother me when I'm in character. Just like Meryl, I'm a Method actor. How am I supposed to center myself as Donna with you prattling on about budgets and ticket sales?" She was berating Neil, who was on her heels, trying to appease her.

"I am so sorry, Blanche. That's why you're a star."

Blanche shrugged out of her fur and threw it backward over Neil. He stopped short to wriggle himself free and let out a steadying breath.

"Why do you let her walk all over you like that?" Aunt Ginny asked.

Neil looked from me to Aunt Ginny. He gave Aunt Ginny a shy smile. "It's complicated."

He continued down the aisle toward the stage and Aunt Ginny muttered, "It always is."

Aunt Ginny took off her sweater to reveal another passive-aggressive T-shirt. This one was pale blue and had *Being a phony must be exhausting for you* written across the front in black.

"I'm going to go say hello to Blanche before checking my traps."

Sawyer shook her head. "We're going to have an old lady catfight before the week is over."

We joined Fiona and Mrs. Sheinberg, who were sewing sequin trim on the costumes. Fiona handed us needles and thread with some trim and a couple of white satin tunics. "Since you're here, you can help with the bric-a-brac."

Mrs. Sheinberg showed us where to attach the trim on the sleeves. "Thanks, bubbeleh. We need all-hands on deck if we're going to get these finished by opening night."

Sawyer and I tried to thread our needles, but it was a lot harder than we remembered from seventh-grade home ec class.

Sawyer squinted at the tiny metal stick. "Is this a regular-size needle?"

Fiona handed her something that looked like a nickel with a metal loop on the end. "Here. Use the needle threader before you hurt yourself. I was just telling Miriam here that I haven't seen much of Royce since he's been home from New York. He's been having trouble learning his lines, so he's been coming up here after hours to practice. Don't say anything, he doesn't want anyone to know."

I tried jamming the white thread into the loop. "He's been coming back after the Senior Center closes? How's he getting in?"

"That nice boy, Neil, gave him a key," Fiona answered.

Neil was paying the piano tuner.

Mother Gibson was setting the stage for the first scene. Blanche appeared and snapped at her. "Where is my watering can?! I'm supposed to have it when I walk out of the taverna!" Blanche strode up to Mother Gibson and put her finger in the older woman's face. "If you don't get your act together, I'm going to find another stage manager who can do the job!"

Mother Gibson calmly replied, "If you don't get your finger out of my face, you'll need to find a proctologist to remove it surgically."

Blanche pulled her hand back and turned on her heel. Neil went over and patted Mother Gibson's shoulder and said something to her that we didn't hear. When he walked away, she joined us.

Mother Gibson flopped down on the theater seat. "That woman wants to be snatched bald. As if I know what she did with her props." She took the needle away from Sawyer, who still hadn't been able to thread it, and jammed the white floss through the eye before handing it back.

Fiona shook out the satin pants she'd finished trimming at the ankles. "Blanche is a horrible person. Always has been. The only one she's not been snapping at is Royce, and that's because she's trying to get her claws into him."

I tried to line up the trim with the cuff of the satin sleeve for the third time. "What were you and Neil discussing so intently?"

Mother Gibson took the costume out of my hand and pinned the trim into place. "He wanted to know if Blanche and Royce were an item in high school since they had such natural chemistry onstage. I told him he was out of his mind."

We all looked onstage, where Royce had his arms folded across his chest looking blankly into the lights and Blanche was haranguing him about memorizing his lines again. *Oh yeah, there's that chemistry now.*

Fiona picked up another satin tunic and started to measure out more trim for the neck. "I told Neil the same thing earlier this week. Blanche and Royce were only partners onstage. He couldn't stand to look at her offstage. He only had eyes for Ginny."

I smiled to myself.

"Now my Iggy . . ."

Oh God, here we go.

Iggy sat up straighter at the piano and leaned hard in our direction.

"My Iggy had a high school girlfriend and she was a real beauty. Laura, I think her name was."

"Nicole." Iggy whispered her name, giving away that he was eavesdropping.

"Right, Nicole. I thought for sure they would get married. He met her in fencing. My Iggy has a master's degree in fencing, you know."

We all stopped our sewing and looked at Iggy. He was squeezing the roll of chub that hung over his pants, making it look like his gut was talking.

"My Iggy was quite the athlete. There was nothing he couldn't do. He went to college on an athletic scholarship. He was headed for the Olympic team, but an injury forced him out."

Mrs. Sheinberg furrowed her brows. "Are we talking about that Iggy?" She looked toward the piano. "The one picking lint out of his belly button?"

"Iggy!" Fiona chided.

Iggy jerked upright.

Mrs. Sheinberg whispered to me and Sawyer, "You see what happens when you have a baby near menopause?"

Neil clapped his hands. "Let's clear the stage for the scene between Tanya and Pepper. Where is Thelma?" Mrs. Davis took the stage and was joined by one of the "young" seniors, who was in his late sixties, and Iggy started playing the musical accompaniment for "Does Your Mother Know."

Blanche led Royce backstage with a sly look on her face, and Aunt Ginny stormed out from behind the backdrop.

Sawyer looked up from concentrating on her stitches. "Uh-oh. She looks mad."

That's a glare that could fry an egg. "Maybe there is more to Royce and Blanche's relationship than we know."

Fiona and Mrs. Sheinberg looked at each other and shared a laugh. Fiona jabbed a bejeweled finger in my face. "That would be the day. Any man who wants to get involved with Blanche Carrigan is taking his life into his hands."

Sawyer looked up for the first time from concentrating on her stitches. "Why is that?" Sawyer pulled her thread tight and all her stitches slipped through the fabric and out the other side. "What?!"

Mother Gibson chuckled. "You forgot to knot the end, child."

Fiona pinned the trim in place on a new pair of pants and switched garments with Sawyer, who now had to thread a new needle. "Because Blanche killed her first husband with rat poison."

I dropped my needle. "Are you sure?"

Mrs. Sheinberg waved Fiona off. "That's a bunch of hearsay. The police verified that her husband got hurt on the job building the Springfield Inn."

Mr. Ricardo and Duke joined us from the row ahead, balancing backward in the seats on their knees.

Duke took a drink from a bottle of water. "I remember that. The guy had fallen from the rafters and landed on a shaft of rebar and was pierced through the stomach. He pulled it out and drove all the way home to his wife, that crazy SOB. He bled out in the car."

I finally found my needle and managed to prick myself picking it up. I got a spot of blood on the costume and Mrs. Sheinberg took it away from me with a sigh.

Fiona jabbed her needle through the fabric in swift strokes. "That was her second husband. Her first husband died at home after a bout of so-called tuberculosis. The death was ruled natural causes, but they don't know what I know."

"Which is?" Mr. Ricardo prompted.

Fiona tied her thread in a knot. "Blanche used to come in to the Villas Five and Ten where I was a counter clerk. My boss, Gunter, was the shady sort, you know the kind. He used to import various contraband like Cuban cigars, Russian caviar, and French opium cigarettes. We kept them behind the counter with the absinthe. Miss High-and-Mighty came in every week for a pack of cigarettes and a box of rat poison."

"Did she live in Wildwood?" Sawyer finally got her needle threaded and showed it to me triumphantly. "I heard they used to have a lot of rats."

Fiona bit her thread off with her teeth. "She lived in a dinky little apartment in the Crest; that's not the point. I always thought it was so ridiculous that someone with that big a rat problem would have the nerve to look down on a single girl trying to make a living on a dollar an hour. Then I read a dime novel where the wife killed the husband by putting rat poison on his cornflakes. That's when I figured out what she was up to."

Duke rolled his eyes. "Okay, Columbo."

Sawyer and I gave each other a look. *I wonder how many murder plots are based on paperback mysteries?*

Mr. Ricardo asked, "Did you report her to the police?"

"I had no proof. Gunter would have had my head if I got the Five and Ten involved with the cops. And it's not like it would have brought the poor man back."

"Wait a minute." Duke leaned so far forward in his seat, it was a wonder he didn't topple over the back. "Are you telling me the Five and Ten sold contraband?"

"Not just contraband. Sunday was Gunter's busiest day because of all the back-door liquor sales when it was illegal for the liquor store to open." Fiona took a hot-pink minidress and matched it up to a spool of thread and handed it to me. "Old Gunter got away with a lot of illegal imports because it was the sixties. No one was watching the little shop selling penny candy and nickel postcards."

The musical number hit a snag and Bebe was called to the stage to walk Tanya and Pepper through their choreography again.

Duke ran his hand over his goatee. "I spent twenty years on the vice squad. We never got a single lead about the Five and Ten."

Mr. Ricardo slapped Duke on the back. "Just imagine all the other things you probably missed "

Mother Gibson snickered. "I'm sure you tried really hard."

Duke's face was running through a myriad of expressions. "I . . . I gotta take a powder."

I had to hold in a laugh because he looked like he was about to lose his doughnuts. The poor guy's brain must have been going tilt. He left his seat and muttered his way out of the auditorium.

Fiona started tacking the gold sequins to another pink minidress. "I don't know why he's going on like that. What's the big deal? Gunter's dead, we're friends with Cuba, and the Five and Ten is long gone. What's he going to do about any of it?"

A loud pop jerked all our attention to the stage. A splattering of blue paint was seeping through the Kalokairi cove backdrop. Bebe dove to her belly on the stage and covered her head with her hands. Aunt Ginny jumped to her feet. "Ah ha! I caught you, you sneaky little cop! Come on out here and face the music, Duke."

Duke answered from the back of the theater. "What? I'm right here."

Mrs. Davis tried to see behind the backdrop. "Who is that? Who's back there?"

There was a scuffle in the side curtain, then a furious, paint-splattered Blanche Carrigan was prodded out, aided by Mrs. Dodson's cane in her back. Aunt Ginny's trap had caught its prey.

Chapter Seventeen

We were all stunned. Aunt Ginny tramped onto the stage, taking off her earrings. "Just what did you think you were doing, Moira?!"

Sawyer grabbed my arm in a panic.

"Oh no." I was on my feet in a flash and speeding toward the stage as fast as a forty-plus-year-old chubby girl can. "Aunt Ginny, no!"

Neil was on the other side and had Blanche around the middle. "Now, ladies, let's be civilized about this."

Mrs. Davis, who was already onstage and in the perfect position to intervene, fished a cell phone out of her tube top. "Hold on! Hold on! How do I record?!"

Mrs. Dodson rushed to her aid. "It's the red button under the camera. Hurry up."

One of the big guys down in front was motioning to Aunt Ginny. "Go for the eyes!"

Fiona screeched, "She's been sabotaging Royce's play. I bet she sent him that death threat too!"

Blanche took a swing at Aunt Ginny. "You stupid tramp. You've ruined my Hermès blouse."

Aunt Ginny bobbed and came back with an uppercut. "That's what you get for sabotaging my backdrops, you conniving harpy!"

Royce tried to calm the ladies, but his presence just egged them on.

It finally took Bebe to settle them both down. She stood between the ladies and had a hand on top of each head. "Blanche honey, you're covered in paint. There's no coming back from that one. You'll have to own it. And, Ginny, you can scratch her eyes out if you want, but you'll mess up your manicure. Wouldn't you rather just bask in the glory that this will be spread all around town before dinner?"

The ladies stopped struggling, but not before Aunt Ginny gave me an elbow to the gut.

"Oof."

"Sorry, Poppy Blossom."

I was doubled over trying to catch my breath. "I'm fine."

Neil ran a hand through his white hair. "Okay. Let's regroup. It's perfectly natural for tempers to flare in a production the closer we get to opening night. Everything will work itself out."

The mast of the yacht chose that moment to fall over again. The two guys in front started to giggle, but Neil's eye went to Piglet in the back row. Piglet appeared to be rather disgruntled about the whole thing and was angrily taking notes on his tablet.

"Why don't we break for lunch? I'll take care of the backdrop. Everyone can get cleaned up." His eyes darted to Blanche. "And we can meet back here in an hour and we'll start with the duet between Royce and Blanche about lost love. It will be a technical rehearsal. Poppy, be ready with those lights, and, Iggy, you're good to go on the piano tuning, yeah?"

Iggy and I nodded, although my heart wasn't in it.

Mrs. Dodson tapped her cane on the stage. "What are you going to do about Blanche?"

Mrs. Dodson threw her hands to her hips. "She's obviously been the one sabotaging the props. She's trying to ruin the play."

Royce rubbed the back of his head. "That wooden oar really hurt."

Blanche was rather indignant for a woman with paint dripping off her nose. "I have not touched the props. And I would never threaten Royce; we're partners. I've only been messing with Virginia's backdrops as a practical joke. A little stage prank. I didn't mean anything by it."

Aunt Ginny shook her head. "Where's my purse?"

I remembered the brass knuckles and gave Neil a desperate look. "Do something. Now."

Neil clapped his hands. "Okay, let's break."

I took Aunt Ginny by the arm while Neil cleaned up the paint explosion backstage. Mrs. Davis and Mrs. Dodson followed close behind us giggling. Mother Gibson made a shadowboxing bob and weave to Aunt Ginny before they all broke out in giggles.

Aunt Ginny wiped the tears from her eyes. "Royce, want to join us for lunch?"

Royce grinned but shook his head. "I'm going to stay and go over my lines while everyone is at lunch."

Aunt Ginny waved goodbye to him. "Okay, where do we want to go eat?"

Mrs. Davis offered, "How about the Lobster House?"

Mother Gibson swatted the suggestion away. "We just had that. How about Russo's for cheesesteaks?"

I wanted to scream, *Yes!* But Aunt Ginny shook her head. "Too far." Then Aunt Ginny gave me a sly look. "How about Mia Famiglia?"

You're killing me, old woman.

Sawyer had snuck up behind me. "I haven't had a good fettuccine Alfredo in forever."

"We were there just a couple of months ago."

"Yeah, but I didn't get the fettuccine. I got the spaghetti Bolognese."

Skinny girl problems.

Aunt Ginny grinned. "The chef might be Poppy's mother-in-law one day."

I tried to laugh off Aunt Ginny's nonsense. "What? No, she won't." *Kill me now.*

Sawyer's eyes tried to pop out of her head. "Ooh."

I glared at her, but she made kissy sounds, like she had the nerve not to be intimidated by me at all.

"Where are your keys?" I asked Sawyer.

She held them up. "Right here."

I grabbed them. "Good. I'll drive the ladies while you go with Aunt Ginny."

The blood drained from Sawyer's face. "I'm sorry, I'm sorry, I'm sorry."

Aunt Ginny took Sawyer by the arm and dragged her toward the exit. "Come on, kiddo. It's just a few blocks away. I know a shortcut, so we can beat everyone else there."

Sawyer tossed me a pleading look over her shoulder.

I grinned and waved her keys.

It didn't take long before we were all seated in the terracotta ristorante of Chef Oliva or, as Gia called her, Momma. Of course, the ladies teased me about Gia all the way over here, but Sawyer needed a stiff drink when she arrived, so I'd say their little bit of teasing was harmless.

Momma was wearing a flour-sack dress and a faded, flower-printed apron, and she was as sweet as Lucky Luciano when he'd been crossed. She came out to greet our table of six and tried to set me on fire. She acted like she was lighting the candle, but I knew what she was up to.

Five of us received a smile. I received a scowl and a dirty hand gesture. After complaining about me in Italian to the waiter, she went back to her stainless-steel lair of bubbling cauldrons and pasta torture devices.

"So . . ." Our waiter took a step toward our table and gave me a timid smile. "The lady is gluten-free. Any other allergies I should know about?"

I held my tongue. My list of problem foods was too long, and Momma wasn't far enough away. "We'll just keep it at gluten for now."

I ordered a chicken Caesar salad and we settled in to chat. Sawyer calmed down enough to stop gripping the linen tablecloth by the time the salads were delivered and was able to join us.

Mother Gibson brought up what we'd all been waiting to talk about. "Edith, the look on Blanche's face when you marched her onstage dripping with blue paint."

We all laughed so hard, it took several minutes for us to calm down and switch topics.

Aunt Ginny passed around the bread basket. "I wouldn't put it past Blanche to be behind that threat Royce received. She's obviously trying to ruin the play. Stage prank my foot."

I passed the bread to Sawyer as fast as I could. "Why would Blanche try to sabotage the play? She's the lead across from Royce. She has nothing to gain with it being canceled."

Aunt Ginny's forehead furrowed. "Maybe she was trying to keep me too busy to spend time with Royce outside of practice. That harlot."

Mrs. Davis nodded along. "His sister seems very keen on him spending all his time at home."

Mrs. Dodson spoke in hushed tones. "There have been a lot of strange doings. What I want to know is . . . is someone trying to actually hurt Royce or just scare him away?"

Sawyer came alive. "Whoa. You should have heard what Fiona was saying during rehearsal about Blanche's first husband and his mysterious death."

Mrs. Davis had Sawyer elaborate, then added, "We'd always heard those rumors, but the police never found any evidence of wrongdoing."

Aunt Ginny made a face. "Meh. The police in this town wouldn't know a crime scene if you wrote them a script for it."

Mother Gibson emptied a couple of Splendas into her iced tea. "I don't know. Duke McCready seems like he knows what he's doing. He sure is in great shape after all those years chasing bad guys around the shore. I wonder if he works out."

Mrs. Dodson rolled her eyes. "You're only saying that because you have a crush on him."

Mother Gibson giggled. "Yeah, I do."

That made me smile and I tried to hide it from the ladies.

Mrs. Davis caught me. "And what are you snickering about over there, Missy?"

"What? Nothing."

Sawyer kicked me under the table and winked at me.

Mrs. Davis had a teasing gleam in her eye. "Let me tell you something. No matter what age you are, falling in love feels the same. Doesn't it, Ginny?"

Aunt Ginny choked on her tea and spit some of it out. "Don't pull me into this."

Mrs. Dodson poked Aunt Ginny with her fork. "Deny that you have butterflies every time you look at Royce."

Aunt Ginny blushed. "I feel like I'm seventeen again." Then she giggled until she snorted.

Sawyer's mouth dropped open and I kicked her.

Mother Gibson speared an olive from Mrs. Dodson's plate. "See, you're never too old for romance."

Thank God their pasta arrived to keep them busy for a while.

A little over an hour later, we were back at the Senior Center. Everyone was congregating down by the stage, waiting for the technical rehearsal to begin. The curtain was down and the lights were off. Ernie Frick was sitting in the front row on his cell phone until he saw Royce arrive with a cheeseburger from the fast-food place down the street.

"Hey, there's the star now." Royce and Ernie clasped hands and chatted quietly.

Everyone was chattering about the problems we'd had so far. Part of the backdrop needed to be repainted, again. The seniors were still having trouble with the dance numbers. Smitty would have to come back to repair the yacht.

Mr. Ricardo jabbed Royce in the side. "It doesn't help that you break into Shakespeare every time you forget your lines either!"

Royce rocked back on his heels. "I do?"

Most of the ladies made faces at one another but wouldn't comment.

Ernie chuckled. "Royce is one of a kind. That rare talent that made him the love of London's West End. Shakespeare stays with you forever."

Fiona patted Royce's arm. "That's right, Boodaloo." She glared at Mr. Ricardo. "Some people are just jealous."

Royce dabbed his forehead with his handkerchief. "If you ask me, the problem is the schedule. We need to delay the opening to the fourteenth."

That made me laugh. "I'm surprised you believe that old theater superstition, Mr. Hansen."

Royce wagged a finger in my direction. "No Broadway

theater would dare to open on Friday the thirteenth. You'd be inviting the jinx." He looked around and saw the frightened faces staring back at him and gave a nervous laugh. "I mean, I never put too much stock into theater hoodoo. Plus, we're so far off-Broadway here, I'm sure we're perfectly safe."

He didn't look convinced and everyone laughed uneasily.

Blanche threw her cape over the first three seats on the second row. "Please. We're doing *Mamma Mia!* It's not exactly *Phantom*, is it? Besides, if you want a curse, you've got a living, breathing one right here in Ginny's niece."

I had one hand on Aunt Ginny's arm to hold her back. "What did I do?"

"From what I've seen in the paper, everywhere you go, a body drops. They'll have to start calling you Jessica Fletcher."

I wanted to let Aunt Ginny have a go at her. I opened my mouth to defend myself, but Mr. Sheinberg cut me off.

"What a buncha *mishegas*. Friday the thirteenth. Meh. Let's get cracking. I want to be home tonight before they call the lotto."

Aunt Ginny glared at Blanche. "I agree. You're all being ridiculous."

Mr. Sheinberg pulled the rope to lift the curtain and stopped halfway up.

There, at center stage, under a baby-pink spotlight, was Duke McCready. His eyes were blank. His head twisted at an impossible angle. He had taken his final bow.

The biddies gasped, and everyone took a giant step away from me, like I was somehow responsible for the curse.

Aunt Ginny fanned herself. "Then again, maybe we should move the opening to the fourteenth."

Chapter Eighteen

Fiona screamed, "Oh my God, he's dead! He's dead!" then passed out.

Iggy ran to her side and patted her hand. "Mother! Mother! Are you okay?"

Sawyer started to cry, and Mr. Ricardo patted her on the back.

Piglet made his way toward the stage, wringing his hands. "Oh no. Oh no no no no no. This is no good."

"Are we sure he's dead?" Ernie Frick asked. "Maybe he just nodded off."

Mrs. Dodson poked me in the side. "Poppy, go check."

"Why do I have to go check?"

Mrs. Davis took some unsteady steps backward. "Because you have the most experience with checking dead bodies."

"I do not." *Oh wait, that's probably true.*

My protest was falling on deaf ears. Blanche was silently rocking in her seat, gently crying. Aunt Ginny was holding

on to Royce with her face buried in his chest. The Sheinbergs were huddled together, praying.

Mother Gibson was noticeably pale. "Please, honey."

I went up on the stage and slowly crept over to Duke's
broken body. My heart was lodged in my throat. I didn't
have to check for a pulse to know he was dead. No one
could survive a neck injury like that. His eyes were open, his
skin was pale even in the pink glow of the spotlight, like all
the blood had drained from his body even though there was
only a pool of it under his head, presumably caused by the
fall. But for the sake of the others, I leaned down and put my
fingers where his artery would be. His neck was still warm.
I touched the part of his wrist that was outside of the spotlight and it was exceptionally cooler but not cold. He hadn't
been dead long. Of course, he was alive an hour ago, when
we broke for lunch.

I looked into the crowd of expectant eyes and shook my
head. Many of the seniors started to weep. Duke had been
their friend. He was one of them. His grandson was coming
for a visit next weekend.

Mother Gibson cried out, "Who would do this? Why
would someone want to kill Duke? He was a nice man."

I looked down at Duke and quickly blinked a tear away
before it could fall. There was a slip of paper sticking out of
his breast pocket. "Does anyone have a handkerchief or a
scarf?"

Mrs. Davis pulled a handkerchief out of her bustier and
handed it up to me. *I'm going to try not to think about where
that's been.* I used the fabric to pull the paper from out of
Duke's pocket and opened it. It looked like it had been hastily
ripped in half. My heart gripped in my chest as I read it.

"What is it, Poppy?" Aunt Ginny called to me.

The biddies all huddled up to the edge of the stage.

"It seems to be a suicide note."

The crowd of seniors gasped and started murmuring to one another. "No way. Not Duke."

Piglet's hands shook as he pulled out an iPhone. "Well, I'm ca–calling the police." He didn't get any argument from the rest of us.

The two gorillas who had been hanging around in the front row fought each other to dislodge themselves out of their seats. They took one look onstage and shot out of the emergency exit.

I wanted to point out that we probably shouldn't let them leave what might be a crime scene, but my voice wouldn't cooperate.

Neil strode in from the back of the auditorium. "Okay, I know we've had a rough start to today's practice, but I think we can make this afternoon a lot of fun."

Yeah, I'm pretty sure that's not gonna happen.

Bebe appeared on stage from the back exit, by Royce's dressing room. "Sweet corn puddin', what is happening here?"

"Duke is dead." I looked up into the rafters and my eyes fell on a section of the railing that was broken through. "It looks like he fell from the catwalk and broke his neck."

Neil stopped short, then ran the length of the auditorium and leaped to the stage. "What happened? Did anybody see him fall?"

Bebe looked at the catwalk, then at Duke. She crouched down beside him. "Aww. Poor man. What a horrible way to go."

I tried to reassure everyone. "It had to be very quick. I'm sure he didn't suffer."

Bebe put one large hand on Neil's shoulder and one on mine. "What can I do to help? Do you need me to find a place to hide the body?"

A breeze blew through the room and was quickly followed by sirens in the distance.

Bebe's hands dropped back to her side. "I've got to go." She gingerly stepped backstage and out of the exit toward the costume closet Royce used as a dressing room.

Bebe wasn't the only one who was suddenly very nervous. I tried to return the suicide note inside Duke's front pocket, but it got hung up on a button and I had to jam it into his blazer instead.

One of Cape May's finest entered the little theater and came down to the stage. "Okay, everyone. I am Officer Birkwell. Officer Consuelos is securing the building and will be in momentarily."

I looked at Officer Birkwell, then Aunt Ginny. We both looked around Officer Birkwell and down the aisle, waiting for a certain little blond cop who had been the bane of my existence since I returned to Cape May and she'd arrested me for killing a cheerleader. As if.

Officer Birkwell took the stage and briefly examined the scene. "Who's in charge here?"

Neil raised his hand. "I am. Neil Rockford."

"Can we have some more light please, Mr. Rockford?"

Neil jumped toward the light booth. "Of course." He turned the stage lights up to full power, and I had to shade my eyes until they adjusted.

I'm sure the police deal with murder investigations every day. Maybe Officer Birkwell doesn't even remember me or Aunt Ginny.

"I want everyone to stay where they are." He scanned the room. When he came to Aunt Ginny, he flinched and reached for his side arm. "Mother of God!"

Oh. He does.

Aunt Ginny gave him a lopsided grin. "Where's Amber?"

He looked around until he spotted me near the light booth and sighed. "Officer Fenton is on another assignment, but it appears that I owe her twenty dollars now. Ms. McAllister, why am I finding you so close to the deceased?"

I took a step forward. "This is Duke McCready. We were rehearsing a play for the Senior Center. We broke for lunch, and when we returned we found him like this."

Officer Birkwell dropped to a squat. "Did anybody touch the body or interfere with the crime scene?"

"Um." I could feel a band of sweat start to form under my Spunks. "I took his pulse on his neck and his wrist . . ."

Officer Birkwell turned his face to me and cocked an eyebrow.

"They wanted to be sure."

I gave Piglet the eye and hoped he wouldn't be a snitch about me taking out that note.

Officer Birkwell considered the seniors for a moment, then nodded. "Why don't you take a seat until I can get your statement?"

Phew. I hopped down from the stage and joined Sawyer and Aunt Ginny in the front row while he got a list of everyone's names from Neil.

Mrs. Davis and Mrs. Dodson pulled me into a huddle. "What did the note say, Poppy?"

I couldn't keep the tremble out of my voice. "Something about he can't go on. His lover broke up with him and he was depressed."

The ladies looked dubiously at one another.

"That's a load of pig snot," Mrs. Dodson said. "Duke was a career cop. If fifty years on the force didn't break him, retirement and a little lady trouble wasn't going to do it."

Mother Gibson joined us. "I didn't know he had a girlfriend. Duke would never do something like this. He was so excited about his grandson's visit this weekend."

Mrs. Davis looked at the stage. "Did the note look like it was Duke's handwriting, or do you think someone forced him to write it?"

"It was typed."

Seniors were filing in late from lunch. The cast and crew

members took their seats and were quickly brought up to speed and put their names on the list.

Officer Birkwell was still questioning Neil. "Any idea why the deceased was up there?"

"I can't imagine. Royce is the only one with scenes that enter from the catwalk."

Royce started to cough and had to sit down. He dropped his head down between his knees.

Officer Birkwell motioned around the theater. "Who else had access to this room who isn't here now?"

Neil's hands shook. "Just, uh, the carpenter, Smitty. Uh, the choreographer, Bebe. There were two men who've been hanging around, but I don't know their names."

"You just let anyone hang around the building?"

"Well, it's open to the community until nine, and they weren't hurting anyone."

Aunt Ginny narrowed her eyes. "They sure shot out of here the minute trouble was afoot."

Mrs. Dodson tapped her cane. "Oh yes. They wanted to retreat before the law arrived. Very sketchy, if you ask me."

I hesitated to say anything, knowing the world of trouble I'd be in when I got home, but I tend to blurt things out when I'm nervous and I was sweating so much my Spunks were hydroplaning right now. "Royce stayed after to run lines today."

A collective gasp rolled through the seniors. My hair felt as though it were on fire between Aunt Ginny's flaming scowl on one side and Fiona's glare from hell on the other.

"Royce would never!"

"Poppy, how could you!"

Mr. Ricardo came to my aid. "That's right. Royce did stay here alone."

Royce was pale and shaky. "Is this a dagger I see before me . . . but no, I did not commit such a foul act as this."

Officer Birkwell's eyelids went to half-mast. "Were you here all afternoon, sir?"

"Aye. But I was in my dressing room running my lines. And then I went to get a cheeseburger."

"Was anyone with you?"

Royce shook his head no.

Ernie raised his hand. "I was with my client the entire time."

Royce looked confused but didn't contradict his agent.

Officer Birkwell was joined by Officer Consuelos, who donned plastic gloves and gingerly searched Duke's clothing. He pulled out the note that I'd returned a few minutes earlier.

Aunt Ginny was doing her part to cover my tracks. "Oh my goodness, whatever in the world is that?"

Officer Consuelos showed the note to his partner, and a cell phone on a selfie stick came slowly poking out from backstage over their heads. I looked around and didn't see Mrs. Davis next to me anymore. *Oh my lord, what is she doing?*

There was a very quiet *tchk* sound that ten people tried to cover by clearing their throats at the same time. *Subtle*. Then the selfie stick pulled back in and the phone disappeared.

Officer Birkwell looked at the group of us. "What was that?"

Aunt Ginny looked in the rafters. "Squirrels?"

I shrugged. The seniors made a unified front that no one had heard anything. Mrs. Sheinberg said it must be her hearing aids acting up and the officers went back to their search of the crime scene.

Ernie Frick called Royce into the shadows on the side of the aisle. He handed him a flask and Royce took a deep drink before handing it back.

Royce was shaking. "That was supposed to be me."

Ernie turned sympathetic eyes on the aging actor. "How can you say that?"

"I was supposed to make my entrance from that catwalk today. I've received death threats. I'm telling you, Ernie, someone is trying to kill me, and they got Duke instead. I have to drop out before someone else gets hurt."

Ernie looked around to see if anyone was listening. Aunt Ginny, Sawyer, and I made ourselves look like we were busy in conversation.

Ernie put his hand on Royce's back. "Maybe you should drop out. Broadway is waiting for a Royce Hansen comeback. I have a lot of other clients clamoring for this one-man show, but I brought it to you, Royce baby! You've always been my favorite. This kind of offer doesn't come along every day."

Royce nodded slowly.

Ernie patted him on the shoulder and looked around before going back to his seat.

Fiona pounced on Royce the moment Ernie was gone. "What was that two-bit scoundrel trying to get you to agree to?"

"Now, Fee, settle down."

Officer Birkwell went up on the catwalk and took some pictures while Officer Consuelos scanned the stage and surrounding area for evidence. I heard sirens getting closer, and before long the ambulance arrived and Duke was prepared for transport.

It was a shock for everyone to see the body bag roll down the aisle.

Officer Birkwell pointed to me and Aunt Ginny. "You two are with me."

We followed him out past Officer Consuelos interviewing Piglet, who gave his name as Terrence Nuttal. "I've been here every day. It's my job. This whole place is a death trap, if you ask me. I'd be looking into that carpenter."

Office Birkwell led us into the main hall. "Okay, ladies, I

know we've had some problems in the past." His eyes bore into Aunt Ginny's. She responded by giving him a toothy smile. "But I want you to promise me that you'll not interfere with police business this time."

I raised my hand and belted out, "Absolutely."

But at the same time Aunt Ginny was saying, "I'm not promising anything."

I sighed. Officer Birkwell sighed. Aunt Ginny dug her heels in.

He tried to appeal to her with logic. "Mrs. Frankowski, there is nothing for you to get involved in. This is an unfortunate situation, but it looks like a suicide."

"Hogwash!"

Office Birkwell gave Aunt Ginny a dry look. "You want to elaborate on that?"

Aunt Ginny folded her arms across her chest and stared Officer Birkwell down. "I overheard Duke talking with Neil this morning between scenes. He was buying two tickets for Friday night's opening performance. One for his daughter and one for his grandson. Does that sound like a guy who's gonna throw himself off the catwalk three hours later?"

Officer Birkwell's eyes bored into Aunt Ginny. "He left a note. It's a suicide." He made some notations in a little flip book. He asked us the usual: alibi, motives, etc. Aunt Ginny and Duke were friends, but they weren't that close, and I'd just met him. Then he asked all the same questions again but trying to trick us with different wording. We answered them again the exact same way. After about thirty minutes, he said we were free to go. "And I'm begging you to go straight home."

Aunt Ginny smiled angelically. "Why, Officer Birkwell, of course we will. Just as soon as we get our pocketbooks and sweaters."

He went back into the theater to collect more statements. We waited a couple of minutes till he was good and distracted with Fiona and Iggy, then we slinked down to the front.

Mrs. Davis had her phone out and the ladies were examining the screen.

Sawyer waved to us to hurry. "Look, Mrs. Davis got a good shot of the suicide note."

Mrs. Davis read the screen. "'I can't go on like this. Life is pain. How will I live without my lover? The pain is too unbearable. Tell Christopher I'm sorry.'"

Aunt Ginny shook her head. "It's rather a bit melodramatic for a cop, don't you think?"

The ladies shook their heads in agreement.

Mrs. Davis scrunched up her nose. "And who in the world is Christopher?"

Aunt Ginny answered. "Maybe it's his grandson."

They were trying to decipher the note, but I found myself drawn to the catwalk. Something wasn't right.

Mother Gibson said, "It doesn't sound like him at all. He was so excited about his visit. It was all he talked about."

The skin on the back of my neck prickled and I made a face.

Aunt Ginny nudged me. "What is it? You just thought of something, didn't you?"

Five sets of eyes were grilling me so hot, I thought my skin would tan. "Why would he crash through the bar of the platform? That would only slow him down and be a lot of extra work. All he had to do was climb in front of the bar and jump from there."

Everyone's eyes followed mine and looked at the catwalk.

"Oh sweet Jesus," Mother Gibson sighed out. "Do you think it was an accident? Maybe he fell."

"Then where did the suicide note come from?"

Mrs. Dodson shook her head slowly in thought. "Maybe he was pushed."

Mrs. Davis added, "But who would do such a thing? He didn't have any enemies. He could be a pain in the butt, but he was well-liked."

Sawyer said, "Maybe a criminal he put away tracked him down and forced him onto the catwalk and pushed him off. Then left the note to throw off the police."

"How did they know Duke would be here and working on *Mamma Mia!*?" I took Mrs. Davis's phone and pulled the photo back up. "The suicide note is carefully typed and double-spaced. Whoever did this didn't just walk in here and catch Duke by surprise. They planned it and made props. And I doubt he would follow an ex-con up on the catwalk."

Aunt Ginny shook her head. "I think we're missing something obvious. Royce and Duke were about the same size. And Royce has been getting threats. Maybe whoever killed Duke thought they were killing Royce and didn't realize until it was too late that they got the wrong man."

I gave Mrs. Davis her phone back. "Royce has only been back in town for a few weeks. Everyone local who knows him is here."

The ladies' eyes grew big and Sawyer let out a little whimper. "Not again."

Aunt Ginny scanned the room of cast and crew. "Maybe it wasn't a local."

"Whether the victim was supposed to be Duke or Royce, the killer is most likely someone in this room."

Chapter Nineteen

No one had the heart to continue for the day. Aunt Ginny handed me the keys to Bessie. She was too flustered to drive after the horrible events that had transpired. I dropped her at home and suggested she lie down for a while.

It was still early, and we were waiting on word as to whether the entire play would be canceled or if today's rehearsal would be rescheduled for tomorrow, so I walked over to La Dolce Vita to do tomorrow's baking just in case.

The exhaustion was catching up to me. I forgot to put the sugar in a batch of brownies and had to throw them out and start over. I'd yawned my way through two lattes and was about to start on a third when Gia laughed at me and shook his head. "What is wrong with you? Are you sleeping enough?"

I nodded, then shrugged. "I've been getting up at five every day to exercise."

"Why do you have to get up so early?"

"If I don't do it before I come here then go home and make Tim's desserts, it won't happen."

"Is this exercise that important to be like this all day?"

"Well, it is because I'm not losing weight." I didn't finish grousing about my weight problems and lack of weight loss until I had thrown together two batches of muffins. I asked myself several times why I was telling Gia all this. I even tried to get myself to stop talking at one point, but my mouth blew right by me. He listened without adding comment, just nodded. When I was finished airing my grievance with my body, he helped me put the twenty-four-cup commercial muffin pans in the oven.

"Why are you trying to lose weight? You are beautiful."

Wow, these Spunks are doing a better job than I thought. I suppressed a giggle. "I want to look better." *Just in case I ever have to get naked.*

"Why don't you accept that you are gorgeous right now just the way you are? Then if you want to exercise to be healthy and strong, you can do a little at a time without killing yourself."

I stared at him.

"If you are worn out, maybe you are doing too much."

I kept staring.

He waved his hand in front of my face. "Bella?"

I was trying to convince myself not to jump into his arms. I gave him a grin and he grinned back. "I will definitely keep that in mind."

"Good. I want you around for a long time."

"That reminds me. I don't know if I'll be in tomorrow yet or not. The seniors had a death today. One of the actors fell from a walkway over the stage."

"*Dio mio!* What happened?"

"He fell three stories off the catwalk. It looks suspiciously like a murder dressed up like a suicide. Aunt Ginny and her friends are very upset."

"Of course they are. Is the play canceled?"

"We won't find out until tomorrow."

"Aunt Ginny must be very sad."

"She is. They were friends. As far as I can tell, pretty much everyone there was his friend."

"So why today?"

"What do you mean?"

"They have been practicing for almost three weeks and no one tried to kill him. What changed today?"

"A couple of new people showed up. Two big gorilla types and a little smiley guy who turned out to be Royce's agent, but he seems harmless enough. And Royce has been getting threats, so there is some speculation that the killer thought he was getting Royce and got Duke by mistake."

"If someone was after Royce, they won't quit until they get him. The accidents will keep happening."

We talked about the play and the alleged suicide until I finished the day's baking and had to leave. Gia pulled me next to him and kissed me. "You know, Bella means beautiful. Now please get some sleep tonight."

The two-and-a-half-block walk home stretched out in front of me with way too much time for thinking. I tried to force my mind to think about Duke and that suicide note. The ocean, the cold, will we get snow? Getting the B&B ready for the Valentine's couples. Anything but Gia telling me I was gorgeous.

Figaro was waiting for me in the window. The way his whiskers twitched said he was planning to give me a piece of his mind. I suspected it had something to do with the cherry-red Maserati in my driveway or the devil in a blue dress who threw open the front door.

"I'm baa-aack!"

Oh good. Georgina's here.

Chapter Twenty

I felt like I had barely closed my eyes when my alarm went off. It was pitch dark outside and unless we were about to have a storm, something was very wrong. I threw my hand out to hit Snooze and got a furry nip on the wrist for it. I turned my head to see Figaro sitting on top of my alarm clock. It was four a.m. I pushed him off and reset it, then scooped him close to me to go back to sleep. I was sure it was an extraordinary accident. Until it happened again at four fifteen.

"What are you doing?"

Figaro's whiskers twitched.

"Get off my alarm clock."

"Meow."

I nudged him off the nightstand to the floor and set it again. As soon as I rolled over, he jumped back up and stepped on the Power button again. The sound of ocean waves crashed against my brain.

I turned the light on and glared at him. Figaro responded by sitting demurely next to the lamp and wrapping his tail delicately around his feet. *Well, now I'm too irritated to go back to sleep.* I unset the alarm and got my cell phone to check email and Facebook. Figaro lay down next to me for a nap. *Really?*

I had a one-star review on TripAdvisor from AlicePJones. "The Butterfly Wings Bed and Breakfast is overrun with bedbugs. It was filthy! We asked for a refund, but the dishonest, money-grubbing owner refused. We had to cut our time short and leave early. Our honeymoon was ruined! A-VOID!" My in-box was loaded with alerts. She had posted the same review across all the travel sites.

My eyes would hardly focus. A vein on my neck was throbbing. *What is going on? Is there another bed and breakfast by the name of Butterfly Wings that people are confusing us with?*

I did a quick search. There was a "Butterfly Wing Guest House" in Bucharest, Romania. That seemed far-fetched.

I was full of frustration and had nowhere to funnel it, so I dressed in leggings, a T-shirt, a long sweatshirt, and a knit hat and went out for my three-mile walk down the boardwalk and back.

The temperature was somewhere in the forties. The ocean breeze cut against my skin. My limbs moved like someone had poured concrete through my veins and it was setting. The surf roared like a lion and seagulls battered the wind to stay aloft. Yet somehow, this was more peaceful than the rest of my life. What had I done to make God punish me like this? My anger carried me through my walk and it was over way too soon. The sky was in the beginning blushes of pink when I returned home an hour later.

Figaro assaulted me at the front door, petulant that I'd left without feeding him.

"That's what you get for your passive-aggressive alarm-clock antics. Don't think for a minute that I don't know that was payback for Georgina's arrival."

Figaro curled around my ankles and rubbed his face against my calf.

I picked up his bowl and opened a can of beef tips au jus. "This is way too fancy for you, sir. You are going to get spoiled."

I placed the bowl on the floor and Figaro dove in like he'd been on a hunger strike.

Aunt Ginny came into the kitchen dressed in black slacks, a cashmere sweater, a black pillbox hat with a veil, and wearing three strands of pink pearls. "Good morning."

I blinked at her. "Is the funeral today?"

"These are my mourning clothes."

"And the pink pearls?"

"I still want to look pretty." She looked at Figaro, who was loudly smacking his mouth around his au jus. "Did you just give him that?"

I nodded. "He was starving."

Aunt Ginny narrowed her eyes at Fig. "I just gave him a can of tuna twenty minutes ago."

Figaro paused his gobbling and looked from me to Aunt Ginny, then he doubled down and started eating faster.

"You little glutton!"

Aunt Ginny started the grinder for coffee. "Did you check your email?"

Visions of pummeling AlicePJones floated before my eyes. "For what exactly?"

"Neil sent everyone an update. The cops officially ruled Duke's death a suicide. Since the Senior Center is not an active crime scene, apparently the show must go on. We have a makeup rehearsal this afternoon."

I took my fruit and kale from the freezer and scooped some into the blender. "How do you feel about that?"

"Like Duke's memory is being spit on."

I added my protein powder and almond milk while I considered Duke. "What do you want to do about it?"

Aunt Ginny poured the boiling water over the coffee grounds in the French press. "The girls are coming over this morning to discuss a plan. They want to make sure you'll be here to help us strategize."

Well, that filled me with anxiety. *What do those biddies have planned now? I have enough trouble reining in Cyclone Ginny when she's running solo.*

After I sucked down my smoothie I took a shower. I fought my way into my Spunks, a pair of stretchy black slacks, and a black silk blouse. Then I had to stand in front of the open window with my arms up until I'd stopped sweating enough to apply my makeup. When I returned to the kitchen to start making Tim's desserts for the restaurant, five sets of eyes were lined up at the center island waiting for me.

"Ladies."

"Poppy," four biddies and Georgina said in unison.

Aunt Ginny gave me a smile that showed both rows of teeth and handed me a steaming mug. "I just made a fresh pot."

I took a deep breath. "What am I agreeing to by accepting this coffee?"

Mrs. Davis waved her hand. "Nothing . . . really."

Mrs. Dodson shrugged and tried to look nonchalant. "Too small to go into detail over."

Mother Gibson gave me an innocent smile but refused to incriminate herself.

"Uh-huh." I looked at Georgina. "And what part do you play in this?"

Georgina lifted her palms. "I don't know anything. The ladies filled me in on the terrible tragedy of your dear friend,

Duke. I just happen to agree with them that you would want to help find out how he really died."

Aunt Ginny pushed the coffee six inches closer to me. "Out of the goodness of your heart."

"Nope. No way. The price is too high. If I get involved in this, the whole town will label me a death magnet."

Mother Gibson's eyes softened and she took my hand. "Oh, honey. That ship sailed long ago."

My coffee bribe went down harsh and with the bitter aftertaste of manipulation. I spent the morning making strawberry tarts and chocolate crème brûlée for Tim, while the ladies alternated between buttering me up that I had a heart of gold and calling me the Cape May harbinger of death. I Googled "how to remove a curse put on you by a deranged psychic" but found nothing helpful.

Sawyer's arrival was a welcome distraction because they switched to teasing her and left me alone.

"Guess what I got today?" Sawyer was so excited, she was practically vibrating.

Mrs. Davis guessed something that I dare not repeat, but it made the four other ladies squeal with laughter and Sawyer blush crimson.

"I'm guessing six roses."

She pulled out her cell phone and shoved the screen in my face. "Six roses and a teddy bear." Sawyer broke out in a fit of giggles.

Aunt Ginny sighed. "I miss stuff like that."

Georgina took the phone and passed it around. "To be young and in love again. My little Smitty is romantic, but even he doesn't go in for all this display."

I sprinkled raw sugar over my chilled custards for caramelizing later. "Do you know who's sending the gifts yet?"

Sawyer grinned. "No, but I'm sure it's Adrian."

Mrs. Dodson cocked her head to the side. "Did you ask him?"

Sawyer shook her head no. "I'm waiting for him to expose himself."

Mrs. Davis raised her eyebrows. "I wish I could be there to see that."

Sawyer blushed. "I mean, I'm waiting for him to reveal that he's my secret admirer."

Mother Gibson swatted Mrs. Davis on the arm. "What if it's not him? Who else could it be?"

Sawyer shrugged. "There isn't anyone else, except my elderly neighbor, Mr. Vartabedian."

I started carrying loads of tarts and custards out to the car while the ladies continued to bait Sawyer. They had just about convinced her that Mr. Vartabedian was her secret admirer when I grabbed my purse. I told Sawyer I'd be back in a few minutes and snuck off to Maxine's. I wanted to get these desserts to Tim before I had to make the last-minute preparations for the B&B check-ins today. My night was going to be full at the Senior Center. I had yet to actually practice all the way through the script as one disaster after another had canceled rehearsals. And now that we were missing a lead actor, Sophie only had two dads to choose from. The understudy for Bill would have to step up now that Duke was gone. I was having serious doubts that *Mamma Mia!* would ever launch.

Chapter Twenty-One

Tim was a commanding presence in his chef whites, working two sauté pans at once in the busy kitchen. Three line chefs were at their stations grilling, seasoning, steaming, and plating up a hodgepodge of delights. The kitchen must have been ninety degrees, but the air was aloft with the bouquet of bacon and rosemary, roasted beef, and grilled scallops. My stomach growled. I'd burned through the kale smoothie just getting into my Spunks. *I'm starving.*

Tim gave me a quick smile. "Hey, babe. What'd you bring me?" And in the same breath yelled, "Chuck, get that calamari out of the deep fry!"

"I have some tarts and chocolate brûlées."

Tim nodded. "I don't have anyone who can help you with that just yet. Where's my mash, Juan!"

Juan replied, "Coming up, Chef."

One of the line cooks yelled, "Short rib risotto plating!"

White tickets were posted all along a metal rail over the workstations and more were coming out of a black box on the stainless counter. Servers were grabbing plates of food and hauling them out to the dining room faster than Primo's can wrap a hoagie.

I answered back, "That's okay, I can handle it." I don't think anyone really registered that I'd spoken, but I made myself busy bringing in the trays and storing them in the walk-in refrigerator.

When I'd finished, I found a spot to watch where I wouldn't be in the way. Tim looked over at me and threw me a sexy smile. A warmth worked its way up my body to my ears.

After a few minutes, Tim plated whatever he'd been working on and removed his last two tickets from the rail. "Juan, take over sauté." He came toward me. "Sorry. Sunday brunch exploded today."

"That's okay. I like to watch you work."

Tim raised his eyebrows and pulled me closer. "Do you, now?"

I swallowed, hard. "Uh-huh." He had me by my waist with my back against the freezer.

He kissed me, and I forgot where we were until the sound of the line whooping and catcalling brought me back. Tim fired off a string of expletives at the cooks, then turned back to me. "I'm sorry, babe. Kitchen talk."

I suspected there was a lot more of that when I wasn't around by the way his staff laughed it off. He led me down the hall to his office. "They won't bug us in here."

"I need to talk to you about something anyway."

"What is it?"

"I've been getting a bunch of bad reviews lately."

"Reviews about what?"

"People are saying terrible things about the bed and breakfast." I pulled up Travelguy95's review on Yelp. "Like this."

"So, you have some stuff to work on."

"No, it's not that. These people haven't even stayed with us."

"Oh. So, they're trolls." He pulled me closer to kiss me again.

I held my phone up between our faces. "But what do I do about them?"

Tim shrugged. "Nothing you can do. Trolls are bottom feeders. They love sounding like big shots who know what they're talking about, but they're just opinionated jackasses who feed off negative energy and hide behind their cryptic screen names. I had a guy give me one star because he couldn't get a reservation. How do you rate a restaurant one star when you've never even eaten there?"

"There has to be something I can do. They're going to destroy my business before the season even starts."

A loud clang came from the kitchen. Tim craned his neck. "What was that?!"

Someone muffled an answer.

"I'm sorry. We're really busy and I've got to get back out there before Chuck destroys something."

I put my phone away disappointed. I was really hoping Tim would have a more helpful suggestion. "I understand." *Isn't this why we did Restaurant Week? So Maxine's would pick up clientele.*

Tim gave me a quick peck. "Let's find a time to talk later. I want to talk to you about Valentine's Day."

My heart gave a little flutter. "Oh?"

He started to lead me back into the kitchen. "Yeah. I was thinking about raspberry pavlovas. What do you think about that?"

My heart may have been premature with that flutter. "Oh. Um. They don't keep real well. You have to keep pavlova dry, but you'd know that."

We were back in the fray and Tim called his chefs to attention. "Tell Poppy what feedback we've been getting on her desserts."

The chefs whistled and applauded. Even though I could tell this had been rehearsed, I couldn't stop my eyes from leaking or my lips from trembling with emotion.

"You're a huge hit, babe. We had a lady Friday night who bought an entire cheesecake to take to a party after having it at dinner."

"That's fantastic!" *We should celebrate.*

"Which reminds me, I need a couple more cheesecakes."

Celebration over.

"Ahh!" Juan dropped the au gratin dish of scallops he was taking from the oven.

Tim threw out another shocking string of "kitchen talk" and sent Juan away from the line to ice his hand.

"I think Juan burns himself once a month to get a thirty-minute smoke break. Poppy, can you take over the sauté station while I check on the prime rib?"

What?! Me?? "Oh, yeah sure." I played it real cool. Grabbed a dish towel and took the sauté pan by the handle. Gave the scampi a little flip. Sent a little side-eye to see if Tim had seen me. He hadn't. He was elbow deep in shoving garlic and rosemary into cuts of a rack rib roast. I took the other sauté pan and gave the shrimp a flip. *Look at me. Chef Poppy.*

"Poppy, put some white wine in there and burn it off for me, please."

"You got it, Chef." I poured a little wine in the pan, let it heat up a bit, then tilted the pan to set the alcohol on fire. *I'm doing it. I'm cooking in a restaurant kitchen.*

Chuck sidled up to me. "You're doing great."

"Thank you."

"Also, your dish towel is a little bit on fire."

Oh God! I stamped the towel on the floor and put the fire out. I sent another side-eye Tim's way. His shoulders were shaking over his roast. Of course, *that* he sees.

Chapter Twenty-Two

"Some guests are arriving today. They'll be with us for a week. I know you like to help, but I don't want to have a repeat performance of your recent shenanigans."

Figaro flattened his ears to his head and swished his tail from side to side.

"I need you to try to behave yourself. No stealing bacon off the guests' plates. No slinking into their rooms if they leave their doors open. And no sneak attacks when they walk past the banister, even though Miss New Jersey did have that coming. Do you think you can do that?"

Figaro wasn't as inspired by my pep talk as I'd hoped he'd be. He gave me a yawn and stretched out across my laptop in baguette position.

Aunt Ginny breezed through the kitchen carrying a vase of red roses. "Did you say these go in the library?"

"No, the front entryway, so they're the first thing the guests see when they arrive."

I took the boxes of Godiva truffles up to the Purple Emperor and Swallowtail suites as part of our romance package. I had a couple coming in from Cape Cod tomorrow, but today the Pescatellis were arriving from Philly. They had won the spa prize sponsored by the local radio station that included a stay at the Butterfly Wings B&B with champagne, roses, chocolates, and a couple's massage at the Radiance Day Spa.

I wanted everything to be perfect for both parties. I desperately needed some good reviews to offset the rash of bad press we'd been getting. I had fresh flowers in both rooms. Top-of-the-line toiletries from Crabtree & Evelyn. The towels were super-fluffy Turkish cotton. The sheets were 1,000 thread count Egyptian cotton, and the bathrobes were luxurious American Pima. I had a beautiful chocolate cherry German sweetbread I'd made earlier to serve with French strawberry cream crêpes for breakfast in the morning. You had to admit I was doing my part to support the global mindset.

Georgina clacked her way into the Swallowtail suite as I was fluffing the royal-blue pillows on the queen-size sleigh bed. My blood pressure rose a few points just knowing my former mother-in-law was near. Georgina could push buttons like a black hat hacker bypassing the Pentagon firewall.

"Poppy. Good. I found you. Sometimes I think you're hiding from me."

Obviously not well enough. "What do you need?"

She looked like she was dressed for a rally. Pink silk suit jacket over pink trousers and pink pumps. She was tying a white silk scarf covered in pink hearts around her neck. "I wanted to let you know that I'll be going out in a bit."

"You going to do some makeovers in your pink Cadillac?"

"Makeovers? No. Whatever for?"

I shrugged. "Just a guess."

She fluffed back her brunette wave to put on her diamond earrings. "I'm meeting Smitty at the theater for rehearsal.

He has to check on the sets to make sure nothing has been tampered with. Really, Poppy, is everything in this town falling apart, or is it just what you're involved with? One would think you would have a complex by now."

"Well, not for lack of trying."

Aunt Ginny hollered up the stairs, "Poppy. Connie is on the phone. She wants to know what time you need her here."

Connie was one of my best friends from high school. She had agreed to meet the guests for check-in tonight since I now had to be at the Senior Center rehearsal. I promised her I'd schlep Emmilee to gymnastics and dance while she took Sabrina to a cheer competition later this month. *Sucker. I would have done it anyway.*

"Tell her the Pescatellis are due at five, but if she could be here at four, I'd be forever grateful."

"So, I'll see you up there?" Georgina stared me down like the musical was a ruse and I was about to change the locks as soon as she left the house.

"I'm right behind you as soon as I check the minifridges."

Georgina left looking unconvinced. *What does a girl have to do to reassure her former mother-in-law that she isn't trying to ditch her now that she's moving on with her life?* My conscience suggested the option of *not ditching her* and I told it to shut up.

Everything was in place and there was nothing more I could do. I grabbed my tote bag and said goodbye to Figaro. I shut the door in midflop. *Crazy cat.*

There was a maroon Mercury Marquis parked across the street in front of Mr. Winston's house. *I wonder if that's his daughter, Judy, or if he has company. People on this street get company so rarely. It's sad really. I should take them all some cookies for Valentine's Day.*

* * *

I was a few minutes late getting to rehearsal. Bebe was back in the activity room, leading the seniors who didn't get speaking parts in their moves for the company dance number. Aunt Ginny was off to the side, shaking up a bunch of pink bottles. Neil was in the back of the theater in deep discussion with the man we now knew was Terrence Nuttal, not that we knew anything about him. Although I suspected the biddies would still call him Piglet.

I saw one of the big guys who'd been hanging around the theater open the emergency exit door down at the front, look around the theater, and close the door again. *Somebody should find out what that's about.*

I stopped in the middle of the theater and set down my tote bag, which held my purse, a bottle of water, a salad that I did *not* want, and my copy of the *Mamma Mia!* script with lighting directions, so I could take off my coat.

Smitty was showing off his drill skills on the yacht mast to Georgina. Georgina was pointing out areas he'd missed. Mrs. Dodson, Mrs. Davis, and Blanche were having an argument at center stage about where they were each supposed to stand during the Super Trooper Hen Party scene and Mother Gibson was stomping her foot on one of the Xs and scolding them. "This is your mark. This is always your mark. No one is moving it after you go home, Blanche."

Aunt Ginny came up behind me. She had taken off her sweater to reveal a black T-shirt with silver writing that said *I wish you would suck on a lemon and lose your voice.*

"How'd that one go over?"

Aunt Ginny laughed. "I didn't know anyone could turn that shade of purple."

Fiona and Iggy walked down the aisle past us. From the tremble in Fiona's voice, we gathered that the news had reached them that Royce was considering Ernie Frick's offer for that one-man show on Broadway.

"He can't go. He just can't. He won't be safe."

"He can do whatever he wants, Mother, gahd! He should just go back to New York and forget about this dump."

"How can you say that, Ignatius?! Uncle Royce is family."

"Family doesn't disappear for sixty years."

Aunt Ginny gave me a told-you-so look.

"What? I came back after twenty-five."

Neil hopped up on the stage and clapped his hands. "Okay, everyone. I know we're all devastated about Duke. I can't even begin to know why he would do something like take his own life. I wish he would have reached out to someone for help. If anyone is having problems—no matter what they are—please find someone to talk to. You don't have to struggle alone. We're all family here. Whether we know it or not. Let's share a moment of silence for Duke."

The seniors bowed their heads. I started to bow my head, but a shaft of light from the emergency exit door opening drew my attention. One of the gorillas had Ernie Frick against the brick wall by his throat. The one who came in realized we were having a moment of silence, shut the door, and bowed his head.

When the moment was over, Neil said, "Okay, we open in five days, I've asked Itty . . . er . . . Smitty to repair the catwalk and he's promised that he'll be done shortly."

Smitty wasn't paying attention. He was doing a bit for Georgina with the drill, acting like it was a snake. "Gnahh. Whoop whoop whoop. Wise guy."

Georgina swatted him on the arm. "Cut it out. They're talking to you."

Neil pointed to the catwalk and Smitty gave him a salute.

Neil continued his pep talk with the actors. "So, let's take it from the top and run through it a few times."

Neil started to leave the stage when Mr. Sheinberg called out in a falsetto voice, "Who's going to play Bill?"

"Oh, right. Thank you. Sol Sheinberg will now be performing the roll of Bill Austin, the travel writer."

There was polite applause from everyone except Mrs. Dodson. "No way. I'm not kissing him. He's married."

Mrs. Sheinberg had already taken her usual seat in the third row. "I'll allow it. I could use a break."

Mr. Sheinberg slapped his leg. "Hot diggity!"

Mrs. Dodson stood her ground. "Absolutely not! I'm no adulteress."

Mrs. Sheinberg didn't look up from her sewing. "Trust me, he's no Casanova."

Mr. Sheinberg stopped his little dance. "I got you, didn't I?"

"'Cause I let you."

"Meh. I'm the best thing that ever happened to you."

"That would be the Dr. Scholl's arch supports."

Neil interrupted the couple to encourage Mrs. Dodson, "We don't have time to worry about that right now. We'll work it out in the stage directions. Just take your place, please."

Fiona cried out, "But where's Royce? He left home hours ago. He should have been here by now."

Neil froze. "Royce isn't here? We have to find him. There's no play without Royce."

Aunt Ginny muttered, "No offense taken."

Everything stopped so Neil could panic and run back and forth. The seniors took seats on the edge of the stage facing the audience. Mrs. Dodson and Mrs. Davis were head-to-head in discussion. They both looked up at the catwalk.

That won't end well.

Blanche went back to ordering Mother Gibson around. Mother Gibson went back to praying for God to give her patience not to drag Blanche down by her hair.

Iggy ran a few bars on the piano to warm up, then played an instrumental version of "Rock You Like a Hurricane." He leered at me and I recoiled. Aunt Ginny jabbed me in the side, but she couldn't speak because she was laughing too hard.

Neil finally returned with Royce, who was dressed in a maroon toga with a gold sash. "It's okay. I found him."

Fiona flipped out on Royce, smacking his arm with every word. "Where did you go! You know we have an agreement!"

"Now, now. I'm sorry, Fee. I had to get into character."

Neil explained, "I found him in his dressing room looking for a gold circlet for his head."

"And just who are you supposed to be?" Fiona was clearly still angry.

Royce stood to his full height. "Julius Caesar."

The whole exchange was bizarre, but not half as terrifying as the sight of Mrs. Dodson's purple bloomers on display as she shimmied on her belly with her derrière skyward across the catwalk.

"Oh my God!"

"What is it?" Neil was staring at me. The seniors all turned their eyes my way.

"Um. It's just that . . . uh." I jabbed Aunt Ginny.

"She thought Royce . . . was actually . . . Rex Harrison for a minute."

Neil raised an eyebrow at me. Mrs. Dodson lost her balance and slid forward.

"Help!" I yelled. "Help . . . me. I did think Royce was Rex Harrison . . . here . . . in Cape May. At the Senior Center."

Blanche would cut me no slack. "Rex Harrison's been dead twenty-five years."

A bright light went off behind Neil. Mrs. Dodson was taking pictures of the catwalk damage and had forgotten to turn off her flash.

"Has he?" I turned to Aunt Ginny.

She looked at me. "Wow. Has it been that long? Time flies."

I nodded. "He'll be missed."

Royce looked from me to Aunt Ginny and back to me and shrugged. "Rex Harrison? I get that a lot."

Mrs. Dodson was shimmying backward toward the steps.

I was terrified that she would fall. "Maybe we should all close our eyes . . . and . . ."

Mother Gibson spied Mrs. Dodson. Her eyes got really big and white and she jumped in. "Say a prayer."

"Yes." I snapped my fingers. "A prayer."

Neil shrugged. "Sure. We can say a prayer for a good rehearsal."

Mrs. Dodson's foot missed the step and she dangled off the catwalk.

"Oh Jesus!" Aunt Ginny grabbed my arm in a death lock. "Jesus help us."

Everyone bowed their heads and closed their eyes.

Mrs. Dodson got her foot on the step and we breathed relief.

Mother Gibson took over for us. "Oh God, watch over everyone durin' this rehearsal, no matter what they doin' or what they *should be doin'*. Keep 'em safe, Lord. You too good to us."

Mrs. Dodson reached the bottom of the steps and pulled her dress back down.

"Amen."

Everyone said amen, and Neil started the five-minute countdown to practice. Ernie Frick came in through the emergency exit. He was red around the neck, but that smile was still on his face. The biddies were in a cluster by the light booth, whispering feverishly when Neil handed Blanche a pink bottle, "Here you go, dear," and handed me a contraption with wires and earphones.

"What's this?"

"Your headset. I'll be on the other end when I'm not on-stage."

Blanche opened the bottle and grapefruit soda exploded all over her face. "Ginny!"

Aunt Ginny answered with a practiced naïveté. "Yes? Who's calling me?"

Neil went to get Blanche a towel and I grabbed Mrs. Dodson and dragged her into the light booth with me. "What in the world were you doing up there?" I turned my script to the first scene and set the lights on the panel to their appropriate settings. "You could have gotten hurt."

Aunt Ginny joined us in snickering. "Blanche . . . heee . . . that was fun."

Mrs. Dodson gave Aunt Ginny a thumbs-up. "I knew we needed to get a good picture of that catwalk before Smitty fixed it."

Aunt Ginny choked out a quick laugh. "You probably have months."

The sixty-five-year-old playing the college-aged Sophie was under a soft blue spotlight singing "I Have a Dream." I turned the light down slowly to simulate dusk as the song went on. I turned up the dial listed as "Ripple" to simulate a water effect on the backdrops.

"Well, what did you find?" Mrs. Davis joined us from backstage.

Mrs. Dodson found the picture on her cell phone and we examined it. "The wooden beam was only splintered the last quarter inch or so. Most of the four-by-four was cut with a sharp edge."

Aunt Ginny grabbed the phone. "It's been sawed through."

"Not only that"—Mrs. Dodson paused for effect—"but it's not that easy to get up there."

I gave Mrs. Dodson a reproachful look. "We saw."

"I don't know how Royce does it every practice." She shook my look off. "At least now we have evidence."

Mrs. Davis patted Mrs. Dodson's shoulder. "Great job. It's a good thing you wore new underwear. I like the purple."

I had to adjust the lights up for the Honey, Honey scene, with Sophie and her seventy-year-old college chums.

Aunt Ginny peeked through the side curtain. "How many of us would be able to get up there and be strong enough to push someone off? Duke was in great shape, but most of the seniors have hip replacements and bad knees."

Mrs. Dodson agreed. "Not to mention that Duke probably fought back."

Mrs. Davis grabbed Mrs. Dodson's wrist. "That's our cue!"

I was supposed to turn light 15 "coral ellipsoidal" to power 8 and totally missed it. "Rats!" I tried to focus on my cues and kept getting the lights mixed up. There was no way I was going to get the hang of this by Friday.

Blanche came back on stage for the scene where Donna discovers the men are on the island. She stood in front of Mr. Ricardo and said her line to Royce. "It's you!"

Before Royce could respond, Mr. Ricardo yelled that Blanche was upstaging him again.

Mr. Sheinberg said, "Come on, Toots. You've had weeks to practice already."

Blanche stuck her finger in Mr. Sheinberg's face. "I know what I'm doing, old man. I'm an actor. I need to be able to flow through my scene and follow the muse."

Neil rolled his script like a megaphone. "Blanche, please tell your muse to take her mark!"

Blanche took a giant step to the right, pushed Royce back

from where he was standing, and stomped her foot on the orange X. "Fine! Happy?!"

A Fresnel box light fell from its support beam above and landed square on top of Blanche. She screamed and went down hard.

Mr. Sheinberg replied, "Yeah, that helps."

Chapter Twenty-Three

Royce screamed and stumbled back. "Oh! What ugly sights of death within my eyes!"

Several people rushed the stage. All but Neil went to Royce to be sure he was unhurt.

I got out my cell phone and dialed 911. I wasn't waiting for Neil's approval this time.

"Get this thing off me!" Blanche kicked her feet out and moaned.

Neil tried to help Blanche sit up. "Are you okay?"

"No! I'm not okay." Blanche's breath was coming in short bursts. "I think something is broken."

Fiona had Royce by the hand. "Are you all right, Boodaloo?"

"I told you someone was trying to kill me." Royce took an unsteady drink from the flask Ernie offered him. "Where's my Ginger? Ginny!"

Aunt Ginny went to Royce and took his other hand. "I'm right here, Royce. You're okay."

Ernie led Royce off the stage. "Come on. Let's sit for a minute and catch our breath."

Blanche sat holding her arm. A trickle of blood ran down her temple. "I'm the one who was brutally attacked."

The blood drained from Neil's face. "No, no. Not attacked." He looked up at Terrence Nuttal and said in a breathy half laugh, "No one was attacked. Just an accident. Right, everyone?"

Piglet appeared to be making some more angry notes on his tablet.

Mr. Sheinberg was looking at the light on the floor. "Heck of an accident."

Mr. Ricardo nudged the light with his toe. "That could have hit me. My dancing days would have been over."

Smitty came to look at the light and up at the support it had fallen from. He grunted. "I hung this light myself."

Aunt Ginny muttered, "Well, there's your problem."

Royce was still rattled. "I know that was meant for me. It fell on my mark."

Fiona went to Royce and patted his hand. "You don't have to do this anymore. You know my husband was very generous with me. He left me well off. I can support both of us."

"What about me?" Iggy protested from his seat at the piano.

"Shut up, Iggy!" Fiona screeched. "Uncle Royce is hurt."

I knew I should have just kept my mouth shut, but once again my opinion flew out with reckless abandon. "Well, technically, he's not hurt."

Royce, Fiona, Aunt Ginny, and Ernie all looked at me like I was crazy.

"I'm just saying, nothing actually happened to Royce. The light fell on Blanche."

Royce gave me a pained expression. "I almost died."

From cowardice maybe.

The sirens from the ambulance could be heard getting near.

Blanche moaned, "Royce, come help me. I can't get up."

Neil patted Blanche on the hand. "I think you should just stay put until help arrives."

Blanche lashed out at Neil. "Don't tell me what to do."

"I just want you to be safe."

The biddies stepped over Blanche to investigate the light on the floor. I ushered them over to the light booth to get them out of harm's way.

Mrs. Dodson nodded to herself. "Poppy, I'm telling you. Something is up. Somebody doesn't want this show to go on."

Mother Gibson shook her head. "I thought all the sabotage would end after Duke was killed."

Mrs. Davis counted on her fingers. "And Blanche was the one sabotaging the backdrops. Surely she wouldn't sabotage herself. She could have been killed. And where are those two assassins?" she squealed. "Ooh, here come men in uniform."

"I don't think anyone has determined that those two men are assassins," I said.

Mrs. Davis ushered a challenge. "Then what are they?"

I shrugged. "Maybe they're just fans of musical theater." *Fans who hold agents by the throat outside when no one is looking.*

A team of three EMTs from the rescue squad checked Blanche's vitals and her injuries. They insisted she be taken to the hospital for a CT scan and X-rays, and Neil almost passed out from the shock. He wanted to go with Blanche to make sure she was okay, but she wouldn't allow it.

Blanche was wheeled down the aisle on a stretcher, but as luck would have it, she was just strong enough to make a rude gesture to Aunt Ginny with her good arm on the way by.

Smitty looked at the support beam for a full minute, then

announced, "I'm getting the cherry picker." He left the stage and a few minutes later returned through the backstage exit, wheeling a metal cage on a platform. He plugged in the device, strapped himself in the cage, and pushed a button that started a slow, noisy arm lifting him up to the support beam. "This clamp has been opened all the way. It was just a matter of time before the vibrations made the light fall."

Neil wrung his hands and looked at Terrence Nuttal, then at the two beefy guys in front, then over at Ernie Frick. "Do you think we could just rehang it and declare it a fluke accident? I mean, no one died this time."

Piglet jumped to his feet and stormed from the room. One of the guys in front covered his eyes with his hands and the other zipped his mouth shut. Ernie Frick shrugged his shoulders, which, coupled with his forever smile, gave him the appearance of going along with a good joke.

Neil and Mr. Ricardo hoisted the fallen light up to Smitty. Smitty hollered to Georgina to get new clamps from his toolbox. They argued for a minute over what size clamps and Georgina finally brought him what he wanted. "Be careful up there, honey."

Aunt Ginny and I made eye contact and mouthed "honey?" to each other and snickered.

After reattaching the cables and checking all the lights, and the clamps, and all the other cables, and all the other clamps, Smitty finally made the whirring, grinding descent back to the stage. "Someone had to go up there and fiddle with that light. I made sure they were all secure."

Neil looked at the ceiling. "But how would someone get up there?"

Smitty also looked at the lights and the two of them shook their heads in wonder.

I thought this was obvious, but I wanted to see how long it would take them to come to the same conclusion. Aunt Ginny rolled her eyes, so I knew she was thinking the same thing I was. After a minute Mrs. Sheinberg asked, "Couldn't they just use that same contraption you did?"

Smitty and Neil looked at the cherry picker. Smitty took his hat off and scratched his head. "I guess so. But they would have to have a key to the supply closet. This one has been locked away since I hung the lights. As far as I know, there are only two keys and I have one right here." Smitty held up his key ring and looked at Neil, who remained silent.

Everyone else waited for Neil to address the soft accusation, but he remained tight-lipped. Eventually, he sighed. "Someone stole it from my office, okay. I didn't think I'd have to lock up keys to a room full of tools and toilet paper. Let's take ten and regroup. We really can't afford to miss any more practices. We're going to have to press forward, everyone. I just have a quick phone call to make." Neil took the stage steps two at a time and marched up to Aunt Ginny. "Ginny, darling. Are you ready?"

Aunt Ginny had a blank look on her face. "Hmm?"

"To be my Donna. You're Blanche's understudy."

Royce clapped his hands together. "Huzzah! Oh, Ginger, it'll be so much more fun with you on stage."

Aunt Ginny's mouth dropped open.

Neil put his arm around Aunt Ginny and walked past a few rows of seats, whispering to her. She nodded along. Then he took her hands and gave them a squeeze before leaving the theater in a hurry.

I hightailed it over to Aunt Ginny as fast as my Spunks would allow. The biddies had the same idea and we converged around her.

"What did Neil say?" Mrs. Davis giggled.

"He said he always wanted me to play the part of Donna, but his hands were tied."

"By who?" I asked.

"I don't know. He just said he was overruled and sometimes money gets in the way of art."

Mother Gibson's face lit up. "Are you going to be Donna for the performances?"

"I don't know yet. It depends on how Blanche is after she's discharged. I don't want her to die . . . or anything, but I do hope they find something wrong that requires her not to talk for the next couple of weeks."

"Aunt Ginny . . . no, that's fair." Blanche had been horrible to everyone except Royce.

Mrs. Dodson motioned for us to come closer to her. "Listen. I've been thinking about some of the strange doings in the theater."

My heart sped up and terror began its furry climb up the back of my neck. The other biddies nodded along, their sharp eyes shining with excitement.

"I'm starting a task force."

"You're starting what?" I asked, but I knew the answer would just keep me awake at night.

She tapped her cane. "You heard me. This confirms Duke was not a suicide. I think someone is trying to kill Royce and make it look like an accident. There is a murderer among us and Duke might have been in the wrong place at the wrong time. It's up to us to bring the ruffian to justice."

I looked each biddy in the eye. "Ladies, we need to take these suspicions to the police."

"Police? *Pshh.*" Aunt Ginny put her hand in the middle. "I'm in."

"No, no, you can't be in. We just got you out of trouble a few months ago."

Mother Gibson put her hand on top of Aunt Ginny's. "I'm in too."

I felt hysteria growing inside me. "Ladies, I really don't want anyone to get hurt."

The other two joined their hands to the pile and four sharp sets of eyes turned my way. "Are you in?"

It wasn't my proudest moment, being shaken down by

four old ladies. I caved under the pressure of their wrinkled little faces and their cataracts. The biddies had assigned me with questioning Piglet, finding out if the two gorillas were assassins, and making a batch of my pecan shortbread for our next council of war session. I felt like I had just been deployed to the bagel brigade on the beach. If I came out of this in one piece, I would still be pecked to death by seagulls.

Chapter Twenty-Four

I slept like the dead and woke up with Figaro's paw over my mouth. "What are you doing?" He retracted his paw and continued observing me. Sometimes I felt like a feline science experiment.

I ran through my morning routine of workout, shower, dress, serve Figaro my overlord his breakfast, choke down a green smoothie while I question my life choices, and finally—coffee. Sawyer arrived to show me the gift of the day, seven roses and a bottle of perfume, and to finagle some coffee and crepes out of me. We were just relaxing into the prebreakfast bliss when my spa guests came down for breakfast. I grabbed the carafes of orange juice and coffee and started through the kitchen door into the dining room.

"Oh. Thank. Gawd. You have cawfee. I thought I would die."

"Babe, there's no way yoose gonna die from not having cawfee for like an ow-wa. There's a Starbucks in Rio Grande, for Pete's sake."

I put my hand out to introduce myself. "Hi, I'm Poppy.

I'm sorry I wasn't here yesterday to personally welcome you to the Butterfly Wings."

They were a young couple, late twenties maybe. The woman was short and dark-skinned, with long, curly brown hair. She popped her gum and grabbed to shake my hand. The rhinestones on her bright pink nails scratched against my thumb. "I'm Val. This is Joey."

"Hey, nice place you got heyea." Joey was a big guy. He had dark hair cut close to his scalp the way men do in the hopes that you won't notice their hair is thinning. He was starting to get lines around his eyes that you get from working outside your whole life, squinting in the sun. My hand disappeared in his rough and calloused paw.

"You're the couple who won the spa package at the Chamber's Mansion."

Val giggled and grabbed Joey's arm. "Yeah. We never been to a spa before. I can't wait to see what they can do with this one."

Joey smiled down at Val. "Oh, I'm gettin' the works. They gonna paint my toenails and pluck my eyebrows."

Val giggled again. "We got married a few months ago but didn't have the money for a honeymoon. This is the first time we been away togetha. Joey, I bet the spa has those one-size-fits-all robes for you to wear."

"Whaddya talking about? They gonna hafta sew four towels togetha to wrap me up for the massage table."

I found myself giggling along with Val. "Well, help yourself to the coffee and juice. I've made a chocolate-cherry tea bread with white chocolate chips and I'll bring it right out. And this morning we're serving French butter crepes with strawberries and cream."

Val's eyes sparkled with delight, but Joey crinkled up his nose. "Don'cha got no eggs or bacon or nothin'? How'my supposed to get full on cake and ooh-la fancy crepes?"

"The crepes do come with sausage links."

"Do you got like thirty or forty of 'em?"

Val popped her gum. "Joey's not usedta eatin' this fancy stuff." Only she didn't say *stuff*.

The front door opened, and three biddies tiptoed as loudly as possible down the hall while "whispering" to each other.

"Shh, her guests are here."

"We're not too late for breakfast, are we?"

"If we are, she can make us something else."

I adopted the rule that if I don't look at the ruckus, it isn't really happening. Then one of the biddies knocked something over in the hall. "Shh!"

I smiled at Joey and Val. I had small plates of gourmet luxury planned for every day. I would have to rethink my menu for the week. "If you like, I can throw together some scrambled eggs and toast to go along with the planned meals."

Joey's face broke into a smile and he pounded me on the shoulder and sent me back a few inches. "Now you tawkin."

I entered the gossip den and Aunt Ginny had already cracked a dozen eggs. "How'd you know I was going to need those?"

Sawyer handed me the china plate with the tea bread. "We were listening through the door."

I returned again and started warming the crepes and frying the sausages while Aunt Ginny made the scrambled eggs. "So, are you all just here for the buffet or are you going to catch a show?"

Mrs. Dodson took a paper from her purse. "No, Miss Hot Pants. We came to show you this."

I took the paper and examined it. "It's a receipt for six tickets to the Senior Center musical."

"Yeeesss." Aunt Ginny prodded me.

I read it again. "*Mamma Mia!* starring Broadway's Royce Hansen."

Mother Gibson pursed her lips together. "Mm-hmm."

I was obviously missing something. The way they were

watching me was unnerving. I flipped my crepe. *Mamma Mia!* starring Broadway's Royce Hansen. Receipt for six tickets dated November 2. "November?!"

Mrs. Davis smacked the counter. "Now she's got it."

I warmed another crepe. "How in the world did Neil sell tickets to a musical he hadn't announced yet?"

Aunt Ginny dumped the eggs on a hot platter. "It's worse than that. Royce didn't even come home until after New Year's Day."

"Neil must have worked it out with Royce to star in the play last fall." I warmed another crepe and Sawyer started rolling them with strawberries and mascarpone.

Aunt Ginny shook her head. "I asked him. Royce said the first time he heard about the musical was two days before tryouts."

"Are you sure he didn't just forget?" I gave the other ladies a look that they returned.

Mrs. Dodson snuck a sausage off the plate and popped it in her mouth. "Neil was selling tickets before anyone knew there would be a play and the star had no idea he had signed up for it."

I nudged the plate to the other side of the island. "Wouldn't that be ticket fraud? Why do you think he would do that?"

Now Mrs. Davis could reach the sausages and she snatched one. "Money laundering."

I gave the ladies an incredulous look. "Money laundering?"

Georgina entered the kitchen and snatched a sausage off the plate.

Mrs. Dodson nodded sagely. "And word on the street is, it will not go well for Neil if the play flops."

"Word on what street?" I asked them. "Who is saying these words? Is the Gambino family going to whack Neil if he doesn't have a Broadway star in the Cape May Senior Center musical? Where do you guys get this stuff?"

The four biddies shrugged and gave one another cryptic looks. Georgina and Sawyer giggled to themselves.

Sawyer picked up the plate of scrambled eggs. I plated three sausages next to three crepes on both plates and we went out to Val and Joey.

Val fanned herself with her hands over her plate. "Oh my gawd, just look at that. They are so fancy."

Sawyer put the plate of scrambled eggs in the middle of the table and Joey dumped them all onto his plate on top of his crepes. He handed the platter back to an openmouthed Sawyer and gave her a smile. Sawyer followed me back to the kitchen with her empty platter and shocked expression.

I looked at the receipt again. "How exactly did you all come by this?"

Mother Gibson, the retired Baptist Sunday school teacher, shrugged and took a bite of her smuggled sausage. "We stole it."

I pointed to the other biddies, who all had managed to sneak sausage from the platter. "I think these guys are a bad influence on you."

She smiled at the other ladies.

Georgina handed me the plate of cold crepes and looked to the frying pan, then back to me. It looked like I was making crepes for a few more this morning. I started warming the first one and Sawyer cut more strawberries.

I was just flipping the first crepe when I heard Val scream. "Oh my gawd, what is that?"

Followed by Joey. "Gawd, Val, ya killed it."

"No, I didn't, it just fell ovah."

I looked at Aunt Ginny. "Did you remember to lock Figaro up this morning?"

Aunt Ginny rolled her eyes up to the ceiling. "Uhhh . . ."

So much for my pep talk.

Chapter Twenty-Five

I cleaned up from breakfast and made some tour sugges-
tions for Joey and Val. Figaro scratched and meowed at
the door until I let him in, so he could meow and scratch at
the door for me to let him back out. He came back in to
watch me get dressed and judge my choices.

I tried the jeans again. Nope. I was forced to resort to
clean Spunks and leggings of loathing yet another day. Then
a pink T-shirt and a pink flannel button-down to cover the
lumps in my leggings and I was done. This was as good as I
was capable of right now. Figaro cataloged my every move
with the same look I get on my face when I watch episodes
of botched plastic surgery gone wrong. I kissed him on the
forehead and told him I'd see him later. Right now, I was off
to Gia's. Valentine's Day was Saturday and I had a whole
week of holiday-themed baking planned.

I was surprised to open the back door to the coffee shop
and find Gia standing in the kitchen drinking an espresso.
"Ciao, Bella."

We went out to the bar to sit, and I caught him up on the most recent disaster that was the senior center musical. "Now Blanche is in the hospital. There's a really good chance that Royce was the intended target for both of the attacks."

"What makes you think that?"

"He's the only one who enters from the catwalk and that light did fall right where he was supposed to be standing in that scene."

"But how did it fall? And how did the person who made it fall know Royce would be onstage at the time?"

"I dunno."

"Are you sure Royce isn't the one who killed Duke? You said he stayed during lunch to practice. Maybe Duke followed him up on the catwalk and they had an argument."

"What motive would Royce have for killing Duke? He's been gone for sixty years. Plus, he seems to be really shaken up about the attacks."

"Yes, but he is an award-winning actor, isn't he?"

I nodded.

Gia shrugged. "So maybe the nice-guy routine is an act."

I wondered if the absentminded professor routine was also an act.

"Do you think someone really wants to kill Royce? Or Duke? Maybe they just want to shut down the play altogether and Duke was an accident."

"Who would want to shut it down? The seniors would be devastated if the play was canceled."

"What about the agent?"

"He wants to take Royce back to New York for a comeback, but he just got here. I'm wondering about the sister. She has a hold on Royce about something. I could see her wanting to have the play canceled so Royce would be home with her. She keeps reminding him that he's been gone for sixty years."

"I have six sisters and two brothers. I understand why he'd stay away that long."

"I grew up an only child. I would love to have had a big family. It sounds like fun."

Gia pulled me close and whispered in a seductive voice, "Maybe one day you will see just how very wrong you are."

I giggled and swatted him on the shoulder.

"I will make you a latte."

I nodded and tried to focus on my baking. Today's agenda was the Stud Muffins and Baby Cakes, along with heart-shaped linzer cookies. I needed to make enough for the coffee shop and the B&B. I started compiling all the ingredients on the silver-flecked granite countertop. I built the linzer cookie dough first, so it had time to chill, and placed the butter and sugar in the bowl of my Professional KitchenAid stand mixer that Gia had specially painted to look like a peacock as a gift to me. That seemed like ages ago and it was only, what? Three months or so? Things have moved very fast since I've come home to Cape May. Maybe it's the salt air that makes everyone so driven. In Virginia I'd be in bed reading a book right now. Or at least on the couch watching cooking shows and thinking about reading a book.

Gia placed a special coffee drink with a heart design in the foam on the counter next to me. "Do you have plans for Saturday night?"

"No, not yet."

"Can I take you out for Valentine's Day?"

My breath caught in my throat. Valentine's Day is a big step in a relationship.

"You mean a lot to me, so I have something special to give you."

I think I know what it is too and I'm not sure I'm emotionally ready to receive it.

Gia grinned. "Don't look so nervous, Bella. You will like this, I promise."

"I'm sure I will." I tried to smile bravely. *I'm not worried about not liking it. I'm worried I forgot how to do it.*

He took a step closer and twirled his finger around a curl of my hair that had sprung loose from its kitchen braid. It was such a simple yet intimate gesture. "So, what do you say?"

"Gia!" Karla's voice punched me in the face. "You're wanted!"

Gia frowned and let loose a string in Italian. "I'll be right back." Another string in Italian carried him out to the coffee bar.

I started measuring my dry ingredients for the strawberry chocolate chip muffins. If I was honest, I wanted to go out for Valentine's Day. I hadn't been on a date in years. Even with John, we got to the point where we'd rather stay home and eat potpies than have a crowded, overpriced reservation. Now I think we were just taking romance for granted. Of course, with John, the romance was subtle. I was surprised that Tim hadn't asked me to do anything on Saturday. After that whole let's-give-it-a-go spiel. Maybe with Tim the romance is subtle too.

Gia returned muttering to himself in Italian. *Speaking of stud muffins.*

"Now are you going to let me take you out for a romantic dinner or not?" he teased.

"Yes, but we'll have to do it on Monday. I'm promised to do the lights for the musical on Valentine's Day."

"We'll think of something." He started to kiss me. I knew I was supposed to stop him to be fair to Tim, but Karla called him out to the dining room again and saved me the trouble.

Leave it to me to pick the most romantic holiday of the year to swear off making out. Three hours later, I had a dozen of each kind of muffin and two dozen raspberry linzer cookies to take home to my guests, leaving several dozen of each for Gia to sell. I had to get back to the B&B to make white chocolate raspberry cheesecakes for Maxine's. *Why did I agree to all this?* My conscience reminded me that it was because I couldn't say no to Tim. I wondered if I'd be able to say no to Gia when the time came to choose.

Chapter Twenty-Six

I pulled up at the Senior Center for rehearsal. Aunt Ginny had gone ahead of me because I had to leave Tim's cheesecakes home to cool. I was going to leave them on the counter, but Figaro was looking shifty and I knew he was plotting something, so I left them in the oven with the door cracked open. Tim was sending Chuck to pick them up.

All the parking spots in the front were taken, so I had to drive around to the side. I almost ran over the curb when I saw the display in front of me. Mrs. Davis appeared to be hovering off the ground in some boxwoods and azaleas while peering into a window. I looked at the ground and realized Mrs. Dodson was on her hands and knees in the bushes and Mrs. Davis was standing on her back.

Oh, this is not good. I crept over to them and whispered, "What in the world are you doing?"

"*Shhh!*" They both shushed me, and Mrs. Davis absently swatted in my direction. "We're spying on Neil. He's up to something."

"What makes you think he's up to something?"

"He keeps going into his office and locking the door."

"So? People do that. Maybe he doesn't want to be disturbed."

Mrs. Davis blew me off. "I bet he's got a pile of money in that desk drawer with a lock. That's where all the laundry schemers keep it."

They're going to be arrested or sued before this week is over. "I really don't think Neil is laundering money through the Senior Center. He's way too nice to be up to anything nefarious. Now get down from there before you get hurt!"

Mrs. Davis ducked down and Mrs. Dodson grabbed my ankle. "*Shhh.* The thugs are coming out."

I pulled a boxwood leaf out of my hair. "You can see that in Neil's office?"

Mrs. Dodson took a receiver from her ear. The other end of the wire was plugged into her cell phone. "*Shhh.* Lila's been on the inside shadowing them. She says they're heading this way."

The emergency exit door opened on the far end of the building and the two big guys came out with Ernie.

Mrs. Davis hissed in my ear, "They must have something on Smiley because they keep dragging him outside."

We couldn't hear what the men were saying, but it looked intense because Ernie had finally lost the grin from his face. The men pushed Ernie against the wall and he pleaded with them, "I've got it covered."

The men dropped him and went back inside. Ernie got up and smoothed his sport coat over his turtleneck while looking around. After about a minute, he pulled out a cell phone and walked around the corner to the back of the building.

Mrs. Davis jumped down from Mrs. Dodson's back. "That was mighty fishy, Edith."

Mrs. Dodson sat up and spoke into her phone. "Tango, this is Foxtrot, come in."

Good Lord, what now?

Mother Gibson's voice came through the speaker. "Tango here. Go."

"Smiley has gone around the back. Get your eyes on him."

"Ten four. Rooster guarding the front."

"Ladies," I persisted, "are code names really necessary?"

Mrs. Dodson looked at me like I was an imbecile. "We have to speak in code in case anyone overhears us."

Mrs. Davis shimmied up her tube top. "All the spies use code names. I'm Sexy Knickers."

Mrs. Dodson narrowed her eyes at Mrs. Davis. "We agreed on dances. You're Hokey-Pokey."

"I never agreed. I'm being called Sexy Knickers and that's that!"

"If someone overhears voices coming out of these bushes, code names aren't going to help you."

Mrs. Dodson narrowed her eyes at me. "That's why we're whispering and using earpieces. Good heavens, do you think we were born yesterday?"

I was about to tell Mrs. Dodson, aka Foxtrot, that she didn't whisper as quietly as she thought when I heard footsteps crunching through the dead leaves coming our way.

"Who's over there?"

It was Neil.

Mrs. Davis pushed me out of the bushes and hissed. "Distract him!"

I flopped out on my knees and extracted myself from the branches. "Sorry, Neil. Just me."

"What in the world are you doing in there?"

"Um. I thought I lost an earring."

Neil looked at the cluster of bushes. "Against the building?"

"Yeah, it kind of . . . flew through the air . . . and . . . rolled."

He headed toward me. "I'll help you look."

I lunged toward him. "Oh no! It's fine. See." I held my earlobe out. "I found it."

I crawled close enough for Neil to squint at my neck. "How did you ever find that in the bushes?"

I took his arm and led him back toward the front of the building. "The light hit it at just the right angle."

"Wow, that was lucky. Have you seen Thelma and Edith? I want to go over the finale again."

We walked past the coat closet and I spied Aunt Ginny's red hair peeking out from between a tan raincoat and a bright blue parka. "No, I haven't, but I'm sure *Edith and Thelma will be in right away for practice.*"

The red hair in the closet started to quiver.

Neil let me drag him down the hall. He was apparently used to these ladies controlling him to some degree. "So how is Blanche?"

He brightened. "She's going to be fine. Just a broken collarbone. It will heal, but she's out of the play, I'm afraid."

"That's too bad." *I wonder if that sounded sincere enough?*

"Thank goodness Ginny's ready. She'll be fantastic."

"She's been practicing her lines at home."

"She's wonderful onstage with Royce, don't you think?"

"Oh yes."

"Don't you think they make a natural couple?"

"Um, yeah. As far as I can see."

Neil patted my arm. "Me too. I hear they were a serious couple in their youth."

I nodded. "Before Royce started his career in New York."

We entered the theater to see that Blanche had resumed her role of making everyone miserable. She was wearing a complex sling over her neck and around the back of her champagne pantsuit and standing at center stage. "Where is that two-bit hack, Ginny? I know she is behind the attack on me yesterday. I'll sue, Neil! Do you hear me!"

Neil rushed down the aisle to Blanche's side. "Honey, please calm yourself before you strain your injury."

"Don't you tell me to calm down! This was finally my chance to be back in the spotlight. I know I was targeted by that spiteful crow. She's always been jealous of my talent."

"Woo. That'll be the day." Aunt Ginny had snuck up behind me in the sixth row. Her red T-shirt said *Sucks To Be You*.

I gave her a light glare. "Rooster, I presume."

She gave me a toothy grin.

Blanche was so angry she was spitting. "You see how she's been baiting me with her shirts . . . and her . . . smug looks?"

I whispered to Aunt Ginny, "What looks have you been giving her?"

Aunt Ginny shrugged. "Beats me. She's delusional."

Neil put his hand gingerly on Blanche's back. "Honey, please, let's go sit down and rest. Do you need anything? Is it time for your pain meds?"

Blanche angled her body stiffly until she was glowering at Neil. "I don't need anything! But I'll tell you this: Your little play will fail."

Aunt Ginny breathed out like a bull about to charge and I put a hand on her arm. "Don't let her get to you."

Blanche tried to stab at Neil with her good arm, but she grabbed at her shoulder and moaned in pain. "If you don't take Virginia Frankowski out of this play, bad things will happen. I'll make sure of it. And you already know you don't want to mess with me, Neil."

Blanche started the slow process of storming off the stage with a broken collarbone and Neil crept with her down the aisle. "Now, dear, don't do something you'll regret. Why don't you let me take you to lunch?"

Blanche shot another black look at Neil. "Not until you get rid of Frankowski."

Aunt Ginny scowled at Blanche as she limped past. Then I heard the bud in Aunt Ginny's ear crackle. "Sexy Knickers to Rooster." Aunt Ginny ignored her. "Sexy Knickers to Rooster." I was about to nudge Aunt Ginny when Mrs. Davis sighed loudly. "Fine! Hokey-Pokey to Rooster."

Aunt Ginny grinned to herself. "Yeeees?"

"Do you have eyes on Papa Bear?"

I followed Aunt Ginny's gaze to the back of the theater, where Blanche had left and Neil was flopped down in one of the theater seats rubbing his eyes with his fists. "I see him."

"Keep him occupied. We're going in."

"Roger."

"Please don't tell me you're helping those ladies spy on everyone. What happens if someone sees you?"

Aunt Ginny shrugged. "We're old. People expect us to be eccentric."

Royce came from backstage with his arms outstretched. "There's my Ginger. How's my best girl today?"

Aunt Ginny giggled. "Well, I'm doing just fine, Royce. How're you?"

I quietly gave a little cock-a-doodle-do.

Aunt Ginny nudged me and through gritted teeth said, "Go keep Neil distracted."

I smiled at Royce. "You look very handsome."

Royce rocked back on his heels. "Thank you . . . my lovely. And how good to see you again."

"Are you ready for rehearsal?"

"I am ready as Freddy."

Aunt Ginny took Royce's hand in hers. He gave her a big smile. "Hey! There's my Ginger. How's my best girl today?"

Aunt Ginny cocked her head to the side and gave Royce a grin. "I'm fine."

I left Rooster and Royce to their flirting and joined Neil just as he was getting up. "How are you doing?"

He gave me a tired smile. "I'll be glad when this is over."

You and me both. "Can I ask you something?"

He started to head out of the auditorium and I followed him.

"Sure. Anything for you."

"What did Blanche mean by saying your play will fail?"

Neil chewed his bottom lip. "Oh, that."

"It's obvious something is going on. She threatened you in front of everyone."

"Well, you may as well know. It will all be in the meeting notes by next month. Blanche is on the board of the Senior Center committee. She was only willing to approve the play if she was given the lead."

So many things make more sense now.

"She's furious that she's been sidelined because of an injury that, of course, she blames Ginny for causing."

"Which is preposterous." I grabbed Neil's arm and stopped him in the front foyer.

Neil nodded. "Of course. But now she's threatening to rescind the activities budget for the year."

"Can she do that?"

Neil nodded. "She has the authority, and the other committee members are afraid of getting on her bad side. And honestly, so am I."

This hasn't been her bad side? I had an image flash in my mind of winged demons in the fires of hell.

Neil looked around to be sure no one could hear him. "The thing is, I've already invested the entire budget into this one play and it's only February. We need to make a return or my seniors will have to do jigsaw puzzles and adult coloring books for the rest of the year. Not to mention I could lose my job."

"I was wondering, when do tickets go on sale?"

"Oh, um." Neil began to examine a sign-up sheet for a book club.

Behind Neil, Mother Gibson kept her eyes on me as she

tiptoed over to his office door and opened it. Mrs. Dodson and Mrs. Davis looked up from his desk, surprised. They appeared to be trying to get that drawer open.

Neil reached out and put his hand on my arm. "I have to get my production notes from my desk. Will you excuse me."

Danger, Will Robinson!

"Neil!"

He froze.

"Before you go . . ." *What will hold him here? He's a man . . . so . . . flattery.* "I've noticed that you're really talented onstage. You're going to give a fantastic performance as the groom." *Even though the bride is in her late sixties.* "In fact, you have a wonderful singing voice. Did you do theater in high school or college?" *He's smiling. This is good.*

Neil shoved his hands into the pockets of his tan Dockers and rocked back on his heels. "Well, I grew up in a family where theater was encouraged. We often put on plays in the backyard for the grandparents. But then, they were always a very captive audience."

A bright flash went off from Neil's office and I felt a grimace climb across my forehead. Really, sometimes my face has a mind of its own.

Neil flinched. "Not captive. I mean generous. You know. They could leave whenever they wanted." He chuckled.

"Of course." I laughed. "Grandparents . . . And high school? Did you ever try out?"

Neil grinned. "I was Harold Hill in my senior production of *The Music Man*. They said I was very good. A natural con artist."

Huh . . . "How about that."

Mother Gibson poked her head out of the office and gave me a thumbs-up. She was followed by Mrs. Dodson, who was looking around furtively and skirting the wall, and Mrs. Davis, who was brandishing her cell phone and mouthing, "We got the goods."

The ladies forgot about Neil's door and it shut with a loud kerplunk! Neil spun around and saw three guilty faces looking back at him. Mrs. Dodson was spread-eagle against the tan tiles of the wall.

"Hello, ladies," I said too loudly. "Did Aunt Ginny send you here to get me?"

Mrs. Davis asked, "Who?"

But Mother Gibson was a little quicker. She gave me a slow nod. "Yes. Yes, she did." She put her hand out to me. "Come, child. Your aunt needs you."

I waved to Neil. "Have a good practice today."

Neil was still watching the group of us with a furrowed brow when we disappeared down the hallway and into the theater.

"That was too close, ladies. You've got to be more careful."

Mrs. Davis held up her cell phone again. "Yeah, but we got it."

"Got what?"

"Evidence."

"Evidence of what?"

Mrs. Dodson took the cell phone away from Mrs. Davis and swiped at the screen. "We found something in that locked drawer. See." More swiping. "It was right here."

Mother Gibson let out a low rumble. "Giiiiirrrrrrl. What happened to that picture?"

A very flustered Mrs. Davis grabbed the phone back. "I took it."

Mrs. Dodson handed the phone to me. "See if you can find it."

I went to their gallery and found several blurry photos of documents and showed them.

Mrs. Davis blushed. "Well, they were rushing me."

Mrs. Dodson glared at her. "You were the one who said panoramic shots would be best."

I held up the phone. "What am I supposed to be looking at?"

Mrs. Davis huffed and shoved her phone down in her strapless bra. "We found an insurance policy for a million dollars."

"A million dollars! For what?"

Mother Gibson crossed her arms over her ample chest. "Well, it had Neil's name on it."

The biddies looked at one another. Mrs. Dodson answered for them. "It looked very important, so we took pictures to show to you, but . . ."

Mrs. Davis shook her head. "Poppy, you need to see it for yourself. I'm sure it's evidence."

"How in the world am I going to do that?"

Mrs. Davis shrugged. "I don't know. You'll have to be sneaky about it."

"That's a good tip. I'll try that." I gave her a pointed look.

Mrs. Davis put her arm around my shoulders. "I saw Royce's name on it."

Okay, keep talking, I'm listening.

Before I could agree to do anything, Neil came back in the theater and called the room to attention.

I whispered to the ladies, "I'll see what I can do." And we headed down to the stage, where Smitty and Georgina were doing a safety check to make sure nothing had been tampered with overnight. Georgina, who obviously attained her depth of experience inspecting construction sites by running society luncheons and fund-raisers, declared everything satisfactory. The seniors decided to take a chance and practice despite the expert opinion that was offered.

Practice was good. Great even. I hit my light cues on time. Bebe was able to direct the dance sequence with no one getting hurt. Royce had some trouble with his lines, as per usual. He called Mr. Sheinberg Mercutio a few times. Then he thought he was supposed to be involved in a sword fight dur-

ing the disco scene and had to be reminded of what play he
was in again. But none of the lights fell off the crossbar, so
all in all a greater success than most days.

Practice concluded for the night and Aunt Ginny sidled
up to me. "I'm exhausted. I can't wait to get into a hot bath
and go to bed."

Royce came up behind her and poked her in the ribs. She
jumped and giggled. Then he kissed her hand. "How about
we go to dinner tonight, Ginger?"

Aunt Ginny batted her eyes. "Oh, Royce, that would be
just divine."

I whispered in her direction, "What about going to bed?"

She whispered back, "We'll see how it goes."

Fiona marched up and grabbed Royce's arm. "No way,
Royce. You promised you'd come home with us. I've been
slaving over a pot roast all day."

Iggy was slumped behind her. "No, you haven't. The
Crock-Pot's been doing all the work."

Fiona stamped her foot. "That is beside the point. You
were gone for sixty years!"

Royce turned on her and snapped, "Well, you're not
going to make me a prisoner for the rest of my life because
of it! I'm going out with Ginny and that's final!"

We were all kind of stunned that he'd stood up to her,
Fiona most of all. Her lip started to tremble, and she ran
from the room. Iggy flashed Royce a venomous glower and
ran after Mummy Dearest.

"Now." Royce took Aunt Ginny's hand. "Where were
we, love?"

Aunt Ginny giggled and leaned into Royce. "What time
do you want to pick me up?"

Royce grinned at me. "How about you make the reservation for the three of us and I'll meet you two young ladies
there?"

I started to protest. "I don't want to intrude on your night out."

Royce waved off my concern. "Nonsense. I plan on being in Ginny's life from now on. I want to get to know you better."

Aunt Ginny gave me a look with stars in her eyes. How could I say no?

Royce and Aunt Ginny giggled all the way down the aisle to the exit. I was collecting my things to follow behind them when I heard the most unpleasant sound behind me.

"McAllister."

I closed my eyes and tried to wish it away. I couldn't believe I had gone three whole weeks without a sighting or a blood sacrifice, but now here she was. I clicked my heels together three times. When I opened my eyes and turned, she was still there. I said "Abracapocus!" No change. "Pocuscadabera!"

"What are you doing? Are you having a stroke?"

I sighed. "What can I do for you, Amber?"

"We need to talk."

Chapter Twenty-Seven

"I can't control these ladies any more than I can swim across the Atlantic Ocean. Besides, you're the police officer. Why don't you just tell them about the complaints?"

Amber's radio crackled on her hip and she turned the volume down. She was in uniform right up to her mirrored sunglasses that she pushed up to the blond bun wound tightly on top of her head, making her eyebrows unnaturally arched. Or maybe that superior ego was permanently etched on her face from her cheerleading days where she ruled Cape May High with perky manipulation.

"For some reason, these ladies listen to you. I blame senility. I want you to convince them to stop looking into windows and taking things from area businesses in the name of investigating."

"I'll try, but what have they done that's been so bad, really?"

Amber took out her black notebook and flipped a few pages. "The owner of Shear Delight Hairdresser said the ladies stole a receipt from her file box that she needs for her taxes."

"Okay, but in their defense, they thought it was evidence of a money-laundering scheme."

Amber's face remained impassive. I realized that if she tried to raise an eyebrow under current circumstances, her bun could pop like a tick. "Three ladies with white hair and dark sunglasses, one African American, one with a cane, and all three in orthotics, have reportedly harassed area businesses about 'back-room deals' and snooped around local offices looking for 'smoking guns.'"

"I think smoking guns here means more evidence of early ticket sales."

"Blanche Carrigan and Fiona Sharpe have both reported figures with white hair trampling their hydrangeas and spying into their front windows leaving the scent of Icy Hot behind. I can only assume it's the same characters."

"Or it could just be some fans of the theater looking for an autograph."

"And Neil Rockford has reported that they damaged the lock to one of the drawers on his antique partner's desk."

I swallowed hard. "How does he know it was them?"

"It's a strong suspicion. He's refusing to press charges, but he filed a police report for the insurance claim."

"I'll talk to them."

"What are they up to, McAllister? This has to be about more than money laundering through ten-dollar tickets for local musical theater."

I knew I couldn't trust Amber to be impartial. She'd hated me since middle school, when she joined the popular crowd and I became an anchor on her social life. She'd had one vendetta aimed for me after another since I returned for our reunion and fate sprinkled my life with her bitter hostility.

"I don't have all day, McAllister. I have another case."

"It's about the death of Duke McCready."

Amber gave a single nod. "The suicide?"

"Duke McCready was their friend. They knew him really well and none of them believe his death was a suicide."

"You're not playing detective again, are you? 'Cause I'm not going to like it if you're involved."

"I was right here when we found the body."

"There was a note."

"Who rips a piece of paper haphazardly from a notebook, then formally types a message on it saying goodbye?"

Amber shrugged and her bun bobbed slightly on her head. "People do lots of things when they're depressed, McAllister. There's no rhyme or reason."

"Duke wasn't depressed. He had a lead role in a play and his grandson was coming for a visit this weekend to see him in the play."

"If I recall, his note said he'd just suffered a breakup. That can set a lot of people over the edge."

"If Duke had a lover, it was a secret affair. No one had ever seen him on a date or heard him talk about a girlfriend."

Amber put her notebook away. "So. Lots of people like to keep their romantic lives private. Not everyone flaunts their love triangles around town."

"What is that supposed to mean?"

Amber put her hands up. "Hey, I'm not judging you. I get it. You're back in town, recently widowed, hooking up with your old boyfriend and a piece on the side. Nobody's business but yours. But you mark my words, the way those two men were fuming at each other at the culinary school the last time you interfered with a crime scene . . . I've investigated enough domestic disputes and crimes of passion to know you have trouble on the horizon."

How did this become about my love life? I tried to calm down and let her intrusive analysis roll off my shoulders. "This isn't about me. It's about Duke McCready. The ladies have evidence that the catwalk was tampered with, and a lot of strange things have been going on in the theater."

"There is not a thing I can do about any of that, McAllister. I'm not the officer in charge of the case. I've got my own investigation in progress. I'm only here to follow up on the nuisance report. I wish I were more surprised to find out that you're involved."

"That's hardly fair."

"Save it. If you have evidence to share about Duke McCready, call Officer Birkwell. You should probably have that number memorized by heart."

Amber strode back up the aisle to the exit and I imagined going William Tell with that bun on her head. One day she would need my help. And I wasn't sure I'd be inclined to give it to her.

Chapter Twenty-Eight

"Why do I have to go with you? I'm going to be like a third wheel."

"You heard Royce. He said we'll be spending a lot of time together. He wants to get to know you."

"He knows me just fine." *Especially if he's a murderer.*

"Royce never had children of his own, I think he wants a family."

"He has Fiona and Iggy."

Aunt Ginny made a face and stuck her tongue out.

"Okay, fair enough, but does he have to get to know me tonight?"

"Hey, don't get sassy with me. I'm not the one who invited you."

"But why'd you pick there of all places?"

"You have to face your fears sometime."

I stomped upstairs to my bedroom on the third floor as Aunt Ginny hollered behind me, "We have to leave in twenty minutes."

I was more than a little bit put out. I was furious. About

what, I didn't really know. Just a general anger because I don't like being told what to do, I guess. I'm fortysomething years old. When do I get to do what I want?

I'm not dressing up, I'll tell you that. I pulled out my long black skirt and wine-colored chiffon blouse. I did have melted chocolate on my pink flannel from making Stud Muffins earlier. I got dressed and put on a pair of tall black boots. Then went to the bathroom and brushed out my braid, creating a giant, frizzy helmet over my head. *It would serve them right if I went just like this.* I sprayed my frizz down with a misting bottle and conditioning oil until I had tamed it into soft waves. I freshened up my makeup and considered lining my eyes with thick black rings to punish Aunt Ginny. Only she would rise to the challenge and request the table in the middle of the room. If I showed up at Maxine's with giant frizzy hair and black rings around my eyes, I'm the only one who would be uncomfortable. Tim would find the whole situation hilarious.

My phone buzzed. I had a review alert from Yelp. I held my breath. GnobtheGnome left me one star. He said my bed-and-breakfast was infested with fleas from a mangy cat. Tears welled up in my eyes and I wanted to snuggle Figaro for the unjust slander he had no idea he'd received. My cat is not mangy! Why is this happening? Is this Joey and Val? GnobtheGnome's profile says he's from Delaware. So, not Joey and Val from Philly.

Well, it was worth a shot. Someone was targeting the bed-and-breakfast, or me specifically. A dreadful thought crossed my mind and I checked the reviews for La Dolce Vita. There had been two one-star reviews left in the last two days. Both reviewers said the coffee was great, but the baked goods brought the score down. One reviewer said, "Beware! Not really Gluten-Free. I've been sick all day since eating one of La Dolce Vita's muffins. I should sue! Someone needs to report them to the health department." The other review was just as spiteful. To make my humiliation worse, Gia had responded very professionally to both reviews, saying he thanked them for coming in, and La Dolce Vita has only the highest-quality gluten-free ingredients and a strict adherence to quality control. He was sorry they didn't have a good experience and that he hoped they would find another place more to their liking.

I wiped tears from my eyes before I remembered I was wearing mascara. I checked Maxine's Bistro, but the reviews of late were all good. There was even a couple who raved over the new dessert menu, so that was promising.

Aunt Ginny hollered for me to *get the lead out*. I cleaned the mascara from around my eyes and grabbed my purse before heading downstairs.

Joey and Val were in the library in front of the fire on their cell phones. Figaro was in Val's lap and she was petting him. He looked at me through slits for eyes. I told them we'd be back in a couple of hours and that they should call my cell phone if they needed me. They waved us on.

I was getting Aunt Ginny settled in the passenger seat of my car when I noticed that maroon Marquis was still parked on the street down a ways from Mr. Winston's house. *His daughter doesn't usually stay but a few hours when she visits. I hope everything's okay.*

Maxine's had a decent crowd for a Monday night in February. About half the tables were occupied. The hostess took our coats and led us to the main dining room in front of the fireplace. Royce stood when we entered. "Here's my girl." He handed Aunt Ginny a dozen red roses and kissed her. Then he surprised me and handed me a dozen pink roses. "And for her lovely granddaughter."

Aunt Ginny corrected him as she took her place by his side. "Niece."

Royce looked surprised. "She's your niece?"

Aunt Ginny nodded. "I never had children."

Royce raised his eyebrows. "Five husbands and you never had children?"

Aunt Ginny shrugged. "Well, the five husbands often acted like babies, so that made up for it."

Royce laughed rich and deep. It was easy to see how he had made a living on Broadway with that voice.

"Mr. Hansen," I said, "everyone is so excited to have a professional actor in the play. I'm curious, how did you hear about the Cape May Senior Center musical?"

Royce grinned broadly. Clearly, we were talking about a subject he was very comfortable discussing. "I was eating my lunch at Carnegie Deli when I got an email from Neil. He said he was the new director of the Senior Center in my hometown, and would I like to star in a play for charity."

Aunt Ginny and I looked at each other. Aunt Ginny picked up her water glass and asked me around the side of it, "What charity exactly?"

Before Royce could continue, our waitress came over to tell us tonight's specials. I wanted to order the seafood pasta in the worst way. Instead, I begrudgingly asked for the filet mignon and steamed broccoli. I feel like something is very wrong with your relationship to food when you grieve over having to suffer through a thirty-dollar steak and broccoli when all over the world people are eating a handful of rice every few days. *Maybe I need therapy.*

The waitress left, and Royce continued his story. "I was surprised to hear from Neil because no one knows my personal email address but family and close friends. But apparently, he'd been writing letters to my agent for months." Royce laughed. "They must have gotten lost in the mail. Ernie said he never got a single one. Can you imagine?"

Aunt Ginny and I made eye contact again. Aunt Ginny muttered, "Yes, that is hard to believe."

"Well, I had just closed a run of *A Christmas Carol* a few nights earlier, to great reviews—really, the press in New

York is just fabulous. And I was wondering what my next project should be."

The sommelier, who, I happened to know, was just Carlos the waiter unless someone wanted to order wine, came and suggested a bottle of Pinot Grigio or Picpoul de Pinet to go with Royce's and Aunt Ginny's dinners. Royce chose the Picpoul and Carlos went to fetch it.

"Then the strangest thing happened."

"What was that?" I asked.

"I got a call from Fee, telling me she needed my help, and could I please come home. Well, I took that as a sign from the universe and moved back to my old stomping grounds to help out my sister."

I nodded along. "That was very nice of you. So, when did you agree to do *Mamma Mia!*? After you knew you were coming home to Cape May?"

Royce grinned at me blankly. "Did I tell you about *A Christmas Carol*?"

Aunt Ginny cocked her head to the side like a bird. "You may have mentioned it, yes."

"Fabulous reviews. The press in New York is just fabulous."

Carlos returned with the wine and Tim came with him bearing baskets of bread. "Hey, gorgeous. Carlos said you were out here, and I wanted to deliver these to you personally." He placed the basket of rolls in front of me with a grin. "I made them special for you." He said hello to Aunt Ginny while I sniffed my basket.

I looked under the cloth napkin expecting to see snowflake rolls like Aunt Ginny and Royce were digging into. But instead, I had corn muffins.

"Gluten free and with a side of honey butter."

"Ooh." *Okay, did I just shudder in delight over corn muffins and honey butter? I really do need therapy.* I bit into one. "You did a great job, I love them."

"I figure I need to come up with some gluten-free dishes to take care of my girl."

Aunt Ginny kicked me under the table.

"I'm thinking about adding them to the bread basket every night, so I have something gluten free if it's requested."

"I think that's a wonderful idea." I introduced Tim to Royce and they shook hands.

"Make sure you save room for dessert. Tonight's special is white chocolate raspberry cheesecake." He winked at me. "And so far, I've already sold out of one."

"I'm not surprised," Aunt Ginny said. "I got to lick the bowl and it was purty good."

Royce smiled. "You do a good business here, I take it?"

"We've been booming since Restaurant Week last month. I'm going to have to hire more staff when the *South Jersey Dining Guide* comes out."

Maxine's was doing well. I was relieved that the bad reviews hadn't reached Tim. "I got some more trolls today."

Tim took my hand in his. "I'm sorry, Mack."

"They're attacking the coffee shop now because I do the baking."

He shook his head. "Not cool."

"Are you sure there's nothing I can do to stop it?"

"Short of hiring a PR firm and a lawyer, there's nothing I know of. Besides, all the reviews are coming from different accounts, right?"

"Yes, but most of them are brand new and they always leave one or two reviews for someone else, usually five star."

Tim shook his head. "Yeah. That's how they get around being flagged as fake. Unfortunately, I think you're just going to have to ride this one out."

Royce and Aunt Ginny gave me sympathetic smiles even though they had no idea what I was talking about.

The waitress came over carrying a tray and placed two plates piled high with seafood pasta in front of Aunt Ginny and Royce. Then she placed the filet mignon and steamed broccoli in front of me. "Bon appétit."

My imagination played Def Leppard's "Bringin' on the Heartbreak." *I really do need therapy*.

Tim stood to go. "I'll let you enjoy your dinner. You made great choices. And Poppy, let's get together in the next couple of days. I have something very important I want to ask you." He winked.

Aunt Ginny kicked me under the table again. Her eyes were as big as the scallops nestled in her angel hair.

Chapter Twenty-Nine

I had a nightmare that I cheated on my diet with marshmallow Peeps. I woke up in a cold sweat. Figaro was watching me calmly from the end of the bed. I sensed his thoughts were, *Where are these Peeps you speak of?*

"Fig, it was horrible."

Figaro bit my foot. Fig had a different concept of comfort than the rest of us.

"Okay, that's rude."

My cell phone chimed, and I looked at the screen. It was a selfie of Sawyer with eight roses, a box of Godiva chocolates, and a gigantic smile.

I got out of bed and tried to shake off the dream. I took a deep breath and ran through my yoga workout and my morning routine. Fig led me down the backstairs to the kitchen as if I'd forgotten where it was and I sat at the table with a carton of sugar-free coconut yogurt while Aunt Ginny heated water for coffee.

"It's silly to let it upset you this much. It didn't happen."

"It felt very real."

"So, what if you did eat the Peeps? Life is too short to obsess over a few carbs."

"I'm trying really hard right now. Don't you think I need to lose some weight?"

Aunt Ginny gave me an appraising look. "You could stand to lose a few pounds in the middle there, but everything else is fine."

"That's a small comfort."

"I just think you're going overboard with it. How much kale can a person eat?"

I went to the oven and shook the Southwest breakfast casserole. It was just about set. I turned the oven off and left the door open a crack, so it would finish baking on carryover heat. "Well, nothing else is working."

"You already walk three miles a day, do yoga, and eat practically nothing but vegetables. At some point you might just have to accept that this is you and be okay with that."

Crazy woman, crazy talk.

The timer went off that the coffee was ready, so I plunged the press. "This is the happiest part of my day."

A clicking sound thumping into the cabinets drew my attention and I had to extract Figaro from the empty yogurt cup he had lodged on his head. His pink tongue fought furiously to catch the last schmear.

Aunt Ginny peeked into the dining room. "The silver fox is early."

Charles and Barbara Ainsworth had arrived from Cape Cod yesterday afternoon for a romantic Valentine's week getaway. Charles had the chiseled features and a strong body used to hours on the StairMaster. His gray hair and tailored sport coat gave him a George Clooney/Richard Gere kinda vibe and I had to drag Aunt Ginny away from the door before she started drooling.

I took the carafe of coffee out to the sideboard with the cream and sugar. "Good morning, Mr. Ainsworth."

He held up a finger. "Ah-ah. Remember, you're to call me Chigsie. All my friends do."

I smiled and handed him a china cup and saucer. "All right, Chigsie."

As if on cue, his wife came through the sitting room. "And call me Bunny. Bar-bara sounds like my mother."

Bunny had all the earmarks of having been a trophy wife twenty years earlier. Platinum blonde, French tip manicure, dripping with diamonds, and a body that had put in many hours with a personal trainer or tennis coach. "I just love your little inn, Poppy. It's so quaint."

"Thank you. It's been in my family since the 1800s."

"How delightful." She helped herself to the coffee, black, one Splenda, I noticed.

"And how did you like the Purple Emperor suite?"

Bunny reached out and touched my arm. "It's darling! I've always wanted to sleep in a four-poster bed, haven't I, Chigsie?"

"You have."

"We have an antique, hand-carved French Provincial at home and it's nice to have something rustic for a change. It makes me feel like I've stepped back in time. And those sheets are divine. I must know where you bought them."

"I'll try to get you the name of the store."

I went back through the kitchen door and ran into Aunt Ginny holding out the carafe of juice in one hand and the muffin basket in the other. "Let me help you."

"You just want to get a better look at Chigsie, don't you?"

"Maybe."

"What would Royce say about that?"

"Who cares? He doesn't own me."

We carried the items into the dining room, where Bunny was reading the stamp on the bottom of the china cups. "I just love antique china. I have a vintage set of Limoges Nosegay, service for ten. It's such a darling little pattern. So happy."

Aunt Ginny added the juice to the sideboard while I placed the muffins on the main table and described them.

Bunny threaded her arm through Chigsie's. "I have my stud muffin right here." She gave him a brilliant smile that he returned.

Aunt Ginny turned on the charm that was usually reserved for the man at the deli counter and the volunteer fireman handing out the bingo cards. "So, what brings you to America's oldest seaside resort?"

Chigsie pulled out a chair for Bunny. "We usually winter in the South of France this time of year."

Bunny picked up the story from there, as seemed to be their custom. "Chigsie works in finance and he has clients all over the world. Have you been to Nice?"

I shook my head no. Aunt Ginny said yes.

"Monte Carlo?"

Again, I said no. Aunt Ginny said yes.

"Marseilles?"

This time we both said no.

"They are so beautiful. And the food is so fresh. You could just pick lemons and oranges right off your trees and eat them."

Val and Joey meandered in, having just rolled out of bed. Joey was scratching his stomach and yawning. They were both barefoot and in their pajamas, not that we minded, but it caught Bunny off guard and she paused in her story.

Val said, "Good morning," and pulled out a chair. Figaro slid out from under the table on top of it. "Yay, I win a cat." Val picked Figaro up and nuzzled him before placing him on the floor. "I just love those little heart-shaped sandwich cookies you put out for tea yesterday, Poppy. What are they called?"

"They were raspberry linzer hearts."

Bunny was nodding in agreement. "They were fabulous. You must give me the recipe, so I can have my cook make them for society luncheons."

"I'd be happy to."

Figaro was attempting to get into Val's lap—to get closer to the food; he wasn't fooling anyone—and Aunt Ginny scooped him up and gave him a warning look. Figaro touched Aunt Ginny's nose with his paw.

I wanted to hear the end of the Ainsworths' story so, after introducing the couples to each other, I said, "So why not the Mediterranean this year?"

"Oh." Bunny shook herself as if she'd totally forgotten that was where she was going. Chigsie chuckled, amused by her. "We are expecting our first grandbaby in three weeks."

Everyone gave the required "awws."

"We don't want to go too far away in case our daughter, Blake, needs us."

We left the couples to chat and I got the Southwest casserole while Aunt Ginny brought in the salsa and sour cream.

Joey was especially excited with this morning's breakfast. "Yeah! Now that's what I'm tawkin about!"

Bunny looked at the casserole and asked, "What is it?"

I explained it, and even though she looked scandalized at the list of ingredients, she tried a tiny spoonful anyway. "My trainer is going to have to double my Pilates when I get home."

The two couples seemed to get along well enough. We overheard snippets of conversation: Bunny telling Val she'd never stayed anywhere so quaint. Val saying she'd never stayed anywhere so fancy. They both loved it. I had my fingers crossed for good reviews. The men were mostly quiet except for answering their wives with "yes, dears" and "you're right, dears."

They finally went their separate ways, the Ainsworths to go wine tasting and the Pescatellis to look for Cape May diamonds, which are really just quartz pebbles that wash up on the beach. I started to clear the table. When I came back to the kitchen, I ran into Aunt Ginny having a squabble with

Mrs. Galbraith, who I hadn't realized had arrived. I had hired Mrs. Galbraith to be my part-time chambermaid just a few weeks ago when I opened the bed-and-breakfast for a trial run. The domestic service had warned me that she could be demanding to work with, but everyone else was either settled into permanent positions at established B&Bs or they had returned to Eastern Europe when their work visas had expired. Mrs. Galbraith had begrudgingly agreed to come out of retirement to work with me, but she still refused to come in the front door. She said she was professional staff and only guests should use the main entrance. Mrs. Galbraith always parked on the side at the back of the driveway and came in the back door through the mudroom.

There was currently a line being drawn in the sand over a furry, gray feline.

"That animal has no business being around food preparation and service. And furthermore, it sheds so much, my vacuuming takes twice as long as should be necessary."

I was steeling myself for Aunt Ginny's volley of insults when she picked up Figaro and stomped off to her bedroom. Mrs. Galbraith had the smug look of one who had just won an argument, until Aunt Ginny returned with Figaro under her arm. He was now wearing a bright orange vest that said "emotional support companion" on the back. I choked on my eggs.

Aunt Ginny put Figaro on the floor and he went right to biting at his vest.

Mrs. Galbraith sputtered for lack of a better argument and Aunt Ginny produced a formal document declaring Figaro's support status. "I'm old and frail. Are you going to deny me my only comfort at the end of my life?"

What am I, beans on toast?

Mrs. Galbraith narrowed her eyes at Aunt Ginny. "If he is a registered service animal, why is this the first time I'm hearing about it?"

"He doesn't like to brag."

Mrs. Galbraith took her carrier of cleaning supplies and bolted from the kitchen like a cannonball.

I tried to wipe the smile off my face so Aunt Ginny would know I was serious. "Why do you have to antagonize Mrs. Galbraith?"

"Because she's a mean old bat."

Figaro ran backward from the kitchen out to the hallway, trying to escape from his bondage.

"She's coming in early every day to back me up because I have to do quadruple duty now with the play."

"She still doesn't have any right to tell me what I can do in my own home. She makes me depressed. I'm too old to go on antidepressants."

Figaro galloped sideways back through the kitchen toward the dining room, trying to outrun the vest.

Aunt Ginny was bent over double, laughing. "See, I feel better already."

Chapter Thirty

I spent the morning making raspberry rose macarons for La Dolce Vita. Gia came in between customers to attempt sneaky displays of affection that I had to deftly block. He took that as a challenge and his approaches became more and more cunning. Once he even had Karla call me into the coffee bar and hand me two lattes so I couldn't move fast enough to get away from a kiss. Karla thought this was hilarious and said that Gia thought we were playing a game, and the more I tried to block his advances, the more fun he was having, trying to outwit me. My resolve at not showing affection was melting faster than the white chocolate in the rose ganache.

I finally had to kiss him goodbye, a very long kiss goodbye that almost turned into something else until Karla called him out to make a flat white. I gave a tinkering finger wave and snuck out the door while I still had the resolve to do so and made the quick drive over to the Senior Center.

* * *

I parked and walked up the path to the front door, where a giant Amazon box hissed at me. "Poppy."

I peeked under the lid of the recent delivery. "Who is that?"

"It's me, Thelma."

"What are you doing in there?"

"Guarding the perimeter."

"Of course you are."

She handed me a bright yellow walkie-talkie. "Here. We've hidden a few of these around the property with the listening volume turned down. This one's yours."

The high-tech device was made in the likeness of SpongeBob SquarePants. I'm sure it was the model the KGB used as well. Mrs. Davis gave me a salute and I saluted back before closing her cardboard lid. *What have I gotten myself into?*

Bebe was running the seniors through the chorus again. I had to do a double take. Georgina was in the midst of the dancers. She waved when she saw me. "I'm in the play. Mrs. Spisak dropped out because she didn't want to be attacked. Isn't that great?" She swiveled her hips in time with the music. I gave her a smile and a thumbs-up. *Good luck, Bebe.*

Neil was in his office with Piglet. Piglet glowered and shut the door as I passed by.

Royce was gingerly picking his way across the catwalk over to Donna's balcony while Blanche was onstage badgering Aunt Ginny. "Stay away from Royce or I'll make your life a living hell."

"I'll do whatever I want, Moira." Aunt Ginny took off her sweater and her passive-aggressive T-shirt of the day said *You're shallow. How's that working out?*

Blanche popped a couple pills and stormed off the stage.

Smitty was sitting in the seats the two gorillas usually occupied while the gorillas and Ernie were not in the building. *It figures that the very people I need to question are nowhere around.* I took a seat down in front next to Mrs. Sheinberg to await the opening of rehearsal before I realized Fiona was in the middle of an Iggy story.

"He's very graceful. You should see the pirouettes he can do when he dusts. My Iggy has a master's degree in gymnastics, you know."

I was sucking on a mint that flung itself to the back of my throat and I choked on Fiona's words. A woolly, white head with a tinge of blue hovered up from the end seat two rows ahead of us and I heard the feverish whispering of Mrs. Dodson in her walkie-talkie.

Mrs. Sheinberg gave Fiona a look that said, *God will strike you down for lying before this day is over.*

"No, it's true. He can still do a backflip. Iggy, show the ladies your backflip."

"*Uckhhhhh,* Mo-ther."

"Iggy!"

Iggy dragged himself away from the piano while his mother continued her delusional bragging. "I told you my boy was talented. Not there! Go up onstage. Ginny, get out of the way. Iggy is going to do a backflip."

Aunt Ginny pointed. "That Iggy? Are you sure?"

"Of course. Show them, Iggy."

Mrs. Davis shot down the aisle. "Wait, I have to see this."

Mother Gibson stuck her head out from the set foliage where she had been "conducting surveillance." Mrs. Dodson raised herself all the way up from her hiding place in the second row.

Iggy took a deep breath, bent his knees, and did two back handsprings across the stage and ended with a backflip to stunned silence.

"See! I told you my Iggy went to college on an athletic scholarship."

Mr. Sheinberg pointed out that he wobbled on the landing, to which Iggy snapped, "I'm almost forty years old, give me a break!"

Aunt Ginny blurted out, "You're not forty yet?"

Mrs. Davis converged onstage with Mother Gibson and Mrs. Dodson. They joined Aunt Ginny and there was a lot of whispering and looking from Iggy to the catwalk. It was not subtle, but fortunately, Fiona was too caught up in all things the delightful Iggy could do to add up their implications.

"My Iggy is a true Renaissance man. We watch *Jeopardy!* together every night and he knows *all* the answers. He has a degree in alternative philosophy."

Iggy was coming back down to the piano. He hefted his baggy jeans over the stretched-out band of his tighty-whities and kerflumped onto the bench.

Mrs. Sheinberg shook her head. "Exactly how many degrees does that boy have?"

"Six so far. He is still deciding what he wants to do when he grows up."

Mrs. Sheinberg's beady black eyes flashed. "The *schmegegge* is forty and still lives at home. The time for deciding has been over for twenty years."

Fiona crossed her arms in a huff and started a good, long pout that was interrupted by Neil.

"Okay, everyone, three practices till opening night!" Neil came down the aisle and clapped his hands. "Let's get another tech rehearsal behind us. You're all doing very well."

I made my way up onstage to the light booth and put on my headset. Terrence Nuttal, aka Piglet, ducked behind the stage curtains on the far side of the stage and was poking around behind the backdrops.

I was about to ask Neil what he was doing when the biddies cut me off.

"Poppy. Did you see that?" Mrs. Dodson jabbed her cane in the direction of the stage. "That boy can do acrobatics."

"I saw. That Iggy is full of surprises."

Mrs. Davis clutched at my sleeve. "He could easily get up on that catwalk and push poor Duke off."

"But why would he do that?"

Mother Gibson shrugged. "Well, honey, I have no idea. But most of these seniors would break a hip climbing the stairs or fall off from vertigo. No way they could wrestle against someone fighting back."

"Royce and Mr. Ricardo just snuck across a few minutes ago."

"And if one of them so much as sneezed, the paramedics would be on the way right now."

Mrs. Davis added, "Maybe Iggy has had some run-ins with the law. He could be the head of a local drug smuggling ring. Maybe he held a vendetta against Duke for a past arrest."

"Does Iggy strike you as motivated enough to head up a drug smuggling ring?"

Mrs. Dodson took her cane and pulled the side curtain out of the way.

Iggy sat at the piano, biting his nails. Fiona yelled at him and he stopped and sat up straight.

"If he was going to kill anyone it would be Fiona," I added.

My walkie-talkie crackled and Aunt Ginny's voice came through. "What if he thought he was killing Royce? You know he doesn't think of him as family. We heard him say so."

I picked up SpongeBob. "How do you know what we're talking about?"

Aunt Ginny answered me. "We put a walkie-talkie in the light booth."

"Where?"

"Taped under the panel."

I ran my hand under the box and felt a hard-plastic rectangle with a pointy head in the shape of SpongeBob's starfish friend, Patrick. I gave the biddies a look that I hoped would be disapproving. Three sets of eyes blinked at me innocently.

Mother Gibson patted her fade. "You never know what you might pick up backstage."

I don't know how Amber expects me to keep them out of trouble. I need a SWAT team just to keep an eye on them. "What motive would Iggy possibly have to try to kill Royce?"

"Life insurance?"

"Inheritance?"

Iggy started to play the intro music for rehearsal.

I shook my head. "As wealthy as Fiona is, I don't think Iggy would have a strong motive to kill anyone. I also don't think he'd be able to work up the energy to do it unless they offered a master's degree in it."

Mrs. Dodson and Mrs. Davis heard their cue and rushed off to take their places for their scene.

Mother Gibson stood next to me and flipped through the pages on her clipboard. "I don't know, Poppy. There are more actors in this room than just the ones onstage." She went off to make sure her props were ready to go and I adjusted the lights to my first setting.

Blanche heckled the practice from the back row and accused Aunt Ginny of being an overactor. Aunt Ginny was getting madder by the minute.

Royce went through the balcony scene from *Romeo and Juliet* instead of the loft scene with Donna. Aunt Ginny tried prompting him with the right lines, but Mother Gibson had to feed them to him from backstage.

Mr. Sheinberg delivered his lines like he was Miracle Max from *The Princess Bride*. "Oy, Donna. Whachu got that's worth living for?"

Neil asked him what he was doing and he answered, "Trying to add a li'l pizazz."

Then there was Mr. Ricardo, who was flirting with Mrs. Davis. Neil finally had to yell "Cut" when Mr. Ricardo pinched Mrs. Davis's bottom.

"Um, Mr. Ricardo. I think we need to have a chat about your character."

"Okay."

"You're playing Harry Bright."

"And I'm doing it really well."

Mrs. Davis giggled.

Neil nodded. "Yes, but Harry isn't going to come on to the ladies and flirt with them, is he?"

Mr. Ricardo winked at Aunt Ginny. "I think Harry would want to make the most of his time on this island around so much beauty."

Neil paused. "Mr. Ricardo, you do know that Harry is gay, don't you?"

"What?"

"Harry Bright is gay. That's why you have the line that Donna was the last girl you ever loved."

"I thought he was being romantic."

"No. He's being gay."

Mr. Ricardo's eyes were darting from Neil to the ladies to the floor. He ran his hands through his silver-tinged hair and walked in a circle, taking deep breaths. "I don't think I can be convincing as a gay man. What about my reputation with the ladies? Everyone knows I'm the Don Juan of the Senior Center."

Neil lifted his palms to the ceiling. "That's why it's called acting. Professionals do it all the time."

Mr. Ricardo shook his head. "Harry could convert. He could experiment with all the ladies and one by one, they could change him. They could bring him out of the closet as a sexual-heterosexual."

Mrs. Dodson snorted and Mrs. Davis rolled her eyes. The actress playing Sophie slapped Mr. Ricardo in the face.

"What? What'd I say?"

Neil shook his head. "It doesn't work that way."

"Well, could it?"

Mr. Ricardo appeared ready to bolt when Royce saved the day. "You know, Colin is a good friend of mine. He played Harry in the movie and the ladies love him."

Mr. Ricardo brightened. "Really?"

Royce nodded. "Had to beat them off with a stick after that role. I think it made him even more irresistible."

"Okay, I'll give it a try, but don't blame me if no one believes it."

Neil breathed a gust of relief and we got back to it.

We were in the nightclub scene and all the seniors were stomping around to "Voulez-Vous" when SpongeBob picked up the crackle of a conversation. I moved the side curtain to the left and saw Ernie Frick and the two gorillas arguing in the back row, where Piglet usually sat. I had to remove my headset and put my walkie-talkie up to my ear to hear them clearly.

"I told you to be patient."

"We're out of patience, Frick."

"Have I ever let you down before?"

"If you had, you'd be dead."

Ernie let out a nervous chuckle. "Okay, calm down, guys. You'll get your money."

One of the thugs leaned in to Ernie. "I would hate to see something happen to your star talent because you didn't honor your commitments."

To my horror, I saw Mother Gibson creeping against the back wall, holding the boat oar in front of her.

Ernie pointed to her. "Hey, who's that?"

I didn't think, I just reacted, and flashed the lights onstage. All three men turned to the stage to see what was happening and Mother Gibson slipped by, forgotten. I heard Neil through my abandoned headset on the board and grabbed for it.

"Sorry, Neil, my hand slipped."

The song finished, and we went to intermission. Mrs.

Dodson and Mrs. Davis announced they were going after the assassins and I cut them off. "Stay right where you are. Someone has to stay here to keep an eye on Iggy. I'll go talk to Ernie."

I ducked out of the booth while Neil gave the actors some pointers and Mr. Ricardo flexed his stringy arms for Aunt Ginny. I scanned the auditorium for Ernie and didn't see him, so I headed off the stage and out the emergency exit door. Ernie was alone and on his cell phone. He tucked it into his breast pocket when he saw me. "Hello there."

"I thought I'd get some fresh air." My breath came out in smoky puffs and I swung my arms back and forth, like that was going to generate more oxygen.

"Yes, well." Ernie chuckled. "This is a good place for it."

"So, you live in New York?"

Ernie squinted with that perpetual smile and bobbed his head back and forth.

"I bet you have a lot of clients waiting for you?"

"Definitely. Night and day, they are calling me. I was just talking to Uma before you came out."

"Wow, who else are you representing?

"Oh, A-listers. Josh Groban, Bette Midler, Idina Menzel."

"I had no idea. That must be very exciting. And Royce is one of your best?"

"Royce is my favorite. That's why I'm trying to help him make a comeback. He's much too talented to end his career now."

"Is that what you're working on with those other two men you are always talking to?"

Ernie gave me half of a head shake. "Oh. No . . . Finn and Winky represent the largest advertising firm on the East Coast. Bennet and Darcy. They're big fans of Royce."

"Big fans?"

He nodded vigorously. "Most definitely. They want Royce to do a quick spot—that means a fifteen-second commercial—for the New York Arts Program. We've been working out the details between rehearsals."

"I see. Would they pay Royce for that or would you have to pay them?"

Ernie made gurgling sounds while he tried to come up with an answer. "It's for charity. Royce is very charitable."

"It's funny, they don't look like advertisers. Some of the seniors thought they looked like gangsters." I laughed. Ernie laughed. Ernie's laugh had an edge of terror in it.

He pulled out his phone. "I'm sorry, I have to take this. Hello?"

Finn and Winky with Bennet and Darcy. What a ridiculous cover story.

I opened the emergency exit door to get back to my post and Google the advertising firm when I heard a loud crash combined with Aunt Ginny's scream of terror.

Chapter Thirty-One

A rapid stream of complaint wriggled its way out from the fallen canvas. "I will knock you flatter than a flitter, Blanche, you butt-faced baboon. You just wait till I get out from under this hickey."

Neil and Smitty were lifting the heavy backdrop off Aunt Ginny's little body, but I ran over and threw it off like I was powerlifting a Volkswagen off a toddler. "What happened?"

There was panic in Smitty's cow eyes. "I checked these sets myself. I've even come in every day to make sure they're safe. Someone is tampering with them; look, the support struts have been sawed through."

Aunt Ginny's forehead had a gash over her right eye and she growled, "Blanche!"

I looked to the back row, where Blanche had been camped out earlier, whistling a gallows tune. It had been abandoned.

"That vindictive strumpet is behind this. I know she is." Aunt Ginny scanned the auditorium through angry slits.

"I don't see how she could with a broken collarbone. Of

course, you have been baiting her all week with those T-shirts."
I helped her down to a seat while Neil pushed everyone back.

"Let's give her some space, please. Will someone please get the first aid kit?"

Royce jumped into action and ran to Fiona. "Do you still have those swabs and gauze pads?"

Fiona clutched her purse to her chest. "What?"

Royce fanned his fingers. "In your bag. Come on, Fee. Ginny needs first aid. Now is not the time to be shy about your issues."

Fiona spoke through clenched teeth. "I don't know what you're talking about."

Royce grabbed her purse and ran to Aunt Ginny's side, fishing around in the flamingo-print tote.

Fiona called after him, "Royce, no!"

He ignored her and dumped the contents. "Hold on, Ginger, I'll take care of you." Gauze pads, alcohol wipes, and Band-Aids scattered on the worn, red-velvet seat. Royce grabbed an alcohol wipe, tore it open with his teeth, and dabbed at Aunt Ginny's forehead. She winced at the icy sting.

I scanned the paraphernalia from Fiona's purse and didn't really see anything incriminating to account for the fuss she was making until Neil pointed at the pile. "What are they doing in there?"

Fiona stormed over and grabbed a yellow box. "It's none of your business. It's no one's business."

Iggy placed a hand on his mother's shoulder. "What's the big deal? So you have colitis. It's not a crime."

"Iggy!"

"Not that," Neil shouted. "That!" He picked up an item and held it out to Fiona. "What are my keys to the equipment room doing in your purse?"

All eyes shot to Fiona.

She sputtered. "What? I don't know. I've never seen them before."

Aunt Ginny winced in pain. "I don't suppose there is a saw in the equipment room, is there?"

Fiona backed away from Neil. "Somebody obviously dropped your keys into my purse. I've been sitting in here working on costumes every day since we started this stupid musical. My fingers are practically raw from the sequins. Anyone could have dropped something into my purse when I wasn't looking."

Mrs. Sheinberg nodded. "The noodge's telling the truth. She's been working next to me every day. She didn't have time to ransack the toolroom."

Mrs. Dodson tapped over to Aunt Ginny's side on her cane while peering at Fiona. "You could have come back up here after hours and done your dirty work."

"I've been home with Royce every night, isn't that right, Boodaloo?"

Royce looked at the ceiling.

Aunt Ginny held the gauze against her forehead. "You weren't home with him last night. We were out to dinner until well past ten."

Iggy put his hands on Fiona's shoulders. "If you all think my mother is capable of working that machine to sabotage the lights and saw through the backdrops, you're a bunch of idiots."

Fiona patted his hand. "Thank you, Iggy."

Mr. Sheinberg shoved his hands in his pockets. "Hey, maybe your mother isn't the one who took those keys. You look like you'd be able to figure out that contraption. And you're strong enough to do some damage on the set, eh? I think we should call the cops."

Fiona's lip trembled. "I don't care what you say. My Iggy wouldn't do something like that. He is home with me every night on his GameBox. You should test those keys for fingerprints. You won't find mine on there. Or Iggy's."

Iggy glared at the group of us. "Go on, call the police. We have nothing to hide. We're only here to keep an eye on Royce."

Fiona smacked his arm. "Iggy."

He spun her around and led her back to her seat. "Well, we are."

Neil took Aunt Ginny's hand. "We will get to the bottom of this. Can you tell me what happened, darling? Why were you even over there? That was where Royce was supposed to enter the scene."

"I don't know. One minute I was running my lines for act two and the next I was hit on the head. Will I have a scar?"

"No, I don't think so. It's very superficial."

"Thank God, I think this is my good side."

Neil took Aunt Ginny's hand in his. "If you need to sit this one out, it's okay. It's more important to me that you're safe."

"No, I think I can manage."

I looked around and didn't see Piglet anywhere. "Neil, I saw Terrence Nuttal going backstage before rehearsal began. Do you know what he was doing?"

Neil looked sheepishly from Aunt Ginny to me. "He said he wanted to inspect the set to be sure it was safe."

Aunt Ginny deadpanned, "Well, he did a fabulous job."

"Exactly who is he and why is he here?" I asked.

Neil's Adam's apple bobbed in his throat and his eyes darted around the theater. "He's working here."

Aunt Ginny scrunched up her face. "Doing what? All I've seen him do is sit in the back there and frown at rehearsals."

Neil cleared his throat. "It's complicated. But you know I wouldn't do anything to hurt you, don't you?"

Aunt Ginny blinked a couple of times. "I know that, Neil."

Neil patted her hand. "Good. I'm going to go check on the backdrop now." He rejoined Smitty to reinstall the backdrop.

Aunt Ginny slid her eyes to me. "What do you suppose that was about?"

"I don't know. Did you notice he mentioned that you were hurt where Royce was supposed to be standing?"

"I did catch that."

Ernie had cornered Royce on the other side of the auditorium. They were sharing a silver flask that Royce was tipping back like water to a desert nomad. Ernie was fast-talking about something and Royce was nodding along with whatever it was.

"Do you think Ernie could be trying to hurt Royce?"

Aunt Ginny shook her head. "But why? You don't kill your cash cow."

"Then again, how much do you really know about Royce?"

Aunt Ginny's eyes were set on fire. "I hope you're not suggesting what I think you're suggesting, Missy."

"I'm not suggesting anything. But you haven't seen Royce in sixty years. How do we know he didn't tamper with the backdrops one night when he was up here practicing?"

"I know Royce better than that. He would never hurt me. People don't change that much, Poppy Blossom. And Royce has always been the good sort."

My eyes followed Terrence Nuttal up to the stage, where he had a camera and started taking pictures of the backdrop.

Blanche had vanished. The biddies had also vanished, but I knew they hadn't gone far.

"Aunt Ginny, will you be okay if I leave you here for a minute?"

"I'm all right."

I went onstage and looked at the backdrop Smitty and Neil were trying to repair. I asked Smitty, "What do you think?"

He took his baseball cap off and scratched his bald head. "We'll have it fixed in a jiff. I'm using screws this time to make it extra sturdy, but that won't prevent someone from coming in here and making new cuts. Without the stabilizers, anyone could tip the backdrop over with a little force."

I looked at Terrence Nuttal. "What were you doing back here earlier?"

He turned pink and blinky. "I was inspecting the set to make sure it was safe."

"And you didn't notice that someone had sawed through the support braces?"

It was hard to believe, but he turned a deeper shade of pink. "I didn't notice the cuts. I'm not in the construction business. I was looking for something more obvious."

"Like what? A bomb? A coyote with an anvil and a sign that says ACME?"

His mouth puckered and he started to sputter. "Now see here, madame."

"What exactly is your job here, Mr. Nuttal?"

Before he could turn puce or answer my question, the police arrived, and he squirmed away.

Officer Birkwell stood in the center aisle looking around and shaking his head. "We got a call that there has been another accident and someone else is hurt?"

Royce pointed to Aunt Ginny. "My Ginger was nearly crushed."

Fiona leaped up, "And my brother was next to her when it happened. He was lucky to escape in one piece."

Aunt Ginny looked from Royce and Fiona to Officer Birkwell. "I'm fine. Just a little banged up, but I'll live."

Officer Birkwell walked over to Aunt Ginny to examine her forehead and ask her some questions. SpongeBob crackled to life in my pocket and Mother Gibson's voice came through like a tire losing air. "*Pssssssst.*"

I looked around until I spotted the biddies peeking out from behind the curtains stage left. Mother Gibson was holding a walkie-talkie shaped like an octopus.

"*Pssssssssssssst.*"

Mrs. Davis crooked her finger for me to join them.

"What? Ow!"

Mrs. Davis was really strong for a woman of her age. I rubbed my arm where she'd grabbed me and hauled me into a curtain tornado. The four of us stood enshrouded by 360 degrees of red theater curtains.

"Poppy!" Mrs. Dodson shook my wrist. "Do you think Royce dropped those keys in Fiona's purse when we hauled it over to Ginny?"

All three sets of eyes were looking at me expectantly. "Well, I don't know. It's possible. It would have been a good opportunity to cover his tracks if he was the one who had taken them."

The biddies did not like that answer at all. "We have to protect Ginny. What if he's the one who pushed Duke off the catwalk?" Mrs. Dodson said.

"He did stay here to run lines when we all went to lunch. And you see where that's got him." Mrs. Davis rolled her eyes.

Mother Gibson shook her head. "Uh-uh. I think Fiona stole those keys herself. She been trying to get Royce to quit the play and stay home with her to watch Turner Classic Movies since he got here."

Mrs. Davis fished a little pink notebook out of her bra and flipped some pages. "Fiona said that Royce was up here practicing late every night. He would have had plenty of time to sabotage the props and the sets."

I didn't disagree with them, but I tried to inject a little reason into the conversation all the same. "But why would he do that, ladies? Why join the play only to sabotage it? If Royce wants to ruin the play, all he has to do is drop out."

Mrs. Dodson shot up her hand. "What if it's a stunt, for publicity? What if Royce is planning on going back to New York after all and it will be all over the news that his last production was cursed, like *The Phantom of the Opera*?"

"I have a hard time believing the Senior Center musical would hit the Broadway trade news."

Officer Birkwell's voice punctured through our cocoon. "Ladies, you do know those curtains are only going down to your calves, don't you? I can see your feet."

The ladies looked to me to come up with a plausible explanation.

I unwound our little group from the curtains to face him. "Hello, Officer Birkwell. We were just doing an acting exercise."

His mouth was set in a grim little scowl. "Uh-huh. I need the four of you to listen to me very carefully. You seem to be under the misguided notion that you are private investigators. Now don't give me those innocent looks. I know you've been sneaking around, looking into windows, and breaking into offices. It has to stop before someone gets hurt. I know you miss your friend. It was a terrible thing that happened here the other day. If you want, I can arrange for a grief counselor to come in and talk to you."

Mrs. Dodson looked down her nose. "We don't need a grief counselor. What we need is a police investigation. What are you doing about all the accidents that keep happening?"

"And the sabotage," Mrs. Davis added.

"Those can all be chalked up to old equipment and human error."

Mother Gibson gave him a look you would give your child caught in a lie. "And the threats?"

Officer Birkwell shifted on his feet. "Mr. Hansen has decided not to file an official complaint. Now please, leave the police work to the professionals before one of you ends up injured or arrested. And Poppy, Officer Fenton told me to tell you: if there are any more complaints registered, she's holding you personally responsible."

Chapter Thirty-Two

I wish the drive home from the Senior Center took longer, because a few blocks did not give me enough time to cool off. Who did Amber think she was? Threatening to hold me responsible if these ladies get any more complaints. I can barely control myself, let alone a group of stubborn biddies who have their minds made up. In their heads, those ladies were conducting an FBI sting rivaling that of capturing Osama Bin Laden, and they were going to get their man.

If truth be told, I was more concerned about Royce and his relationship with Aunt Ginny than anything else. I didn't want to see her get hurt. She was so trusting that he was the same man she fell in love with when she was sixteen. How can you expect to know a person after so much time has passed? People change. And there was something not quite right about Royce. Of course, people could say the same thing about Aunt Ginny, but she was just a little eccentric. At least that was my take on things.

I pulled into the CVS parking lot and pulled out my cell phone. Royce said he'd just finished doing a run of *A Christ-*

mas Carol and he was fabulous. Was he Hugh Jackman fabulous or the kind of fabulous I am when I sing "Total Eclipse of the Heart" in the car? I needed to confer with the internet.

I found a few reviews for Royce's most recent play online that ranged from eight to ten stars. *Playbill* gave a favorable report of Royce's "avant-garde rendition of Ebenezer Scrooge with a side of Hamlet." *Variety* said, "Royce Hansen does it again and freshens up a Christmas classic with a keen mashup and brilliantly delivered satire." And the New York Theatre Guide claimed "All we want for Christmas is Royce Hansen as Julius Caesar Scrooge. Brilliant!"

Then there was a rough review from the *New York Times*. "Don't mess with the classics." And one from the *New York Post*, "Charles Dickens and William Shakespeare should rise from their graves and come back to haunt Royce Hansen for desecrating their works." *Ouch*. It was obvious that Royce had been influenced by his time with the Royal Shakespeare Company. Was he reliving the glory days? Or did he even realize it was happening?

I was starving. I had a salad covered with almonds and tears of disappointment hours ago and the satisfaction lasted about as long as it took me to notice Smitty eating a Wawa hot dog. I could see the candy aisle in the CVS from the car. Across the street was a gourmet cheese shop and behind me was a bakery. It was like being in the first level of Dante's Hell with the little old ladies who brought store-bought pies to the church bake-off.

My heart sped up from being in the Snickers bar hot zone. I forced myself to turn my attention to the belly roll flopped over my yoga pants. It was a couple of dress sizes bigger now than when I first woke up this morning. I put the car in reverse and left the parking lot for the safe haven of home and lack of tasty choices.

The maroon Mercury was still parked across from us at the edge of Mr. Winston's yard. And everyone knows you aren't being a nosy neighbor if you take a gift. I reached in the back seat for the bag of linzer hearts and took them with me to Mr. Winston's door.

"Ho, Poppy, what's doin'?"

I held out the bag. "I brought you some cookies for Valentine's Day."

Mr. Winston's bushy, black eyebrows shot up to his snow-capped hairline. "Cookies, eh." He took the bag. "What information are you angling for?"

I felt the roots of my red hair blush. "What, no—I—okay, is your daughter here?"

"No, I haven't seen Judy since New Year's. She's bringing me some homemade TV dinners this weekend, though. Do you need me to give her a message?"

"No, I was just wondering if that was Judy's car. It's been parked there for a week." I pointed to the car and used big hand gestures. Mr. Winston was very hard of hearing and there tended to be a lot of misunderstandings.

He nodded. "I noticed that. I was going to bring you an Entenmann's raspberry Danish tomorrow and ask you if it was one of yours."

"No, it's no one at our house. Have you seen anyone come or go by it?"

His busy eyebrows wiggled down on his forehead. "No, I don't think it's for sale. At least, no one has looked at it that I've noticed."

I was pulling the plug before I got in too deep. "Okay, thank you. Enjoy the cookies."

Mr. Winston lifted the bag and gave me a grin. "Tell Ginny I said hello."

I walked over to the car and peered in through the windows. The floor was littered with coffee cups and fast-food wrappers. There was a device on the dashboard that was plugged into the lighter. It looked like a giant, black eyeball. *If that's a speaker, it's going to run the car battery dead be-*

fore the owner comes back. I took a closer look at the device and saw what looked like a high-tech camera lens. *Oh my God. It's a security camera and it's facing my house.* The lens blinked, and I noticed a green light was on.

Someone was watching me. I turned and fled into the house, flung the latch on the door, and locked it as if the camera could sprout legs and run in after me. I felt like there were spiders crawling up my arms and I had to swat them off. I told myself I was being ridiculous. The driver probably broke down and left a security camera plugged in to be sure no one stole the car before they could come back to retrieve it. I paced around the foyer for a couple of minutes until an idea came to me. I ran to the laundry room and found an old blanket Aunt Ginny used on the beach for the Fourth of July. It was a hundred years old, butt ugly, and miserably scratchy. You'd rather sit on hot rocks. No one in their right mind would have it. I grabbed the blanket and took it outside to the abandoned Mercury. I skirted the edge of the yard to try to sneak up behind it—I didn't want to show up on camera—and threw the blanket over the car, covering the windows. There. Now at least they weren't spying on my house, and if someone came to steal the car, they'd be caught on camera when they removed the blanket.

I was proud of myself for my quick thinking and bravery. I went back inside much relieved. I still threw the latch and set the alarm. Then I scooped up my companion cat and ran up the stairs with him to hide under the covers.

Chapter Thirty-Three

The brilliant sunrise of a Cape May winter is a lie. The peachy-pink glow is a bouquet of empty promises of warmth and comfort mocked by the frigid wind blowing off the Atlantic Ocean. Even the seagulls sit with their wings wrapped around themselves, too disgruntled by the cold to dive-bomb passersby for potential smackerals.

This morning in particular, the cold was cutting through my fleece like tiny ice daggers, while the roar of the waves brought little comfort to the ache in my bones or the unsettled gnawing in the pit of my stomach. Someone was watching my house. Maybe. Probably. What were the odds that the abandoned Mercury with dashboard security camera was a fluke? Maybe the owner ran out of gas and had no idea of the agitation they were causing me. What were the odds that Amber would run the plates for me? *Yeah. About the same as the odds that I'd be a size five by this summer.*

I turned the final corner back to the house and stopped short. The blanket was missing. I fast-walked across the street to come behind the car to see if maybe it had slid off the back and was lying on the ground. The blanket was gone. And the green light was still on.

I crossed the street to my house and stomped up the porch steps. I couldn't take it anymore. I was going to ask Officer Birkwell to look into the owner of the car for me. I did have his number memorized, even though I wouldn't admit it to the insufferable Amber.

I opened the front door and was hit in the face with a back-draft of heat that felt like an inferno after the hour I'd spent walking the boardwalk at daybreak. Figaro was sitting at the bottom of the stairs, his head stuck through the armhole of his orange companion vest. I pulled his head out and shifted the vest back around. "Don't look at me like that. This wasn't my idea."

I shed my layers on the way up the backstairs to shower and change before making today's crabs Benedict and citrus salad. An hour later, I was buzzing around the kitchen with Aunt Ginny making coffee and peeling tangerines.

Aunt Ginny handed me two mugs and I filled them with steaming Ethiopia Guji. Figaro hobbled his way into the kitchen. He had worked his front paw through the neck hole of his vest and Aunt Ginny had to right him and twist it back into place again. He celebrated by biting at the neck strap while spinning in a circle, which caused Aunt Ginny to choke out a cackle.

"Ahem."

Aunt Ginny and I shot up straight and Figaro paused his spinning when we heard the formidable Mrs. Galbraith.

I gave the older woman what I hoped was a pleasant smile. "Good morning. Would you like some coffee?"

Mrs. Galbraith critically eyed Figaro, who was critically eyeing her back while scratching at his vest with his back leg. "No, thank you. I had my tea and toast before I came to work."

Aunt Ginny muttered under her breath, "Well, don't get carried away."

Mrs. Galbraith ignored Aunt Ginny. "I'm going to get the laundry done so I can change the linens while the guests are away. In the meantime, I felt I should share my concerns with you."

I stirred coconut creamer into my coffee. "What concerns are those?"

"I think the couple in the Swallowtail suite may be stealing from you."

"Joey and Val? Why would you think that?"

"When I made their beds yesterday something in the room looked different. I can't put my finger on it, but something is missing."

"Maybe they moved something. People sometimes rearrange things when they stay to make room for their own stuff."

"I can't see how that's possible, seeing as how their personal belongings are strewn about without care."

Aunt Ginny gave me a look over her coffee and took an English muffin out of the toaster.

"Not to mention," she went on, "they keep asking me what things are worth."

"I think they're just curious."

"Then they are curious about the china, the silver, the painting in the hall, and the crystal vase in the library."

I grinned at Mrs. Galbraith. Joey and Val had definitely gotten under her skin. "They're young and just starting their life together. I think they're just excited to be here and experience something outside their normal routine."

"Perhaps that's it. But I thought you should know that something feels off about them. I am much more comfortable with the couple in the Purple Emperor suite."

"The Ainsworths," I offered.

She nodded. "They're a delight. I met the missus in the hall and she asked for a corkscrew. You can tell they know how to conduct themselves in fine surroundings."

Aunt Ginny let out the tiniest of snorts.

"And the gentleman gave me a sizable tip yesterday when they requested tea service in their room. Only people of quality do that anymore."

Figaro ran around the island with his ears pinned to his head and skidded through the kitchen.

Aunt Ginny was pouring chocolate syrup on her English muffin. "Well, we are all about quality and breeding here."

I turned my attention back to Mrs. Galbraith, who was now frowning at Aunt Ginny. "I'm glad you're getting some decent tips with so few guests in the house. I'm hoping we fill up for the summer. I already have a few reservations for March and April."

"Yes, well . . . tipping isn't like it used to be. At least the Ainsworths are making up for the lack of tips from the other two suites."

I blinked a couple of times. "Have you been servicing the Adonis suite?"

"Well, I should hope so. She has the sign out requesting housekeeping."

Figaro flopped over and was wiggling across the floor on his back.

Aunt Ginny and I stared at each other, speechless. Georgina was in the Adonis suite and she wasn't a paying guest. She was—dare I say—family since she was my former mother-in-law, and she had a ten percent investment in the Butterfly Wings B&B. Since she'd become enamored with my handyman a few months ago, her drop-in visits had become a lot more frequent. *I should have fired Smitty when I had the chance.*

Aunt Ginny laughed. "Where are you going to put her when we have no vacancy?"

Mrs. Galbraith narrowed her eyes at Figaro. "I'm not sure how you are going to keep that animal in residence with a full house."

"I'm advertising us as cat friendly."

Mrs. Galbraith looked like she was choking on a peach pit. "Well, we shall see how that pans out. And I want to remind you that I will require my overtime rate this week from all the extra hours spent covering for your absence."

"Yes, of course."

Figaro skidded in front of Mrs. Galbraith and flopped over to attack the underneath of his lopsided service vest.

Mrs. Galbraith picked up her laundry basket. "And I may need hazard pay." She left the kitchen with her head high and her nose skyward.

Aunt Ginny gave me a wry look. "What she needs is for somebody to remove that stick from her butt."

I sputtered on my coffee and had to wipe some off my T-shirt. Figaro rolled his eyes up to mine and I said the magic word. "Eat?"

He sprang to all fours like he'd been vaulted out of a jack-in-the-box. I adjusted his vest and filled his bowl with some of the crab for the morning's Benedicts. He and Aunt Ginny were both smacking their mouths around their breakfasts when I heard Sawyer come in the front door and call down the hall. "Hellooo."

I was getting a coffee mug down for her when she came around the corner. "I got nine roses today! And you'll never believe what else came."

Aunt Ginny crossed the kitchen and poured herself another cup of coffee. "A pony?"

Sawyer giggled. "A freezer chest full of gourmet ice cream."

"Adrian made you ice cream?"

"That's what I thought at first too." She took a Mason jar out of the cabinet and filled it with water. "But they were shipped from an artisanal ice cream company in New York."

"That's weird. You would think a chef would make his own ice cream if it was a gift." I sprinkled chopped mint over the medley of citrus segments and topped the salad with a dusting of pink sugar.

Aunt Ginny is always one who believes in poking the bear. "It sounds like Mr. Vartabedian has been busy."

Sawyer looked from Aunt Ginny to me and poured herself a cup of coffee. "Adrian doesn't want to give himself away. I think he's playing it cool. He keeps denying everything, but I know it's him."

Aunt Ginny took the citrus salad out to the dining room and came back with her report. "The eagles have landed, and guess which crow will be joining them?"

My jaw dropped. I peeked through the door to the dining room and Georgina had poured herself a cup of coffee and was having a little tête-à-tête at the table with Bunny. "She wants me to wait on her now?"

Sawyer split open an English muffin for the toaster. "I'll help you."

I started spinning the water with a touch of vinegar for poaching the eggs and gave my hollandaise a little whisk so it wouldn't split. "Are you sure Adrian isn't denying everything because he really isn't behind it?"

Sawyer shook her head "I don't think so. I think he's trying to make up for all our missed dates and rain checks."

"Why are you missing dates?"

Sawyer sighed. "It's not been easy dating a chef. He's never available to go to dinner. He works nights and weekends and every holiday. Most of our dates have been at his restaurant when he takes a break, or we'll meet at the twenty-four-hour diner at midnight when he gets off. It's only been getting worse since Restaurant Week made him more successful. I think he's being extra-romantic to make up for it."

Aunt Ginny grunted. "You're scaring her off, girl."

Sawyer must have seen the distress on my face because

she added, "Oh, but I'm sure it will work for you. You and Tim have such history. Plus, you'll be working with him, so you can sneak off whenever business is slow."

I gently cracked an egg into the spinning, simmering water and watched the white wrap around the yolk. I set my timer for three minutes and cracked another egg into the identical pot next to it.

Sawyer and Aunt Ginny practically pushed me out of the way to see into the pans. "Where'd you learn to do that?" Sawyer asked me, her eyes excited.

"Julia Child."

They were both so impressed, I felt like a celebrity for a minute. Then Georgina burst in through the kitchen door. "How much longer, Poppy? I have to get to the theater early to practice my number. I've been given a starring role in *Mamma Mia!* now that the cast is shorthanded."

Aunt Ginny cocked an eyebrow. "You're starring in the play now? As what?"

The timer went off and I removed the eggs with a slotted spoon, trimmed the sides, and placed them on piles of buttery crab meat nestled on the toasted English muffins. I topped each Benedict with a cloak of hollandaise before starting on two more eggs.

Georgina rolled her shoulders back and stood taller. "I'm Greek villager number six, but I lead off the "Dancing Queen" number through the audience, so it's an important role."

Aunt Ginny picked up the plates and handed them to Georgina. "Well then, by all means, you should do the honors with the first two eggs."

Georgina took the plates and tried to balance them carefully to not drop the strawberry fans and mess up the presentation. "There was talk that I might have my own dressing room."

"I heard that too." Aunt Ginny gave her a gentle push toward the door. "It says janitor's closet right now, but don't let that deter you. Just push the mop out of the way and pull on that spandex." Aunt Ginny gave us an evil grin. "Now to spill something at the right time."

Sawyer laughed. "You're so naughty."

"Don't tell her that. It just makes it more fun for her."

Chapter Thirty-Four

Aunt Ginny had gone to meet the other biddies for coffee and Sawyer and I were cleaning up from the morning's breakfast service when there was a tap on the kitchen door from the dining room. It was Bunny Ainsworth.

"Sorry to disturb you, but I wanted to let you know that breakfast was delicious."

"Thank you. I'm so glad you enjoyed it."

"Chigsie said he had never had a better eggs Benedict anywhere."

"Well, I take that as a huge compliment."

"We were also wondering if you could set something up for us. We'd love to see inside some of these beautiful Victorian houses. Do you think you could arrange a couple of tours for us?"

"I can make some calls. I know both Angel of the Sea and the Physick estate offer tours for a small fee. Where else did you have in mind?"

"We were thinking the Queen Victoria and maybe a couple of the smaller ones. Could you arrange that? Money is no object; we can pay for their time."

"Let me see what I can do and I'll let you know tonight."

Bunny grabbed my hand. "Wonderful. Thank you so much, dear."

Sawyer was pouring herself another cup of coffee. "You want me to call a couple for you? I know the manager of the Queen Victoria."

"No, I'll do it. I have to establish a relationship with the other B&B owners sometime. You know what you can do for me? Look up Bennet and Darcy in New York and see if it's an advertising firm."

While Sawyer was searching on her phone, I called and left a message for Officer Birkwell about the Mercury across the street that was plaguing my sanity. Then I pulled out my laptop and started calling around to see who would let the Ainsworths have a private tour of their B&B. Most places were happy to oblige, especially those who charged a fee. My last call was to the manager of the Queen Victoria. It was one of the most beautiful Victorian homes on the tour circuit with its Edwardian porch, Italianate Ville turret windows, and red-cedar-sloped mansard roof. It sat on one of the most picturesque corners of the historic district. I got a young lady named Carol on the phone and introduced myself as the owner of the Butterfly Wings Bed and Breakfast.

"Right. Virginia Frankowski's place. How's it going?"

"It's going well. We won't have our big grand opening until the season starts, but we have a few guests."

"Sure. Business will really pick up after Easter if we have good weather."

"I have a couple right now who would love to have a tour. Do you think that could be arranged?"

"I don't see why not. As long as it's not during breakfast. When did you have in mind?"

We worked out the details and she gave me a couple of windows to offer them. Then I told her I'd have to come take the tour myself one day. I'd always wanted to see inside.

Sawyer set her phone down and mouthed to me, *No Bennet and Darcy advertising firm.*

Aw, Jane Austen will be so disappointed. Then I remembered that Ernie had told me he was staying at the Queen Victoria. "You know, Carol, I think a friend of mine is staying with you: Ernie Frick. I think he just got into town a couple of days ago."

"Oh yes, Mr. Frick. He's very nice. Always smiling."

"Yes, that's him."

"But Mr. Frick has been here much longer than a couple of days. He checked in almost three weeks ago."

"Three weeks ago? Oh, I must have misunderstood him. I thought he had just arrived Friday afternoon."

"Not unless there is more than one Ernie Frick. Your friend is booked for the whole month."

"Have his cousins come to visit him yet? They're big guys, you can't miss them. Winky and Finn?"

"Not that I've seen. But I'm only here part time."

I thanked Carol for her help and a thought struck me. "Have you ever heard about any of the B&Bs leaving bad reviews for other B&Bs online?"

She was quiet for a moment. "I'm not aware of that happening, but business can be very competitive."

I thanked her and we agreed to be a resource for each other in case we ever had an emergency, although I think that would probably happen to me long before she would need anything, and I hung up the phone.

Sawyer gave me a questioning look. "So?"

"Ernie Frick has been here for almost a month. Three weeks longer than he said."

"Holy moly. What's he been doing here all this time?"

"That's a good question. And why would he lie about it?"

"Well, he lied about Bennet and Darcy too, so he's hiding something."

I heard the front door open and the bell chime in the kitchen. The biddies were back and they sounded excited about something. That could only mean trouble.

"Do not tell Aunt Ginny or the biddies what we found out. I could see them kidnapping Ernie and interrogating him with a flashlight. Amber has it in her head that I'm responsible for all their behavior all of a sudden."

The biddies came around the corner, their eyes sharp and excited. Sawyer and I gave them sweet smiles. "Hello, ladies. What have you been up to?"

"Poppy, we have a great idea."

Oh dear lord. "Oh?"

"We are going to break into the Senior Center after midnight to get that insurance policy Neil had in his drawer."

An image of four little old ladies in sensible shoes playing gin rummy in a jail cell floated into my mind.

Sawyer looked at the ceiling and started to hum.

The ladies were looking at me with glee, like they were expecting praise. I had to think fast. "You know what?"

They shook their heads.

"I have a more pressing assignment for you."

Their eyes got wider and they leaned in expectantly.

"But you have to keep it hush-hush. If word gets out that we're looking for something, it could be a problem for us."

Mrs. Dodson tapped her cane. "Okay, well, quit dawdling. What is it?"

"I need you to do some digging into Ernie Frick and his agency. He told me those two gorillas were in advertising and Sawyer can't find their agency online."

The ladies were all grinning now and standing a little taller. Mrs. Davis practically gushed, "What do you want us to do?"

"Aunt Ginny, do you have your old theater magazines?"

Aunt Ginny blushed. "I may have one or two around here, somewhere."

Mrs. Dodson gave Aunt Ginny a look and Mother Gibson laughed out loud.

"Great. I need you all to comb through whatever Aunt Ginny has to see if you can find any references to Ernie's business, his clients, any arrest records, and anyone named Winky or Finn. You may need to search on the internet too. We need to figure out what kind of person Ernie is and who else he represents. Are they happy with him? Got it?"

The ladies agreed and followed Aunt Ginny to collect their research materials.

Sawyer grinned. "That should keep them busy for a while."

My reveling in cleverness was cut short when I got an email from one of my April guests canceling their reservation. The reason they cited was "Too many bad reviews have left us feeling nervous about our stay. We've decided to stay somewhere with a higher rating."

While Sawyer read the email, I lay my head on the table. I wasn't upset. I was too numb and confused to be upset. So, I just lay there feeling doomed.

Sawyer put my phone down and drummed her fingernails on the kitchen table. "Let's call Kim. She may know someone who can help."

Kim was one of our oldest friends, who had an eclectic personality that included half a shaved head, full-color tattoo sleeves, and a pet iguana named Betsy. "Why would Kim know someone?"

"Because she worked for the Tropicana years ago, setting up the nightclub acts. Maybe she knows someone in public relations we could talk to about how to fix this."

"It's worth a shot." I dialed Kim's cell.

"Laughing Gull Winery, Kim speaking."

"Hey, it's Poppy."

"Hey, girl. What's up?"

"I'm having a PR nightmare and Sawyer said you used to set up nightclub acts for the Tropicana and might know someone."

"If by 'set up' you mean made a spreadsheet after the talent manager secured the booking, then yes." Then she spoke to someone nearby, "This is free if you join the wine club today."

I whispered to Sawyer, "She only kept the records."

Sawyer's face fell. "Oh."

Kim came back on. "But I do know people. What kind of problem are you having? I could call Margaret and ask her for a referral."

I filled Kim in on the outbreak of fraudulent reviews. While I was talking, the biddies began to emerge from Aunt Ginny's lair. They were dragging clear plastic bins full of back issues of theater magazines, *Playbills*, and newspaper clippings. Mother Gibson gave me a shocked look and rolled her eyes at the amount of stuff that was coming out of Aunt Ginny's storage. Aunt Ginny declined to make eye contact.

Kim had to ring up a customer, but when she came back, she said, "Girl, that's messed up. Don't people have anything better to do than trash each other online? That's twelve dollars."

Mrs. Dodson dragged a storage bin out backward and stopped in front of me to catch her breath. "Where can we set up our command center?"

I flicked my eyes to Sawyer, who had to swallow a laugh.

"Why don't you start in the sunroom? I'll bring in a folding table and some chairs."

Mrs. Dodson nodded and motioned for the other biddies to cart everything to the back of the house.

"I'm sorry, Kim. What were you saying?"

"That's okay. I can hear the clatter in the background. Let

me call my old booking manager at the Trop and I'll get back to you."

"Thank you."

"Do you want me to leave you a positive review on Yelp?"

"No. I don't want to do anything shady." *At least not yet.* "But you could leave Gia a good review if you'd like. You've been in there."

"Yeah, lots of times. I'll do that."

I hung up feeling a little more optimistic. I started to tell Sawyer what Kim had said, but I was waylaid by Mrs. Davis.

"We're going to need legal pads, pens, strong coffee, magnifying glasses, Post-it notes, and that pecan shortbread we tasked you with a couple of days ago that you haven't made yet."

Sawyer snickered. "What have you done?"

I got up to retrieve my purse. "It looks like I'll be running to CVS after I get them set up. I should have sent them to do research at the library."

"It's too late now, they've gone Woodward and Bernstein all over the sunroom."

"I just hope they find something useful."

Chapter Thirty-Five

I left for rehearsal before Aunt Ginny and her crew could be pried away from their Broadway gossip columns. They shooed me off and sent me away. I was informed to "stall" if they didn't arrive in time. I thought their expectations of me might be a little on the high side.

Georgina had cornered Neil in his office and had a script in his face, trying to convince him that the stage directions were better her way. Royce and Ernie were in the craft room on the other side of the foyer, sitting at one of the tables. I went in to eavesdrop while trying to look like I wasn't eavesdropping. I stood at the vending machine trying to decide between buying a pretend Coke or buying a pretend Sprite. No way was I going to pretend to buy an old-lady nutritional shake, even if this was all a ruse.

Ernie was plying Royce with something from his ever-present silver flask and telling him all the reasons why now was the perfect time for a comeback.

"I'm not sure I can get away, Ernie, old man."

"Of course you can, Royce baby. Just think about the star

treatment waiting for you backstage. Evian water and top-shelf scotch in your dressing room, a daily fresh muffin basket and those little packs of chocolate macadamia nuts you like. You know I'll take care of you. What my stars want, my stars get."

"Fee will never let me go."

"She has her son. He looks like a very capable young man."

I forgot that I was supposed to be covert and accidentally snorted out loud. Ernie and Royce stopped talking and I felt them watching me. I took a dollar out of my wallet and fed it into the machine. *Nothing to see here. Just getting some water.*

I could see Ernie's reflection in the vending machine glass. He was motioning for Royce to follow him out of the craft room for privacy. I punched in the number for spring water and kept my eyes on their retreat.

My purchase hit the exit chute with a loud *thunk*. I reached in to retrieve my spring water and pulled out a vanilla old-lady shake. *Oh, come on! I can't even get Aunt Ginny to drink these.*

I tossed it in my tote bag and trudged down the hall to the theater. I didn't see Royce and Ernie anywhere.

Fiona was sitting in her usual spot in the second row on the right—which I think was stage left? I don't know. Blanche had cornered Royce's sister and was trying to force an alliance. Fiona was scanning the room, desperate for an escape. She even called out to me to save her. "Poppy, oh good. All ready for the lights tonight?"

"I think so. With a good team effort."

Blanche screwed up her face when she saw me. "I hope your aunt fails miserably."

"That's the spirit." I said it more for me than for Blanche, but she turned pink and sucked in all the air that was around us.

Fiona must have realized she was in the strike zone and

immediately tried to change the subject. "Have you seen Royce?"

"He was in the craft room with his agent."

"Oh no. What were they doing?"

"Just talking, as far as I could tell. And drinking scotch, I think."

Fiona squirmed in her seat. "I knew it. That man won't stop until he entices my brother back to New York. Royce is not supposed to be drinking alcohol with the medicine he's on."

I thought about the three glasses of wine Royce had at dinner the other night and decided not to mention them. "What medicine is he on?" I asked.

Fiona looked uncomfortable. "I can't really talk about it."

Blanche sat back with a smug look on her face. "That's an old agent trick. Ernie is keeping his client pliable so he's easier to manipulate. They do it all the time. It's one of the reasons I left acting. Agents only want to use you."

"You're one to talk."

We had forgotten about Iggy, as I suspect happens a lot. He sits so quietly until Fiona yells at him to change something that you learn not to look at him. But now we noticed he was watching us from the piano bench and the look in his eye was not a friendly one.

"You've been trying to seduce Royce since he got home. We know what you're up to and it won't work. He won't marry you. You're not getting his money."

Blanche threw her head back and laughed. "That's a good one. You think I'm after Royce's money. Honey, I have my own money. If anyone has their hooks into your uncle, it's Mummy Dearest." Fiona started to sputter, but Blanche talked right over her. "Well, I have news for you both. It won't work. You can try to make Uncle Royce believe you're a nice little family, but he already told me he's leaving all his money to the Cape May Community Theater. You won't see a dime."

Iggy sprung up like a rocket with his hands clenched into

fists. He looked like he planned to tear Blanche a new one,
but he stormed out of the theater, which was weird in itself
because I had never seen him apart from Fiona. I kept waiting for him to jerk backward and yelp like he had on a shock
collar and had ventured too far from the safe zone.

Blanche laughed again and then noticed Royce walking
with Ernie. She abandoned us to latch on to Royce before
anyone else had a chance.

Fiona was so visibly upset that I regretted my uncharita-
ble thoughts about her and Iggy earlier and tried to comfort
her. "I'm sorry, Mrs. Sharpe. Are you okay?"

She snuffled and nodded. "I don't know why anyone
would think we are after Royce's money. My husband left
me very well off. I have my own money."

I nodded. "I know."

"Okay, everyone, let's get rehearsal started. I feel good
about tonight." Neil came down the aisle excited and raring
to go and I didn't see the biddies anywhere.

"Um, Neil." Everyone's eyes turned to me and I felt like
an idiot. How I hated talking in front of a group of people.
"Do you think we could do some vocal exercises before we
begin?"

Mr. Sheinberg waved his hand in my direction. "We don't
need no exercises. What's to exercise? Just say the words
and get on with it."

Mr. Ricardo agreed. "I am rather interested in getting
things going. I have a hot date after rehearsal tonight."

The senior playing Sophie said, "With what, a TV dinner
and HBO? You got nothing."

Neil looked like he was starting to get antsy that he would
lose their focus, which was easy to do, and said, "Let's just get
tonight started, shall we?"

I went to my cage and put on my headset. I set my dials to
my first light cue, then took out my phone to call Aunt
Ginny. Sophie was sending her letters to her potential dads,

and Aunt Ginny was going to voice mail. *Great. Thank God this isn't opening night.*

Neil came over my headset, "Poppy, where are Ginny and the other ladies?"

"Uh . . . aren't they here? I thought I saw them in the craft room."

"I need them down here. Thelma and Edith go on in a minute."

I tried to talk some sense into my jitters. *What are you so nervous about? It's not your fault if the practice is delayed. Calm the heck down.*

Just as "Honey, Honey" was wrapping up, four out-of-breath biddies popped into the cage from the side curtain. "We have it!"

Mother Gibson was holding up an old copy of *Backstage Biz Magazine* in victory.

I took the magazine and changed my light dial. "What is it?"

Aunt Ginny, Mrs. Davis, and Mrs. Dodson shook with excitement.

"Hold on, Poppy Blossom."

"That's our cue."

"Be right back."

They ran off to do their scene and left me with Mother Gibson, who grinned like a cat finally let out of its cage.

"Honey, that there is the smoking gun. It's a regular column called "Despicable Agents" from the back of the magazine."

I read the article and my eyes caught the words "Frick Agency" and "bankrupt."

"When was this?" I asked.

Mrs. Dodson was on stage, mouthing, *Don't start without us!*

Mother Gibson acted like she hadn't seen it. "'Bout four

years ago. It says Ernie's clients have been leaving him in droves."

"Does the article say why?"

Aunt Ginny was saying her lines, but she was backing up closer and closer to the cage. When she got close enough, she turned her head and hissed, "Hold on till we get back!" The music intro played for the "Money, Money, Money" number and she had to go back to her mark while the rest of the company joined her onstage for the dance number.

Mother Gibson didn't get to be in the spotlight very often, so she ignored their warning looks. "Misappropriation of funds. Child, it seems that Ernie wasn't giving his clients their fair share of the box office take. He was keeping more than his ten percent."

"Is Royce his last remaining client? Did you happen to see who else Ernie represents?"

Mrs. Davis ran to the cage, out of breath. "There is a list," she gasped. "Of Ernie's clients on his website." She gasped again. She did a box step back to the stage and gave a shimmy to the music.

Mother Gibson pulled out another piece of paper from a folder and handed it to me.

Mrs. Dodson was dancing over with her cane. When she got close enough, she threw her hip to the side. "But when you look up each actor." She did a pivot step and threw her other hip to the side. "Their personal websites list different agents."

Mother Gibson shook her head and laughed to herself. "Honey, he's hurting. His clients have all left him and lawsuits are pending."

I examined the paper and saw that several of Ernie's clients were bringing a class action suit against him. When I looked up, Aunt Ginny was standing at the cage with her arms crossed and her eyes near slits.

"I thought we agreed we would all tell Poppy together.'"

I realized the music had stopped and I quickly adjusted the lights for the dock scene. Royce was making his way across the catwalk to make his entrance on the yacht. *I wonder if he overheard us talking about his agent?*

Mrs. Davis took the client list from me. "What if one of these actors has been trying to hurt Royce so he'd leave Ernie too? Then they'd have another voice in their lawsuit."

I looked at the list. "Have you happened to see Bette Midler around the Senior Center in the past couple of weeks and not mentioned it?"

Mrs. Davis's countenance fell. "No, I guess not."

Aunt Ginny shot a final dirty look at Mother Gibson for starting without them. "I think Ernie has been trying to scare Royce into quitting the show so he'd go back to New York and he could keep skimming from his shows."

Mother Gibson let the dirty look roll off her back like it didn't affect her at all. "Maybe he mistook Duke for Royce and scared him so bad, he broke through the catwalk."

I nodded. "That's a good theory, but someone sawed the railing. I did find out today that Ernie has been here a lot longer than he led us to believe. Three weeks longer."

The ladies grabbed on to one another.

Mrs. Davis whispered, "He could be the saboteur."

Mrs. Dodson held up her hand. "Now we just have to prove it."

I wanted to call Officer Birkwell and hand everything over to him, but I had learned enough from the past few months to know that it was useless to call the police until I had some hard evidence. I also needed to keep the biddies occupied so they wouldn't put themselves in a dangerous situation. "Why don't we do a little more digging . . ."

"Forget that!" Mrs. Davis bobbed her head to the side. "We need to corner Ernie and trick him into confessing."

Two words came to mind and the second was "no." "How about instead, I ask Royce a few questions?"

Aunt Ginny shook her head. "No. Royce won't know anything. And he thinks Ernie is great. He probably has no idea he's been stealing from him. If we're going to question anyone, it needs to be Ernie."

"Okay, fine. I'll question Ernie, but I need you ladies to stay out of it and let me do it alone. If we're all there, we'd be sure to spook him."

The ladies huddled together and whispered to one another.

Neil crackled in my headset, "Poppy, where's my baby spot for 'Thank You for the Music'?"

Oh crap. I forgot about this stupid headset. Had Neil heard us talking earlier? "Sorry." I adjusted the dials until a soft pink glow filled the stage.

The ladies broke from their huddle and Aunt Ginny spoke for them. "You have six hours to question Ernie and get some answers. After that, we initiate Operation Shock and Awe."

Chapter Thirty-Six

"Six hours! What am I, a magician?" The last thing I needed was for these ladies to initiate whatever Operation Shock and Awe was supposed to be.

I waited until rehearsal was over. As soon as the seniors finished practicing for their second encore number, which seemed optimistic, I ripped off my headset and went in search of Ernie. He wasn't in the auditorium. Before I checked the various activity rooms, I ducked out the emergency exit, where he could usually be found up against the wall. Ernie wasn't outside, but Winky and Finn were. I'd never been this close to them before. One of them had very short-cropped, dark hair on a squarish head and no neck. He was built like a giant, menacing LEGO. The other had a head like a watermelon and wore a gold hoop in one ear. He jumped and had to juggle his cell phone when I flung the heavy metal door open.

"Have you seen Ernie?"

The LEGO recovered first. "No. Who's looking for him now?"

"I am."

"Does he owe you money?"

"No."

"Well, whatever you do . . . don't lend him any."

I gave him a nod. "Noted." I started to shut the door, then paused and opened it again. "Ernie said your names were Finn and Winky."

They looked at each other. The one who looked like Mr. Clean, if Mr. Clean had had a hard life, said, "I'm Winky. Ernie shouldn't be so free to pass around our names without giving a proper introduction."

I looked at the LEGO. "So, you must be Finn."

The LEGO nodded, which looked hard to do since he had no neck. "That's right."

"And you guys are with Bennet and Darcy?"

"Who?"

"How do you guys know Ernie?"

"We're in the same book club."

"Uh-huh. And why have you been hanging out here all week?"

Finn answered, "We're big fans of musical theater."

"I don't suppose you work in advertising?"

They gave me quizzical looks and shook their heads. Then Winky shrugged and said, "But we do send messages. And you really don't want to be on the receiving end of one of our messages, ya know?"

"Okay. Bye now." I shut the door and headed up the aisle out of the theater. *Ernie lied. The gorillas are lying. The biddies might be right about them being assassins. I want a doughnut.*

No Ernie in any of the rooms, but I did run into Blanche standing outside the front lobby in the parking lot. She was pacing back and forth, muttering angrily and smoking a long, golden cigarette that smelled faintly of cherries. She stubbed it out in a hurry when I approached her. "Is the nightmare over for the day?"

"They are just discussing whether or not to run through the big company numbers again."

"Like it'll help."

"Have you seen Ernie?"

"No. But it's creep agents like him who ruined my career."

"I thought you said you quit the theater."

Blanche threw me a look brimming with hostility. "I left because I realized show business was full of manipulators and creeps."

"Does that include Royce?"

"Royce and I were fabulous together. Everyone on Broadway knew we were a package deal."

"Then why did you come home?" I thought I saw a flash of annoyance in Blanche's eyes, and then it was gone.

Blanche rubbed her arm and adjusted her sling. "I started getting offers that Royce wasn't getting and it put a strain on the partnership. I didn't want to ruin a friendship, so I took a sabbatical."

"So, you were planning to return sometime?"

"At first. But then Royce moved to work with the Royal Shakespeare Company. I fell in love and got married. End of story."

That last bit was delivered without much conviction. "If you were a package deal, weren't you upset when Royce left New York to go to London? Do you blame him for killing your acting career?"

Blanche turned on me and spat out the words, "No, I don't blame Royce. I blame Virginia Frankowski."

Crap. Out of the corner of my eye, I spotted Ernie getting into a car and driving off. He must have gone out the emergency exit while I was talking to this hot mess.

Blanche poked me with her good arm, then winced.

"This was supposed to be my big comeback and she ruined it for me!"

"Your comeback? From the Senior Center play? How was that gonna happen?"

Blanche sneered. "You're as stupid as your aunt, you know that. Ernie Frick is a talent agent. He was going to be so impressed watching me perform that he signed me on as a client. But Ginny made sure that wouldn't happen. I'll never forgive her for this." Blanche was wild-eyed by the end of her rant and her nostrils were flaring. "She's going to get hers, though, don't you worry about that." Blanche turned and strode down the sidewalk toward the parked cars, holding her sling with her good arm.

I don't know which one dodged a bigger bullet. Blanche or Ernie.

"Poppy!"

Oh no. Here came Aunt Ginny and the biddies. Practice must be over.

Mrs. Dodson pointed to the parking lot. "Was that Ernie we saw leaving?!"

"Um . . . yes, I believe it was."

Mother Gibson gave me a sweet smile. "Did you talk to him?"

I could feel their beady little eyes boring into mine. "I got caught up with another . . . situation."

Mrs. Davis patted me on the back. "It's okay. I'm sure you'll have a chance to talk to him tomorrow."

Oh. Okay. This was going much better than I'd expected. "Thank you, ladies, for understanding. It's not like he's going anywhere. He's booked his room until the fifteenth."

Aunt Ginny grinned at me. "Honey, could you please take us to the drugstore? I need some corn pads and Thelma's out of denture cream."

Mrs. Dodson chimed in. "I'd like to pick up some of that Metamucil too."

"Sure." They were taking it easy on me, so the least I could do was take them to CVS.

We piled into my car with Mother Gibson in the passenger seat and the other biddies smooshed in the back. They were very quiet; then Aunt Ginny said, "Turn left up here."

"That's not the way to CVS."

"CVS doesn't carry my brand of denture cream," Mrs. Davis said.

"And I have a coupon," Mrs. Dodson added.

I turned left as Aunt Ginny directed. "Which drugstore are we going to, then?"

"I don't think you know it." Mother Gibson smiled at me.

I had an uneasy rolling start to form in my stomach.

"Turn right!" Mrs. Dodson practically shouted from the back seat.

I jerked the wheel to the right and the car screeched into the turn. "Okay, a little more notice next time, please." We drove a few more minutes and I kept glancing in the rearview mirror. "What are you all doing back there? Playing a game?" Aunt Ginny was huddled over a cell phone and Mrs. Dodson and Mrs. Davis were scrunched up next to her.

"Take this left! Take it now!" Aunt Ginny was waving her arm madly.

I slammed on the brakes and waited for an oncoming truck to pass us. Mother Gibson was holding on to her purse as if it were an airbag. I turned left down a gravel road, and at the next driveway, Mrs. Dodson said, "Stop! This is it."

We were at a long, brown building with a flat roof. There were only a couple of windows, one on either end, and they were covered in blackout paper. Next to the front door there was a neon sign for Coors that was flickering like a bug zapper in a swamp. "Whaaaat? Where are we, ladies? No way this is your drugstore."

I looked in the rearview mirror and Aunt Ginny gave me a toothy grin. "You can wait in the car if you want."

Two Harleys pulled into the gravel lot and parked next to the row of chrome hogs. The bikes rocked side to side as their leather-clad drivers dismounted and took off their helmets. "You're going in there?" I asked the biddies incredulously.

They all nodded, straight-faced.

"For what?"

"To question Ernie." Aunt Ginny spoke like she was telling a five-year-old to wash their hands for dinner."

"Ernie?"

Mrs. Dodson took a breath. "It's time for guerrilla tactics, Poppy."

Mrs. Davis gave me a sweet smile. "You failed in your mission to talk to him, dear. This is Operation Shock and Awe."

Chapter Thirty-Seven

*O*kay. *I didn't realize I was the one to be shocked and awed or I would have devised a contingency plan. Or at least bought a milkshake to buck up my nerves.*

I looked around the car. Mother Gibson shrugged and tipped her head, like I should have known this was going to happen.

"How do you even know Ernie's here?" I asked them.

Aunt Ginny held up her cell phone. "Because while he was in the men's room we installed a Friend Finder app on his phone. We've been tracking him."

Her phone showed a GPS map with a blinking red light in our location. I felt myself starting toward hysteria. "You can't go in there, ladies. It looks like a seedy dive bar. People aren't in there drinking tea and knitting."

"We know that." Mrs. Davis shook her head.

"We aren't afraid," Mrs. Dodson added.

"That's what has me the most worried. You probably should be afraid."

Aunt Ginny reached across Mrs. Dodson. "Well, I'm going

in there. I didn't come all this way to sit in the car and moan about it."

"Stop." I held up my hand.

Aunt Ginny looked at me expectantly.

Why, why, why? "I'll go. If you all promise to stay here until I get back. I'll see if I can find Ernie and ask him some questions."

The ladies consulted one another and agreed that I could go in—but "only if you leave the channels of communication open," Mrs. Dodson said.

"How do you expect me to do that?"

Aunt Ginny held up her phone. "Call me. Then put your phone on Speaker. I'll mute mine."

Mrs. Davis pointed at my phone. "But don't shove your phone down your pants or we won't be able to hear anything."

I looked from one face to another. "Where did you all learn to be this devious?"

Mrs. Dodson answered. "Honey, we've lived through the fear of being bombed by the Russians, race riots, Vietnam, Nixon, Watergate, and Bill Clinton."

Mrs. Davis added, "But mostly from *Murder, She Wrote.*"

The biddies all nodded in agreement. So I called Aunt Ginny's phone, then I personally put it on mute because, fool me once . . . and I steeled myself to enter the biker bar.

The room was dark, loud, and full of bad decisions and future regrets. Two pool tables sat in a large area on the left. They were currently occupied with a burly contingent of bikers. A stage with a live band was on the right. They weren't the worst I'd ever heard, but I suspected their secret was they sounded better closer to last call. Straight ahead of me through copious amounts of smoke, some of it not yet legal in New Jersey, was a very busy bar with several flatscreen TVs on the back wall. They were showing a football game, a hockey game, horse racing, and a rerun of *Friends*.

I found Ernie wedged in between a very heavy man with quite a bit of plumber's crack showing, and an older woman in a tight red dress who was either very drunk or very cheap. I put my cell phone in the front pocket of my plaid fleece and said, "I've got him. I'm going in."

A chair flew by my head halfway up to the bar and a woman yelled, "Sorry!"

"Ernie Frick?"

Ernie's grin finally disappeared. He blinked at me a couple of times while formulating a cover story. "Hey, Poppy. Fancy meeting you here. I just found this little place today on Yelp. They are supposed to have great wings."

The bartender slapped a receipt on the counter in front of Ernie. "You're paying up front tonight, Frick."

Ernie gave me a hollow smile and pulled out a credit card. I noticed he had a racing form in front of him. "Do you follow the horses?"

He shrugged. "No, not really. Just a little vacation fun."

I believed that as much as I believed that credit card was going to go through. "Do you have a minute? I was hoping I could ask you a couple of questions. Could we sit?" I pointed to an empty table.

Ernie looked at the television. "I don't really have the time right now."

The bartender gave me a chin nod. "There's a two-drink minimum, ma'am."

Ma'am. What the crap? I pulled out a twenty and looked at Ernie. "I only came in for a couple of minutes to talk to my friend and buy him a drink or two, but if he's too busy, I'll just go."

Ernie's eyes lit up and he hopped off his barstool, which was kind of a long way down for him. "Poppy, what's the rush? Come, let's sit." He took the twenty and slapped it on the counter. "Two scotch and sodas, please."

"I don't really drink, Ernie."

"That's okay, they're both for me."

We found a table and Ernie pulled out a seat with a prime view of the horse race. I sat across from him with my back to the bar and hoped I could lure his interest away from the television. He checked his watch. "Okay, what's up?"

"Remember when you told me you were very busy with clients?"

Ernie's grin was back and he nodded like he was laughing at an inside joke.

I pulled the magazine column out of my back pocket and unfolded it. "This fell into my hands today. This says your clients have all left you and some of them are bringing lawsuits. Ernie, you're broke. Why did you lie to me?"

Ernie took a swig of the scotch the bartender placed in front of him. I noticed no change made its way back to me. "It's a setback. A misunderstanding. You know how celebrities can be. They live in a bubble where everyone loves them. They don't understand how much work goes into keeping them relevant. A little sexual misconduct or racist Twitter rant and they become unemployable. Then they want to blame the agent because they aren't getting the roles they want."

The door opened, and four little biddies entered the bar with Agent Rooster in the lead.

Ernie cocked his head again. "Are you okay? You look like you're going to be sick."

I took a deep breath and let it out. "Just a little pain."

Ernie was leaning to look around me to watch the television. I tried to match his lean to bring his focus back to me. "Some people are worried that you're putting Royce in danger. He doesn't appear to be entirely well."

Ernie cocked his head to the side like a bullfrog who had just spotted a tasty fly. "I would never do anything to put Royce in danger. He's my best client."

What in the world? The biddies were chatting up the bikers. They were picking up pool sticks, and Mrs. Davis threw a stack of money on the table. Mrs. Dodson was rubbing one of their tattooed biceps. I had to get them out of here quickly. "I think you mean Royce is your only client, and I thought he just retired. Is that why you've been pushing him to go back to New York for a one-man show. Is it the money?"

Ernie finished his scotch and picked up mine. I felt the fumes burn my eyes. "Royce is very talented. I hate to see a talent like that go to waste."

"What about the flask I keep seeing you pass to Royce? His sister says he's on medication and shouldn't be drinking alcohol."

Ernie was watching the television now. His eyes were bulging and he had that faraway tone to his voice. "Royce is a grown man. He can make his own decisions. He's gotten along all these years without his sister dictating his every move." He started whispering to himself and I could hear other bar patrons joining in. "Come on . . . come on . . . You can do it, baby . . . Yes!"

I turned. We were midrace and the outcome seemed very important to more than a few people in the room.

"What! No no no no no! Come on, Fairy Dust! Nooo." Ernie dropped his head in his hands and I was afraid to speak. He picked up the racing sheet and tore it in pieces. A woman in a purple sweater punched the man next to her in the face and he fell off his barstool.

"I take it your horse didn't win."

"I wish that was all it was."

"Better luck next time."

Ernie snorted like I'd said something sarcastic.

I could see the bikers arguing with the biddies and the hair on my neck started to tingle. I stood up to make a beeline to haul Aunt Ginny and her crew out the door. "One more thing, Ernie. I know that you've been at the Queen Victoria for almost a month even though you said that you'd just arrived.

Have you been sabotaging the play to make Royce think he's in danger?"

Ernie lost his smile again and his little eyes issued a challenge. "Why would I do that?"

"So he'd drop out. Maybe you're desperate enough to scare Royce into returning to Broadway. You clearly need the money, so you created a few accidents. I don't think you were trying to hurt anyone. But things have gotten out of control."

"Be careful what you insinuate. Royce is worth nothing to me if he's hurt. If you're suggesting that I would put Royce's life in danger to make a few bucks, I'm going to be mad. I can make people very unhappy when I'm mad. I could start with Royce's relationship with Mrs. Frankowski. Royce listens to me. All I have to do is tell him to call it off and he will. I don't think your aunt would be very happy with that, do you?" He stood up, grabbed the half-empty glass of scotch, and casually walked back to the bar.

I caught up with the biddies at the pool table, where their stack of money had grown. Aunt Ginny jumped when she noticed me staring her down and she tossed her pool stick to the biker next to her. "What? I don't know how to play pool."

"What's going on here?"

A biker with a long, red beard and a chain going from his ear to his lip gave me a pleading look. "Are these ladies with you, miss?" I had to crane my neck to look him in the eye. He had the name Mousie embroidered on his denim vest.

"I'm afraid so."

"They just conned us out of two hundred dollars."

Mrs. Dodson shrugged. "You knew the terms."

A short biker with a face tattoo practically whined, "But you cheated."

Mrs. Davis shrugged. "You didn't say no cheating."

A man dressed from head to toe in denim wearing a Breton cap replied, "I didn't think we had to say it."

Mother Gibson giggled. "Well . . ."

Aunt Ginny picked up the stack of money. "Now you know."

She started to push past me and I put my arm up. "Ladies, give the nice bikers their money back."

"No, we won it fair and square," Mrs. Davis said.

I cocked my head. "Did you?"

The biker with the red beard chuckled. "They can keep it. But we won't fall for that is-this-how-you-play-pool line again. You old ladies are sneaky."

I mouthed apologies to the bikers and ushered the ladies out to my car. "What happened to the lines of communication? You were supposed to be listening in the car."

Aunt Ginny held up her phone. "That app drained my battery. And Edith had to pee."

Mrs. Dodson said, "Oh rats. I forgot to do that."

Mother Gibson nodded. "And they do like to run a pool table."

"Next time I want you to tell me what you're planning. Don't just lead me on a wild-goose chase. I nearly fainted when I saw you all come in there. What would I do if something happened to one of you?" I started the car and pulled out of the parking lot. I hoped my silence would shame them for tricking me.

I thought Aunt Ginny was remorseful for her actions until she said, "Can we stop by CVS on the way home? I actually do need those corn pads."

Chapter Thirty-Eight

The ladies were raising havoc in the CVS. I waited in the car so they'd be someone else's problem for a few minutes. I turned up "We Built This City" on the radio and stretched my neck from side to side to try to relieve some of the tension they had caused. My cell phone dinged: Ciao! I looked at the screen, and Gia was asking me to stop by for a minute. He wanted me to try a new after-hours drink. Every cell in my body cried out "ruse"! But I caught myself grinning and said I'd be there in a couple of minutes.

The ladies made their way back to the car with the CVS manager carrying several boxes and bags for them. I helped him put their stuff in the trunk and they took their places in the car. "They played the helpless-little-old-ladies card again, I see."

The store manager gave me a weak smile and I nodded back and patted him on the shoulder. I climbed in and told the ladies I had to stop by the coffee shop, but I'd only be a minute. They reassured me that it was no inconvenience. I thought they owed me ten minutes even if it was an inconvenience after what the swindlers had done to me.

I parked in the alley behind La Dolce Vita and went through the back door. Gia heard the bell ring and came back to greet me. "Bella, I missed you today." He pulled me into a hug and kissed the top of my head.

"I missed you too. Boy, it has been a day. I can't stay long. I have Aunt Ginny and the biddies in the car."

"I think I've come up with the perfect Valentine's cocktail and I want your opinion."

The bell jingled at the front of the shop, signaling a customer had arrived.

Gia took my hand and led me to the front. Aunt Ginny and the biddies were taking off their coats and setting to roost at two of the tables.

"What are you guys doing in here? I'm only going to be a minute."

Mrs. Davis threw her scarf and gloves on the table next to hers. "We want coffee."

Gia's warm hand rested on my back just under my neck. I could hear the amusement in his voice. "Go sit down. I will bring the cocktail to you."

"Cocktails?" Aunt Ginny squealed. "We're having cocktails?"

Mother Gibson smiled at the others. "I'll just have a decaf, please. And some of those pink pastries Poppy keeps complaining about."

I blinked a few times, trying to come to terms with what was happening. Gia took the ladies' orders and I helped him get their desserts from the pastry case. By the time he had made all their coffees, Royce had showed up with Fiona and Iggy in tow.

Aunt Ginny patted the seat next to her. "Royce! Over here."

I gave Aunt Ginny a look. "How did Royce know we were here?"

She gave me an innocent head bob. "I have no idea."

Fiona answered. "Ginny called us from the car."

"I was only in here a minute."

"I'm a fast talker."

"Oh, you're not telling me something I don't know." I put the plate of linzer heart cookies on her table, a plate of macarons in front of the other biddies, and took Royce, Fiona, and Iggy's coffee orders.

When I took them over to Gia, he gave me a wink. "We make a good team."

"Yeah? What kind of mental health insurance do you offer?"

"Whatever it is, it's not enough, *cara mia*."

I felt warmth grow from the center of my chest out to my fingertips. I took the coffees out to Royce and his family with a little more lightness in my step.

Royce took his cappuccino and gave it an appreciative sniff. "I will have to make this place one of my regular haunts from now on."

I gave him a grin. "You should give Gia a couple of pictures of yourself in costume from some of your Shakespearean plays. I bet he'd put them up on the wall."

Royce lit up. "I would love that."

Aunt Ginny covered his hand with hers. "That's a wonderful idea, Poppy."

I sat at the table across from Royce. "Since I have you here, I was wondering if I could ask you a question, Royce."

"Sure, anything for Ginny's granddaughter."

"Niece."

He looked at Aunt Ginny in surprise. "She's your niece?"

Aunt Ginny flicked up her eyes to me for a second and took a sip of her cocktail. "Yep."

"Well, how about that."

I nodded and gave him what I hoped was an encouraging smile. "I wanted to ask you about your time in New York on Broadway. Specifically, about working with Blanche."

Royce knitted his brows together and stared at his cappuccino foam.

"Blanche has said that the two of you were a package deal."

He looked up again and there was sadness in his eyes. "We were at first. Before I stabbed her in the back."

The door opened and the bell jingled. It was Sawyer. "I thought I saw you all in here. At least I saw Aunt Ginny's red hair. So I closed the bookstore and came over." She gave me a hug and waved to Gia. He was bringing a tray of sample cocktails over. "What are you all doing here?"

Mrs. Dodson took a pink drink from the tray. "Having cocktails. Join us."

Mrs. Davis giggled. "The more the merrier."

Sawyer knew that if all the biddies were in here with me, it wasn't my idea. She gave me a silly grin and took the cocktail Gia offered her.

Mother Gibson blew on her decaf. "Royce was just telling us about double-crossing Blanche."

"Oh." Sawyer sat at the table with Fiona and Iggy. She noticed Iggy for the first time. He was making an awkward attempt at a smile. She paused for a beat before recovering and returning his smile. Sawyer had always had a tender heart. She was a late bloomer in high school, so she bypassed the mean girl genes that often came with good looks.

Gia pulled up a seat next to me and put his arm around the back of my chair.

Royce took another sip of his cappuccino and continued his story. "Blanche and I had made a promise to each other that we would stick together no matter what. It was a foolish pact we made when we were eighteen." He quickly looked at Aunt Ginny. "It wasn't a romantic pact. Strictly professional. We thought we would be able to get each other parts if we made ultimatums to the directors. It was so arrogant of us to think that we were that talented that casting would bow to our demands. There are thousands of actors trying out for a scant handful of roles. One director offered me the role of Gideon in *Seven Brides for Seven Brothers*. I told him I would only take it if he gave Blanche a part. He laughed in my face and told me never try out for one of his shows again. And there were seven brides to cast. I learned really fast that you can't dictate anything on Broadway."

Fiona tut-tutted. "Blanche was holding you back, dear. You know that. You had plenty of directors tell you that she was no good."

Royce sighed. "I tried for a while to honor our agreement, but I couldn't get any work. No one wanted to cast Blanche. They said she didn't have 'it.' And together, *we* didn't have 'it.'"

"Having the right partner is a must," Gia said. His hand was starting to feel very warm on my back and my neck was getting loosey-goosey.

Royce nodded. "Absolutely. Casting directors said she was lacking in talent and the few roles she did get, she made the wrong kind of name for herself."

"How so?" I asked.

"She was a terror to work with. She'd get a part in the chorus on some off-Broadway production, then make herself a right diva with it. You can't make demands of the producer when you're in the chorus. It isn't done. You can't even do it when you're the lead until you've got some clout behind you." Royce stared off into space, apparently lost in memories, or maybe just lost.

Aunt Ginny gave Royce's hand a pat. "Is that why she came home after only a couple of years?"

Royce came back to us. "Who?"

Aunt Ginny cleared her throat. "Blanche."

"She'd been writing letters to some fella and she left New York to be with him. I heard she got married not too long after that. Frankly, I'm surprised she's been interested in me after the last fight we had. She said I'd ruined her life."

Fiona chimed in. "She used to call the house and demand that we give my brother messages from her. My mother couldn't get her off the phone fast enough. We had to change our number over and over, but she always managed to discover it again."

Mother Gibson nodded her head thoughtfully. "If I remember right, she came home and married Vernon Keller right away. No children. He died not too long after. Sad."

Iggy spoke up, and Sawyer nearly jumped out of her seat. I think she'd forgotten he was there. "Now she has her eyes set on Uncle Royce."

Royce patted his check with his hand. "I never expected to see Blanche when I came home."

Aunt Ginny laughed. "Then you've forgotten just how small this island is."

Fiona sniffed. "Well, that can happen when you're gone for sixty years. We barely saw you except for a couple of holidays."

Royce met Fiona with pleading eyes. "Fee. Actors work on weekends and holidays. It's very hard to have a family life and keep distant relationships. The only night the theater is dark is Monday."

Fiona soured even more. "Well, you could have tried harder. It's not like I could come to you. I was busy raising Iggy."

Mrs. Dodson leaned in to Mrs. Davis. "She'll be raising Iggy till the days she dies."

I was suddenly aware that Gia was rubbing the back of my neck with his thumb. He said, "It must have been hard on you being away from your loved ones for so long. I know how important family is for me."

Aunt Ginny tried to kick me under the table.

Gia said, "Ow." Then he told Aunt Ginny, "You're off by a few inches."

Aunt Ginny blushed, something that happens about as often as she filters what she says.

I got up to clear the empty coffee cups and Mrs. Dodson and Mrs. Davis offered to help me. It didn't take long for the other shoe to drop. They cornered me as soon as we got in the kitchen. "You know, if Royce has a fortune, when he dies it would go to Fiona and Iggy."

"I think I heard that he's leaving it to a community the-ater charity."

"Pshh." Mrs. Dodson tapped her cane. "A family mem-ber could contest that if it came to it. And he's not dead yet. There's still time to convince him that family should come first."

Mrs. Davis leaned in even closer in case she could be heard in the other room. "Maybe that's why Fiona keeps re-minding Royce that he's been gone. To get him to see that he owes her."

"Maybe," I said, "but Fiona claims to be very well-off fi-nancially. I'm not sure she has a secret plan to get Royce's estate. Do we even know if Royce has an estate? Maybe he spent all his money on fancy living in New York."

Mrs. Dodson shook her head slowly. "No, I don't think Fiona is doing as well as she claims to be. For one thing, Iggy keeps trying to discourage her from spending money. Did you see how he wouldn't let her order the large cappuccino? And whenever we're together, he tries to get her to split a sandwich with him instead of ordering her own."

"Maybe he's looking after her health."

Mrs. Davis patted my arm. "Maybe he's trying to make sure that inheritance is there for him one day. We need to find out."

"We need to mind our own business."

The ladies ignored me and strolled back to the dining room. As soon as Mrs. Dodson sat down, she said, "Fiona, I've heard so much about your lovely home and your expertise with entertaining. What a wonderful gift to have. Oh, I have a fun idea."

Oh no.

Fiona raised her painted-on eyebrows.

Mrs. Dodson took that as encouragement to continue. "You should have an afternoon tea to celebrate Royce's return to the shore."

Fiona didn't look too sure of that idea, so Mrs. Davis jumped in to help. "I bet you have some exquisite china, don't you? You always go on about the lovely things your late husband bought for you."

Iggy shifted uncomfortably in his seat. "I don't think now is a good time for that."

"I do." Fiona blushed. "I have the most beautiful set of Royal Albert Yellow Roses."

Aunt Ginny looked from Mrs. Davis to Mrs. Dodson and somehow figured out what they were up to. "And that way we can hear more about the impressive Iggy too."

Fiona sat up straighter and a grin slowly creaked its way across her face. "That would be a wonderful idea. We should do it right after the play is finished."

"Nonsense," Mother Gibson said. "Honey, we're old. We might not have that long. Let's do it tomorrow. I'll bring the cucumber sandwiches."

Et tu, Mother Gibson?

Mother Gibson returned my side-eye with a side-eye of her own. "Poppy will bring some of these pink cookies."

Mrs. Davis and Mrs. Dodson were pleased as punch to have outsmarted Fiona and circumvented me. I could see them plotting something terrifying as they finished their pastries.

Later, Gia and I did the dishes while the biddies finalized plans for their tea party. I filled Gia in on recent discoveries and told him how this tea party was a ruse to snoop around Fiona's house and try to get information about Royce's estate and Fiona's wealth.

He was no help at all because he found it hilarious that I was being *handled* by four senior citizens and they had me backed into a corner.

Sawyer said good night and Royce left with Fiona and Iggy. The biddies went to wait in the car to give me a chance to say good night to Gia. Aunt Ginny said she was timing me and I had five minutes.

Gia gave me a lovely kiss that I was supposed to block. I was so flustered that when I picked up my purse, it tipped over and my old-lady shake fell out. I considered kicking it under the refrigerator before Gia could see it, but he was too quick. He picked it up and handed it to me.

"I forgot that was there. It's not mine."

Gia raised an eyebrow.

"Okay, it is mine, but I bought it by accident. It was supposed to be water." I could feel my face getting hot. "I'm not old."

Gia leaned against the counter with his arms crossed and was giving me enough rope to hang myself.

"I mean, I'm not young anymore, but I'm not old-lady-shake old." I cleared my throat and waited. Outside, Aunt Ginny honked the horn.

Gia laughed. "I think you are just right." He kissed my forehead. "Now take your *nonna* shake and call me tomorrow."

Aunt Ginny honked the horn again.

"If they haven't killed me by then."

Chapter Thirty-Nine

"These Spunks have seen better days."

Figaro sniffed at my tourniquet of delumping.

"I don't think they were intended to be washed every night."

Figaro sat to his full height and blinked at me, which I took to mean, *I don't think they were intended to be stretched to within an inch of their life every day.*

I tried to put on my dress pants without the Spunks, but I still couldn't button them. I considered using rubber bands like a pregnant woman, but the many wardrobe malfunctions I've had over the years flew to my memory like a cautionary tale. *Another day in the sausage casing it is.*

Why isn't this diet working? I could have been eating pizza and not losing weight. I dressed in a pink, flowery blouse appropriate for afternoon tea and finished my hair and makeup. By the time I'd made it to the kitchen to start the breakfast service, Aunt Ginny had fed Figaro and filled the carafe with French press Guatemalan.

"Did you hear the fracas last night?"

I picked up a coffee mug. "No. What happened?"

"Joey and Val had quite an argument."

"About what?"

"Apparently, something went wrong at the massage."

"Oh dear."

I got out my breakfast ingredients. Today I was serving a breakfast version of peach cobbler with custard sauce and baked eggs in ham cups with crème fraiche and herbs. Aunt Ginny liked to keep an eye on the dining room through the crack in the kitchen door and she finally gave me the "go" command. "Three out of four have landed."

I took the peach cobbler in to the table, and Aunt Ginny followed me with the custard sauce. Joey was sitting at the table by himself looking a little worse for the wear. "Good morning. Will Val be joining us?"

Joey's eyes wouldn't meet mine. "She don't feel good this morning."

"Oh, I'm sorry. Does she need anything?"

"No. She'll be all right."

Georgina flounced into the dining room wearing a black leotard, white tights, a one-shouldered pink sweatshirt, and pink leg warmers. She had her hair piled up and held together with a sweatband. I was sure Georgina had never worn a sweatband a day in her life.

Aunt Ginny brought in the baked eggs, took one look at Georgina, and almost knocked over the cranberry juice.

Georgina took her seat at the head of the table. "Good morning, everyone. I need a good breakfast today, Poppy. It's going to be a grueling practice."

"Sure. And you've got that big shower finish to get through."

Georgina blinked at me a couple of times with her baked egg on the way to her plate.

"If you want to practice, I can spray you with the hose in the kitchen."

I saw the tiniest flicker of a grin on Joey's face.

My cell phone buzzed in my apron pocket and I gave Georgina an innocent smile. I handed Bunny the list I had put together of possible homes to visit. "Here are a few places that would love to give you a tour. Just call them when you're on your way and they'll be ready for you."

"Thank you, Poppy. We can't wait to get into some of these, can we, Chigsie?"

Chigsie didn't look up from his newspaper. "Yes, dear."

On the way back into the kitchen, I noticed Figaro sitting on the top shelf of the curio cabinet next to a statue of a Siamese, frozen in place like he was trying to blend in. His orange vest had turned around backward, and he had one paw sticking out of the neck hole. I hoped none of the guests had noticed him and I made eyes at Aunt Ginny. I rolled my eyes over to Figaro, who didn't twitch a whisker.

Aunt Ginny walked over, tucked his paw in, spun his vest around, then picked up the empty coffee carafe and went through the kitchen door, leaving him there like a bookend.

That wasn't exactly what I'd had in mind. My cell phone buzzed again. When I got back in the kitchen, I checked my messages. Three missed calls from Tim and a selfie from Sawyer, posing with ten roses and a scented candle. I sure hoped Adrian would be able to fulfill these unspoken promises he was making.

I called Tim while I had a minute, before the next carafe of coffee was ready.

He answered on the first ring. "Hey, gorgeous."

"Good morning."

"First of all, I'm crazy about you."

I giggled. "O-kay. I think you're pretty neat too."

"Second, I know Valentine's Day is Saturday."

"Yeees." *I hope he isn't about to ask me out for the same time I'm supposed to go to dinner with Gia. See, this is why I didn't want to get involved with both of them. I'm not made out to be a player . . .*

"I'm sorry I won't be able to take you to dinner or anything."

Oh.

"This one's a double whammy, being a holiday and a Saturday."

"Oh right. I guess you'll be pretty busy."

"We've been booked solid for it for a month. We can't even take a walk-in. But you can come hang out with me if you want. I might not be able to really pay attention to you because we'll probably be in the weeds all night, but I'd love to have you here."

"You know, that's okay." *If I was a jerk, I'd tell him I have plans with Gia.* "Don't worry about me. We can do something after the holiday."

"I knew you'd understand. You get what it's like to be a chef."

I swelled with pride. If he was trying to butter me up, he was on the right track.

"There is one thing I need to talk to you about."

"What's that?"

"You know those bad reviews you've been getting?"

"The ones that're keeping me awake at night? Haven't seen them."

"Well, they've kind of jumped over to Maxine's now."

The bottom fell out of my good mood. "Are you kidding me?" I put him on Speaker and started scrolling through the review sites.

"We've had three in the past week and they're all blaming the desserts as the problem."

"Do you see what I mean? This isn't a fluke, Tim. This has to be personal. Every place I've made food for is getting bad reviews all of a sudden. Someone is out to destroy me. Do you think it's a rival bed-and-breakfast?"

"Well, let's not get carried away yet. I'm not worried about the reviews because I think they're pure garbage. All we get in-house is praise for your stuff. I've had to put the kibosh on the staff from eating the desserts because we're running low as it is. Chuck can't stay out of that mousse."

In the background, I heard Chuck. "It's like peanut butter crack."

I would have giggled had I not been so miserable. CWKlinger left Maxine's Bistro one star saying, "This was the worst cheesecake I've ever had. Whose idea was it to put chocolate and Grand Marnier together?" *Then why did you order Grand Marnier chocolate cheesecake, CWKlinger, you idiot! It wasn't exactly a surprise.*

Tim purred comforting words. "I don't want you to be upset by this, Mack. I just wanted you to hear it from me first. We're going to figure this out together."

Aunt Ginny put a cup of coffee down in front of me and I gave her a grateful smile.

"Thanks, Tim."

"On another note, do you think I could put in a big order with you for the weekend?"

I laughed to myself. "Are you sure you want to use me in light of the reviews?"

"Hey, if people didn't love your desserts so much I wouldn't have to keep begging for the goods."

I smiled. "Okay, lay it on me."

"So how about four cheesecakes—two chocolate orange and two white chocolate raspberry—two trays of crème brûlée, three peanut butter mousses, and I need a big-finish dessert. What do you think?"

"I'd go with Strawberries Romanoff Shortcake. I've already got the orange liqueur, so I can macerate the berries for you. I can make a sheet pan of vanilla bean pound cake, and you can have Carlos—*the sommelier*—flambé them before spooning over ice cream if you really want to up the wow factor."

"Oh my God, Mack, that's genius. I'll have Chuck deliver the ingredients this morning, plus it'll get him out of my hair for a while—and don't worry about the reviews, I'm on it."

We hung up. *Now* he's on it.

Chapter Forty

The morning had gotten away from me, and I called Tim and told him that he would have to have Chuck swing back to pick up the desserts. I was so far behind schedule that I almost sent Aunt Ginny to Fiona's by herself until Mrs. Galbraith kindly offered to take the cheesecakes out of the oven when they were done.

"I really appreciate your flexibility this week, Mrs. Galbraith."

The older woman flicked her frown up to a straight line, which from her was as good as a smile. "At time and a half, it's no trouble at all."

Oh, right. "Well, you're in charge until Connie can get here tonight to take over."

Aunt Ginny came down the hall dressed in a tea-length, pink satin gown and white opera gloves. She pointed at Fig. "Figaro, you're in charge."

Figaro stretched and attempted to scratch the wicker umbrella basket by the front door. Mrs. Galbraith snapped her fingers. "Stop it!"

Figaro shot up the stairs with his ears flattened and we heard him gallop down the hall in protest as we left for the tea party.

Fiona lived in a little cottage a few blocks off the beach. It was robin's-egg blue with white trim, and there were giant hydrangeas planted on either side of the front porch that would be gorgeous come springtime. She had a pink Valentine's flag hanging next to the front door with two bunnies hugging each other surrounded by hearts. There were statues of bunnies all through the yard. Bunnies on swings, bunnies in wheelbarrows, bunnies under mushrooms, bunnies selling carrots at a farmstand.

Aunt Ginny gave me a wry look. "Someone likes rabbits."

"I would say so."

Fiona answered the door. "We were wondering what was keeping you."

I handed her a plate of chocolate-dipped shortbread. "I'm sorry, I had a rather large order to fill for my friend's restaurant."

"That's okay, I was just about to pour the tea." Fiona led us through a maze of Longaberger baskets and Marie Osmond dolls to a sitting room with floor-to-ceiling curio cabinets overflowing with Precious Moments' figurines, bright Murano glass clowns, and vintage perfume bottles. My eyes had trouble taking in the cornucopia of colors and shapes.

Aunt Ginny whispered, "Holy Mother of God."

There were a few places where I could just make out the blue wallpaper with yellow butterflies peeking out behind massive paintings of Harlequins. There wasn't a bare surface in the room. Every table, shelf, and box window was covered with some kind of collectible, down to the stuffed white Persian in a wicker basket sitting on the faded mauve wall-to-wall carpet.

The other biddies were lined up in a row on a rose chintz sofa, raptly watching our faces with a tenuous hold on their glee, waiting to see which of us would crack first.

Royce stood to hug Aunt Ginny and then hugged me before taking his seat on a folding chair next to Fiona.

I spun in a slow circle, taking it all in. "Wow, Fiona. You have quite the collection of . . . everything."

Fiona produced a brass bell from her voluminous dress pocket and gave it a jingle. "My late husband, Edgar, was very generous. He indulged me in whatever I wanted."

Iggy appeared much like Lurch from *The Addams Family*. Wearing black jeans, a short-sleeved, buttoned-up plaid shirt, and a mustard-colored bow tie. He was clearly not on board with this plan.

"Iggy, bring the sandwiches now, dear."

Iggy trundled back out of the living room in a snit.

Fiona sat on a pink chair shaped like a giant clamshell. "Well, make yourselves at home."

I looked around and decided to move the stack of Fingerhut catalogs off the edge of the love seat so I could sit next to Aunt Ginny.

Iggy returned with a tower of tea sandwiches that would put the Ritz to shame. Cucumber cream cheese, egg salad, cheese with chutney, and little roast beef with horseradish cream on minibaguette rounds. I hadn't expected to be tempted this afternoon and I died a little inside when they passed around the plates. Aunt Ginny was too busy snuggling up to Royce on the other side to feel my pain.

Mrs. Dodson was shifting her eyes back and forth in the direction of the hallway.

What? I mouthed to her.

She made eyes at Mother Gibson, who then touched the statue on the table next to her of twin dolphins jumping over a manatee. "Fiona, is that Capodimonte?"

"Why yes, it is. I just love the detail on the manatee's face, don't you?"

Mother Gibson was looking at the statue like it was a vampire squid. "Yes, I've never seen anything like it."

Mrs. Dodson leaned in to me and through gritted teeth said, "Go check Iggy's room."

"Check it for what?"

"Anything incriminating."

I drained my teacup and went in search of whatever would placate the biddies and keep them from making a scene later. I crept down the hallway toward the sounds of gunfire and explosions coming through the crack of a door. The glow of a huge television illuminated Iggy slumped in a beanbag with a video game controller in his hands. The only other furniture in the room was a low table and the corner piece of an old sectional. Iggy hadn't noticed me, what with the busty alien on screen diverting his attention, so I slinked further down the hall.

Next was a purple bedroom that matched the living room in style and substance. This was obviously Fiona's. There was so much to look at. My eyes darted from porcelain dolls to Beanie Babies to wooden angels to Winnie the Pooh china. There were even a few packages that hadn't been opened yet sitting next to the bed. I felt a migraine coming on. Also, I kind of wanted a grape Nehi.

I forced myself to shut the door and keep going until I found a neat and tidy bedroom with one queen bed, a matching dresser and nightstand with a model of the Starship *Enterprise*, and in the corner, a little desk. I glanced back down the hallway to make sure that Iggy was still occupied in his space battle and crept into the room and over to the desk.

Iggy had been in the process of balancing Fiona's checkbook and doing the bills. The checking account was in the negative by a couple of hundred dollars. It was easy to see where the problem was. The credit card statements read like the inventory of an Amazon warehouse. Line after line of small purchases to the Home Shopping Network, Figi's, Harry & David, Seventh Avenue, and the Franklin Mint. You name it, Fiona bought it.

I leafed through the stack of bills sitting next to the checkbook and saw that the mortgage was past due. I gently placed it back on the desk and my eyes caught the edge of something familiar peeking out from under a Roaman's Plus Size Clothing catalog. I slid the women's catalog to the side and revealed an insurance policy with MetLife. I unfolded it to the declarations page and read. The insured was Royce Hansen in the amount of $250,000, and the beneficiary was listed as Fiona Sharpe.

"Who said you could come into my room?"

I jumped and fumbled the policy. I tucked it, unfolded and sloppy, under the stack of bills and grabbed a bobblehead doll from the top of the desk and spun around. "Is this your room? I'm so sorry. I got lost looking for the bathroom and my eye caught your fabulous little . . ." *What the heck is this? A baseball player?* "Bobblehead. I collect these too. Is this one Derek Jeter?" *I hope Derek Jeter is a baseball player. Or at least a real person.* I had no idea where that name came from.

Iggy snatched the bobblehead from my hands. "It's Luke Skywalker. Why are you touching my things? Were you going through my bills?"

"No. Not on purpose."

"Then why are they all messed up? I had them perfectly

lined up with the grain of wood." He patted them back into a perfect stack.

Psycho. "You see, what had happened was, I came in to look at your Luke Skywalker guy and accidentally knocked your papers off your desk." I ran my hand down my hip and tried to look seductive and not desperate. "Sometimes these things have a mind of their own."

Iggy's eyes narrowed to slits that would give Fig a run for his tuna.

Seduction fail. "I picked them up and thought I'd put them back the way you had them. I'm so sorry if I got them out of order."

Iggy leaned in close to my face to try to see the back of my retina. My ophthalmologist stood further away when she was checking for glaucoma. I felt a trickle of sweat run down the center of my Spunks. I reached out and flicked the bobblehead and said in my most awkward Darth Vader wheeze. "Luke . . . I am your father."

Iggy was not amused. He spun like a revolving door and pointed to the hall. "Get out. If I find you in here again, I'll call the police and have you arrested for trespassing."

I made it to the hall and turned around. "I don't think you can be arrested for trespassing in one room when you're an invited guest."

Iggy slammed the door in my face.

I took a step back. *Whoa. That was all kinds of weird.*

Then a little bell rang, and Iggy's door flew open again. He grabbed my arm and marched me down the hall to the living room.

Fiona didn't see anything unusual about her precious baby boy manhandling a guest, even though manhandling is definitely not proper afternoon tea party etiquette. "Please bring in the scones, Ignatius."

My trajectory flopped me next to Aunt Ginny on the love

seat and I rubbed my arm. Iggy had a much more volatile temper than I would have pegged him for. I had half a mind to file a complaint with the Emily Post Institute.

Aunt Ginny gave me a raised eyebrow and said nothing.

The biddies enjoyed their fancy tea biscuits while my stomach growled. I took a strawberry from the side of the plate and popped it into my mouth. It would have been better cooked into jam and spread on a scone, but whatever. Fiona was droning on about Iggy's master's degree in electrical papier-mâché or some such nonsense, but I couldn't shake my thoughts from that life insurance policy. The question that kept rolling around in my head wasn't why Fiona was the beneficiary for Royce; she was his sister. The question was why did Iggy have the policy on his desk next to all those overdue bills? And why did someone who wore the same shirt with a hole in the armpit for three days in a row suddenly turn into Rain Man when money was involved?

After the sweets course, where I scarfed down one of my gluten-free shortbread cookies. Or maybe three. I was sure I'd worked off at least four cookies' worth of calories just staying alive at Fiona's house for two hours. In fact, I ate the fourth cookie and called it even.

I thought I might have to fake an injury to escape, but it was finally time to leave for dress rehearsal. It was an exciting night for the biddies and they were abuzz about the final practice before their "big debut." They kept snickering to themselves, and the more they snickered, the more nervous I became about what they might have planned.

Aunt Ginny left me in the foyer to powder her nose. I hoped she wasn't going to try to get into Iggy's room. She'd never make it past Fiona's purple nightmare. But a minute later, she raced past me. "Fiona, thank you for a lovely tea. You have a lovely home. We'll have to do it again sometime.

Bye." Aunt Ginny rushed down the porch steps and hot-
footed it to the car.

I turned and gave Fiona a weak smile. "Thank you for
your gracious hospitality." I hoped she'd remember those
words when Iggy filled her in on my scouting mission down
the hall. I pulled away from the curb and gave a final wave
to Fiona, who was watching from the front door. Two windows down, I was being grilled by Little Lord Fauntleroy
himself.

Chapter Forty-One

Aunt Ginny recoiled from the passenger window. "Whoa, what'd you do to him?"

"Touched his bobblehead."

"I hope that isn't what it sounds like."

"If it was, I'd be bathing in peroxide right now. Why'd you fly out of there like the place was on fire? You didn't start another fire, did you?"

"You're going to have to let that go sometime."

"Not today."

"I spotted something while the rest of you were being hypnotized by those Marie Osmond dolls."

"Their eyes kept following me. I think that house was designed by the Russians for sensory overload training."

"That would explain why Iggy hasn't managed to escape. Maybe he has Stockholm syndrome."

"I don't even want to talk about Iggy. My arm still hurts."

Aunt Ginny pulled a framed photo out of her purse. "Look what I found."

"You stole something from Fiona's house?"

"It will take years before she notices it's missing."

I glanced at the picture, then crawled to a stop in the middle of the road. Calm down. It's February in Cape May. Rush hour is three seagulls in a crosswalk. "Is that who I think it is?"

Aunt Ginny nodded. "I was so surprised, I dropped a cucumber down my dress. I still have to fish it out when I get home."

"We have to ask her about this."

"I doubt she'll tell the truth. They obviously kept it hush-hush."

"Y'all said Duke wasn't seeing anyone, but here he is, cozied up with Fiona at some restaurant, and not that long ago from the looks of it. I want to know why she didn't mention this when we found that suicide note."

Aunt Ginny took the picture from me so I could drive. "I want to know how he went on a date with Fiona without Iggy sitting in between them."

We made a quick pit stop at home so we could change. I had to get on my black pants, black T-shirt, and black shoes—the official uniform of backstage crew. Aunt Ginny rushed off to change into her Donna overalls and I checked email while I waited. Another troll had left me a bad review for the Butterfly Wings B&B. I didn't have time to deal with it right now, so I tossed my phone in my tote bag. Joey and Val came in holding hands and giggling. They'd obviously made up, thankfully. The last thing I needed was a review that my house split up marriages.

Aunt Ginny finally emerged, and we said goodbye to Connie, who was graciously covering the B&B for a couple of hours, and headed to the Senior Center. We were the last to arrive. Everyone else was in the auditorium. Royce was leading the actors in a few vocal exercises, Bebe was warming the dancers up for their first company number, and Neil was consulting with Mother Gibson over props and stage directions.

I dropped my tote bag in a seat and took the picture from Aunt Ginny.

She was reluctant to let go of it. "What are you going to say to her? You're not going to tell her I stole it, are you?"

"I might tell her you're a kleptomaniac. It wouldn't be your first time, would it?" I issued a challenge with my eyes.

Aunt Ginny blushed to the roots of her dye job. "I'm sure they have a yardstick in the craft room if you're getting too big for your britches," Aunt Ginny issued a challenge of her own.

We narrowed our eyes and glared at each other. "Well played, old lady."

Aunt Ginny winked at me and sashayed down the aisle to find Royce.

I went and sat next to Fiona. She looked up from her crochcting. "I hope Iggy wasn't rude to you this afternoon. He hasn't had many girlfriends, plus he was an only child, so he never really learned how to share his toys."

Does she think I'm Iggy's girlfriend? "No, he was fine. I think he stayed in his room most of the time."

She shook her head. "I told him he's never going to find a wife if he spends all day playing Space Wars."

I wanted to tell her that the video games were probably not Iggy's biggest problem in finding a wife. Very few women were going to be attracted to a forty-year-old man who still lived with his mother, but I refrained. I was still stinging from Aunt Ginny's fat joke.

I handed the photo to Fiona. "Mrs. Sharpe, I have an embarrassing confession to make. I think I accidentally knocked your picture into my tote bag when I was at tea. I just wanted to apologize and return it."

Her eyes softened, and she touched the glass with a gnarled

finger. "Oh, look at him there. This picture is almost five years old. That was our first date, you know."

"You look happy together."

"He was such a gentleman. He took me to dinner and to see three of the Four Tops at the Tropicana in Atlantic City. I didn't know at the time that Duke hated casinos. After he'd been on the vice squad he didn't want anything to do with gambling. He said it was like taking his work home with him. He was a lifer, you know."

"What's a lifer?"

"Being a cop was the only job he ever had. He joined the force straight out of high school. He told me he'd covered just about everything. Robberies, murders, runaways. Once, he got called for a seagull trapped in a house." She chuckled at the memory.

"Did many people know you were going out?"

"No. He was a very private person. And we only dated on and off for about a year, but it didn't go anywhere."

"Were you the one who called off the relationship, then?"

Fiona looked back down at her bright orange yarn and started whipping her crochet hook through the little holes. "No. Duke said he was looking for a companion who could take off at any time and go anywhere. I'm a single mother and Iggy takes a lot of my attention, I can't be footloose and fancy free."

I felt a wave of sadness for Fiona. She could have had love again, but she was afraid to take the leap. "I'm sorry."

She gave me a bright smile. "It was a long time ago."

Neil finished running the actors through warm-ups and told everyone to take their places to begin final rehearsal. I got set up in the light booth with my headset, my script, and my booklight so I could read my script, and I was adjusting the dial to the moonlight setting for the show opening. I noticed a pink scrap of paper stuck on the side of the cage. I pulled it off and read, "You were warned."

What? . . . Is someone threatening me? I looked around the cage to see if there were any more notes stuck elsewhere or maybe fallen on the floor. There was a puddle forming under my feet. It was coming through the stage curtain and heading toward a frayed electrical cable from the light board that was skimming the floor. My last thought was, *this is gonna hurt.* I saw a flash and smelled burning rubber. Then everything went black.

Chapter Forty-Two

I didn't feel pain. I felt anger. Anger and hunger. Partly because I'd only eaten four cookies and a strawberry, and partly because I thought I smelled bacon. Aunt Ginny was hovering over me and snapping her fingers in my face. "Poppy. Poppy."

The biddies reminded me of the three good fairies from *Sleeping Beauty*, tutting and fretting and muttering to each other.

And Georgina pushed her way past Aunt Ginny to take my shoulders and shake me until my head flopped back and banged the floor. "Stay with me, Poppy. Say something."

"Did somebody try to kill me? Because if I find out someone tried to kill me and I didn't eat any of those scones, I'm going to be super pissed."

"She's delirious. Give her some room."

"I am not delirious. I'm furious." I pulled myself up, using the chain links of the cage. There was a pile of shop towels on the floor mopping up the water and the lights were out. I pointed to the shop towels. "Whose water was that?"

Everyone looked at one another like I was speaking Chinese. "I said, whose water was that!"

Aunt Ginny took my arm. "Honey, no one saw anything. Lila saw the spark and then you were thrown to the back of the cage."

Mother Gibson helped Aunt Ginny lead me to a seat. "We turned off the power and called the rescue squad. They're on their way."

"I don't need the rescue squad!" I was shouting, and there was a loud buzzing in my ears, and I smelled like bacon. I was really annoyed.

Neil came over with the first aid kit and applied ice to the back of my head. "You're bleeding. You must have cut yourself when you hit the cage. You'll probably need a tetanus shot." He flinched and leaned far away from me. "Ginny?"

Aunt Ginny reappeared. "Yeah, she's pretty mad. What do you need, honey?"

I thought for a few seconds, then gave my list of demands. "I need coffee. Not that crap in the lounge either. Someone go to Wawa and get me an extra-large medium roast with cream and sugar. And I want a sandwich. Get an Italian hoagie from the deli while you're there."

Mrs. Davis squatted down next to me. "Honey, you can't have gluten, remember?"

That was not what I wanted to hear. I was about to make more demands when a very good-looking EMT gave me a smile. "What happened here?"

"I need a sandwich."

He nodded his head. "I think she's in shock."

They took my vitals and wrapped me in a blanket, which I thought was stupid because I wasn't cold. After a while, Mr. Ricardo arrived with my coffee.

"Thank you. See, you I like."

Then he handed me a wrapped, gluten-free chocolate cupcake and my opinion of him skyrocketed. I was so excited that I announced to the room, "It's okay! I have cake." Cake that I shoved into my mouth, chipmunk-style. As I gnawed through the frosting, my thoughts swirled. Angry thoughts. Revengey thoughts. Thoughts of punching somebody in the throat. *I know somebody messed with that light panel. Water doesn't spill itself. I keep trying to mind my own business and these old ladies suck me back in. I'm not a cop. Why can't they accept that? There's not a thing I can do to bring justice for Duke, and now I've made somebody mad enough to try to electrocute me. I'm a nice girl. Nice girls don't get electrocuted.*

My thoughts went to Iggy and how mad he was that I'd been in his room. *I'm probably the only girl who has been in that room for ages. He should have been grateful. Of course, there's also Ernie Frick, who I cornered while he was losing money on the horse race. He threatened me, then he drank my whiskey. And the two big guys who are always down in front. I forget their names again. Fred and Barney? That sounds right. Where are they right now? And Blanche threatened me. Well, actually, she threatened Aunt Ginny. That's okay, I'll add her to the list anyway.*

"You okay, McAllister?"

"Uhhck." *Amber.*

"It's nice to see you too."

"I ate all the cake."

"Uh-huh." Amber turned and spoke with Neil and Aunt Ginny. She was holding the pink scrap of paper from the cage. "And no one saw anything strange? No one lurking around the light booth?" Aunt Ginny and Neil shook their heads and she asked them some more questions about my behavior over the past few days.

Amber crouched in front of me. "You know, you bring this on yourself. What were you and the fossil squad up to that someone would try to hurt you this time?"

"They hustled some bikers playing pool, so I gave them magazines to read."

"Fine, don't tell me."

"Did you check for fingerprints?"

"Check what, McAllister?"

"The cables, the water bottle."

Amber folded her hands together under her chin. "There is no water bottle."

"That's not possible. Then where did the water come from?"

Amber shrugged, then got up and rejoined Aunt Ginny and Neil.

The cute EMT came back and asked me if I wanted to go to the hospital.

"I do NOT want to go to that place."

He smiled. "Okay. Well, I want you to take it easy for a few days. You're very lucky. Your rubber girdle absorbed most of the shock. You're bruised, but you'll be okay."

My girdle? I blew on my coffee and contemplated moving back to Waterford.

"Are you sure you're okay, ma'am? You look pale and your eye is twitching."

"It does that sometimes." *Like when people call me "ma'am."*

He begrudgingly agreed to let me stay and made me sign a paper saying I'd turned down his generous offer for an inflated medical bill. Everyone left me alone until I finished my coffee. Mostly because I glared at anyone who came near. I was starting to feel a little more like myself, albeit a less enthusiastic version than I was this morning. Aunt Ginny took me to the bathroom and cut my Spunks off me with craft scissors. The stomach panel had fused together like a radial tire and I smelled like the vacuum when the belt slips off the roller and overheats.

"Are you sure you want to do this?" Aunt Ginny handed me a wet wipe from her purse and I rubbed it over the tread marks. "No one would blame you if you quit now. We could just leave the lights on one setting the whole time."

"No, I'm in it with you till the end. But I don't think those lights are going to work. Some of the cables were pulled out and stripped. I'm pretty sure that's bad. And I'm not going back in there until it's fixed."

"Well." Aunt Ginny made a face. "While you were drinking your coffee and growling at people, Iggy was rewiring the light board."

"Say what now?"

"Didn't you hear Fiona say he has a master's degree in electrical engineering?"

"No. I tune out whenever Fiona mentions *Iggy*."

"Apparently, he not only has it fixed, but he's made a couple of upgrades."

"How do we know I wasn't just on the receiving end of one of his upgrades?"

Aunt Ginny sucked in her cheeks. "We don't know, honey."

I marched out of the ladies' room and found Iggy sitting at the piano. "Did you tamper with the light board because I was in your room?"

He had the nerve to look at me like I was the crazy one. "What? No. And I just fixed it for you."

"Yeah, I heard you have a master's degree. How do I know you aren't the one who rigged it to electrocute me in the first place?"

Iggy gave half a laugh. "You don't need a degree to pull wires out and pour water on them. Besides, we were both at my house all afternoon."

"You got here before me. How long does it take to cut some wires?"

I wanted to rip into Iggy some more, but he had a master's degree in alibis.

Neil took me by the hand and led me away. "Okay, dear. I know you've had a terrible shock. Oh, sorry. Poor choice of words. Are you sure you're all right? We really need to start dress rehearsal now. Why don't you sit in the audience until you're ready to join us?"

Neil went to lead the actors in some warm-up exercises while I fumed from my seat. In two weeks, there had been four injuries and a death. Royce, Duke, Blanche, Aunt Ginny, and now me. If we chalked the death up to an accident or suicide, which I didn't think it was, that was still way too many injuries to be random. The biddies were right: someone was deliberately trying to shut down the play and enough was enough. I had to figure out who was behind these accidents before they had a chance to make another one occur, or one of the biddies "investigated" the wrong place at the wrong time and had an accident of her own.

None of the seniors had any reason to want to shut down the play as far as I could tell. They'd worked too hard on it. Blanche would like to see it fail now that she wasn't in it, but she'd been hanging out here every day hoping Aunt Ginny would get hurt so she could have her part back.

Fiona would love to have Royce stay home with her, but I didn't think she wanted it badly enough to harm anyone. And I didn't think she'd be able to accomplish most of the sabotage by herself.

Iggy was certainly capable. And that life insurance money could pay a lot of late bills and keep them from losing their house. But Fiona had Iggy on a short leash and I didn't think he would have been up here without her.

Could they have planned it together? Fiona was living in a fantasy world where butterflies were made of gold and nickels grew on rosebushes. But she clearly idolized her brother. If Iggy was out to kill Royce for the life insurance, Fiona would have no part in it. No, something didn't feel right about it being the two of them.

And I knew something was off about Royce. Could all of that doddering be an act to cover his sabotage? But what did he have to gain?

No one had less of a motive to kill Royce, and more of a motive to scare him into quitting the play, than Ernie. He'd love to get Royce back to New York, where he made a commission on him. And just where was Ernie Frick tonight when I was being barbecued?

I walked over to the gorillas in the front. "Finkle, Winny, outside. We need to talk." I went out the emergency exit and the men extracted themselves from their tiny seats and followed me.

"You okay, little red? That was a pretty big owie you got back there. You want Finn to go have a talk with someone?"

"I'm fine. I still smell smoke, but I'm fine. I need to ask you about Ernie."

The two men exchanged looks.

"I know he's a gambler. I assume he owes you or your boss money?"

They stared at me blankly.

"I've seen you out here with him pinned against that wall. I figure you're trying to shake him down to pay his debts."

Finn spoke for both of them. "We cannot confirm or deny these rumors, but let's just say that hypothetically you're right. What will you do with this information?"

"I don't know yet. But it's not about you. I think Ernie's behind all the accidents that have happened in the theater. I think he's been trying to scare Royce back to New York, where he makes a sizable commission from his performances. Do you know when Ernie arrived in Cape May?"

Winky answered. "About a month ago."

Finn shrugged. "We heard that Royce Hansen was in the

musical, so we tracked Ernie here. We knew he'd eventually show up and we could encourage him to pay Big Louie back."

"How much money does Ernie owe Big Louie?"

Winky answered. "About two hundred Gs."

"Whoa. Have you ever seen Ernie hanging around the Senior Center by himself?"

"His car was here this afternoon when we arrived, but we didn't see him with a saw or catch him sabotaging anything if that's what you're hoping for."

"What about last Thursday, the day Duke died? Ernie didn't officially show up until Friday, but could he have pushed Duke off the catwalk while we were all at lunch?"

They both shook their heads. Finn answered, "We didn't see him all day. He was probably holed up at that dive bar he's been hanging out in."

"Where is he now?"

"In the wind. But he'll show by tomorrow night. As long as Royce is here, Ernie won't be far behind."

I looked the men over. "If Ernie isn't here, why are you?"

Finn answered. "We told you, we're big fans of musical theater."

Winky pulled his cell phone from his back pocket and pulled up the *Backstage Pass Theater Blog*. "I promised my readers I'd post about Royce's debut with the Senior Center. We have a huge following waiting to see if he'll perform the role as it's written or put the bard's twist on it."

"I don't think he's doing it on purpose. I think he may be ill."

Winky put the phone back in his pocket. "We know. It's been coming on for a while. It's why he retired from the big stage."

Finn heaved a sigh. "Royce Hansen was one of the greats, but nothing lasts forever."

The side door opened and Neil poked his head out. "Poppy? Do you think you feel up to maybe doing the lights for us?"

"No one else is willing to step foot in the cage, are they?"

"No."

"I'll take a look, but if I see any wires or water, I'm going home."

Finn tapped my shoulder. "You don't know us, you never seen us. Forget our names. 'Kay?"

Winky shook his cell phone at his side. "Oh, but please follow our blog. BackstagePass.com."

I looked from one to the other. Finn shrugged. "It's a side business we're trying to get off the ground and there's a lot of competition. Bloggers are cutthroat."

I gave them a silent nod and went back inside.

Neil grabbed my wrist and practically ran up the steps. "Come on, I'll go in first." He led me to the booth and went inside the cage. Everything looked dry and in order. Neil turned on the master switch and turned all the dials up to ten one by one. "You see. It's all fixed."

"If I get even the smallest shock from static electricity I'm coming out of here swinging."

Neil swallowed hard. "I wouldn't blame you."

The biddies kept their distance. In fact, everyone approached with caution. We went through the numbers one after the other without pause. There were no bursts of random Shakespeare or frustrated stage directions. They finally had a handle on the script.

Piglet approached me during the intermission. I had been trying to corner him for days and now that I was locked in a cage, here he was coming to talk to me. "Excuse me, Miss McAllister, is it?"

"I only have a couple of minutes before the actors come back out. What do you need?"

"We haven't been properly introduced, but my name is Terrence Nuttal. I represent the Actors Equity Insurance Overwriters United." He handed me a card and held out a little pink hand for me to shake.

"You couldn't work in a sometimes Y?"

He remained expressionless.

I handed him his card back. "Is this a joke?"

"I assure you it is not. I've been here these past two weeks to oversee the safety of this production."

"Uh-huh. And how's that working out for you?"

"It—it's not." He took out a handkerchief and mopped his forehead. "It's not going well. I've never seen so many accidents on one show."

"What is it you want from me?"

"In light of your misfortune earlier this evening, I have some papers I'd like you to sign. Just a formality, you know. You're obviously in good health, knock on wood." He knocked on the light panel.

"You know that's the equipment that nearly electro-cuted me."

"Oh dear." He jumped back and scurried out of the cage.

The seniors had made their costume changes and were taking their places onstage ready for act two. My time was short, and Mother Gibson was about to raise the curtain, so I just scanned through the papers he'd given me. "These are release of liability forms. You want me to sign saying I won't hold the Senior Center responsible for the attack and sue them?"

"We don't know that it was an attack, per se."

"It melted my Spunks."

"It's just a formality." He took a pen out of his pocket and tried to pass it through the cage. "And it's just for the pro-duction policy. If you want to sue the county, that's your business."

Iggy started playing the music to open act two. "I'm sorry, Mr. Nuttal, but I'll have to get back to you."

His face fell. He returned his pen to his breast pocket. "Okay, then. Please get them back to me as soon as possible.

It's imperative that I have them before the play opens tomorrow night."

He left me alone and I rolled up the papers and shoved them in my back pocket. *So that's what he's been doing here all this time. Making sure no one can make a claim against the insurance policy he's underwritten. I wonder if that's the insurance policy in Neil's office. And what's so significant about tomorrow night?*

Dress rehearsal was fabulous. I thought the seniors would be thrilled, but Royce and Neil were more worried than I had seen them all week. Then there was Blanche, stirring the pot. She gave a standing ovation. "Woo! That was the best dress rehearsal I have ever seen. Congratulations, suckers."

Royce sat on the edge of the stage with his head in his hands and Neil just stood silently looking around like he'd lost his best friend. Aunt Ginny gently shook Royce's shoulder. "What is wrong with you?"

"Will the line stretch out to th' crack of doom?"

Neil answered Aunt Ginny's confused look. "There's an old theater adage that the worse the dress rehearsal before opening night, the better the show will be, and vice versa."

"Well, surely that's just a superstition. Isn't it?"

Neil gave her a weak smile. "Don't worry. I'm sure everything will be fine."

He didn't look sure of anything.

"What in the world do you think that was about?" Aunt Ginny plunged herself into the passenger seat of my car. "They've all given me the heebie-jeebies. I don't care what they say, I was fabulous tonight."

"I think I'll call Amber and tell her about Ernie. I don't trust him. If he's been setting traps to scare Royce out of a local musical that runs for all of two nights, I'm afraid he's desperate enough to keep going. Who knows what kind of time line he's on and what threats he's trying to run from? Finn and Winky seem like nice guys until you're the one whose feet are dangling beneath you."

"Are you listening to me?"

"What?"

"I said I was really good tonight. It's only polite for you to agree with me."

I responded in a flat tone. "You were an acting goddess. You made the role of Donna come alive. Eat your heart out, Meryl Streep."

"Well, you don't have to be so flippant about it."

"My tongue still tastes like metal."

Aunt Ginny patted my knee. "I'm sorry, honey. What can I do for you?"

I pulled into the driveway and parked. "I've got to make a call. Can you tell Connie I had an emergency and I'll talk to her tomorrow?"

"Yes, of course."

While Aunt Ginny went inside, I pulled out my cell phone and called the police station and asked for Officer Fenton. After a minute, I was put through.

"This had better be important, McAllister. I'm on a stake-out."

"I got to thinking after you left about the accidents and how they might be connected."

"Go on."

I filled her in on everything I knew about Ernie Frick. How he was bankrupt, his previous clients were suing him, his gambling problem, and my recent discovery that he owed Big Louie enough money to justify sending in the muscle— although I left Winky's and Finn's names out of the conversation. "Ernie was seen lurking around the Senior Center this afternoon. I'm sure he's the one who sabotaged the light panel and set me up to be electrocuted."

"I think you mean shocked. It's doubtful you would have died from it."

"The bruises on my rib cage disagree with you. And I know you believe Duke's death was suicide, but we really think he fell victim to one of Ernie's traps. The railing on the catwalk was sawed through. And now that I'm thinking about it, Duke was on the vice squad. He probably busted Ernie in one of those backroom gambling dens. What if Ernie killed Duke to enact his revenge, then tried to cover it up by creating the other accidents? Are you laughing at me?"

"I'd be lying if I said no."

"Come on, Amber, you have to see the absurdity of that suicide note."

"It's hardly a smoking gun."

"And we found an ex-girlfriend, but she says Duke did the leaving and that was five years ago."

Amber sighed. "I'll give Officer Birkwell a call and have him pick Ernie up for questioning. Duke's daughter and grandson are coming in tomorrow for a copy of the police report. I want your word that you won't say one thing to them about your conspiracy theories. They've been through enough without having to listen to you."

"Absolutely. I'll stay out of it."

"Good. If that's all . . ."

"Where are you? This connection is fabulous. It's like I'm in the same room with you."

Amber paused. "We have new cell service. I have to go." She clicked off, leaving me more and more convinced that Ernie had killed Duke. I just wished I'd figured it out sooner. Maybe I could have stopped him before so many people got hurt.

Chapter Forty-Three

The next morning, I woke up stiff and sore. The adrenaline had worn off from my vicious attack. My headstone almost read "electrocuted by puddle." The pain had crept its way up my body overnight and Figaro was performing shiatsu on the worst of the bruises. I didn't even try to yank my remaining pair of Spunks over my swelling. I did, however, consider framing them as a memorial.

I did not have the energy to work out, but I did get on the scale to see if it felt sorry that I'd been attacked. It did not. No downward movement there. I picked up the scale, walked to the bedroom window, opened it, and threw the scale out. Then I sent off an email to my new alternative wellness physician, Dr. Melinda, to complain that my body didn't seem to realize that if you eat less and exercise more, weight was supposed to come off. Maybe my fat cells needed hypnothcrapy.

I finally made my way downstairs to get breakfast going. I would be glad when Sunday morning checkout came. I was exhausted. I'd basically been working four jobs. But nothing wore me out more than running interference between disaster and those biddies.

I put on a thick, long-sleeved sweatshirt and retrieved Aunt Ginny's ancient Belgian waffle maker from the hidden pantry at the bottom of the backstairs. It made the most beautiful waffles, but it was manufactured before protective casing and safety regulations. You were expected to be smart enough not to touch it when hot. Clumsy people like me are the reason everything today has a bajillion safeguards built in. I had never once used it without giving myself a third degree burn—hence the sweatshirt.

Aunt Ginny made the coffee while I fed Figaro a can of Luxe roast beef tips with baby carrots and early peas. It slid out of the can in a glop of brown that didn't resemble anything like the description, but Figaro dove on it anyway. Then I showed Aunt Ginny how to form a strip of bacon into the shape of a heart before baking it and filled her in on my conversation with Amber last night.

"Why would Ernie go to all that trouble to get Royce to quit the play this late in the game?" Aunt Ginny waved around a strip of bacon to untangle it. "Tonight is opening night and tomorrow the show closes. What was he going to do? Scare Royce back to New York an hour before the final curtain call? It's not like he'd be working tomorrow."

The front door chimed, and Sawyer came down the hall. Aunt Ginny and I waited for the gift-of-the-day announcement. She came around the corner wearing a giddy smile.

"Well?" Aunt Ginny put her hands on her hips. "Where's the pony?"

Sawyer held up her phone. "Eleven roses and a bottle of champagne. They were waiting outside my door in a basket this morning."

I poured the batter for my first red velvet waffle into the iron and carefully closed the lid. "Did Adrian declare himself yet?"

Sawyer shook her head no. "Not yet. But this is the most romantic thing I've ever heard of. What if he proposes tomorrow?"

Aunt Ginny and I passed a wary expression. "Are you ready for that? You've only known him a few weeks."

Sawyer poured herself a cup of coffee. "No. But it would be fun to be asked. I've only been single for six months and that was after a couple of years of separation and divorce during the great hooker parade that my ex grand marshaled. I don't want to be married again. At least not yet. We haven't even done a lot of serious dating because he's always in that restaurant. What exactly are you making there?"

I looked up from dislodging a dark pink waffle and poured the batter for the next one. "Red velvet waffles with raspberry plum compote and cream cheese drizzle."

Aunt Ginny held up the sheet pan of bacon to show it off before putting it in the oven. "And I'm making bacon hearts."

"Oh man. Is there enough for me too?"

Aunt Ginny nudged her in the side. "The line starts behind me."

"There is if you make me another cup of coffee."

Sawyer laughed. "Done." She took my mug and filled it up. "Did anyone special ask you out for Valentine's Day?"

I gave her a sly grin. "As a matter of fact, Gia and I are going to dinner, but not until Monday night because of the cast party after the play tomorrow night."

Sawyer smiled. "And Tim?"

"Nothing yet. He wants to do 'something,' but not tomorrow because he's booked. He has me making another sheet of pound cake. Carlos flambéed the Strawberries Romanoff and word spread through the dining room and they sold out. Once one guest has flaming fruit tableside they all want it. Plus, I have to go to the coffee shop and make some champagne cupcakes and a large batch of linzer hearts. Gia has orders for a party tomorrow."

Georgina breezed into the kitchen in a pink swing dress topped with a silver cardigan and helped herself to a cup of coffee. "Good morning, everyone. I'm so excited for tonight I'm bursting. How are you feeling, Poppy? Are you going to be all right to do the lights?"

I pried another waffle off the iron and started the next. "I'll be there. I know it's really Neil's job to call Smitty, but I'd feel better if he did a little inspection before we do the mini run-through this afternoon. Do you think you could let him know for me?"

Georgina nodded with her eyes as she sipped her coffee. "Already on it. He's going over this morning. He wants to double-check the work that was done on the light panel so you don't get hurt again."

My heart melted a little. My handyman had become family just as much as my crazy former meddle-in-law.

"Plus, I asked him to make sure everything was working for my performance tonight."

Oh, moment over.

Georgina spied the clock and said, "I'd better get out there so you can start serving."

Aunt Ginny rolled her eyes and shook her head and Sawyer stifled a giggle. Then I got the high sign that Bunny and Chigsie had entered the dining room. We took carafes of juice and coffee in and said good morning.

"How did you enjoy the tours yesterday?"

Bunny clapped her hands. "Beautiful. Just beautiful. Thank you so much for setting them up."

Chigsie looked around his newspaper. "Is the Abbey open all year or are they seasonal?"

"I'll have to find out for you. B&Bs can change their hours as the season dictates, and I don't know what plans they might have."

Chigsie nodded and went back to the finance section.

We returned to the kitchen and I plated waffles drizzled with cream cheese icing and a little custard dish of compote on the side. I placed two hearts of bacon next to the waffle, then I finished with a fanned strawberry on an orange slice and a dusting of powdered sugar. Aunt Ginny and Sawyer were standing there with hands out ready to receive and deliver the dishes.

When they returned to the kitchen, I handed Aunt Ginny the plate for Madame Georgina and she stuck her thumb in Georgina's compote. "Oops." She gave a devilish grin.

Aunt Ginny came back to report that the breakfast was "delightful," and she gave a little bow, making Sawyer and me giggle again.

As soon as Joey and Val were served their waffles, I heard Joey yell, "Sweet!" and Val say, "My gawd, like the cake? Awesome!"

Sawyer started making a plate for her own waffle. "This one's extra, right? You couldn't have two more different couples this week if you tried."

"There's something endearing about Joey and Val. I just think they're so sweet."

"Well, I think they're up to no good." Mrs. Galbraith had arrived and was greeting the day with her usual level of crotchetiness. "I left you a note yesterday that there is something else missing from their room. I'm not familiar enough with the contents yet to be able to put my finger on it, but I think they're stealing from you."

"Good morning, Mrs. Galbraith. Would you like some coffee?"

Mrs. Galbraith looked at me down her nose and over her bifocals. "No, I would not."

Sawyer cleared her throat and sat at the kitchen table to wolverine her waffle just as Aunt Ginny returned to the kitchen. She took one look at Mrs. Galbraith and stopped short. "Oh."

I started to make Aunt Ginny's plate. "I really don't think they're stealing, Mrs. Galbraith. I bet if anything is misplaced it will turn up when they leave. They may have moved things around a bit."

The chambermaid crossed her arms in front of her chest. "I've also noticed the antique silver candy dish is missing from the library. Did you move it?"

I shook my head no and looked at Aunt Ginny. She shook her head no as well. "We haven't moved it."

"Well, it isn't there."

Figaro came from the hall and launched himself at the back of Mrs. Galbraith's uniform. She jumped and hollered, "Aah. Stop it." Then she turned back to me. "You're the boss, Poppy. I'm just warning you that those kind of people can't be trusted. You might want to lock up the rest of the valuables before it's too late." Mrs. Galbraith turned and walked out and down the hall. Figaro ran after the dangling thread hanging off the bottom of her uniform. By the time she got to the end of the hall we heard her yell, and a second later, Figaro came galloping back to the kitchen.

Sawyer looked up from her empty plate. "What does she mean by 'those kind of people'?"

I gave Sawyer a wry look. "She means young."

Aunt Ginny took the plate I offered her and joined Sawyer. "And we've noticed the battle-ax equates low tippers with criminals."

Sawyer looked at me with wide eyes. "Do you think they're stealing from you?"

"No, of course not." I joined her and Aunt Ginny at the table with my coffee and a plate of bacon. "I'm sure they're not."

Aunt Ginny poked her fork at Sawyer. "Make sure you get a good seat for tonight. I don't want you to miss the big finish we have planned."

"Isn't the big finish 'Waterloo'?"

Aunt Ginny gave us a terrifying grin. "Not tonight it isn't."

Chapter Forty-Four

There are some images you can never recover from, no matter how many cat videos you watch on the internet. I had not seen so many old people in their underwear since the movie *Cocoon*. The seniors had designated the large activity room as their changing area and were all in the process of getting into their costumes—I hoped. Why they were changing here I wasn't sure. Some of their costumes were just regular clothes they could have worn from home. One look at Mr. Ricardo in his red satin boxer shorts that said Love Machine over the butt and I was rendered speechless for a good ten minutes. Neil had even brought in a couple of bonus biddies to do hair and makeup.

I went into the little theater and spotted Smitty and Georgina down by the stage. Georgina had dressed at home, thank God. I don't think I could have looked her in the eye had she been in the melee of Cross Your Heart bras and tightywhites. Smitty gave me a hug. "How you doin', Boss?"

"I'm okay. A little sore. A lot sore. How does everything look?"

"I can't find anything broken, sawed, or tampered with, and I've been through it all twice."

"I feel better knowing you've checked." *I must have some brain damage.*

The biddies rushed down the aisle to meet me. "What did you find out?"

I filled them in about my call with Amber this afternoon. "Ernie is in police custody right now. And one of the things they are going to question him about is Duke's death. But there were no eyewitnesses, so they would really need a confession to prove it."

Mrs. Davis rubbed my back. "You're a good girl, Poppy. Be careful tonight just in case that rascal left any traps that we didn't find. Edith and I are going to go run surveillance in the activity room."

"The room where everyone is changing?"

Mrs. Dodson blushed. "Is it?"

While I waited, I decided to run through email. One troll had left another Yelp review. Another had left a Google review for Maxine's. And a third for La Dolce Vita. Oh good, a trifecta of idiots. I was too numb to be outraged at this point. Or maybe that was the brain damage.

"Poppy?"

I looked over my shoulder and saw Officer Birkwell coming down the aisle. "Hey. How's it going?"

"Good. I just wanted to give you an update on Ernie Frick."

"Did he confess?"

He tilted his head from side to side. "He confessed to several acts of minor sabotage, including leaving threatening notes in his client's dressing room and tampering with props."

"Did he admit to trying to electrocute me?"

"He only admitted to tampering with the electrical when

we told him we pulled his prints off the cable. That and he had electrical burns on his hands from stripping the wires without cutting the main power. He called it a stage prank. He denied tampering with the light that fell on Ms. Carrigan, but I suspect that he was behind that too. We can check it for prints, but it's probably too late. We'll need you to fill out some forms when we charge him."

I chuckled. "He's lucky he didn't kill himself."

"We picked him up at the urgent care last night when the APB went out. I think the shock did something to the muscles in his face. He won't stop smiling."

"That's just how he looks. Did you ask him about Duke?"

"Well, that's what I wanted to talk to you about. It seems Mr. Frick has an airtight alibi for the afternoon that Duke died."

That took the rise out of my biscuits.

"He was at a biker bar over on Seahorse. Not only did the bartender and about ten other people confirm that he was there all afternoon, he's on the security footage as well. If someone really did push Mr. McCready off that catwalk—and I'm not saying that they did—it wasn't Ernie Frick."

I thanked Officer Birkwell and moped in my seat for a few minutes after he left. The ache in my side was getting sharper. I reached into my tote bag and took out a bottle of water and some Tylenol. That's when I spotted the release of liability papers that Terrence Nuttal had forced into my hands. He said it was imperative that they were signed by tonight. Why? What happened after tonight? And someone else died on this stage two weeks ago. If they died from an accidental fall, surely that would be a big concern to an insurance underwriter. Would it be a big enough concern to cover up the accident and hastily make it look like a suicide? My biscuits started to rise again. I had to get a look at that insurance policy. And I knew just where to look.

I pulled SpongeBob out of my tote bag and turned it on. "Is anyone there? Foxy Lady? Big Momma? I don't remember your names."

Mother Gibson's voice came over the walkie-talkie—quiet and scratchy, but I could hear her. "Tango here."

"I'm going in the lion's den to look for the million-dollar policy. Can you cover me?"

"We got your back."

I calmly walked down the aisle as some of the early birds were making their way to their seats for the performance. When I got to the hall, I found Aunt Ginny, arm in arm with Neil, leading him down toward the theater. She was praising him for his work on the play, and when she passed me she tucked a key into my hand. Mrs. Dodson and Mrs. Davis were standing in front of Neil's office handing out programs to people who were arriving. The programs were really last week's lunch menu, but most of the patrons figured it was part of the play and didn't question it until Mrs. Sheinberg handed them the real program inside the theater doors. Mrs. Dodson gave me a wink and the ladies stood shoulder to shoulder to cover my entrance to Neil's office. I shut the door behind me and went right to the desk.

The bottom drawer was locked, but the biddies had done so much damage with a letter opener that all I had to do was shake it a couple of times and it jimmied open. I rifled through files marked "building plans," "receipts," and "board minutes"; I couldn't find anything incriminating. Then, I saw it. On the bottom of the drawer, lying under the hanging files. I glanced at the door to be sure no one was coming. The policy issued by the Actor's Equity Insurance Overwriters United and signed by Terrence Nuttal. It was a million-dollar umbrella policy in case anyone got hurt on the premises while working on the play. No wonder Mr. Nuttal wanted me to sign the release form. Mrs. Dodson started talking very loudly outside the door and I knew someone must be coming. I started to skim faster. Neil had taken out the policy to cover the investment in the Senior Center musical. It looked like he had invested thousands of dollars in the theater and advertising for the production of *Mamma Mia!* And there was something called a keyman rider.

My walkie-talkie crackled, and Mother Gibson said, "It's getting hot. I'll meet you at the extraction site."

What? I clicked on to respond to her. "Where is the extraction site?"

Then I heard a tap on the window.

Oh no. Outside the door, one of the ladies was tapping "SOS," and Mrs. Dodson was talking loud and fast. I could hear a set of keys jingling on the doorknob and Neil saying, "Not again. Wait, Terrence has a set. Terrence!"

I shut the desk drawer and lifted the window. Mother Gibson and Mr. Ricardo were waiting outside, standing on box crates that were part of the village scenery.

"I don't think I can do this," I hissed.

"Honey, you got no choice, now jump."

I stood on a box of computer paper that, thankfully, was unopened, hoisted myself halfway through the window, and got wedged like Winnie the Pooh in the honey tree.

"I'm stuck."

Mother Gibson and Mr. Ricardo grabbed my wrists and yanked me out of the window and right out of my yoga pants. The boxwoods and my dignity would never recover. I yanked the spandex flag from the window latch, hopped into my pants, and took off running to the front of the building, clutching the policy.

I shoved the papers inside my shirt and entered the lobby just as Neil and Piglet were coming out of the office with a headset. "Poppy, I was looking for you. I need everyone backstage. The curtain goes up in fifteen."

"Sure, Neil, on my way."

I trotted down to the stage, gave a quick wave to Sawyer and Smitty in the fourth row, grabbed my tote bag, and ducked into the light booth. Terrence Nuttal trotted in right behind me.

"Do you have my papers, Miss McAllister?"

"Not yet. I may not sign them. I might want to keep my options open."

I watched him closely for his reaction. He turned pink and wiggly. "Well, th–that would be terrible for the theater."

"Terrible for the theater? Or terrible for the insurance company?"

"Terrible for Mr. Rockford. He'll lose everything." Terrence Nuttal scurried away from the booth and disappeared offstage. I could see him through the crack in the side of the curtain talking to Neil down by the piano. How would Neil lose everything over an accident claim? I pulled the policy out of my shirt and gave it another look. If I understood what I was reading, the umbrella policy came with a sizable deductible that Neil would be on the hook for if anyone sued. But the keyman rider insured Neil's investment in the play against the death of Royce Hansen. So, if anything happened to Royce, if he died before the play was over, Neil would collect a quarter of a million dollars.

Oh my God. Could the catwalk and falling light have been staged by Neil in an attempt to kill Royce? I couldn't believe it. There had to be a logical explanation. Neil wasn't capable of killing anyone. He was one of the kindest people I'd ever met.

Then again, I reflected on the past six months and wasn't so sure anymore. I'd learned that anyone could be capable of murder if they were pushed too far. Still, it was starting to look like Duke had simply been in the wrong place at the wrong time. Neil could have killed him by mistake. That did explain why Neil didn't want to call the police or ambulance when the accidents happened. And it gave him a strong motive to make Duke's accident look like a suicide. I had to warn Royce. There was still time for Neil to stage an accident. He could be in danger.

Chapter Forty-Five

The lights flashed the two-minute warning for the audience to take their seats and Neil came backstage. I shoved the policy into my tote bag under my wallet.

Neil gathered the cast and crew together for a final pep talk. I tried to pull Royce aside, but Blanche walked backstage. She handed Aunt Ginny a bouquet of lilies. "For you, dear." Then she yelled, "Good luck, everyone! May the ghost of *Macbeth* shine upon you."

Royce yelled, "Gaaah!" and jumped backward, crossed his fingers, and spun around three times. Then he spit on the floor. He told everyone else to follow suit and they did, except for Mr. Sheinberg, who went straight to the spitting part. Then Royce took a nip from a flask that was in his pocket, which Fiona promptly took away from him.

Blanche left the stage laughing and Royce had to give himself a three-minute time-out. He sat in the corner muttering, "Hell is empty, and all the devils are here."

Neil tried to be encouraging, but the general feeling was that we were doomed.

I tried once again to get Royce's attention, but Iggy started playing the overture and he climbed the steps of the catwalk to make his entrance.

I put on my headset, dialed in my lights, and said a prayer for him not to fall. The curtain rose and Sophie made her entrance. It wasn't a big theater, but from my vantage, it looked like every seat on the right was taken.

While I waited for the "Honey, Honey" number to finish, I texted Smitty. Did you check everything?

He had forgotten to turn his sound off and I heard Moe say, "Wise guy," from somewhere in the audience.

He texted back, Yes. Don't worry. *I'd worry less if he wasn't the same handyman who accidentally wired my door-bell to turn off the porch light.*

Mrs. Davis and Mrs. Dodson made their entrance as Tanya and Rosie. Mrs. Davis had the first line of the scene, but she froze when she saw the audience. She stood under the orange glow of the simulated sunshine and stared into the audience with her mouth open. Mrs. Dodson jabbed her in the back with her cane. When that didn't snap her out of it, Mrs. Dodson prompted her. "I bet you don't want to take one more step in your heels, do you?"

Mrs. Davis dumbly shook her head no.

Neil made a circular motion with his hand to *keep going*, so Mrs. Dodson said both her and Tanya's lines until the senior playing Pepper took the stage and goosed Mrs. Davis. "Sehsugleymon."

Mrs. Davis yelped and gave a little hop. Then she slapped him and said, "Sorry, I don't speak Greek."

Then the men made their entrance for the dock scene. The audience was twittering with amusement, which stopped everything backstage. We all looked around at one another to try to figure out what was so funny on the other side of the backdrop. I looked around the curtain and right away noticed Mr. Ricardo's red boxers showing through his white pants under the bright lights. One of the men in the audience called for him to turn around so they could read the back and he obliged. That caused a louder gale of laughter from the audience, which made Royce more nervous, and after a long pause he said, "Alas, but we have seen better days."

The audience laughed even harder, then Mr. Ricardo skipped a couple of lines and went straight to "I'm rather impressed. I thought I would have to sleep with the goats."

Mr. Sheinberg was completely lost by this time, so he snapped his fingers side stage. "Line."

Mother Gibson whispered, "'Give me goats over camels.'"

Mr. Sheinberg hollered, "Huh?"

Mother Gibson whispered loud enough to be heard by the first few rows of the audience. "'Give me goats over camels.'"

Mr. Sheinberg acted as though he had never heard the line before. "Camels? Oy, are there supposed to be camels?"

The audience laughed harder this time and Mr. Sheinberg lit up like a firecracker.

Neil directed Mother Gibson to send Sophie out early to move on to the next scene because this one was hopelessly lost.

Sophie was pushed out onto the stage in the middle of eating a Kit Kat. She muttered an apology. "I get low blood sugar." Mother Gibson reached her hand out from backstage and took the candy away from the woman.

Sophie got the men back on track until it was time to sing. Mr. Ricardo was supposed to have a guitar in the boat, but he couldn't find it, so he ad-libbed, "Well, I'd play my guitar along with you, Sophie, but it appears to be missing from the boat that I rode in on."

There was a whistle, then a guitar flew over the backdrop from backstage and Royce caught it and handed it to Mr. Ricardo. "Here you go."

"Thanks."

I could see Winky and Finn in the front row beet-faced from laughing.

Aunt Ginny entered the next scene carrying her watering can. She was supposed to bump into the men and be surprised. When she yelled, "What are you doing here?" Royce answered, "I'm doing a play at the Senior Center."

Aunt Ginny was so stunned that she missed her cue for the song and had to come in on the second line. The audience was laughing so hard at this point. I don't think anyone noticed.

When the song was over, she came to my booth. "Did you see that? He didn't even know we were in the middle of the show."

"I saw it."

But then Aunt Ginny realized she'd forgotten her watering can onstage and the stage crew had changed the scene to Tanya and Rosie's bedroom. "Oh no."

I clicked on my headset. "Forgot the watering can."

Mother Gibson clicked back. "On it."

Tanya and Rosie were sitting on the bed discussing Donna's situation when Mrs. Dodson's cane inched out from the side of the stage in front of the scene and snagged the watering can, scraping it backstage before the "Chiquitita" number.

Georgina led the chorus up the aisle for "Dancing Queen." I heard the audience roar with laughter in the middle of the number, but I couldn't see what happened. Then Mother Gibson clicked over the headset and told me between gasps of laughter that the sequins on Georgina's costume sleeve caught Dicky Crebb's toupee and ripped it off his head on the way back down the aisle. It was flying back and forth with her arm movements like she was flinging a hamster.

Neil brought down the house in his "Lay All Your Love on

Me" duet with Sophie, even though she looked old enough to be his mother. Then Sophie got a crick in her back crawling on the stage toward Sky and the seniors in the chorus had to improvise the dance scene to include picking her up and carrying her around the stage flat on her back. One of the stage crew had to prop her up in front of a potted palm in the scenery for her to ask Mr. Sheinberg if he was her dad.

He replied, "Oh God, I hope not."

Neil wiped a tear from his eye. "That scene always gets me."

The music picked up and the chorus with Georgina rejoined the stage for the nightclub scene at the end of act one. Mother Gibson couldn't get the fog machine to work. Mr. Sheinberg and Mr. Ricardo were carried off by the dancers as the story goes, but they kept sneaking back onstage to dance with the ladies. The dancers carted them off again, but they went across the catwalk and entered from the other side of the stage. Since Sophie had hurt her back in the beach scene with Neil, she couldn't perform the faint at the end of "Voulez-Vous" like she was supposed to, so Mr. Sheinberg decided to add some drama of his own to make up for it. He clutched his chest and dropped to the stage. "Goodbye, cruel world."

Neil came in over the headset. "What is he doing? Bill doesn't die! He has to be in the next act."

Mr. Sheinberg flopped over to his stomach and groaned. "Oh, the pain." He kicked out his leg. "I'm dying. I think it's my heart!"

Mother Gibson had to go out and fetch him. She dragged him offstage as the curtain was going down. We could still hear him groaning over the audience's applause. "Oy, my heart. Wait! It's a false alarm. It was just gas." The houselights came on, announcing the intermission. Royce grinned at me and Aunt Ginny. "I think that went rather well."

The seniors had fifteen minutes to change for act two. I

followed them to the dressing room. I wanted to catch Royce and warn him, but he'd been cornered by someone with a microphone.

While I stuffed the biddies into their wedding party costumes, they wanted to know what I'd found in Neil's desk. I filled them in on the keyman policy and the suspicion that I didn't want to have.

"I don't believe it." Aunt Ginny shook her head. "Neil? Trying to kill Royce?"

Mrs. Dodson shook her head. "You just never know about some people. I blame a poor upbringing."

Mother Gibson clicked in my ear. "Two minutes."

"We have to get back." I led the biddies out into the hall. Royce was being interviewed by *Cape Gazette* newspaper, Fiona standing proudly at his side. When we passed we heard him say, "And that's why I'm leaving my estate to the Cape May Community Theater Program."

Even Fiona's orange lip stain turned pale. "You what?"

Royce patted her hand. "I thought I told you that, Fee."

Aunt Ginny picked up her speed. "We better get in there quick. Don't want to be late for curtain call."

Mrs. Davis chuckled behind her. "You don't want to get caught in the undertow of that drama about to roll out."

We hustled backstage behind the curtain.

Iggy started the act two overture and Aunt Ginny and Sophie took their places for the opening scene. The curtain rose, and before Aunt Ginny could say, "What's going on, Sophie?" everything stopped for a ruckus in the theater.

"I can't believe you would treat your own family this way!"

"Fee! Sit down."

"Don't you tell my mother to sit down! She has worshipped the ground you walk on, and you care only about yourself."

I peeked around the corner to see Blanche staggering up

the aisle clutching her arm, either drunk or hopped up on pain medication. "Let her talk. You screwed her over just like you screwed me over. It's time everyone in here knew about it. The great Royce Hansen. Broadway's leading man. A liar and a cheat."

Camera flashes were going off all over the audience. Mother Gibson clicked through my headset. "This'll be all over the news tomorrow. That fella in the center there is with Channel Eight."

Fiona turned on Blanche. "Stay out of this, Moira!"

Neil jumped onstage and held up his hands. "I am so sorry, ladies and gentlemen. We'll be just a moment. Royce." He started motioning to Royce to join him onstage.

Royce went up the steps and Blanche yelled, "Are you his little lapdog now? You always do what the director says, don't you, Royce? Always have to be the director's pet. Well, you know he's hoping you die during the play."

A collective gasp went through the room. The fog machine chose that minute to finally kick in and a blue-white mist curled its way around the stage, making it look like a graveyard.

Royce was shocked. "You—you poisonous, bunch-backed toad. Thine face is not worth sunburning."

Blanche was enjoying the spotlight. "You didn't know, did you?"

Neil spoke into his headset. "Someone please call security."

Mother Gibson answered, "We don't have security."

"Then call the police."

Blanche gave a hollow laugh. "I'm the one who approved the policy. If Royce gets hurt and dies during the play, Neil collects two hundred and fifty thousand dollars. What do you think of that, Fiona? I bet you'd like to get your hands on that kind of money."

All eyes were on Neil. The auditorium was silent. The seniors started creeping out onto the stage. First the lady play-ing Sophie shuffled out holding her back. "Is that true, Neil?"

Then Mrs. Davis joined her. "It was you, wasn't it? Those accidents were aimed for Royce."

Mrs. Sheinberg stood up from the second row. "What about Duke? Did you push Duke off the catwalk thinking he was Royce?"

Bebe cried out from somewhere on the wing, "Am I still getting paid?"

Even the audience members got in on it and started jeer-ing at Neil like they were at *The Rocky Horror Picture Show*. "Murderer!"

Neil turned pale. "I haven't been trying to kill Royce." He looked around frantically. "That policy is to take care of my mother in case something happens to Royce. You can ask my insurance provider. He's been here all week, doing safety audits. Terrence?"

A tiny Piglet voice squeaked, "Over here."

Blanche yelled, "You can't talk your way out of this. You killed Duke because you thought he was Royce! You're as greedy as the rest of them!"

Neil's arms dropped to his sides. "I didn't kill Duke. And I would never try to hurt Royce. I love Royce. He's my fa-ther."

Everything went still. Royce clutched his heart and had to sit down on the bed onstage.

"I put this play on to bring Royce back to Cape May. I started selling tickets months ago to build the stage. I even enlisted his sister's help to contact him. I'm ashamed to admit that I made you think this was all for charity, so you'd say yes."

Royce stared at Neil. "You're my son?"

I took a good look at Neil. How did we not notice it before? The same eyes. The same jawline. Even the body language was the same.

Neil nodded. "I saw you at the Broadhurst last year and paid someone to let me in your dressing room, where I stole a glass and some of your hair. I know that sounds creepy, but I had to be sure. I have a DNA report. I didn't want to tell you until I found out who my mother was."

Royce stared at Neil, looking for the resemblance. "Who is your mother?"

"I don't know. I've known I was adopted my whole life. My adoptive family said I was born in the Cape Admiral Home for Unwed Mothers in the spring of 1954, and that my father had gone to Broadway to be a star. All I was left with was a little, yellow, knitted blanket that had embroidered on it, 'I'll always love you, Pickle.' I've been following your career closely. I thought this play would be a chance to find out who my mother was. That's why I put you together on stage. You see, I've narrowed it down to Blanche, your old partner, and Ginny, your high school girlfriend."

My brain turned to cotton. I was afraid to move.

Blanche shook her head. "I'm not your mother. I never had children."

I looked at Aunt Ginny, but her face was the color of ash. She wouldn't look me in the eye but turned and ran off the stage and out of the theater.

Mrs. Dodson stood up and silently went after her, followed by Mrs. Davis and Mother Gibson. None of them spoke a word.

Chapter Forty-Six

I took my headset off and placed it on the light panel. Then I left the stage and went in search of Aunt Ginny. She would get no judgment from me. I found the group of ladies huddled around her in the activity room.

I went to her side and put my hand on her shoulder. Behind me, I heard Royce. "Ginny?"

Aunt Ginny wouldn't look at him.

Neil came in and squatted down in front of her. "I'm so sorry to do things this way. But I have to ask. Are you my mother?"

"No. I am." Mrs. Dodson stepped forward, her eyes cast on the linoleum tiles.

Neil stood up to face the old woman, whose lined face and mournful eyes told of a life of regret. "You? I didn't even have you on my radar."

"I wasn't in a relationship with your father. I made a mistake. An illicit, one-time fling. Something that was very taboo back in my day."

Aunt Ginny kept her eyes forward but reached her hand up to cover her friend's.

Mrs. Dodson seemed to gain both courage and shame at Aunt Ginny's touch. Her voice was heavy with emotion. "We were all infatuated with Royce. But he and Ginny were going steady. We thought he was going to propose after graduation. Then one night, after a football game, I fit into those poodle skirts back then. Royce had been flirting with me and he invited me to park. I was over the moon. I thought he loved me. He didn't. It was foolish and treacherous. Ginny was my best friend and what I did was unforgivable. I never told Royce. I never told any of them."

Aunt Ginny cut in. "We didn't need to know."

"The girls stood by me through the whole thing. Ginny drove me to the home for unwed mothers and named you Pickle. Lila made your blanket, and Thelma embroidered your name on it." Mrs. Dodson's lip began to tremble. "Giving you up was the hardest thing I've ever done, but I was eighteen and my family would have disowned me. No one would give me a job. How could I take care of you?"

Aunt Ginny gazed lovingly at her. "Why didn't you tell us it was Royce?"

"I was ashamed. You do foolish things when you're young and you think you're in love. I've lived with the shame my whole life. Oh, Ginny, can you ever forgive me?"

Aunt Ginny stood up and wrapped her arms around Mrs. Dodson's neck. She turned around to face Royce and slapped him across the face. "I don't know if that's for being unfaithful to me or for almost destroying Edith's life. But you deserve it for both."

Royce's eyes were misty. "I'm not the same man today that I was in my youth. I carried on behind your back, but you were the only one who had my heart, Ginger." Then he turned to Mrs. Dodson. "Edith, I don't know what to say. You didn't deserve to go through that. Do you forgive me?"

Mrs. Dodson finally looked Royce in the eye. "No. Not yet."

"When?" he pleaded.

"I'll let you know."

Aunt Ginny and Mrs. Dodson hugged and were quickly surrounded by a teary-eyed Mrs. Davis and Mother Gibson. The four of them had carried the secret for over sixty years. Their friendship had created a bond to last a lifetime.

Sawyer made her way to my side with tears streaming down her cheeks. We grasped each other's hands. Mrs. Sheinberg handed us tissues she'd plucked from her sleeve.

Aunt Ginny reached for Neil and called him Pickle. Then the ladies opened their arms and drew Neil into their hug. In a way, they were all part of his story.

The room broke into applause, and we were stunned to find that the audience had crammed into the activity room behind us. They seemed to be under the impression that this was all part of the play. Someone said it was a big, twist ending.

The biddies looked at one another and Aunt Ginny whispered, "What do we do?"

I shrugged. "Take a bow?"

So, the biddies, Neil, and Royce took an awkward bow. Neil hollered for everyone to make their way back to the theater for the finale number, where the cast performed their two encore songs.

When the final curtain dropped, Neil took the microphone one last time. "Thank you for indulging our Friday the thirteenth surprise ending for *Mamma Mia!* And for those of you who would like to come back tomorrow, you can see a different Valentine's Day ending, one that will very likely be more traditional."

Royce was next to my light cage, watching Neil handle the disaster with grace. The audience was eating it up. "Oh yeah. Now I see the resemblance. He gets that from me." Royce grinned at Aunt Ginny. She returned a tight-lipped scowl.

I gave Aunt Ginny a bouquet and kissed her on the cheek. "You were wonderful." The seniors milled through the audience, being greeted by everyone and receiving flowers. Smitty had a bouquet for Georgina. Mr. Ricardo had a dozen roses and he handed one out to each of the ladies.

Mrs. Dodson and Neil stayed to themselves, off to the side. I imagined that Neil had a lifetime of questions.

Everywhere we turned, Aunt Ginny received praise about the play.

"What a clever twist at the end."

Aunt Ginny replied, "Yes, wasn't it."

"A play within a play."

"Who saw that coming?"

Sawyer joined me as soon as she could make her way through the crowd and we left Aunt Ginny to her fans. "Oh my gosh. Did you know?"

"I had no idea. I think only Mrs. Dodson knew."

"I can't imagine holding on to a secret like that my whole life."

A trim woman with golden-brown hair approached us in the back of the theater. She wore a black dress and carried a beaded black purse. A teenage boy followed two steps behind her, staring at his shoelace dragging on the ground. "Are you Poppy?"

"Yes."

She put out her hand. "I'm Abby. Duke's daughter. This is my son, Kevin."

Kevin looked up for a brief moment, said a quick "hi," then fixed his eyes back on his feet.

So, Duke's grandson is not Charles. I took Abby's hand and gave her a squeeze. "Nice to meet you. This is my girl-friend, Sawyer."

Sawyer also made introductions.

"I'm so sorry about your father," I said. "I hope that little weird ending to the play didn't upset the two of you."

She gave me a tiny smile. "My father was a cop for fifty years. One thing he taught me was how to spot the truth. That was no twist ending."

"You saw through the PR speech, huh?"

Her smile broadened. "I was actually touched that some of Dad's friends are still trying to avenge his death."

"People here loved your dad. They're having a hard time making peace with what happened."

Abby looked at her son and back to me. "That's what we wanted to talk to you about. The lady who played Tanya said I should see you about the suicide note."

I looked across the room, and Mrs. Davis gave me a little nod.

"What's on your mind?"

She sat her purse on the seat next to her and took a breath. "The police showed me the suicide note. That doesn't sound anything like Dad. His lover left him? Dad didn't have lovers. He was dating some of the ladies here, but he wasn't looking for a fling. And who is Charlie?" Her eyes darted uncomfortably to Kevin for a moment. "He was lonely. He told me he wanted to get married again, but the ladies here were all enjoying the single life. They'd already gone the marriage-and-children route and didn't want to give up their independence." She gave a laugh. "He said a couple of them wanted to play the field."

I looked around. "I would say he was right on."

"I wanted to ask your opinion. Does that note sound like my dad to you?"

I felt an uncomfortable knot form in the pit of my stomach. We had run down every lead we could find, and all signs pointed to Duke's death being suicide. I couldn't lie, but I also didn't want to give her false hope either. "To be honest, I didn't know your dad. But the couple of times I talked with him, he was very excited about Kevin's visit. He had written a play and he wanted Kevin to see him perform it."

Kevin was focused on the floor, but I thought I saw a drop of water fall to his feet.

"He clearly loved his grandson very much, and I know he was proud of him."

Abby's face lit up with thanks. "He and Kevin had a pretty special relationship. Dad regretted not getting to see me grow up all those years he was on the force. Kevin was his second chance."

Kevin looked up and I gave him a smile. "He wanted to show you the play he'd written about his time on the force."

Abby laughed. "Oh, we know all about it. Dad has been regaling us with his true crime stories ever since he retired a few years ago. I had to tell him to cut back on the grisly murders and riots and stick to the safe topics, like robbery and breaking and entering."

"I was under the impression that Duke was mainly on the vice squad, arresting gamblers and smugglers."

"Oh no. He was on vice for about twenty years, but he started out as a beat cop and got called into whatever crime happened in his jurisdiction. He used to obsess over this one robbery in 1963: First Bank of Sea Isle. He called it the one that got away. They never caught the two guys that did it and they made off with a half a million dollars. I bet it's in his play."

I stared at her for a long minute.

"Are you okay?" she asked me.

I nodded absently.

Sawyer placed her hand on my back. "What is it?"

"I think we know why Duke was killed."

Chapter Forty-Seven

I left the theater early and went home to search for Duke's script. Aunt Ginny had thrown hers in the trash, but mine had to be around here somewhere. Unless Aunt Ginny had destroyed it. Or Mrs. Galbraith had thrown it out. Or Figaro. Figaro could have done any number of things with it. My eyes were burning. *I can't keep getting up early to exercise and make breakfast, then stay up late.* I finally had to concede that tomorrow was another day. I made sure the porch light was on for Aunt Ginny. That car was still out there. I was beginning to think it was abandoned. I made a mental note to call and have it towed away in the morning. Then Fig and I went up to bed. I decided not to work out in the morning and set my alarm for an hour and a half later. I was beyond exhausted and no one wants puffy eyes on Valentine's Day. I stretched out on the bed toward all four corners, something that was just starting to not feel lonely, and Figaro curled up in the crook of my neck and purred me to sleep.

I woke up before the alarm with him curled into my back.

It was such a small thing, but it brought me great joy. "Do you want a Valentine's Day treat?"

Figaro worshipped the treats. As long as they had no nutritional value, weren't a disguised health supplement to clean his teeth or dissolve hairballs, or had a pill stuffed into them. I felt him stretch and meow. He started to purr before I could get the bag in my hand. I fed him a couple while telling him what a pretty boy he was. "You're my fluffy valentine, aren't you?" He gave me a tolerant look while chomping the shrimp nugget on one side of his mouth. I left him a few more on the nightstand and went to get ready for my day.

I was giddy. There was a surge of excitement flowing through me like it was Christmas. I pulled up a YouTube tutorial on Valentine's Day makeup. I wanted to look beautiful and romantic today, like I just stepped off a magazine shoot. I followed the instructions exactly. When we were done, the presenter looked like the spokeswomen for celebrity makeup and I looked like a Disney villain. I washed it all off and started over with a much more reasonable goal. Namely, don't look like the sea witch.

Today was going to be special. I pulled on black pants—real pants. Pants with a zipper and buttons. There was a lot of spandex, but it still counted. I'd finally discovered the secret to getting pants to fit: buy bigger pants. I topped off the outfit with a wine-colored, flowy tunic and black heels that I would regret wearing by ten. Change in plans: I took off the heels and put on flats. I only wear heels when I want to impress someone. I left the room, then came back in and grabbed the heels because you never knew.

Aunt Ginny was in the kitchen, working her way through a valentine box of Russell Stover. She was wearing a dark red swing dress and red bedroom slippers. I walked over and gave her a hug.

"What's that for?"

"I just love you."

"I already ate all the caramels."

"That's okay. Where'd you get that?"

"The biddies and I went to the VFW last night. They were giving them out to all the ladies."

"The biddies?" I reached for the coffee beans and tried to act cool. "Who might that be?"

Aunt Ginny took out a dark chocolate ball. "We know you call us 'the biddies.' Thelma thinks it should be our gang sign. We're having jackets made."

I started the water and opened a can of tuna for Fig, who was putting on the full-court press. "My sweet boy gets a special breakfast today."

"What are *we* having?"

"You're having an insulin shot. I'm making strawberry cheesecake pancakes with heart-shaped sausage patties and heart-shaped lobster quiches."

The front door opened and the three biddies chattered their way down the hall. I made a fist and gave them a peace sign over my heart and they returned it. "Good morning, everyone. What brings you here so early?"

"Ginny invited us for breakfast."

I cut my eyes to Aunt Ginny.

"Did I forget to mention that?"

The kettle whistled and I poured the water over the coffee grounds while the ladies filled me in on the events of last night after I left. They'd stayed up until the wee hours, reminiscing and talking about what might have been.

Aunt Ginny poured cream into her coffee. "One thing I know, Royce wasn't going to marry me either way. He had a roving eye and big dreams that didn't involve me or staying in town."

Mrs. Dodson took a sip of her coffee. "I just wish it hadn't been me. I was intoxicated by his charm and his good looks and I let myself believe there were real emotions behind his flattery."

Mrs. Davis held her coffee cup aloft. "Well, we've all been there."

The biddies joined in the toast and I lifted my cup along with them. I got an email response from Dr. Melinda. Her encouragement was to focus on the real issue, my health and not my looks. *Plbbt!* I read part of the message out loud. "'There is a lot more to weight loss than the medical community understands, and they now know that the old calorie/exercise model is outdated and doesn't fit every circumstance.'"

The ladies raised their mugs and we toasted again. Dr. Melinda wanted me to make an appointment for some time next week. I added that to my mental to-do list.

The front door chimed just as I was putting the heart-shaped pans of lobster quiche in the oven. Sawyer dragged herself around the corner looking like someone who'd won the lottery but lost the ticket. "What's wrong. Didn't you get your valentine gift of the day?"

Sawyer dropped onto the stool at the island. "I got it."

Aunt Ginny poured Sawyer the last cup of coffee. "Was it something terrible?"

Mrs. Davis lowered her eyes. "Was it dirty? Is that the problem?"

Sawyer shook her head. "No. It was a dozen roses and an engagement ring."

We all yelled in surprise. "An engagement ring? Adrian proposed?"

Tears welled up in Sawyer's eyes. "Not Adrian. You were right. The gifts were from my neighbor, Mr. Vartabedian. He needs a green card or they're going to send him back to Bulgaria." Fat tears rolled down her cheeks.

"Oh, honey, I'm so sorry." I put my hand on her shoulder and rubbed her back. "Did you say yes?"

Sawyer jerked her eyes to me and her mouth flopped open. I started to giggle. She tried to keep a straight face, but the biddies started tittering and she let out a snicker.

We laughed for a good ten minutes. When we finally calmed down, Sawyer said, "Adrian thinks I've been cheating on him with Mr. Vartabedian." And we all started up again.

I had met Sawyer's neighbor once when she was out of town and I went to pick up her mail. He was about ninety pounds and a hundred years old, with a shock of white hair that stood straight up on top of his head, and he smelled like cabbage and boiled eggs.

When we calmed down for the second time, Sawyer picked up her coffee and said, "Did you know there's a bathroom scale on the front lawn?" That was all we needed to start laughing again. No one else knew why it was funny, but we laughed anyway.

Georgina waltzed into the kitchen wearing a white dress with a red scarf covered in hearts tied around her neck. "What's so funny?" That set us off a fourth time.

While I made the pancakes, I told everyone about my talk with Duke's daughter last night and my suspicions that there was something in Duke's script that got him killed. No one had seen my copy of the script, but Mother Gibson said she thought hers was home on her dresser. "I'll look for it when I get back and bring it tonight."

Sawyer poured us both another cup of coffee. "What are you doing today? Do you want to go for coffee? After we have this coffee." Sawyer held up her cup.

Her audacious wantonness with coffee was one of the many things I loved about her. So we made plans to go out that afternoon to cheer ourselves up from our lack of weight loss and appropriate male suitors. Then everyone helped me with breakfast. And when I say helped, I mean they got in the way and ate like they were at Benny's all-you-can-eat buffet.

Mrs. Galbraith let us know she did not approve of Figaro's official orange companion vest being blinged out with rhinestone hearts, and she did not approve of him being in the dining room while the guests were eating. I peeked through the door and saw Figaro standing on his hind legs and pawing at Chigsie's very expensive sport coat, trying to coerce some sausage from him.

I was about to retrieve the pest when a loud banging on the front door interrupted me. "Who in the world is that?" The biddies and Sawyer followed me into the hall to see what the commotion was about.

"Police, open up."

I threw the door open to find Amber on my porch flanked by two officers I didn't know. "What's going on?"

She handed me a search warrant. "I need to look around."

"Oh look, one more visit and you get a free hoagie. What could you possibly want in my house?"

"We've been on the trail of a couple of art thieves and I have reason to believe they're staying here."

"I don't have any art thieves here."

Mrs. Galbraith stepped forward. "Now wait a minute, Poppy. I told you things were missing from the Swallowtail suite." She jerked her eyes in the direction of the parlor, where Joey and Val were stock-still in the doorway, watching.

"Yeah, but . . ."

Amber cut me off. "Were you aware that many of the homes in this neighborhood have been robbed over the past three weeks?"

Aunt Ginny hollered from the back of the foyer, "It wasn't me!"

Amber stepped inside and the officers took off, one up the stairs and one down the hall. "We've been following the thieves since the APB came out of Rehoboth that they were heading this way. They've been hitting B&Bs up and down the East Coast for months. All reported small, expensive antiques missing."

"How did you know they were staying here?"

"We've been staking out the whole neighborhood."

I looked outside at the car across the street. "Is that why that's been there?"

Amber's commanding facade slipped and she snapped at me. "Yeah, and you almost blew the whole op with that ridiculous blanket."

"Well, you should have told me."

"It's called undercover, McAllister!"

Officer Consuelos, who hadn't been on the porch when I opened the door, came up the steps with Bunny Ainsworth in handcuffs. "She climbed out the upstairs window and jumped from the drainpipe. I caught her when she tripped over a bathroom scale lying in the yard."

One of the other officers was coming down the steps behind Chigsie, who was also in handcuffs. Chigsie was bleeding from a cut on his forehead. The officer met my stare. "He tripped over the cat."

Figaro trotted down the steps and tried to trip Chigsie again. The third officer went up and brought down a shopping bag full of jewelry and stolen antiques—and my expensive new bathrobes—and Amber read the pair their rights.

Mrs. Galbraith stood off to the side, shamefaced, wringing her hands in her uniform apron. Aunt Ginny started poking through the bag and Officer Consuelos had to tell her to stop before she contaminated the evidence.

Bunny lost her refined demeanor and had a few artful phrases for Amber. Needless to say, she denied having any knowledge of the events and blamed it all on Chigsie.

Chigsie said he didn't take anything; it was all done by Bunny.

Amber silenced them. "I saw you both with my own eyes when you came back from robbing the Queen Victoria." Then she turned to me. "They set up guided tours of prospective marks to check out the security and valuables. Then Bunny excuses herself to use the bathroom, and while she's alone, she stashes the items in a giant purse."

While Amber was postulating on how brilliant she was to unravel the crime, Figaro was pawing at Chigsie's coat. Chigsie couldn't do anything in handcuffs, so he shook his leg at Fig. "Get off me, you stupid cat."

Figaro's claw got stuck and he ripped a hole in the lining. Aunt Ginny's antique silver candy dish fell out and landed at Figaro's feet.

Aunt Ginny pointed at the sport coat. "I think there's your giant purse."

Mrs. Galbraith was so upset, she had to sit down on the steps. Aunt Ginny smacked Chigsie's hand. "How dare you steal from me, you heathen!"

Amber flushed a little pink and said she had to get them down to the station for processing. Officer Consuelos was staying to collect statements and go through each room looking for evidence.

I snuggled Figaro, who wasn't the least bit interested in being snuggled. He still had sausage on the brain. Mrs. Galbraith apologized to Joey and Val for jumping to conclusions. They took it in stride. Joey said, "I thought it was weird when I came out of the shower and found Bunny in our room. She said she must have got the rooms mixed up. I thought she was trying to see me naked."

Val took his hand. "That broad would have to go through me first." Only she didn't say "broad."

After a while, the biddies left to take naps. They wanted to be fresh for their big surprise ending since they didn't get to do it last night. Sawyer and I cleaned up the dining room.

Aunt Ginny said she was feeling poorly and too full to help, so she flopped in a dramatic pose on the settee in the front parlor. Then she overheard me telling Sawyer I was meeting Gia for a special coffee date in less than an hour. "Sawyer, tell Poppy she has to choose between Tim and Gia. No one likes a love triangle."

Sawyer raised her eyebrows.

I hollered back, "I've only been home six months!"

"Who can't decide in six months?"

"Besides, no one said anything about love. It's not a love triangle. It's more of a make-out triangle. Oh wait. That sounds worse."

Sawyer grinned but made no comment.

Aunt Ginny was full of advice from her fainting couch. "If you learned anything from me last night, it's that men are not worth getting giddy over. Don't let a man cause drama in your life."

Someone rang the doorbell and Aunt Ginny used all the energy she'd recovered in the past three minutes and popped up before Sawyer and I could get over there to answer it. Royce stood on the front step with a dozen roses in one hand and a box of chocolates in the other. "Please forgive me, Ginger. I was such a fool."

Aunt Ginny's hand flew up to her throat. "Oh, Royce. Well, I don't know. You hurt me pretty bad, not to mention Edith."

"I'll make amends with Edith, but you can hardly hold me accountable for leaving when I didn't know about the baby."

"Well, that's true enough."

Aunt Ginny took the roses and chocolates from Royce and handed them to me and Sawyer.

Royce took Aunt Ginny's hand. "Alas, my fair one, the course of true love never did run smooth."

Aunt Ginny tittered. Her eyes met mine and she shut it down.

"Come to brunch with me?" Royce pleaded.

I piped up on Aunt Ginny's behalf. "She's way too full and feeling kinda poorly."

Aunt Ginny tittered "Poppy, you're such a kidder. I'm fine." She shot me some daggers, then turned sweetness and light back to Royce. "I'd love to go to brunch. Let me get my wrap." She reached up and took her white wool wrap off the coat stand. Royce helped her into it and led her out the door. She poked her head back in before she shut it. "Do what you want with the men . . . and don't eat my chocolate!"

Chapter Forty-Eight

"Keep a special eye on Figaro. Ever since he found that candy dish he's been unusually good." Figaro was sitting pretty on the steps, watching me get my coat. He hadn't tried to stalk me, swat me, or wriggle out of his vest once since Amber left. "If that isn't proof that he's up to something, I don't know what is."

Mrs. Galbraith, humbled from her errant accusations, promised to be mindful of her fluffy nemesis. I had a hot date with a gorgeous Italian and slipped on my heels.

Gia had set a folding table in the kitchen. It was covered with a white tablecloth and had two taper candles burning in the middle. China cups and plates were laid out for brunch, and a single red rose sat in a vase in the center.

"Look at how fancy." I giggled.

"I wanted today to be special since we can't go to dinner until Monday." He helped me out of my coat and hung it in his office. When he returned he held out a black-velvet ring box. "For my Bella."

"Ooh. A gift." My blood was thudding in my ears. There was no way this was what it looked like. It was much too early. I lifted the latch and pulled out a red ribbon. Attached to the ribbon was a little silk bag, and inside the bag was a pair of tiny blue crystal earrings. "Oh, Gia. They're gorgeous. I think it's too much. This had to . . ."

He cut me off with his lips. "Shh. None of that. I want you to have them." He kissed me long and hard, with all the emotion that had been building between us for six months. "Poppy. Do you not know yet that I love you?"

It was as if the floor had dropped out from under me on one of the old boardwalk rides. He loved me. And I knew in my heart that I loved him too. But something held me back and the words wouldn't leave my mouth, so I reached up and let my kiss tell him how I felt.

Gia looked deep in my eyes and read the writing on my heart. "I am a jealous man and I don't want to share you."

I nodded.

He grinned. "Think about that while I get the coffee. Sit." He picked up a remote and started the music playing "Unchained Melody."

I sat at the table feeling helpless. What was I going to do? How did I feel about Tim? If my head had any answers, my heart was beating too loud to hear them. The only things I knew for sure were that I wasn't ready to jump into the unknown yet and I wanted to put on these earrings.

Gia had convinced Momma to make a gluten-free breakfast cake for us, and there was booze in the coffee. I was feeling very loose and giggly while we talked about Gia's five-year-old son, Henry, and the rest of his family. I had apparently dodged a bullet by not meeting most of them yet. Gia wanted to introduce me, but now he had me terrified. We talked about Duke and his play, and Gia agreed with me that his script held a likely source of motives. There was a lot of just looking at each other and smiling. I didn't want it to end because I was afraid guilt over Tim would spoil the memory of today.

We cleaned up and Gia made me two coffees, sans liquor, to take to meet Sawyer in her bookstore for my next coffee date. Gia gave me a long kiss goodbye in the front dining room amid the snickers of his sister, Karla, and the crushed stares of the young ladies who were hanging out, hoping to catch his eye today. "Think about what I said. I want you to be all mine, Bella." Then he gave me a smile. "I'll see you tonight for the performance. I hope it's just as exciting as you said last night's was."

I floated across the courtyard to Sawyer's *Alice in Wonderland*–themed bookstore. The first thing she noticed was the blue earrings. "Oh my God, let me see them!"

"Aren't they pretty? What do you think they are? Topaz?"

Sawyer gave me an incredulous look. "Ah, Poppy, those are blue diamonds."

"What? No." I gave her a hard look, so she'd be sure to know I thought she was crazy.

She got out her phone to fact-check me. "I'm telling you, I know what I'm talking about. I almost bought a blue diamond necklace in Jamaica. See." She held up her phone and showed me a picture. "Gia spent a small fortune on you."

I couldn't process that right now, so I reverted to what I was comfortable with. Snark. "Well then, we both got diamonds today."

Sawyer rolled her eyes and giggled. "I'm so excited for you. I think Gia is wonderful." Then she stopped with her coffee halfway to her lips. "But what are you going to say to Tim?"

"I don't know. Gia told me he loved me."

"Do you love him?"

"Yes. But I'm still as in love with Tim as the day we broke

up. How can I commit to either one under these circumstances?"

"Does Tim want to be exclusive?"

"A month ago, I would have said yes, I thought this was our second chance, but now I think he really did just want me to make desserts for Maxine's. If only I had a sign that we had a future together . . ." I let the words trail off, knowing it would mean saying goodbye to Gia, and I wasn't ready for that.

I reached in my tote bag and dug around for a pack of tissues. I pulled out a wad of paper. "Look. It's Duke's script. I've been carrying it back and forth to the theater the whole time."

Sawyer and I leafed through it, looking for a crime that could possibly be linked to someone in the play. I turned the page and my eyes nearly burned through the script. There was Duke's suicide note. Ripped right from his own script. He had been talking a jumper off a ledge. "I have to call Officer Birkwell." Dispatch put me through and I had to leave him a voice mail. I frowned at Sawyer and threw my phone back in my bag. Immediately, it dinged that I had a new review. I found a scathing Facebook post by Luv2Fly. "The Butterfly Wings B&B was the worst place we've ever stayed. The owner promised us a suite and when we arrived it was a dingy little room on the third floor with the bathroom down the hall." It went on from there. I handed Sawyer my phone. "Do you see what I'm dealing with? I really hope Kim gets some answers from her old PR boss."

Sawyer's face scrunched up as she read the review. She tapped the screen a couple of times, then her eyes grew big and white. "Oh my God!" She jumped to her feet.

I jumped to my feet, even though I had no idea what was going on. "What? What is it? Do you know who Luv2Fly is?"

"Not yet. But we're going to find out. Come on."

She ran out the door holding my phone in front of her like a tricorder. "Whoever just left this review on Facebook has location finder on. It says they're just around the corner. Let's catch them."

She locked the bookstore and we took off down the mall. I wished I'd changed back into my flats now that I was prancing over the bricks. *I hope Gia isn't watching this.*

"They just checked into the Ugly Mug!"

We crossed Jackson Street, and the balls of my feet felt like I was walking on knives. *Why do we do this to ourselves? Who said this was sexy?* I saw my reflection in a shop window. I looked like a round stork trying to walk a tightrope. I slipped the shoes off and ran the rest of the way barefoot.

Sawyer bounced past the greeter and into the dining room of the Ugly Mug. There were only a couple of booths occupied. She ran up to the first couple. "Are you Love2Fly?"

They shrugged and shook their heads, like *please don't hurt us, deranged lunatic.*

I saw a man sitting by himself and ran to him. "Are you leaving reviews as Love2Fly?"

"What?"

I repeated, "Are you Love2Fly?"

He shook his head. "No, I hate flying."

Sawyer had moved on to the waiter and asked who just arrived in the last couple of minutes, but someone caught my eye in a dark booth. "Oh no, she didn't!" I marched right over to Joanne Junk and grabbed her table. "Do you really hate me that much? High school is over, Joanne. What do you think you're doing?"

She had a tuna melt halfway to her mouth.

"Eating?"

"I know we've had some bad blood, but this is too far."

Joanne looked about as confused as I felt. She blinked a

couple of times and Swiss cheese dripped onto her My Little Pony sweatshirt. "I don't know . . ."

She didn't say any more because Sawyer cut her off. "Poppy!"

I spun my head around and Sawyer was jerking hers to the other side of the restaurant. Sitting in the back corner with a pink baseball hat pulled down over her blond curls was Tim's old mentee, Gigi. She had promised to destroy me when Tim rejected her. I'd thought she meant that metaphorically. I was wrong.

I looked back at Joanne. "Never mind." Then I joined Sawyer to face the troll.

Tim's fellow chef and mentee had declared her love for him and he'd turned her down . . . for me. She'd promised to make me regret it. I opened my mouth to tell her just what I thought about her trying to ruin my business with her lies, but Sawyer beat me to it.

"What is wrong with you? You hideous little troll. You've been lying about Poppy all over the internet and trying to destroy every business she works with. That's called libel and it's a crime. You just got yourself a lawsuit, you petty little fool."

Gigi's eyes looked like they were going to pop out of her head.

"What's the matter?" I slammed my palm down on her table. "Don't you have anything to say to me in person? Or do you only have nerve when you're hidden behind the internet?"

Gigi pulled herself up to her full height of about five feet. Her voice squeaked. "I don't know what you're taking about. You need to leave before I call the cops."

Sawyer held up my cell phone and took a video of Gigi. "We're here on February 14, 2015, where we've used the location finder on Facebook to track the review left by Luv2Fly.

It's just one bad review in a sea of many left by this woman under various screen names."

Gigi was squirming in her seat. "I haven't left you any reviews. You're crazy."

I grabbed her cell phone off the table and turned it on. She was lunging at me to get it back, but Sawyer was blocking her, still recording.

Her phone opened to the Yelp account she had created under the name Luv2Fly. She had been in the process of leaving me another review when we caught up with her. I held her phone up and Sawyer captured it on video. I tossed it onto the table. "You can try to delete all those accounts, but nothing on the internet ever really goes away. My late husband, John, was a lawyer. They can subpoena all your accounts—Facebook, Twitter, Yelp, TripAdvisor—they'll turn over your data and the records of all the reviews you left. It won't take much to see that all the accounts were created with the same IP address. My lawyer will be in touch."

Gigi's lips started to tremble and her eyes filled up. "You took Tim from me."

"You never had him." Sawyer and I turned and walked out of the Ugly Mug, leaving her there to wallow, unmasked in her disgrace.

"You were awesome in there," I told Sawyer as we walked back down the mall.

"Me? What about you? I wish I had thought about the IP address."

"Yeah, but you're the one who found her in the first place. I don't know anything about Facebook. I didn't know you could do that."

"Apparently, neither did Gigi. Or she would have turned it off." Sawyer handed me my phone and it rang the opening bars of "Crazy Train." "Who is that?"

"Aunt Ginny."

"What's my ringtone?"

"'Count on Me' by Bruno Mars."

"Nice."

"Hello?"

"Poppy?"

"Why are you whispering?"

Aunt Ginny said something I didn't quite get.

"Can you say that again?"

"I said we're in trouble. We broke into the house and they came home unexpectedly. We need you to get over here, now."

"Whose house?" I heard muffled voices talking. "Aunt Ginny! Whose house are you in?"

The line went dead.

"Oh my God, Sawyer. Aunt Ginny's in trouble and I have no idea where she is."

Chapter Forty-Nine

Sawyer took my phone. "I'm downloading a family tracker app." She set up an account pretty fast. "Do you think Aunt Ginny will respond if I send her a link to join your circle?"

"I have no idea what Aunt Ginny will do. The biddies are like spider monkeys. They're cute until you're responsible for them. Then they create mass destruction."

Sawyer drummed her fingers on the back of my phone for a couple of minutes while I bit my nails. "She accepted it. Now we ask the app to find her." She drummed her fingers some more.

"How do you know how to do all this?"

"Kurt. When we were married I installed it on his phone when he wasn't looking so I could follow him and see where he was going. It's how I found out he was cheating on me with the United Bimbos of Cape May County. That and the thong I found behind the Snoopy cookie jar."

Sawyer handed me my phone. There was a map with an icon of a car blinking. "That's where Aunt Ginny is. She's in a residential neighborhood at the Point."

We flew to Cape May Point as fast as I could get my flats on. It was an eight-minute drive down Sunset, but I made it in five.

Sawyer pointed to a gorgeous, yellow two-story beach house on the waterfront. "That one."

Every room facing the ocean had floor-to-ceiling windows. There was a local security sign in the yard. "Are you sure Aunt Ginny is in there?"

Sawyer tapped my screen. "This is where her GPS is coming from. And isn't that her car?"

I pulled over on the side of the road next to Bessie, which was covered with a couple of anorexic branches of dead leaves being used as the world's worst camouflage. "This is a million-dollar neighborhood. Whose house do you think this is?"

"I have no idea. Let's go up and knock. We can say we're selling Avon." Sawyer opened the passenger-side door.

"Shouldn't we call the police?"

"And tell them what? Aunt Ginny broke in, got caught, and is being held hostage?"

"What if you stay here with the car and if I'm not back in twenty minutes, you call the police?"

Sawyer frowned. "But I want to go with you."

"I don't know what I'm walking in to. I don't want us both getting hurt. I'd feel better knowing you're watching my back if things go south."

"All right, but hurry up. Rich neighborhoods give me the willies. So many Pomeranians."

I dashed around the corner and up the wide walkway to the front door. I knew breaking in was out of the question since the owner was home, so I rang the doorbell.

Blanche Carrigan opened the door with her good arm and gave me an appraising once-over. "Poppy. What are you doing here?"

I was rendered speechless.

"Well? Why are you at my house? I'm not apologizing, if that's what you came for."

"Actually . . . I wanted to talk to you . . . about . . ." *What, Poppy, what?* "Aunt Ginny and Royce." *Yeah, that's good.*

"What about them?"

"I think Royce is leading Aunt Ginny on. I think there's someone else he's really interested in. I overheard him talking with Neil after the play last night that he only came back to Cape May to reignite his romance with an old partner."

A smirk crossed Blanche's almost wrinkle-free face. "Well, well, well. Why don't you come in?" She stepped aside for me to enter. I immediately looked around the large foyer. There was a spacious living room on the right and an equally impressive sitting room on the left. In front of me was a wide staircase and down a hall to the back of the house I could see a gorgeous open chef's kitchen. This house was enormous. How in the world was I supposed to find four biddies in less than twenty minutes without looking suspicious?

Blanche led me to the sitting room and motioned for the couch in front of the fireplace. She took a wing chair opposite me. "So what else did Royce say last night?"

"You know, my throat is parched. Do you think I could have something to drink?"

If Blanche was afraid that someone would accuse her of not being a good hostess, she needn't worry. She threw herself out of the chair and loped to the kitchen like I'd asked her to go gluten free—and I would know.

When she disappeared, I shot up and looked behind the couch. Then I crept out to the hall and opened a door. It was a powder room. No biddies. I flew back into the sitting room before she came around the corner.

"Here, I brought you some water."

"Don't you have anything stronger, like some tea maybe?"

She huffed and went back to the kitchen. I sprinted across the hall and checked the living room. The only closet was full of shelves and not old ladies. I sprinted back to the sitting room as Blanche brought in a large glass of tea. "Here. Now tell me about Royce."

"Does this have sugar in it?"

Blanche narrowed her eyes. "Yes."

"I'm so sorry. I can't have sugar. Could I have the water back?"

Blanche yanked the tea out of my hand, splashing some of it on her hardwood floor. She stared me down and I grinned. "It's a really good story."

She left to spit in my water and I jumped back in the hall. I ducked into a room with a cherrywood desk and built-in bookshelves. I looked under the desk. No biddies. "What are you doing in here?" Blanche was standing behind me with the glass of water, and she was looking very agitated.

"I'm sorry. I was looking for the powder room."

"It's in the hall. If you don't really have anything to tell me, I'd like you to just leave."

I went to the door I knew was a powder room and grabbed the doorknob. "Trust me, it's worth waiting for. Royce was in rare form last night, talking about the good old days when the two of you were onstage." I motioned to the powder room. "I'll be just a moment."

Blanche scowled and went into the sitting room to wait. I ducked back into the hallway. This was a growing disaster. Would the biddies be upstairs?

I heard a scratching sound come from under the steps. I turned around and saw a crack in the glossy white paneling. It was a hidden door. I slowly creaked it open and found four little biddies stuffed in a broom closet. I stuck my head in the dark space and whispered, "Dear God, what are you doing in here?"

Mother Gibson held up her copy of Duke's script. "I found it. And look."

It was Duke's suicide note.

"I know. I've seen it."

Mrs. Dodson tapped the script. "It's all about an unsolved bank robbery in 1962 that resulted in a double homicide."

Mrs. Davis hissed, "There is evidence in here that has never been released to the public."

Mother Gibson's hands were shaking the script and the pages were gently rattling. "And, child, wait till you hear this. The cops found a French opium cigarette at the crime scene. Remember what Fiona told us?"

"That's why we're here," Aunt Ginny said. "We were looking for one of those cigarettes or evidence of some kind."

I put my finger to my lips. "Okay, we don't have time for you to tell me all this right now. I have to get you out of here."

The biddies' eyes all widened in horror, and a terror so sharp it could slice through steel shot through me. Aunt Ginny put her arm up and yelled, "No!"

I was hit on the head so hard, it dropped me to my knees. At first all I could see was white-hot light, then stars. Blanche was standing over me holding a life-size wooden duck. "Get up! Now!"

I staggered to my feet, trying to calculate how long I'd been in the house. Sawyer wouldn't be calling the police for at least ten minutes.

Blanche twisted the duck's neck and the back opened. She pulled a gun out of the cavity and pointed it at me. "Go." She prodded us into the sitting room and motioned to the couch. "Sit down." She went over to a desk and pulled out a roll of thick string like you would use to truss a turkey. She tossed it onto the coffee table. "Tie each other up."

None of us moved and she placed the gun against Aunt Ginny's forehead. "I could kill her now. I have enough money to redecorate this room anytime I want."

I picked up the string and started tying the biddies' hands behind their backs.

"Knots. Not Bows."

Then she pushed me onto the couch next to Mother Gibson and tied my hands behind me.

Blanche sat with the gun resting on her knee. "I knew that godforsaken script was going to be a problem the moment he pitched it."

I leaned forward slightly to try to undo my string. "Blanche, what is this about?"

"That stupid play. At first, I only took it to shut him up, but then he kept talking about a bank robbery. Imagine my surprise to read he'd worked the Sea Isle Savings and Loan job in '62. I knew then I was going to have to take care of him."

Mother Gibson wiggled in her seat ever so slightly. "We read the script this afternoon. The official police report said the robbery was pulled off by two men in ski masks, but a bank cashier insisted one of them was a woman. She said she recognized the robber's perfume, but no one took her seriously. You were the other robber, weren't you?"

Blanche grinned. "You bet I was, honey. It was my greatest role, and no one will ever know about it. Vernon planned the whole thing. My first husband was an idiot who liked to hit me for fun, but Vern . . . He had brains. He took a job building the Springfield Inn across the street from the bank. That way he was able to memorize the security patterns and the manager's routine. It was his idea for me to dress as a man and pull the job with him. A real-life Bonnie and Clyde. How do you think I've evaded capture all these years? I had to quit Broadway when Royce got me pregnant, but I put my tricks about stage makeup to good use. The cops were never on my tail because they were looking for two men."

"I thought you couldn't have a baby." Just five more minutes.

"I said I didn't have a baby. I have my first husband throwing me down the stairs to thank for that."

"You gave yourself away with that cigarette," Mrs. Davis said. "The police report said that no tobacco agency sold those on account of them being illegal in the US."

Blanche flushed with irritation. "I made one mistake. I'd hidden in plain sight from that fool for sixty years and then Blabbermouth Busybody goes on about those French opium cigarettes Gunter ordered for me at the Five and Ten. When Duke approached me at practice that day, I saw the way he looked at me. I knew he was putting it together. I waited until he went to lunch and sawed through the railing of the catwalk, so it would fit in with all the other sabotage. Then I waited."

I wasn't getting anywhere with my string. It's a lot harder than they make it look on TV. Then I felt Mother Gibson's hand working at the knot.

Mrs. Davis asked Blanche, "Did you have to kill him? It's not like he could arrest you. The man had been retired for years."

"He cornered me backstage and asked me where the money was. The fool tried to make a citizen's arrest. He said he was going to report it to his old precinct and they'd get a search warrant. Do you know how easy it is to get a search warrant?"

"Yes." I shook my head. "Yes, I do."

"So I let him chase me up the catwalk, and when he caught me at the right spot, I pushed him over." Blanche threw out her bad arm. "Then I ripped that suicide note out of his script and shoved it in his coat."

Mrs. Dodson gasped. "What about your broken collarbone?"

"It's a sprain. Who says I'm not a great actress?"

Aunt Ginny muttered, "Just about everyone."

I glared at her and we had an argument with our eyes.

Blanche toyed with the gun again. "Now what to do with you? I can kill you in the basement and store a couple of you in the freezers, but I don't have room for all of you." She looked at me and Mother Gibson. "Especially you two big ones."

When I get out of this string I'm going to knock you out. "Why kill us now? Duke is dead. The cops have ruled it a suicide. The script is circumstantial. There are no eyewitnesses. And the case wasn't reopened. You obviously have the money to hire a lawyer."

Mrs. Davis added, "That's true. The script says it was never found and the detectives had to give up the search when the trail ran cold. You got away with it. Why don't you let us go? You got everything you wanted."

Mother Gibson had worked the knot free and my hands could move. She held my wrists in place and quietly said, "Not yet."

Blanche's mouth twisted into a hard line. "You better believe not yet. I didn't walk away with everything that was important to me. One of the security guards tried to be a hero and shot Vern in the stomach. We had to kill them. That's when I dropped that stupid cigarette. I had to get Vern across the street and jam a rod of rebar from the Springfield construction into the bullet hole, so the doctors wouldn't report it as a gunshot wound. He bled out in the car on the way to the hospital and I had to drive him home and drag him into the driver's seat."

Mother Gibson threw her head back and shouted, "Roosters like to crow and do the hokey-pokey!"

Blanche was totally stunned by her outburst, but Aunt Ginny crowed like a rooster at the top of her lungs. Blanche jerked the gun to point it at Aunt Ginny, but Mrs. Davis kicked her leg out *to put her left foot in* and knocked

Blanche's arm up to the ceiling. The gun went off and a light dusting of drywall fell from the impact. Mother Gibson smacked my hands and yelled, "Now!"

I grabbed the fireplace poker and whacked Blanche over the head. Blanche went down like a failed Jenga tower.

I kicked the gun aside, then grabbed the string and tied her hands and ankles together.

Mrs. Dodson complained to Mother Gibson, "Why didn't I get to do anything?"

"Because I couldn't think of anything productive to say for fox-trot."

"What about foxes trot? Or foxes like to trot? I could have worked with that."

"What would you have done with foxes trot?"

"I don't know. Get up and dance to cause a diversion?"

I grabbed my cell to call the police in case something had happened to Sawyer while Mother Gibson untied the other biddies. There was no need. Amber and Officer Birkwell threw the door open and burst in, guns brandished, right in the middle of Mrs. Dodson dancing a jig around the body on the floor.

Amber looked from me to Aunt Ginny. "Oh no."

Aunt Ginny cackled and jabbed her thumb in my direction. "You're going to have to start paying us a consulting fee."

Chapter Fifty

"There's no backing out now." Aunt Ginny and the biddies were huddled in the craft room of the Senior Center, where they'd just gotten into costume. Tonight was *Mamma Mia!* the finale and they were up to something devious. "It's all or nothing," Aunt Ginny said.

They nodded and put their hands together in the center of their circle.

Mother Gibson said, "For Duke."

And they all agreed. "For Duke!"

"Are you sure you don't want to tell me what this is about?" I asked.

The four of them gave me the most angelic looks I had ever seen. My spine trembled with premonitions of impending doom.

We had a packed house again. After last night's performance, every senior on the island showed up in hopes of new chaos. Neil had to turn people away at the door for fear that the fire marshal would shut us down.

As for the play, things went pretty much as expected. As

long as you expected Royce to slip in and out of Shakespeare and Mr. Sheinberg to perform another death scene. "Give the people what they want. Just prancing around singing won't put the butts in the seats."

Tonight was the first night the seniors had performed the show's second act, last night's having been preempted by the Jerry Springer tribute to "Who's your mommy?" Recent revelations cast an interesting spin on the play's themes: lost love, unplanned pregnancy, second chances, and discovering your parentage. It was unfortunate that Royce forgot his line in the wedding scene and chose to fill it in with Othello's "I am one who loved not wisely but too well." That brought more than a few snickers, some of them from the audience.

It was an emotional performance, made even more touching by the cast's dedication of the show to their friend Duke. It would have been a tearful ending had there not been one overshadowing incident that will forever live in infamy.

I had turned the houselights up, so the audience could dance along with the third encore number. When the cast sang the final line, "Finally facing my Waterloo," Mrs. Dodson, Mrs. Davis, and Aunt Ginny, who I knew was the ringleader, bent over and mooned the audience. The letters TH EE ND were written in magic marker across their butts.

Neil and Royce, like a set of matched bookends, were first shocked, then laughed and shook their heads. If they didn't know by now there was no controlling the biddies, they were going to learn it soon.

The cast was practically floating when the final curtain fell. Loved ones made a rush for the stage to fawn over the cast. Gia and Sawyer were on Aunt Ginny and me before I had my headset off. "Bella, you were wonderful. And Aunt Ginny, the ending was my favorite."

Aunt Ginny tittered. "It was my idea."

"I figured it was." Gia handed us both bouquets of daisies. "These are for you. I was looking for roses, but all the florists were sold out."

Aunt Ginny and I looked at Sawyer, who had the decency to blush.

The senior ladies had planned a cast party in the dining room right after the show. I was tickled to see my linzer hearts and champagne cupcakes on the "homemade dessert" table. *There's that special order I had to fill.* I relaxed and listened to snippets of conversation around the punch bowl.

Duke's daughter was holding a memorial service on Monday because Duke hadn't wanted a funeral. Everyone in the room was planning to attend.

Some of the seniors who had not been in the play were asking Bebe to start up a dance class for them. She couldn't wait to get started.

Mrs. Spisak asked her, "Where do you get those big, purple glitter boots?"

"Drag Queens R Us."

"Do you think they come in an eight?"

"Well, honey, we can find out."

Royce was still trying to make amends with his sister and nephew.

"Fee, your husband left you all that money. I figured you didn't need mine. Why saddle you with all those taxes?"

"My mother doesn't have any money. She's a shopaholic. I've had to take her credit cards away from her three times. I only moved in to keep her from losing the house."

"That's not true, Iggy. I have your father's pension."

"Mother, his pension is five hundred dollars a month and you'd blow it all at Harry and David if I don't throw the catalog away before you see it."

"Fee, I will make sure that you and Iggy and Neil are taken care of."

"Before you give my mother a check, I'd prefer if you make it straight out to the mortgage company, so she can't blow it on something ridiculous like unicorn china."

"I don't know what I would do without Iggy. He has a master's degree in finance, you know."

Meanwhile, at the other end of the table, Neil was getting to know Mrs. Dodson and she was holding his hand. *Aww, that's so sweet*. It almost brought tears to my eyes.

Gia leaned in to me. "So that's Neil? He looks fantastic for sixty-one. He must have some Italian in him."

I laughed. "Is everyone in your family as vain as you?"

Gia gave me a look of mock horror and touched his palm to his chest. *His tightly chiseled chest*. "You would accuse Giampaolo of being vain? I am hurt."

"Mm-hmm. Would a bacon-wrapped date make it better?"

"It just might."

After a while, Aunt Ginny and I ended up alone together. I handed her a glass of punch, made a toast to *Mamma Mia!* and we clicked plastic cups. "You know, for most of my life it seemed like everyone else was happy and having fun. Their lives were carefree and exciting, while mine was full of anxiety and loneliness. There have been a lot of times when I felt like I was missing out on something. TV shows have the gang sitting in a café laughing over coffee. Love happens at first sight in the movies and they live happily ever after. Every song where the guy promises the girl he can't live without her."

"What a bunch of garbage. Real life isn't scripted and set to music. If it were, I'd always say the right thing."

I giggled. "You've taught me that we have to decide to be happy. These last six months with you have been some of the best times of my life. I'm sure that you and the biddies are going to kill me, but I never knew life could be this much fun. Minus the dead bodies."

"There has been a lot of murder. We might want to find that fortune-teller who cursed you and apologize."

"That's probably a good idea."

We watched Smitty and Georgina laughing and dancing their hearts out to "Fernando."

"Gia hasn't taken his eyes off you all night."

Gia was talking to Sawyer across the room. Our eyes met and he winked at me.

My whole body warmed.

"It's a shame Tim had to work today."

"I'm seeing him tomorrow. Speaking of handsome men. Here comes Royce."

"There's my girl." Royce took Aunt Ginny's hands and pulled her into an embrace. The smooch he wrapped her in made me blush and I wondered if I ought to leave them alone.

"Ginny, I have something I have to tell you."

Whatever it was, I could tell he was dreading it. Aunt Ginny felt it too because her voice cracked. "Okay. What is it, Royce?"

"I haven't been completely truthful with you about why I came home. No, Poppy—you stay. You're important to Ginny and that makes you important to me. I want you to hear this. I'm in the early stages of dementia. I forget things and get confused. Sometimes I'm fine. Then, other times, I find myself wandering around outside and I don't know where I am or where I was going. I might only have a few clear-thinking years left, so Fiona convinced me to come home so she could watch me and keep me safe."

Aunt Ginny reached out and grabbed his hand. "Oh my, Royce. I'm so sorry. Of course, we suspected . . . Is there anything I can do?"

"I'm starting a promising new treatment next week. The

doctors are . . . optimistic. Ginny, I've made a lot of bad decisions in my life, but you were never one of them. Being with you these past few weeks, I've been happier than angels' wings."

Aunt Ginny was a little breathless. "Why, Royce, I feel the same way about you."

Royce dropped down to one knee. The room went still and every eye was on Aunt Ginny and what was to come. Royce took Aunt Ginny's hand in his. "Doubt thou the stars are fire; Doubt that the sun doth move; Doubt truth to be a liar; But never doubt I love."

I thought it was terribly romantic. One look at Aunt Ginny said that she was in full-blown panic. Her lips were moving, but no sound was coming out. Her eyes were bouncing around the room like a pinball machine looking for the nearest exit. All she could get out was, "Uhhh."

I had to do something. Looking up, there on the wall, I saw our salvation. I lifted the plastic cover and pulled the fire alarm.

Chapter Fifty-One

Figaro was doing figure eights around my ankles, oblivious to the red and blue lights that bounced off the mirror in the foyer. The lights went out and I waited for the crackle of the police radio and the inevitable knock on the front door. "Hello, Amber. What can I do for you?"

"You do know pulling a fire alarm when there is no fire is a felony."

"Is it?" I picked up Figaro and snuggled him. "That's a good li'l tidbit to keep in mind, just in case."

Aunt Ginny leisurely strolled down the hall in a bathrobe and bunny slippers. She had her hair thrown up in a couple of cockeyed curlers. "Good evening, Officer. I didn't know we had company, Poppy."

I gave Amber a doe-eyed look. "Is this a social call, Officer?"

Amber rolled her eyes. "Can I come in?"

I opened the door. "Why don't we retire to the library? My aunt and I were just about to have our evening cookies and cocoa." I heard Val snicker from the top of the stairs.

She had nuked the hot chocolate and poured it into a teapot so I could rocket into my pajamas before the police arrived.

Amber took a seat on the sofa in front of the fire and I poured her cocoa into a bone china cup. "How was your day?"

"Cut the crap, McAllister. Iggy Sharpe already ID'd you for pulling the fire alarm. He said to tell you now you're even for touching his Skywalker. I don't even want to know what that means."

I handed Aunt Ginny a cocoa. "Do we know someone by the name of Iggy Sharpe?"

"Doesn't ring a bell. Maybe it's someone from the soup kitchen where we volunteer."

"You're probably right. Or the library where we read to the blind."

"Mmm, true."

"Fine. Whatever." Amber sipped her hot cocoa. "While I'm here, I may as well tell you that the DA doesn't think we have enough evidence to prosecute Blanche Carrigan for the Sea Isle Savings and Loan robbery."

"I was afraid of that."

"The crime is too old; the evidence is gone. Without a confession, we have nothing. I'm afraid Mr. McCready's play is circumstantial at best. But we can bring charges against her for holding you ladies at gunpoint and threatening to kill you and stuff you in a freezer."

"Well, that is something."

Amber sipped her hot cocoa again.

Aunt Ginny lifted a plate of cookies. "Care for a nibble?"

Amber made a face like she was wrestling with herself, then she took a cookie and dunked it in her cocoa. "There is one more thing we might pursue." She popped the cookie in her mouth.

"What's that?" I asked.

"Fiona Sharpe gave us a wild account of Ms. Carrigan

killing her first husband with rat poison. Do you think there's any weight to that story?"

I thought about what Blanche had told us when we were tied up, about her first husband's abuse. "I think there's a very good chance it's true."

"Because we could petition to exhume his body and test it for arsenic. That, plus Mrs. Sharpe's testimony, could bring a conviction for murder in the first."

"What happens if you test the body and don't find anything?"

"I cost the county thousands of dollars and look like an idiot."

"Is that a chance you're willing to take to put her away?"

Figaro jumped up on the couch between Aunt Ginny and Amber. He gave Amber a case of cat stink-eye.

"Shoo. Go away."

Figaro turned around and did a full stretch and lifted his tail in Amber's face. Amber winced, causing Aunt Ginny to giggle. "He really doesn't like you."

"The feeling is mutual."

"Figaro." I nudged Fig off the couch. He flopped over and moaned like he'd been shot.

Amber drained her cup and stood up. "That cat's freaking me out. I gotta go."

"What are you going to do about Blanche?"

"I don't know yet. I'll decide in the morning."

I walked Amber to the door.

"You know, this is the third time I've seen you today because of a crime you're involved in. I have perps on the street who get in trouble less often than you two. Why is that?"

"A psychic put a curse on me."

"You can never be serious, can you?" She called over her shoulder, "Stay out of trouble, McAllister."

I shut the door and joined Aunt Ginny on the couch. Val peeked her head in. "Everything go okay?"

"We're free for another day."

She giggled and said good night.

Aunt Ginny and I figured we might as well drink our cocoa since we had it. She took off her earrings and pulled the curlers out of her hair. "You know, I like my life where it is right now. I don't want to get married again."

"Are you sure? Maybe six is your lucky number."

Aunt Ginny threw a pillow at my head. "I like playing the field. My life is so much fun with the girls and coffee dates and salsa dancing and jet skiing. I don't want to be tied down. I'm having more fun now than I did in my twenties and thirties. You're still a young woman. You have plenty of time for reckless abandon."

"I can't handle reckless abandon. I can't even handle tempered abandon. I don't think I can keep up this pace of making desserts for two places plus running the B&B. Something has to go."

"I hate telling you this, girl. But when the summer comes you're not going to be able to do anything but the B&B. If we get rid of those bad reviews, that is."

"I'm on it. Sawyer saved our life on that one. I have a call with Kim's old boss tomorrow and then I'll call our lawyer if we can't get Gigi to take the reviews down."

Aunt Ginny stretched. "Good."

"What are you going to do about Royce?"

Aunt Ginny made a face. "I don't know. What are you going to do about Tim and Gia?"

"I don't know."

We both sighed. Aunt Ginny stood up. "Well, I'm done in. I'm going to bed." She kissed me on the forehead and took the teapot and cookies to the kitchen.

I tamped down the fire and turned out the library light. I

was getting the teacups when there was a quiet knock at the door. "Who is it?"

"It's Tim."

Tim's hands were full. He had a purple orchid, a stuffed Garfield, and a bakery box.

"What is all this?" I took the orchid and placed it on the foyer table. Figaro eyed it, calculating the quickest path to destruction.

Tim came in and kissed me. "I left a little early. Chuck has probably burned the kitchen down by now."

I took the other gifts and gave Tim a hug. "This is so sweet. Thank you."

"I've wanted to see you all day. Are those new earrings?"

"Uh-huh. What's in the pink box?" I turned on the side table light in the library and we snuggled into the couch.

"Open it."

I untied the string and opened the flaps. It was a delicate tray of four petits fours. "They're beautiful."

"It took me four days to make them. Baking is not my specialty."

"You made these?"

He grinned. "Yep. I used a gluten-free flour mix like you're always talking about. The cake is the same, but each one is a different liquor-infused whipped cream. Try one."

I bit into the pink one. It was filled with chocolate and raspberry cream. "Tim, these are fabulous. You don't need me. You could easily bake on your own." I put the petit four back in the box and licked my finger.

His eyes grew serious and he looked at my mouth. I thought maybe I had icing on my face, but he leaned over and kissed me. And kissed me. And kissed me. If my grandmother were alive, she'd be on her way in here with her crocheting right now.

"Poppy, you know I've always loved you. I was trying to

ask you to be exclusive after the competition. I chickened out because I didn't think you were going to say yes."

"Tim, my heart is in two places."

"I know. But I want to change that. Can't you see this is our chance? We can finally finish what we started in high school. That reunion brought you back to me and I'm not going to let you go again. I should have come after you twenty-five years ago, before you married John. I was stupid. I'm not going to make that mistake again. I want to be exclusive, go steady, make a commitment to date no one else, whatever you want to call it. I don't want to share you anymore. Will you be mine and only mine?"

Recipes

Gluten-Free Baby Cakes

Strawberry Muffins with
White Chocolate Chips

Ingredients

2½ cups gluten-free flour
2 teaspoons baking powder
1 teaspoon baking soda
1 teaspoon sea salt
1½ cups dehydrated or freeze-dried strawberries from
    two 1-ounce bags
1¼ cups milk
2 large eggs, lightly beaten
¾ cup coconut oil, measured then melted
1 cup honey
1 teaspoon strawberry extract
1 cup white chocolate chips
1 cup washed, hulled, chopped fresh strawberries
Pink food coloring (optional)
Sanding sugar (optional)

Directions

Preheat oven to 375 degrees. Line muffin tins with paper liners.

Place freeze-dried strawberries in food processor and process until powder. Keep the lid on for a minute to let the dust settle.

In a large bowl, add gluten-free flour, baking powder, baking soda, salt, and strawberry powder. Mix to combine.

In a separate bowl, combine milk, eggs, coconut oil, honey, and extract. Whisk to combine.

Add the milk to the dry ingredients and stir until just combined. If you want your batter pinker, add a little food coloring until you get the desired shade.

Fold in the chopped strawberries and white chocolate chips.

Spoon the batter into the muffin cups to fill the liners. Top each with a sprinkle of colored sanding sugar if desired.

Bake for 20–25 minutes, or until a cake tester comes out clean and the tops are nicely browned.

Paleo Stud Muffins

Chocolate Muffins with Strawberries and Chocolate Chips

Ingredients

- ¾ cup dehydrated or freeze-dried strawberries, ground to powder from a 1-oz. bag
- 1 cup almond meal
- ¼ cup cassava flour
- ¾ cup dehydrated or freeze-dried strawberries, ground to powder from a 1-oz. bag
- ¼ cup Dutch process cocoa powder
- 1 teaspoon salt
- 1 teaspoon baking soda
- ½ cup coconut oil, measure first then melt
- ½ cup honey
- 1 teaspoon vanilla extract
- 3 eggs, room temperature so they won't solidify the coconut oil
- 1 cup chopped, fresh strawberries
- 1 cup gluten-free, dairy-free chocolate chips

Directions

Preheat oven to 350 degrees. Line a muffin pan with paper liners; set aside.

Place freeze-dried strawberries in food processor and process until powder. Keep the lid on for a minute to let the dust settle.

In a medium bowl, combine almond flour, cassava flour, cocoa powder, salt, and baking soda. Mix together and set aside.

In a separate bowl, whisk together coconut oil, honey, vanilla extract, and eggs.

Add the wet ingredients to the dry ingredients and mix until combined.

Fold in chopped strawberries and chocolate chips.

Spoon batter evenly into your paper liners. Smooth out if you want rounded tops.

Paleo muffins usually look exactly the same when they come out as when they went in.

Bake for 18–20 minutes or until the center is set.

Gluten-Free Cinnamon Streusel Coffee Cake

Adapted from King Arthur Flour

Ingredients

For the streusel topping

1 cup coconut sugar
½ teaspoon salt
½ cup gluten-free flour blend
½ cup almond meal
1 tablespoon ground cinnamon
6 tablespoons butter, melted

For the filling

1 cup brown sugar, light or dark
1½ tablespoons ground cinnamon

For the cake

2¾ cups gluten-free flour blend
1 cup almond meal
1 teaspoon xanthan gum
1½ teaspoons baking powder
1 teaspoon baking soda
1 teaspoon salt
1¼ cups almond milk
¾ cup butter
1½ cups coconut sugar
⅓ cup honey
2 teaspoons vanilla extract
¾ cup sour cream
3 large eggs

Directions

Preheat the oven to 350 degrees. Lightly grease or line with parchment a 9x13 pan.

To make the streusel topping

Combine coconut sugar, salt, gluten-free flour, almond meal, and cinnamon. Add the melted butter, cutting through the mixture until well combined. Set aside.

For the filling

Mix together the brown sugar and cinnamon. Set it aside.

For the cake

In a large bowl, combine gluten-free flour, almond meal, xanthan gum, baking powder, baking soda, and salt. Mix together and set aside.

Beat together the butter, sugar, honey, and vanilla until light and fluffy. Add sour cream. Mix well. Add the eggs one at a time, beating well after each addition.

Add the flour to the butter mixture alternately with the almond milk, beating gently to combine.

Spread half the batter into the prepared pan, spreading all the way to the edges. Sprinkle the filling evenly on the batter. Spread the remaining batter atop the filling. Gently run a butter knife through the pan to swirl the filling into the batter, as though you were making a marble cake. Don't combine filling and batter thoroughly; just swirl the filling through the batter.

Next, sprinkle the topping over the batter.

Bake until golden brown around the edges and a toothpick inserted into the center comes out clean, about 60 minutes. Allow to cool before cutting.

Paleo Carrot Cake Muffins with Rum Raisins

Ingredients

$1\frac{1}{2}$ cups golden raisins
Enough rum to cover, about 1 cup
$1\frac{1}{2}$ cups shredded carrot, about 3 medium carrots
2 cups almond flour
1 teaspoon baking soda
1 teaspoon baking powder
1 teaspoon cinnamon
$\frac{1}{2}$ teaspoon nutmeg
$\frac{1}{2}$ teaspoon ginger
1 tablespoon grated orange peel
3 eggs, room temperature
$\frac{1}{2}$ cup honey
$\frac{1}{4}$ cup almond oil
1 teaspoon pure vanilla extract
Juice from the orange, about $\frac{1}{4}$ cup
$\frac{1}{4}$ cup chopped walnuts
Raisins rehydrated in first step

Directions

In a glass bowl, pour rum over raisins. Cover the bowl with plastic wrap and microwave for 3 minutes. Let sit.

Peel and grate carrots.

Preheat oven to 350 degrees. Line a muffin tin with parchment lines or spray with coconut spray.

In a large bowl, add the almond flour, baking soda, baking powder, cinnamon, nutmeg, ginger, and grated orange peel.

In another large bowl, add eggs, honey, almond oil, vanilla extract, and orange juice.

Pour the wet ingredients into the dry ingredients and mix together. Add the shredded carrots, rum raisins, and chopped walnuts. Combine and scoop into liners.

Bake for 25–28 minutes or until a toothpick inserted in the center comes out clean.

Gluten-Free Cranberry Orange Oatmeal Bars

Ingredients

For the oatmeal cookie base

1 cup Craisins
Enough cranberry juice to cover them (about
    2–3 cups)
1 cup coconut sugar
3 cups gluten-free oats
1 cup almond meal
½ cup cassava flour
2 teaspoon baking powder
1 teaspoon sea salt
½ teaspoon xanthan gum
2 sticks butter, melted
2 eggs, lightly beaten
½ cup honey

For the orange cream cheese frosting

8 oz. cream cheese, softened
1½ cups powdered sugar
1 teaspoon fiori di Sicilia extract or orange flower
    water
1 tablespoon grated orange peel
½ cup Craisins

Directions

For the cookies

Preheat the oven to 350 degrees. Line a 9x13 pan with
parchment paper or spray with coconut spray.

In a glass bowl, pour enough cranberry juice over 1 cup Craisins to cover them. Cover the bowl with plastic and microwave for 3 minutes. Let sit.

In a large bowl, add all coconut sugar, oats, almond meal, cassava flour, baking powder, salt, and xanthan gum. Mix well.

Add the melted butter to the honey and eggs and mix into the dry ingredients. Press half of the mixed crust to the bottom of the pan.

Drain Craisins. Add the rehydrated Craisins on top of the layer of crust. Top with remaining crust and spread over to cover the berries.

Bake for 35 minutes or until golden brown. Let cool

For the orange cream cheese frosting

Beat cream cheese and powdered sugar with an electric mixer until light and fluffy. Add 1 teaspoon fiori di Sicilia extract or orange flower water and orange peel and mix well. Frost bars when cool. Sprinkle with chopped Craisins. Cut into squares—or triangles if you want to imitate a popular coffee chain.

Gluten-Free Apple Pie Crumb Muffins

Ingredients

For the filling

2½ cups chopped apples
½ cup coconut sugar
½ teaspoon cinnamon
¼ teaspoon ginger
¼ teaspoon cloves
1 tablespoon butter for cooking

For the topping

½ cup gluten-free flour
½ cup almond meal
½ cup coconut sugar
6 tablespoon melted butter

For the muffin batter

2 cups gluten-free flour
1 tablespoon baking powder
1 teaspoon salt
1 teaspoon ground cinnamon
¼ teaspoon ground cloves
1 teaspoon xanthan gum
2 large eggs
1 cup honey
1 cup sour cream
1 teaspoon vanilla extract
1 cup coconut oil

Directions

Peel and chop apples. Toss in coconut sugar and spices. Add 1 tablespoon butter to a frying pan and cook apples over medium heat until mostly soft.

Preheat the oven to 375 degrees and line standard muffin pan with paper liners and set aside.

Make the crumb topping. In a small bowl, whisk together gluten-free flour, almond meal, and coconut sugar. Add melted butter and toss with a fork until crumbly.

Make the muffin batter. In a medium-size bowl, add gluten-free flour, baking powder, salt, cinnamon, cloves, and xanthan gum. Mix together and set aside.

In another bowl, whisk together eggs, honey, sour cream, and vanilla until combined. Fold wet ingredients into dry ingredients and mix until combined. The batter will be thick.

Spoon a little batter into each muffin cup, filling less than ⅔.

Add a good tablespoon of chopped apple pie filling in the center of the batter and gently press down to make a well. Top generously with crumb topping

Bake for 18–20 minutes or until the toothpick comes out clean.

Gluten-Free Pink Champagne Cupcakes

I use solid refined coconut oil and vanilla beans
to keep the batter white.

Ingredients

For the cupcakes

1⅔ cups gluten-free flour
1 teaspoon baking powder
½ teaspoon baking soda
1 teaspoon xanthan gum
1 teaspoon salt
¾ cup refined coconut oil (do not melt)
1 cup sugar
3 egg whites
1–2 vanilla beans
½ cup plain yogurt
½ cup pink champagne
½ teaspoon champagne extract

For the frosting

1 cup butter
4 cups powdered sugar
4 tablespoon pink champagne
1 teaspoon champagne extract
Pink food coloring (optional)
Lustre dust (optional)

Directions

For the cupcakes

Preheat oven to 350 degrees and prepare a muffin tin with liners.

In a medium bowl, add gluten-free flour, baking powder, baking soda, xanthan gum, and salt. Stir to combine.

In the mixing bowl of your stand mixer, beat refined coconut oil and sugar until combined.

Add egg whites, vanilla beans, yogurt, champagne, and champagne extract. Mix to combine.

Add dry ingredients to the bowl and mix until smooth.

Divide batter between 12 cupcake liners. Bake 25–28 minutes or until a toothpick inserted in the center comes out clean.

For the frosting

In the bowl of your stand mixer, combine butter and half of the powdered sugar. Mix until smooth. Add champagne and champagne extract. Mix until smooth. Add remaining powdered sugar and mix until fluffy.

Frost cupcakes when cool and decorate with lustre dust.

Grab These Cozy Mysteries from
Kensington Books